I0819453

THE KING IN YELLOW & OTHER TALES OF THE SUPERNATURAL

SIGNATURE EDITIONS

THE KING IN YELLOW & OTHER TALES OF THE SUPERNATURAL

ROBERT W. CHAMBERS

UNION SQUARE & CO.
NEW YORK

This 2025 edition published by Union Square & Co., LLC

A Note on the Text: This book was originally published in installments between 1894 and 1926 and reflects the attitudes of its time. The publisher's decision to present it as it was first published is not intended as endorsement of any offensive cultural representations or language.

ISBN 978-1-4549-6133-8
ISBN 978-1-4549-6134-5 (e-book)

Union Square & Co. books may be purchased in bulk for business, educational, or promotional use. For more information, please contact your local bookseller or the Hachette Book Group's Special Markets department at special.markets@hbgusa.com.

Printed in India

REP

2 4 6 8 10 9 7 5 3

unionsquareandco.com

CONTENTS

THE KING IN YELLOW

To

MY BROTHER

CONTENTS

THE REPAIRER OF REPUTATIONS

"Along the shore the cloud waves break,
The twin suns sink behind the lake,
The shadows lengthen
In Carcosa.

"Strange is the night where black stars rise
And strange moons circle through the skies,
But stranger still is
Lost Carcosa.

"Songs that the Hyades shall sing,
Where flap the tatters of the King,
Must die unheard in
Dim Carcosa.

"Song of my soul, my voice is dead,
Die thou, unsung, as tears unshed
Shall dry and die in
Lost Carcosa."

—Cassilda's Song in "The King in Yellow,"
Act 1, Scene 2

I

"Ne raillons pas les fous; leur folie dure plus longtemps que la nôtre. . . . Voilà toute la différence."

Towards the end of the year 1920 the government of the United States had practically completed the programme adopted during the last months of President Winthrop's administration. The country was apparently tranquil. Everybody knows how the Tariff and Labor questions were settled. The war with Germany, incident on that country's seizure of the Samoan Islands, had left no visible scars upon the republic, and the temporary occupation of Norfolk by the invading army had been forgotten in the joy over repeated naval victories and the subsequent ridiculous plight of General Von Gartenlaube's forces in the State of New Jersey. The Cuban and Hawaiian investments had paid one hundred per cent., and the territory of Samoa was well worth its cost as a coaling station. The country was in a superb state of defence. Every coast city had been well supplied with land fortifications; the army, under the parental eye of the general staff, organized according to the Prussian system, had been increased to three hundred thousand men, with a territorial reserve of a million; and six magnificent squadrons of cruisers and battle-ships patrolled the six stations of the navigable seas, leaving a steam reserve amply fitted to control home waters. The gentlemen from the West had at last been constrained to acknowledge that a college for the training of diplomats was as necessary as law schools are for the training of barristers;

consequently we were no longer represented abroad by incompetent patriots. The nation was prosperous. Chicago, for a moment paralyzed after a second great fire, had risen from its ruins, white and imperial, and more beautiful than the white city which had been built for its plaything in 1893. Everywhere good architecture was replacing bad, and even in New York a sudden craving for decency had swept away a great portion of the existing horrors. Streets had been widened, properly paved, and lighted, trees had been planted, squares laid out, elevated structures demolished, and underground roads built to replace them. The new government buildings and barracks were fine bits of architecture, and the long system of stone quays which completely surrounded the island had been turned into parks, which proved a godsend to the population. The subsidizing of the state theatre and state opera brought its own reward. The United States National Academy of Design was much like European institutions of the same kind. Nobody envied the Secretary of Fine Arts either his cabinet position or his portfolio. The Secretary of Forestry and Game Preservation had a much easier time, thanks to the new system of National Mounted Police. We had profited well by the latest treaties with France and England; the exclusion of foreign-born Jews as a measure of national self-preservation, the settlement of the new independent negro state of Suanee, the checking of immigration, the new laws concerning naturalization, and the gradual centralization of power in the executive all contributed to national calm and prosperity. When the government solved the Indian problem and squadrons of Indian cavalry scouts in native costume were substituted for the pitiable organizations tacked on to the tail of skeletonized regiments by a former Secretary of War, the nation drew a long sigh of relief. When, after the colossal Congress of Religions, bigotry and intolerance were laid in their graves, and kindness and charity began to draw warring sects together, many thought the millennium had arrived, at least in the new world, which, after all, is a world by itself.

But self-preservation is the first law, and the United States had to look on in helpless sorrow as Germany, Italy, Spain, and

Belgium writhed in the throes of anarchy, while Russia, watching from the Caucasus, stooped and bound them one by one.

In the city of New York the summer of 1910 was signalized by the dismantling of the Elevated Railroads. The summer of 1911 will live in the memories of New York people for many a cycle; the Dodge statue was removed in that year. In the following winter began that agitation for the repeal of the laws prohibiting suicide, which bore its final fruit in the month of April, 1920, when the first Government Lethal Chamber was opened on Washington Square.

I had walked down that day from Dr. Archer's house on Madison Avenue, where I had been as a mere formality. Ever since that fall from my horse, four years before, I had been troubled at times with pains in the back of my head and neck, but now for months they had been absent, and the doctor sent me away that day saying there was nothing more to be cured in me. It was hardly worth his fee to be told that; I knew it myself. Still I did not grudge him the money. What I minded was the mistake which he made at first. When they picked me up from the pavement where I lay unconscious, and somebody had mercifully sent a bullet through my horse's head, I was carried to Dr. Archer, and he, pronouncing my brain affected, placed me in his private asylum, where I was obliged to endure treatment for insanity. At last he decided that I was well, and I, knowing that my mind had always been as sound as his, if not sounder, "paid my tuition," as he jokingly called it, and left. I told him, smiling, that I would get even with him for his mistake, and he laughed heartily, and asked me to call once in a while. I did so, hoping for a chance to even up accounts, but he gave me none, and I told him I would wait.

The fall from my horse had fortunately left no evil results; on the contrary, it had changed my whole character for the better. From a lazy young man about town, I had become active, energetic, temperate, and, above all—oh, above all else—ambitious. There was only one thing which troubled me: I laughed at my own uneasiness, and yet it troubled me.

During my convalescence I had bought and read for the first time "The King in Yellow." I remember after finishing the first act that it occurred to me that I had better stop. I started up and flung the book into the fireplace; the volume struck the barred grate and fell open on the hearth in the fire-light. If I had not caught a glimpse of the opening words in the second act I should never have finished it, but as I stooped to pick it up my eyes became riveted to the open page, and with a cry of terror, or perhaps it was of joy so poignant that I suffered in every nerve, I snatched the thing from the hearth and crept shaking to my bedroom, where I read it and reread it, and wept and laughed and trembled with a horror which at times assails me yet. This is the thing that troubles me, for I cannot forget Carcosa, where black stars hang in the heavens, where the shadows of men's thoughts lengthen in the afternoon, when the twin suns sink into the Lake of Hali, and my mind will bear forever the memory of the Pallid Mask. I pray God will curse the writer, as the writer has cursed the world with this beautiful, stupendous creation, terrible in its simplicity, irresistible in its truth—a world which now trembles before the King in Yellow. When the French government seized the translated copies which had just arrived in Paris, London, of course, became eager to read it. It is well known how the book spread like an infectious disease, from city to city, from continent to continent, barred out here, confiscated there, denounced by press and pulpit, censured even by the most advanced of literary anarchists. No definite principles had been violated in those wicked pages, no doctrine promulgated, no convictions outraged. It could not be judged by any known standard, yet, although it was acknowledged that the supreme note of art had been struck in "The King in Yellow," all felt that human nature could not bear the strain nor thrive on words in which the essence of purest poison lurked. The very banality and innocence of the first act only allowed the blow to fall afterwards with more awful effect.

It was, I remember, the 13th day of April, 1920, that the first Government Lethal Chamber was established on the south side of Washington Square, between Wooster Street and South Fifth Avenue. The block, which had formerly consisted of a lot of shabby old buildings, used as cafés and restaurants for foreigners, had been acquired by the government in the winter of 1913. The French and Italian cafés and restaurants were torn down; the whole block was enclosed by a gilded iron railing, and converted into a lovely garden, with lawns, flowers, and fountains. In the centre of the garden stood a small, white building, severely classical in architecture, and surrounded by thickets of flowers. Six Ionic columns supported the roof, and the single door was of bronze. A splendid marble group of "The Fates" stood before the door, the work of a young American sculptor, Boris Yvain, who had died in Paris when only twenty-three years old.

The inauguration ceremonies were in progress as I crossed University Place and entered the square. I threaded my way through the silent throng of spectators, but was stopped at Fourth Street by a cordon of police. A regiment of United States Lancers were drawn up in a hollow square around the Lethal Chamber. On a raised tribune facing Washington Park stood the Governor of New York, and behind him were grouped the Mayor of Greater New York, the Inspector-General of Police, the commandant of the State troops, Colonel Livingston (military aid to the President of the United States), General Blount (commanding at Governor's Island), Major-General Hamilton (commanding the garrison of Greater New York), Admiral Buffby (of the fleet in the North River), Surgeon-General Lanceford, the staff of the National Free Hospital, Senators Wyse and Franklin, of New York, and the Commissioner of Public Works. The tribune was surrounded by a squadron of hussars of the National Guard.

The Governor was finishing his reply to the short speech of the Surgeon-General. I heard him say: "The laws prohibiting suicide and providing punishment for any attempt at self-destruction have been repealed. The government has seen fit to acknowledge the right of man to end an existence which may have become intolerable to him, through physical suffering or mental despair. It is believed that the community will be benefited by the removal of such people from their midst. Since the passage of this law, the number of suicides in the United States has not increased. Now that the government has determined to establish a Lethal Chamber in every city, town, and village in the country, it remains to be seen whether or not that class of human creatures from whose desponding ranks new victims of self-destruction fall daily will accept the relief thus provided." He paused, and turned to the white Lethal Chamber. The silence in the street was absolute. "There a painless death awaits him who can no longer bear the sorrows of this life. If death is welcome, let him seek it there." Then, quickly turning to the military aid of the President's household, he said, "I declare the Lethal Chamber open"; and again facing the vast crowd, he cried, in a clear voice: "Citizens of New York and of the United States of America, through me the government declares the Lethal Chamber to be open."

The solemn hush was broken by a sharp cry of command, the squadron of hussars filed after the Governor's carriage, the lancers wheeled and formed along Fifth Avenue to wait for the commandant of the garrison, and the mounted police followed them. I left the crowd to gape and stare at the white marble death-chamber, and, crossing South Fifth Avenue, walked along the western side of that thoroughfare to Bleecker Street. Then I turned to the right and stopped before a dingy shop which bore the sign,

HAWBERK, ARMORER.

I glanced in at the door-way and saw Hawberk busy in his little shop at the end of the hall. He looked up, and, catching sight of me, cried, in his deep, hearty voice, "Come in, Mr. Castaigne!" Constance, his daughter, rose to meet me as I crossed the threshold, and held out her pretty hand, but I saw the blush of disappointment on her cheeks, and knew that it was another Castaigne she had expected, my cousin Louis. I smiled at her confusion and complimented her on the banner which she was embroidering from a colored plate. Old Hawberk sat riveting the worn greaves of some ancient suit of armor, and the ting! ting! ting! of his little hammer sounded pleasantly in the quaint shop. Presently he dropped his hammer and fussed about for a moment with a tiny wrench. The soft clash of the mail sent a thrill of pleasure through me. I loved to hear the music of steel brushing against steel, the mellow shock of the mallet on thigh-pieces, and the jingle of chain armor. That was the only reason I went to see Hawberk. He had never interested me personally, nor did Constance, except for the fact of her being in love with Louis. This did occupy my attention, and sometimes even kept me awake at night. But I knew in my heart that all would come right, and that I should arrange their future as I expected to arrange that of my kind doctor, John Archer. However, I should never have troubled myself about visiting them just then had it not been, as I say, that the music of the tinkling hammer had for me this strong fascination. I would sit for hours, listening and listening, and when a stray sunbeam struck the inlaid steel, the sensation it gave me was almost too keen to endure. My eyes would become fixed, dilating with a pleasure that stretched every nerve almost to breaking, until some movement of the old armorer cut off the ray of sunlight, then, still thrilling secretly, I leaned back and listened again to the sound of the polishing rag—swish! swish!—rubbing rust from the rivets.

Constance worked with the embroidery over her knees, now and then pausing to examine more closely the pattern in the colored plate from the Metropolitan Museum.

"Who is this for?" I asked.

Hawberk explained that in addition to the treasures of armor in the Metropolitan Museum, of which he had been appointed armorer, he also had charge of several collections belonging to rich amateurs. This was the missing greave of a famous suit which a client of his had traced to a little shop in Paris on the Quai d'Orsay. He, Hawberk, had negotiated for and secured the greave, and now the suit was complete. He laid down his hammer and read me the history of the suit, traced since 1450 from owner to owner until it was acquired by Thomas Stainbridge. When his superb collection was sold, this client of Hawberk's bought the suit, and since then the search for the missing greave had been pushed until it was, almost by accident, located in Paris.

"Did you continue the search so persistently without any certainty of the greave being still in existence?" I demanded.

"Of course," he replied, coolly.

Then for the first time I took a personal interest in Hawberk.

"It was worth something to you," I ventured.

"No," he replied, laughing, "my pleasure in finding it was my reward."

"Have you no ambition to be rich?" I asked, smiling.

"My one ambition is to be the best armorer in the world," he answered, gravely.

Constance asked me if I had seen the ceremonies at the Lethal Chamber. She herself had noticed cavalry passing up Broadway that morning, and had wished to see the inauguration, but her father wanted the banner finished, and she had stayed at his request.

"Did you see your cousin, Mr. Castaigne, there?" she asked, with the slightest tremor of her soft eyelashes.

"No," I replied, carelessly. "Louis's regiment is manoeuvring out in Westchester County." I rose and picked up my hat and cane.

"Are you going up-stairs to see the lunatic again?" laughed old Hawberk. If Hawberk knew how I loathe that word "lunatic," he would never use it in my presence. It rouses certain feelings within me which I do not care to explain. However, I answered him quietly:

"I think 1 shall drop in and see Mr. Wilde for a moment or two."

"Poor fellow," said Constance, with a shake of her head, "it must be hard to live alone year after year, poor, crippled, and almost demented. It is very good of you, Mr. Castaigne, to visit him as often as you do."

"I think he is vicious," observed Hawberk, beginning again with his hammer. I listened to the golden tinkle on the greave-plates; when he had finished I replied:

"No, he is not vicious, nor is he in the least demented. His mind is a wonder chamber, from which he can extract treasures that you and I would give years of our lives to acquire."

Hawberk laughed.

I continued, a little impatiently: "He knows history as no one else could know it. Nothing, however trivial, escapes his search, and his memory is so absolute, so precise in details, that were it known in New York that such a man existed the people could not honor him enough."

"Nonsense!" muttered Hawberk, searching on the floor for a fallen rivet.

"Is it nonsense," I asked, managing to suppress what I felt—"is it nonsense when he says that the tassets and cuissards of the enamelled suit of armor commonly known as the 'Prince's Emblazoned' can be found among a mass of rusty theatrical properties, broken stoves, and rag-picker's refuse in a garret in Pell Street?"

Hawberk's hammer fell to the ground, but he picked it up and asked, with a great deal of calm, how I knew that the tassets and left cuissard were missing from the "Prince's Emblazoned."

"I did not know until Mr. Wilde mentioned it to me the other day. He said they were in the garret of 998 Pell Street."

"Nonsense!" he cried; but I noticed his hand trembling under his leathern apron.

"Is this nonsense, too?" I asked, pleasantly. "Is it nonsense when Mr. Wilde continually speaks of you as the Marquis of Avonshire, and of Miss Constance—"

I did not finish, for Constance had started to her feet with terror written on every feature. Hawberk looked at me and slowly smoothed his leathern apron. "That is impossible," he observed. "Mr. Wilde may know a great many things—"

"About armor, for instance, and the 'Prince's Emblazoned,'" I interposed, smiling.

"Yes," he continued, slowly, "about armor also—maybe—but he is wrong in regard to the Marquis of Avonshire, who, as you know, killed his wife's traducer years ago, and went to Australia, where he did not long survive his wife."

"Mr. Wilde is wrong," murmured Constance. Her lips were blanched, but her voice was sweet and calm.

"Let us agree, if you please, that in this one circumstance Mr. Wilde is wrong," I said.

II

I climbed the three dilapidated flights of stairs which I had so often climbed before, and knocked at a small door at the end of the corridor. Mr. Wilde opened the door and I walked in.

When he had double-locked the door and pushed a heavy chest against it, he came and sat down beside me, peering up into my face with his little, light-colored eyes. Half a dozen new scratches covered his nose and cheeks, and the silver wires which supported his artificial ears had become displaced. I thought I had never seen him so hideously fascinating. He had no ears. The artificial ones, which now stood out at an angle from the fine wire, were his one weakness. They were made of wax and painted a shell pink; but the rest of his face was yellow. He might better have revelled in the luxury of some artificial fingers for his left hand, which was absolutely fingerless, but it seemed to cause him no inconvenience, and he was satisfied with his wax ears. He was very small, scarcely higher than a child of ten, but his arms were magnificently developed, and his thighs as thick as any athlete's. Still, the most remarkable thing about Mr. Wilde was that a man of his marvellous intelligence and knowledge should have such a head. It was flat and pointed, like the heads of many of those unfortunates whom people imprison in asylums for the weak-minded. Many called him insane, but I knew him to be as sane as I was.

I do not deny that he was eccentric; the mania he had for keeping that cat and teasing her until she flew at his face like a demon was certainly eccentric. I never could understand why he kept the creature, nor what pleasure he found in shutting himself up in his room with the surly, vicious beast. I remember once glancing up from the manuscript I was studying by the light of some tallow dips and seeing Mr. Wilde squatting motionless on his high chair, his eyes fairly blazing with excitement, while the cat, which had risen from her place before the stove, came creeping across the floor right at him. Before I could move she flattened her belly to the ground, crouched, trembled, and sprang into his face. Howling and foaming, they rolled over and over on the floor, scratching and clawing, until the cat screamed and fled under the cabinet, and Mr. Wilde turned over on his back, his limbs contracting and curling up like the legs of a dying spider. He *was* eccentric.

Mr. Wilde had climbed into his high chair, and, after studying my face, picked up a dog's-eared ledger and opened it.

"Henry B. Matthews," he read, "book-keeper with Whysot Whysot & Company, dealers in church ornaments. Called April 3d. Reputation damaged on the race-track. Known as a welcher. Reputation to be repaired by August 1st. Retainer, Five Dollars." He turned the page and ran his fingerless knuckles down the closely written columns.

"P. Greene Dusenberry, Minister of the Gospel, Fairbeach, New Jersey. Reputation damaged in the Bowery. To be repaired as soon as possible. Retainer, $100."

He coughed and added, "Called, April 6th."

"Then you are not in need of money, Mr. Wilde," I inquired.

"Listen"—he coughed again.

"Mrs. C. Hamilton Chester, of Chester Park, New York City, called April 7th. Reputation damaged at Dieppe, France. To be repaired by October 1st. Retainer, $500.

"Note.—C. Hamilton Chester, Captain U.S.S. *Avalanche,* ordered home from South Sea Squadron October 1st."

"Well," I said, "the profession of a Repairer of Reputations is lucrative."

His colorless eyes sought mine. "I only wanted to demonstrate that I was correct. You said it was impossible to succeed as a Repairer of Reputations; that even if I did succeed in certain cases, it would cost me more than I would gain by it. To-day I have five hundred men in my employ, who are poorly paid, but who pursue the work with an enthusiasm which possibly may be born of fear. These men enter every shade and grade of society; some even are pillars of the most exclusive social temples; others are the prop and pride of the financial world; still others hold undisputed sway among the 'Fancy and the Talent.' I choose them at my leisure from those who reply to my advertisements. It is easy enough—they are all cowards. I could treble the number in twenty days if I wished. So, you see, those who have in their keeping the reputations of their fellow-citizens, *I* have in my pay."

"They may turn on you," I suggested.

He rubbed his thumb over his cropped ears and adjusted the wax substitutes. "I think not," he murmured, thoughtfully, "I seldom have to apply the whip, and then only once. Besides, they like their wages."

"How do you apply the whip?" I demanded.

His face for a moment was awful to look upon. His eyes dwindled to a pair of green sparks.

"I invite them to come and have a little chat with me," he said, in a soft voice.

A knock at the door interrupted him, and his face resumed its amiable expression.

"Who is it?" he inquired.

"Mr. Steylette," was the answer.

"Come to-morrow," replied Mr. Wilde.

"Impossible," began the other; but was silenced by a sort of bark from Mr. Wilde.

"Come to-morrow," he repeated.

We heard somebody move away from the door and turn the corner by the stair-way.

"Who is that?" I asked.

"Arnold Steylette, owner and editor-in-chief of the great New York daily."

He drummed on the ledger with his fingerless hand, adding, "I pay him very badly, but he thinks it a good bargain."

"Arnold Steylette!" I repeated, amazed.

"Yes," said Mr. Wilde, with a self-satisfied cough.

The cat, which had entered the room as he spoke, hesitated, looked up at him, and snarled. He climbed down from the chair, and, squatting on the floor, took the creature into his arms and caressed her. The cat ceased snarling and presently began a loud purring, which seemed to increase in timbre as he stroked her.

"Where are the notes?" I asked. He pointed to the table, and for the hundredth time I picked up the bundle of manuscript entitled

"THE IMPERIAL DYNASTY OF AMERICA."

One by one I studied the well-worn pages, worn only by my own handling, and, although I knew all by heart, from the beginning, "When from Carcosa, the Hyades, Hastur, and Aldebaran," to "Castaigne, Louis de Calvados, born December 19, 1887," I read it with an eager, rapt attention, pausing to repeat parts of it aloud, and dwelling especially on "Hildred de Calvados, only son of Hildred Castaigne and Edythe Landes Castaigne, first in succession," etc., etc.

When I finished, Mr. Wilde nodded and coughed.

"Speaking of your legitimate ambition," he said, "how do Constance and Louis get along?"

"She loves him," I replied, simply.

The cat on his knee suddenly turned and struck at his eyes, and he flung her off and climbed on to the chair opposite me.

"And Dr. Archer? But that's a matter you can settle any time you wish," he added.

"Yes," I replied, "Dr. Archer can wait, but it is time I saw my cousin Louis."

"It is time," he repeated. Then he took another ledger from the table and ran over the leaves rapidly.

"We are now in communication with ten thousand men," he muttered. "We can count on one hundred thousand within the first twenty-eight hours, and in forty-eight hours the State will rise *en masse.* The country follows the State, and the portion that will not, I mean California and the Northwest, might better never have been inhabited. I shall not send them the Yellow Sign."

The blood rushed to my head, but I only answered, "A new broom sweeps clean."

"The ambition of Caesar and of Napoleon pales before that which could not rest until it had seized the minds of men and controlled even their unborn thoughts," said Mr. Wilde.

"You are speaking of the King in Yellow," I groaned, with a shudder.

"He is a king whom emperors have served."

"I am content to serve him," I replied.

Mr. Wilde sat rubbing his ears with his crippled hand. "Perhaps Constance does not love him," he suggested.

I started to reply, but a sudden burst of military music from the street below drowned my voice. The Twentieth Dragoon Regiment, formerly in garrison at Mount St. Vincent, was returning from the manoeuvres in Westchester County to its new barracks on East Washington Square. It was my cousin's regiment. They were a fine lot of fellows, in their pale-blue, tight-fitting jackets, jaunty busbies, and white riding-breeches, with the double yellow stripe, into which their limbs seemed moulded. Every other squadron was armed with lances, from the metal points of which fluttered yellow-and-white pennons. The band passed, playing the regimental march, then came the colonel and staff, the horses crowding and trampling, while their heads bobbed in unison, and the pennons fluttered from their lance points. The troopers, who rode with the beautiful English seat, looked brown as berries from their bloodless campaign among the farms of Westchester, and the music of their sabres against the stirrups, and the jingle of spurs and carbines was delightful to me. I saw Louis riding with his squadron. He was as handsome an officer as I have ever seen. Mr. Wilde, who had mounted a chair by the window, saw him, too, but said nothing. Louis turned and looked straight at Hawberk's shop as he passed, and I could see the flush on his brown cheeks. I think Constance must have been at the window. When the last troopers had clattered by, and the last pennons vanished into South Fifth Avenue, Mr. Wilde clambered out of his chair and dragged the chest away from the door.

"Yes," he said, "it is time that you saw your cousin Louis."

He unlocked the door and I picked up my hat and stick and stepped into the corridor. The stairs were dark. Groping about, I set my foot on something soft, which snarled and spit, and I aimed a murderous blow at the cat, but my cane shivered to splinters against the balustrade, and the beast scurried back into Mr. Wilde's room.

Passing Hawberk's door again, I saw him still at work on the armor, but I did not stop, and, stepping out into Bleecker Street,

I followed it to Wooster, skirted the grounds of the Lethal Chamber, and, crossing Washington Park, went straight to my rooms in the Benedick. Here I lunched comfortably, read the *Herald* and the *Meteor,* and finally went to the steel safe in my bedroom and set the time combination. The three and three-quarter minutes which it is necessary to wait, while the time lock is opening, are to me golden moments. From the instant I set the combination to the moment when I grasp the knobs and swing back the solid steel doors, I live in an ecstasy of expectation. Those moments must be like moments passed in paradise. I know what I am to find at the end of the time limit. I know what the massive safe holds secure for me, for me alone, and the exquisite pleasure of waiting is hardly enhanced when the safe opens and I lift, from its velvet crown, a diadem of purest gold, blazing with diamonds. I do this every day, and yet the joy of waiting and at last touching again the diadem only seems to increase as the days pass. It is a diadem fit for a king among kings, an emperor among emperors. The King in Yellow might scorn it, but it shall be worn by his royal servant.

I held it in my arms until the alarm on the safe rang harshly, and then tenderly, proudly I replaced it and shut the steel doors. I walked slowly back into my study, which faces Washington Square, and leaned on the window-sill. The afternoon sun poured into my windows, and a gentle breeze stirred the branches of the elms and maples in the park, now covered with buds and tender foliage. A flock of pigeons circled about the tower of the Memorial Church; sometimes alighting on the purple-tiled roof, sometimes wheeling downward to the lotos fountain in front of the marble arch. The gardeners were busy with the flower-beds around the fountain, and the freshly turned earth smelled sweet and spicy. A lawn mower, drawn by a fat, white horse, clinked across the greensward, and watering-carts poured showers of spray over the asphalt drives. Around the statue of Peter Stuyvesant, which in 1906 had replaced the monstrosity supposed to represent Garibaldi, children played in the spring sunshine, and nurse girls wheeled elaborate baby-carriages with a reckless disregard for the pasty-faced occupants, which could probably be explained by the presence of half a dozen trim dragoon troopers languidly lolling on the benches. Through the trees the Washington Memorial Arch glistened like silver in the sunshine, and beyond, on the eastern extremity of the square, the gray-stone barracks of the dragoons and the white-granite artillery stables were alive with color and motion.

I looked at the Lethal Chamber on the corner of the square opposite. A few curious people still lingered about the gilded iron railing, but inside the grounds the paths were deserted. I watched the fountains ripple and sparkle; the sparrows had already found this new bathing nook, and the basins were crowded with the dusty-feathered little things. Two or three white peacocks picked their way across the lawns, and a drab-colored pigeon sat so motionless on the arm of one of the Fates that it seemed to be a part of the sculptured stone.

As I was turning carelessly away, a slight commotion in the group of curious loiterers around the gates attracted my attention. A young man had entered, and was advancing with nervous strides along the gravel path which leads to the bronze doors of the Lethal Chamber. He paused a moment before the Fates, and as he raised his head to those three mysterious faces, the pigeon rose from its sculptured perch, circled about for a moment, and wheeled to the east. The young man pressed his hands to his face, and then, with an undefinable gesture, sprang up the marble steps, the bronze doors closed behind him, and half an hour later the loiterers slouched away and the frightened pigeon returned to its perch in the arms of Fate.

I put on my hat and went out into the park for a little walk before dinner. As I crossed the central driveway a group of officers passed, and one of them called out, "Hello, Hildred!" and came back to shake hands with me. It was my cousin Louis, who stood smiling and tapping his spurred heels with his riding-whip.

"Just back from Westchester," he said; "been doing the bucolic; milk and curds, you know; dairymaids in sunbonnets, who say 'haeow' and 'I don't think' when you tell them they are pretty. I'm nearly dead for a square meal at Delmonico's. What's the news?"

"There is none," I replied, pleasantly. "I saw your regiment coming in this morning."

"Did you? I didn't see you. Where were you?"

"In Mr. Wilde's window."

"Oh, hell!" he began, impatiently, "that man is stark mad! I don't understand why you—"

He saw how annoyed I felt by this outburst, and begged my pardon.

"Really, old chap," he said, "I don't mean to run down a man you like, but for the life of me I can't see what the deuce you find in common with Mr. Wilde. He's not well bred, to put it generously; he's hideously deformed; his head is the head of a criminally insane person. You know yourself he's been in an asylum—"

"So have I," I interrupted, calmly.

Louis looked startled and confused for a moment, but recovered and slapped me heartily on the shoulder.

"You were completely cured," he began; but I stopped him again.

"I suppose you mean that I was simply acknowledged never to have been insane."

"Of course that—that's what I meant," he laughed.

I disliked his laugh, because I knew it was forced; but I nodded gayly and asked him where he was going. Louis looked after his brother officers, who had now almost reached Broadway.

"We had intended to sample a Brunswick cocktail, but, to tell you the truth, I was anxious for an excuse to go and see Hawberk instead. Come along; I'll make you my excuse."

We found old Hawberk, neatly attired in a fresh spring suit, standing at the door of his shop and sniffing the air.

"I had just decided to take Constance for a little stroll before dinner," he replied to the impetuous volley of questions from Louis. "We thought of walking on the park terrace along the North River."

At that moment Constance appeared and grew pale and rosy by turns as Louis bent over her small, gloved fingers. I tried to excuse myself, alleging an engagement up-town, but Louis and Constance would not listen, and I saw I was expected to remain and engage old Hawberk's attention. After all, it would be just as well if I kept my eye on Louis, I thought, and, when they hailed a Spring Street electric-car, I got in after them and took my seat beside the armorer.

The beautiful line of parks and granite terraces overlooking the wharves along the North River, which were built in 1910 and finished in the autumn of 1917, had become one of the most popular promenades in the metropolis. They extended from the Battery to One Hundred and Ninetieth Street, overlooking the noble river, and affording a fine view of the Jersey shore and the Highlands opposite. Cafés and restaurants were scattered here and there among the trees, and twice a week military bands from the garrison played in the kiosques on the parapets.

We sat down in the sunshine on the bench at the foot of the equestrian statue of General Sheridan. Constance tipped her sunshade to shield her eyes, and she and Louis began a murmuring conversation which was impossible to catch. Old Hawberk, leaning on his ivory-headed cane, lighted an excellent cigar, the mate to which I politely refused, and smiled at vacancy. The sun hung low above the Staten Island woods, and the bay was dyed with golden hues reflected from the sun-warmed sails of the shipping in the harbor.

Brigs, schooners, yachts, clumsy ferry-boats, their decks swarming with people, railroad transports carrying lines of brown, blue, and white freight-cars, stately Sound steamers, *déclassé* tramp steamers, coasters, dredgers, scows, and everywhere pervading the entire bay impudent little tugs puffing and whistling officiously—these were the craft which churned the sunlit waters as far as the eye could reach. In calm contrast to the hurry of sailing vessel and steamer, a silent fleet of white war-ships lay motionless in midstream.

Constance's merry laugh aroused me from my reverie.

"What *are* you staring at?" she inquired.

"Nothing—the fleet." I smiled.

Then Louis told us what the vessels were, pointing out each by its relative position to the old red fort on Governor's Island.

"That little cigar-shaped thing is a torpedo-boat," he explained; "there are four more lying close together. They are the *Tarpon,* the *Falcon,* the *Sea Fox,* and the *Octopus.* The gunboats just above are the *Princeton,* the *Champlain,* the *Still Water,* and the *Erie.* Next to them lie the cruisers *Farragut* and *Los Angeles,* and above them the battle-ships *California* and *Dakota,* and the *Washington,* which is the flagship. Those two squatty-looking chunks of metal which are anchored there off Castle William are the double-turreted monitors *Terrible* and *Magnificent;* behind them lies the ram *Osceola."*

Constance looked at him with deep approval in her beautiful eyes. "What loads of things you know for a soldier," she said, and we all joined in the laugh which followed.

Presently Louis rose with a nod to us and offered his arm to Constance, and they strolled away along the river-wall. Hawberk watched them for a moment, and then turned to me.

"Mr. Wilde was right," he said. "I have found the missing tassets and left cuissard of the 'Prince's Emblazoned,' in a vile old junk garret in Pell Street."

"998?" I inquired, with a smile.

"Yes."

"Mr. Wilde is a very intelligent man," I observed.

"I want to give him the credit of this most important discovery," continued Hawberk. "And I intend it shall be known that he is entitled to the fame of it."

"He won't thank you for that," I answered, sharply; "please say nothing about it."

"Do you know what it is worth?" said Hawberk.

"No—fifty dollars, perhaps."

"It is valued at five hundred, but the owner of the 'Prince's Emblazoned' will give two thousand dollars to the person who completes his suit; that reward also belongs to Mr. Wilde."

"He doesn't want it! He refuses it!" I answered, angrily. "What do you know about Mr. Wilde? He doesn't need the money. He is rich—or will be—richer than any living man except myself. What will we care for money then—what will we care, he and I, when—when—"

"When what?" demanded Hawberk, astonished.

"You will see," I replied, on my guard again.

He looked at me narrowly, much as Dr. Archer used to, and I knew he thought I was mentally unsound. Perhaps it was fortunate for him that he did not use the word lunatic just then.

"No," I replied to his unspoken thought, "I am not mentally weak; my mind is as healthy as Mr. Wilde's. I do not care to explain just yet what I have on hand, but it is an investment which will pay more than mere gold, silver, and precious stones. It will secure the happiness and prosperity of a continent—yes, a hemisphere!"

"Oh," said Hawberk.

"And eventually," I continued, more quietly, "it will secure the happiness of the whole world."

"And incidentally your own happiness and prosperity as well as Mr. Wilde's?"

"Exactly." I smiled, but I could have throttled him for taking that tone.

He looked at me in silence for a while, and then said, very gently: "Why don't you give up your books and studies, Mr. Castaigne, and take a tramp among the mountains somewhere or other? You used to be fond of fishing. Take a cast or two at the trout in the Rangelys."

"I don't care for fishing any more," I answered, without a shade of annoyance in my voice.

"You used to be fond of everything," he continued—"athletics, yachting, shooting, riding—"

"I have never cared to ride since my fall," I said, quietly.

"Ah, yes, your fall," he repeated, looking away from me.

I thought this nonsense had gone far enough, so I turned the conversation back to Mr. Wilde; but he was scanning my face again in a manner highly offensive to me.

"Mr. Wilde," he repeated; "do you know what he did this afternoon? He came down-stairs and nailed a sign over the hall door next to mine; it read:

Mr. Wilde,
Repairer of Reputations.
Third Bell.

"Do you know what a Repairer of Reputations can be?"

"I do," I replied, suppressing the rage within.

"Oh," he said again.

Louis and Constance came strolling by and stopped to ask if we would join them. Hawberk looked at his watch. At the same moment a puff of smoke shot from the casemates of Castle William, and the boom of the sunset gun rolled across the water and was re-echoed from the Highlands opposite. The flag came running down from the flag-pole, the bugles sounded on the white decks of the war-ships, and the first electric light sparkled out from the Jersey shore.

As I turned into the city with Hawberk I heard Constance murmur something to Louis which I did not understand; but Louis whispered "My darling!" in reply; and again, walking ahead with Hawberk through the square, I heard a murmur of "sweetheart!" and "my own Constance!" and I knew the time had nearly arrived when I should speak of important matters with my cousin Louis.

III

One morning early in May I stood before the steel safe in my bedroom, trying on the golden jewelled crown. The diamonds flashed fire as I turned to the mirror, and the heavy beaten gold burned like a halo about my head. I remembered Camilla's agonized scream and the awful words echoing through the dim streets of Carcosa. They were the last lines in the first act, and I dared not think of what followed—dared not, even in the spring sunshine, there in my own room, surrounded with familiar objects, reassured by the bustle from the street and the voices of the servants in the hall-way outside. For those poisoned words had dropped slowly into my heart, as death-sweat drops upon a bed-sheet and is absorbed. Trembling, I put the diadem from my head and wiped my forehead, but I thought of Hastur and of my own rightful ambition, and I remembered Mr. Wilde as I had last left him, his face all torn and bloody from the claws of that devil's creature, and what he said—ah, what he said! The alarm-bell in the safe began to whir harshly, and I knew my time was up; but I would not heed it, and, replacing the flashing circlet upon my head, I turned defiantly to the mirror. I stood for a long time absorbed in the changing expression of my own eyes. The mirror reflected a face which was like my own, but whiter, and so thin that I hardly recognized it. And all the time I kept repeating between my clenched teeth, "The day has come! the day has come!" while the alarm in the safe whirred and clamored, and the diamonds sparkled and flamed above my brow. I heard a door open, but did not heed it. It was only when I saw two faces in the mirror; it was only when another face rose over my shoulder, and two other eyes met mine. I wheeled like a flash and seized a long knife from my dressing-table, and my cousin sprang back very pale, crying: "Hildred! for God's sake!" Then, as my hand fell, he said: "It is I, Louis; don't you know me?" I stood silent. I could not have spoken for my life. He walked up to me and took the knife from my hand.

"What is all this?" he inquired, in a gentle voice. "Are you ill?"

"No," I replied. But I doubt if he heard me.

"Come, come, old fellow," he cried, "take off that brass crown and toddle into the study. Are you going to a masquerade? What's all this theatrical tinsel anyway?"

I was glad he thought the crown was made of brass and paste, yet I didn't like him any the better for thinking so. I let him take it from my hand, knowing it was best to humor him. He tossed the splendid diadem in the air, and, catching it, turned to me smiling.

"It's dear at fifty cents," he said. "What's it for?"

I did not answer, but took the circlet from his hands, and, placing it in the safe, shut the massive steel door. The alarm ceased its infernal din at once. He watched me curiously, but did not seem to notice the sudden ceasing of the alarm. He did, however, speak of the safe as a biscuit-box. Fearing lest he might examine the combination, I led the way into my study. Louis threw himself on the sofa and flicked at flies with his eternal riding-whip. He wore his fatigue uniform, with the braided jacket and jaunty cap, and I noticed that his riding-boots were all splashed with red mud.

"Where have you been?" I inquired.

"Jumping mud creeks in Jersey," he said. "I haven't had time to change yet; I was rather in a hurry to see you. Haven't you got a glass of something? I'm dead tired; been in the saddle twenty-four hours."

I gave him some brandy from my medicinal store, which he drank with a grimace.

"Damned bad stuff," he observed. "I'll give you an address where they sell brandy that is brandy."

"It's good enough for my needs," I said, indifferently. "I use it to rub my chest with." He stared and flicked at another fly.

"See here, old fellow," he began, "I've got something to suggest to you. It's four years now that you've shut yourself up here like an owl, never going anywhere, never taking any healthy exercise, never doing a damn thing but poring over those books up there on the mantel-piece."

He glanced along the row of shelves. "Napoleon, Napoleon, Napoleon!" he read. "For Heaven's sake, have you nothing but Napoleons there?"

"I wish they were bound in gold," I said. "But wait—yes, there is another book, 'The King in Yellow'" I looked him steadily in the eye.

"Have you never read it?" I asked.

"I? No, thank God! I don't want to be driven crazy."

I saw he regretted his speech as soon as he had uttered it. There is only one word which I loathe more than I do lunatic, and that word is crazy. But I controlled myself and asked him why he thought "The King in Yellow" dangerous.

"Oh, I don't know," he said, hastily. "I only remember the excitement it created and the denunciations from pulpit and press. I believe the author shot himself after bringing forth this monstrosity, didn't he?"

"I understand he is still alive," I answered.

"That's probably true," he muttered; "bullets couldn't kill a fiend like that."

"It is a book of great truths," I said.

"Yes," he replied, "of 'truths' which send men frantic and blast their lives. I don't care if the thing is, as they say, the very supreme essence of art. It's a crime to have written it, and I for one shall never open its pages."

"Is that what you have come to tell me?" I asked.

"No," he said, "I came to tell you that I am going to be married."

I believe for a moment my heart ceased to beat, but I kept my eyes on his face.

"Yes," he continued, smiling happily, "married to the sweetest girl on earth."

"Constance Hawberk," I said, mechanically.

"How did you know?" he cried, astonished. "I didn't know it myself until that evening last April, when we strolled down to the embankment before dinner."

"When is it to be?" I asked.

"It was to have been next September; but an hour ago a despatch came, ordering our regiment to the Presidio, San Francisco. We leave at noon to-morrow. To-morrow," he repeated. "Just think, Hildred, to-morrow I shall be the happiest fellow that ever drew breath in this jolly world, for Constance will go with me."

I offered him my hand in congratulation, and he seized and shook it like the good-natured fool he was—or pretended to be.

"I am going to get my squadron as a wedding present," he rattled on. "Captain and Mrs. Louis Castaigne—eh, Hildred?"

Then he told me where it was to be and who were to be there, and made me promise to come and be best man. I set my teeth and listened to his boyish chatter without showing what I felt, but—

I was getting to the limit of my endurance, and when he jumped up, and, switching his spurs till they jingled, said he must go, I did not detain him.

"There's one thing I want to ask of you," I said, quietly.

"Out with it—it's promised," he laughed.

"I want you to meet me for a quarter of an hour's talk to-night."

"Of course, if you wish," he said, somewhat puzzled. "Where?"

"Anywhere—in the park there."

"What time, Hildred?"

"Midnight."

"What in the name of—" he began, but checked himself and laughingly assented. I watched him go down the stairs and hurry away, his sabre banging at every stride. He turned into Bleecker Street, and I knew he was going to see Constance. I gave him ten minutes to disappear and then followed in his footsteps, taking with me the jewelled crown and the silken robe embroidered with the Yellow Sign. When I turned into Bleecker Street and entered the door-way which bore the sign,

Mr. Wilde,
Repairer of Reputations.
Third Bell.

I saw old Hawberk moving about in his shop, and imagined I heard Constance's voice in the parlor; but I avoided them both and hurried up the trembling stair-ways to Mr. Wilde's apartment. I knocked, and entered without ceremony. Mr. Wilde lay groaning on the floor, his face covered with blood, his clothes torn to shreds. Drops of blood were scattered about over the carpet, which had also been ripped and frayed in the evidently recent struggle.

"It's that cursed cat," he said, ceasing his groans and turning his colorless eyes to me; "she attacked me while I was asleep. I believe she will kill me yet."

This was too much, so I went into the kitchen and, seizing a hatchet from the pantry, started to find the infernal beast and settle her then and there. My search was fruitless, and after a while I gave it up and came back to find Mr. Wilde squatting on his high chair by the table. He had washed his face and changed his clothes. The great furrows which the cat's claws had ploughed up in his face he had filled with collodion, and a rag hid the wound in his throat. I told him I should kill the cat when I came across her, but he only shook his head and turned to the open ledger before him. He read name after name of the people who had come to him in regard to their reputation, and the sums he had amassed were startling.

"I put on the screws now and then," he explained.

"One day or other some of these people will assassinate you," I insisted.

"Do you think so?" he said, rubbing his mutilated ears.

It was useless to argue with him, so I took down the manuscript entitled Imperial Dynasty of America for the last time I should ever take it down in Mr. Wilde's study. I read it through, thrilling and trembling with pleasure. When I had finished, Mr. Wilde took the manuscript, and, turning to the dark passage which leads from his study to his bedchamber, called out, in a loud voice, "Vance." Then for the first time I noticed a man crouching there in the shadow. How I had overlooked him during my search for the cat I cannot imagine.

"Vance, come in!" cried Mr. Wilde.

The figure rose and crept towards us, and I shall never forget the face that he raised to mine as the light from the window illuminated it.

"Vance, this is Mr. Castaigne," said Mr. Wilde. Before he had finished speaking, the man threw himself on the ground before the table, crying and gasping, "Oh, God! Oh, my God! Help me! Forgive me—Oh, Mr. Castaigne, keep that man away! You cannot; you cannot mean it! You are different—save me! I am broken down—I was in a madhouse, and now—when all was coming right—when I had forgotten the King—the King in Yellow, and—but I shall go mad again—I shall go mad—"

His voice died into a choking rattle, for Mr. Wilde had leaped on him, and his right hand encircled the man's throat. When Vance fell in a heap on the floor, Mr. Wilde clambered nimbly into his chair again, and, rubbing his mangled ears with the stump of his hand, turned to me and asked me for the ledger. I reached it down from the shelf and he opened it. After a moment's searching among the beautifully written pages, he coughed complacently and pointed to the name Vance.

"Vance," he read, aloud—"Osgood Oswald Vance." At the sound of his name the man on the floor raised his head and turned a convulsed face to Mr. Wilde. His eyes were injected with blood, his lips tumefied. "Called April 28th," continued Mr. Wilde. "Occupation, cashier in the Seaforth National Bank; has served a term for forgery at Sing Sing, whence he was transferred to the Asylum for the Criminal Insane. Pardoned by the Governor of New York, and discharged from the Asylum January 19, 1918. Reputation damaged at Sheepshead Bay. Rumors that he lives beyond his income. Reputation to be repaired at once. Retainer, $1500.

"Note.—Has embezzled sums amounting to $30,000 since March 20, 1919. Excellent family, and secured present position through uncle's influence. Father, President of Seaforth Bank."

I looked at the man on the floor.

"Get up, Vance," said Mr. Wilde, in a gentle voice. Vance rose as if hypnotized. "He will do as we suggest now," observed Mr. Wilde, and, opening the manuscript, he read the entire history of the Imperial Dynasty of America. Then, in a kind and soothing murmur, he ran over the important points with Vance, who stood like one stunned. His eyes were so blank and vacant that I imagined he had become half-witted, and remarked it to Mr. Wilde, who replied that it was of no consequence anyway. Very patiently we pointed out to Vance what his share in the affair would be, and he seemed to understand after a while. Mr. Wilde explained the manuscript, using several volumes on Heraldry to substantiate the result of his researches. He mentioned the establishment of the Dynasty in Carcosa, the lakes which connected Hastur, Aldebaran, and the mystery of the Hyades. He spoke of Cassilda and Camilla, and sounded the cloudy depths of Demhe and the Lake of Hali. "The scalloped tatters of the King in Yellow must hide Yhtill forever," he muttered, but I do not believe Vance heard him. Then by degrees he led Vance along the ramifications of the imperial family to Uoht and Thale, from Naotalba and

Phantom of Truth to Aldones, and then, tossing aside his manuscript and notes, he began the wonderful story of the Last King. Fascinated and thrilled, I watched him. He threw up his head, his long arms were stretched out in a magnificent gesture of pride and power, and his eyes blazed deep in their sockets like two emeralds. Vance listened, stupefied. As for me, when at last Mr. Wilde had finished, and, pointing to me, cried, "The cousin of the King," my head swam with excitement.

Controlling myself with a superhuman effort, I explained to Vance why I alone was worthy of the crown, and why my cousin must be exiled or die. I made him understand that my cousin must never marry, even after renouncing all his claims, and how that, least of all, he should marry the daughter of the Marquis of Avonshire and bring England into the question. I showed him a list of thousands of names which Mr. Wilde had drawn up; every man whose name was there had received the Yellow Sign, which no living human being dared disregard. The city, the State, the whole land, were ready to rise and tremble before the Pallid Mask.

The time had come, the people should know the son of Hastur, and the whole world bow to the black stars which hang in the sky over Carcosa.

Vance leaned on the table, his head buried in his hands. Mr. Wilde drew a rough sketch on the margin of yesterday's *Herald* with a bit of lead-pencil. It was a plan of Hawberk's rooms. Then he wrote out the order and affixed the seal, and, shaking like a palsied man, I signed my first writ of execution with my name Hildred-Rex.

Mr. Wilde clambered to the floor and, unlocking the cabinet, took a long, square box from the first shelf. This he brought to the table and opened. A new knife lay in the tissue-paper inside, and I picked it up and handed it to Vance, along with the order and the plan of Hawberk's apartment. Then Mr. Wilde told Vance he could go; and he went, shambling like an outcast of the slums.

I sat for a while watching the daylight fade behind the square tower of the Judson Memorial Church, and finally, gathering up the manuscript and notes, took my hat and started for the door.

Mr. Wilde watched me in silence. When I had stepped into the hall I looked back; Mr. Wilde's small eyes were still fixed on me. Behind him the shadows gathered in the fading light. Then I closed the door behind me and went out into the darkening streets.

I had eaten nothing since breakfast, but I was not hungry. A wretched, half-starved creature, who stood looking across the street at the Lethal Chamber, noticed me and came up to tell me a tale of misery. I gave him money—I don't know why—and he went away without thanking me. An hour later another outcast approached and whined his story. I had a blank bit of paper in my pocket, on which was traced the Yellow Sign, and I handed it to him. He looked at it stupidly for a moment, and then, with an uncertain glance at me, folded it with what seemed to me exaggerated care and placed it in his bosom.

The electric lights were sparkling among the trees, and the new moon shone in the sky above the Lethal Chamber. It was tiresome waiting in the square; I wandered from the marble arch to the artillery stables, and back again to the lotos fountain. The flowers and grass exhaled a fragrance which troubled me. The jet of the fountain played in the moonlight, and the musical splash of falling drops reminded me of the tinkle of chained mail in Hawberk's shop. But it was not so fascinating, and the dull sparkle of the moonlight on the water brought no such sensations of exquisite pleasure as when the sunshine played over the polished steel of a corselet on Hawberk's knee. I watched the bats darting and turning above the water plants in the fountain basin, but their rapid, jerky flight set my nerves on edge, and I went away again to walk aimlessly to and fro among the trees.

The artillery stables were dark, but in the cavalry barracks the officers' windows were brilliantly lighted, and the sally-port was constantly filled with troopers in fatigue, carrying straw and harness and baskets filled with tin dishes.

Twice the mounted sentry at the gates was changed while I wandered up and down the asphalt walk. I looked at my watch. It was nearly time. The lights in the barracks went out one by one, the barred gate was closed, and every minute or two an officer passed in through the side wicket, leaving a rattle of accoutrements and a jingle of spurs on the night air. The square had become very silent. The last homeless loiterer had been driven away by the gray-coated park policeman, the car tracks along Wooster Street were deserted, and the only sound which broke the stillness was the stamping of the sentry's horse and the ring of his sabre against the saddle pommel. In the barracks the officers' quarters were still lighted, and military servants passed and repassed before the bay-windows. Twelve o'clock sounded from the new spire of St. Francis Xavier, and at the last stroke of the sad-toned bell a figure passed through the wicket beside the portcullis, returned the salute of the sentry, and, crossing the street, entered the square and advanced towards the Benedick apartment house.

"Louis," I called.

The man pivoted on his spurred heels and came straight towards me.

"Is that you, Hildred?"

"Yes, you are on time."

I took his offered hand and we strolled towards the Lethal Chamber.

He rattled on about his wedding and the graces of Constance and their future prospects, calling my attention to his captain's shoulder-straps and the triple gold arabesque on his sleeve and fatigue cap. I believe I listened as much to the music of his spurs and sabre as I did to his boyish babble, and at last we stood under the elms on the Fourth Street corner of the square opposite the Lethal Chamber. Then he laughed and asked me what I wanted with him. I motioned him to a seat on a bench under the electric light, and sat down beside him. He looked at me curiously, with that same searching glance which I hate and fear so in doctors. I felt the insult of his look, but he did not know it, and I carefully concealed my feelings.

"Well, old chap," he inquired, "what can I do for you?"

I drew from my pocket the manuscript and notes of the Imperial Dynasty of America, and, looking him in the eye, said:

"I will tell you. On your word as a soldier, promise me to read this manuscript from beginning to end without asking me a question. Promise me to read these notes in the same way, and promise me to listen to what I have to tell later."

"I promise, if you wish it," he said, pleasantly. "Give me the paper, Hildred."

He began to read, raising his eyebrows with a puzzled, whimsical air, which made me tremble with suppressed anger. As he advanced, his eyebrows contracted, and his lips seemed to form the word "rubbish."

Then he looked slightly bored, but apparently for my sake read, with an attempt at interest, which presently ceased to be an effort. He started when, in the closely written pages he came to his own name, and when he came to mine he lowered the paper and looked sharply at me for a moment. But he kept his word, and resumed his reading, and I let the half-formed question die on his lips unanswered. When he came to the end and read the signature of Mr. Wilde, he folded the paper carefully and returned it to me. I handed him the notes, and he settled back, pushing his fatigue cap up to his forehead with a boyish gesture which I remembered so well in school. I watched his face as he read, and when he finished I took the notes, with the manuscript, and placed them in my pocket. Then I unfolded a scroll marked with the Yellow Sign. He saw the sign, but he did not seem to recognize it, and I called his attention to it somewhat sharply.

"Well," he said, "I see it. What is it?"

"It is the Yellow Sign," I said, angrily.

"Oh, that's it, is it?" said Louis, in that flattering voice which Dr. Archer used to employ with me, and would probably have employed again, had I not settled his affair for him.

I kept my rage down and answered as steadily as possible, "Listen, you have engaged your word?"

"I am listening, old chap," he replied, soothingly.

I began to speak very calmly: "Dr. Archer, having by some means become possessed of the secret of the Imperial Succession, attempted to deprive me of my right, alleging that, because of a fall from my horse four years ago, I had become mentally deficient. He presumed to place me under restraint in his own house in hopes of either driving me insane or poisoning me. I have not forgotten it. I visited him last night and the interview was final."

Louis turned quite pale, but did not move. I resumed, triumphantly: "There are yet three people to be interviewed in the interests of Mr. Wilde and myself. They are my cousin Louis, Mr. Hawberk, and his daughter Constance."

Louis sprang to his feet, and I arose also, and flung the paper marked with the Yellow Sign to the ground.

"Oh, I don't need that to tell you what I have to say," I cried, with a laugh of triumph. "You must renounce the crown to me—do you hear, to *me?*"

Louis looked at me with a startled air, but, recovering himself, said kindly, "Of course I renounce the—what is it I must renounce?"

"The crown," I said, angrily.

"Of course," he answered, "I renounce it. Come, old chap, I'll walk back to your rooms with you."

"Don't try any of your doctor's tricks on me," I cried, trembling with fury. "Don't act as if you think I am insane."

"What nonsense!" he replied. "Come, it's getting late, Hildred."

"No," I shouted, "you must listen. You cannot marry; I forbid it. Do you hear? I forbid it. You shall renounce the crown, and in reward I grant you exile; but if you refuse you shall die."

He tried to calm me, but I was roused at last, and, drawing my long knife, barred his way.

Then I told him how they would find Dr. Archer in the cellar with his throat open, and I laughed in his face when I thought of Vance and his knife, and the order signed by me.

"Ah, you are the King," I cried, "but I shall be King. Who are you to keep me from empire over all the habitable earth! I was born the cousin of a king, but I shall be King!"

Louis stood white and rigid before me. Suddenly a man came running up Fourth Street, entered the gate of the Lethal Temple, traversed the path to the bronze doors at full speed, and plunged into the death-chamber with the cry of one demented, and I laughed until I wept tears, for I had recognized Vance, and knew that Hawberk and his daughter were no longer in my way.

"Go," I cried to Louis, "you have ceased to be a menace. You will never marry Constance now, and if you marry any one else in your exile, I will visit you as I did my doctor last night. Mr. Wilde takes charge of you to-morrow." Then I turned and darted into South Fifth Avenue, and with a cry of terror Louis dropped his belt and sabre and followed me like the wind. I heard him close behind me at the corner of Bleecker Street, and I dashed into the door-way under Hawberk's sign. He cried, "Halt, or I fire!" but when he saw that I flew up the stairs leaving Hawberk's shop below, he left me, and I heard him hammering and shouting at their door as though it were possible to arouse the dead.

Mr. Wilde's door was open, and I entered, crying: "It is done, it is done! Let the nations rise and look upon their King!" but I could not find Mr. Wilde, so I went to the cabinet and took the splendid diadem from its case. Then I drew on the white silk robe, embroidered with the Yellow Sign, and placed the crown upon my head. At last I was King, King by my right in Hastur, King because I knew the mystery of the Hyades, and my mind had sounded the depths of the Lake of Hali. I was King! The first gray pencillings of dawn would raise a tempest which would shake two hemispheres. Then as I stood, my every nerve pitched to the highest tension, faint with the joy and splendor of my thought, without, in the dark passage, a man groaned.

I seized the tallow dip and sprang to the door. The cat passed me like a demon, and the tallow dip went out, but my long knife flew swifter than she, and I heard her screech, and I knew that my knife had found her. For a moment I listened to her tumbling and thumping about in the darkness, and then, when her frenzy ceased, I lighted a lamp and raised it over my head. Mr. Wilde lay on the floor with his throat torn open. At first I thought he was dead, but as I looked a green sparkle came into his sunken eyes, his mutilated hand trembled, and then a spasm stretched his mouth from ear to ear. For a moment my terror and despair gave place to hope, but as I bent over him his eyeballs rolled clean around in his head, and he died. Then, while I stood transfixed with rage and despair, seeing my crown, my empire, every hope and every ambition, my very life, lying prostrate there with the dead master, *they* came, seized me from behind and bound me until my veins stood out like cords, and my voice failed with the paroxysms of my frenzied screams. But I still raged, bleeding and infuriated, among them, and more than one policeman felt my sharp teeth. Then when I could no longer move they came nearer; I saw old Hawberk, and behind him my cousin Louis's ghastly face, and farther away, in the corner, a woman, Constance, weeping softly.

"Ah! I see it now!" I shrieked. "You have seized the throne and the empire. Woe! woe to you who are crowned with the crown of the King in Yellow!"

[EDITOR'S NOTE.—Mr. Castaigne died yesterday in the Asylum for Criminal Insane.]

THE MASK

Camilla: You, sir, should unmask.
Stranger: Indeed?
Cassilda: Indeed it's time. We all have laid aside disguise but you.
Stranger: I wear no mask.
Camilla (terrified, aside to Cassilda): No mask? No mask!

—"The King in Yellow," Act I, Scene 2

I

Although I knew nothing of chemistry, I listened fascinated. He picked up an Easter lily which Geneviève had brought that morning from Notre Dame and dropped it into the basin. Instantly the liquid lost its crystalline clearness. For a second the lily was enveloped in a milk-white foam, which disappeared, leaving the fluid opalescent. Changing tints of orange and crimson played over the surface, and then what seemed to be a ray of pure sunlight struck through from the bottom where the lily was resting. At the same instant he plunged his hand into the basin and drew out the flower. "There is no danger," he explained, "if you choose the right moment. That golden ray is the signal."

He held the lily towards me and I took it in my hand. It had turned to stone, to the purest marble.

"You see," he said, "it is without a flaw. What sculptor could reproduce it?"

The marble was white as snow; but in its depths the veins of the lily were tinged with palest azure, and a faint flush lingered deep in its heart.

"Don't ask me the reason of that," he smiled, noticing my wonder. "I have no idea why the veins and heart are tinted, but they always are. Yesterday I tried one of Geneviève's gold-fish—there it is."

The fish looked as if sculptured in marble. But if you held it to the light the stone was beautifully veined with a faint blue, and from somewhere within came a rosy light like the tint which slumbers in an opal. I looked into the basin. Once more it seemed filled with clearest crystal.

"If I should touch it now?" I demanded.

"I don't know," he replied, "but you had better not try."

"There is one thing I'm curious about," I said, "and that is where the ray of sunlight came from."

"It looked like a sunbeam, true enough," he said. "I don't know, it always comes when I immerse any living thing. Perhaps," he continued, smiling—"perhaps it is the vital spark of the creature escaping to the source whence it came."

I saw he was mocking, and threatened him with a mahlstick; but he only laughed and changed the subject.

"Stay to lunch. Geneviève will be here directly."

"I saw her going to early mass," I said, "and she looked as fresh and sweet as that lily—before you destroyed it."

"Do you think I destroyed it?" said Boris, gravely.

"Destroyed, preserved, how can we tell?"

We sat in the corner of a studio near his unfinished group of "The Fates." He leaned back on the sofa, twirling a sculptor's chisel and squinting at his work.

"By-the-way," he said, "I have finished pointing up that old academic 'Ariadne,' and I suppose it will have to go to the Salon. It's all I have ready this year, but after the success the 'Madonna' brought me I feel ashamed to send a thing like that."

The "Madonna," an exquisite marble, for which Geneviève had sat, had been the sensation of last year's Salon. I looked at the "Ariadne." It was a magnificent piece of technical work; but I agreed with Boris that the world would expect something better of him than that. Still, it was impossible now to think of finishing in time for the Salon that splendid, terrible group half shrouded in the marble behind me. "The Fates" would have to wait.

We were proud of Boris Yvain. We claimed him and he claimed us on the strength of his having been born in America, although his father was French and his mother was a Russian. Every one in the Beaux Arts called him Boris. And yet there were only two of us whom he addressed in the same familiar way—Jack Scott and myself.

Perhaps my being in love with Geneviève had something to do with his affection for me. Not that it had ever been acknowledged between us. But after all was settled, and she had told me with tears in her eyes that it was Boris whom she loved, I went over to his house and congratulated him. The perfect cordiality of that interview did not deceive either of us, I always believed, although to one at least it was a great comfort. I do not think he and Geneviève ever spoke of the matter together, but Boris knew.

Geneviève was lovely. The Madonna-like purity of her face might have been inspired by the "Sanctus" in Gounod's Mass. But I was always glad when she changed that mood for what we called her "April Manoeuvres." She was often as variable as an April day. In the morning grave, dignified, and sweet; at noon laughing, capricious; at evening whatever one least expected. I preferred her so rather than in that Madonna-like tranquillity which stirred the depths of my heart. I was dreaming of Geneviève when he spoke again.

"What do you think of my discovery, Alec?"

"I think it wonderful."

"I shall make no use of it, you know, beyond satisfying my own curiosity so far as may be, and the secret will die with me."

"It would be rather a blow to sculpture, would it not? We painters lose more than we ever gain by photography."

Boris nodded, playing with the edge of the chisel.

"This new, vicious discovery would corrupt the world of art. No. I shall never confide the secret to any one," he said, slowly.

It would be hard to find any one less informed about such phenomena than myself; but of course I had heard of mineral springs so saturated with silica that the leaves and twigs which fell into them were turned to stone after a time. I dimly comprehended the process, how the silica replaced the vegetable matter, atom by atom, and the result was a duplicate of the object in stone. This I confess had never interested me greatly, and, as for the ancient fossils thus produced, they disgusted me. Boris, it appeared, feeling curiosity instead of repugnance, had investigated the subject, and had accidentally stumbled on a solution which, attacking the immersed object with a ferocity unheard of, in a second did the work of years. This was all I could make out of the strange story he had just been telling me. He spoke again after a long silence.

"I am almost frightened when I think what I have found. Scientists would go mad over the discovery. It was so simple, too; it discovered itself. When I think of that formula, and that new element precipitated in metallic scales—"

"What new element?"

"Oh, I haven't thought of naming it, and I don't believe I ever shall. There are enough precious metals now in the world to cut throats over."

I pricked up my ears. "Have you struck gold, Boris?"

"No, better; but see here, Alec!" he laughed, starting up. "You and I have all we need in this world. Ah! how sinister and covetous you look already!" I laughed, too, and told him I was devoured by the desire for gold, and we had better talk of something else; so, when Geneviève came in shortly after, we had turned our backs on alchemy.

Geneviève was dressed in silvery gray from head to foot. The light glinted along the soft curves of her fair hair as she turned her cheek to Boris; then she saw me and returned my greeting. She had never before failed to blow me a kiss from the tips of her white fingers, and I promptly complained of the omission. She smiled and held out her hand, which dropped almost before it had touched mine; then she said, looking at Boris:

"You must ask Alec to stay for luncheon." This also was something new. She had always asked me herself until to-day.

"I did," said Boris, shortly.

"And you said yes, I hope." She turned to me with a charming conventional smile. I might have been an acquaintance of the day before yesterday. I made her a low bow. "J'avais bien l'honneur, madame"; but, refusing to take up our usual bantering tone, she murmured a hospitable commonplace and disappeared. Boris and I looked at each other.

"I had better go home, don't you think?" I asked.

"Hanged if I know," he replied, frankly.

While we were discussing the advisability of my departure, Geneviève reappeared in the door-way without her bonnet. She was wonderfully beautiful, but her color was too deep and her lovely eyes were too bright. She came straight up to me and took my arm.

"Luncheon is ready. Was I cross, Alec? I thought I had a headache, but I haven't. Come here, Boris," and she slipped her other arm through his. "Alec knows that, after you, there is no one in the world whom I like as well as I like him, so if he sometimes feels snubbed it won't hurt him."

"A la bonheur!" I cried; "who says there are no thunder-storms in April?"

"Are you ready?" chanted Boris. "Aye ready"; and arm-in-arm we raced into the dining-room, scandalizing the servants. After all, we were not so much to blame; Geneviève was eighteen, Boris was twenty-three, and I not quite twenty-one.

II

Some work that I was doing about this time on the decorations for Geneviève's boudoir kept me constantly at the quaint little hotel in the Rue Sainte-Cécile. Boris and I in those days labored hard, but as we pleased, which was fitfully, and we all three, with Jack Scott, idled a great deal together.

One quiet afternoon I had been wandering alone over the house examining curios, prying into odd corners, bringing out sweetmeats and cigars from strange hiding-places, and at last I stopped in the bathing-room. Boris, all over clay, stood there washing his hands.

The room was built of rose-colored marble, excepting the floor, which was tessellated in rose and gray. In the centre was a square pool sunken below the surface of the floor; steps led down into it; sculptured pillars supported a frescoed ceiling. A delicious marble Cupid appeared to have just alighted on his pedestal at the upper end of the room. The whole interior was Boris's work and mine. Boris, in his working clothes of white canvas, scraped the traces of clay and red modelling-wax from his handsome hands and coquetted over his shoulder with the Cupid.

"I see you," he insisted; "don't try to look the other way and pretend not to see me. You know who made you, little humbug!"

It was always my rôle to interpret Cupid's sentiments in these conversations, and when my turn came I responded in such a manner that Boris seized my arm and dragged me towards the pool, declaring he would duck me. Next instant he dropped my arm and turned pale. "Good God!" he said, "I forgot the pool is full of the solution!"

I shivered a little, and dryly advised him to remember better where he had stored the precious liquid.

"In Heaven's name, why do you keep a small lake of that grewsome stuff here of all places?" I asked.

"I want to experiment on something large," he replied.

"On me, for instance!"

"Ah! that came too close for jesting; but I do want to watch the action of that solution on a more highly organized living body; there is that big, white rabbit," he said, following me into the studio.

Jack Scott, wearing a paint-stained jacket, came wandering in, appropriated all the Oriental sweetmeats he could lay his hands on, looted the cigarette-case, and finally he and Boris disappeared together to visit the Luxembourg Gallery, where a new silver bronze by Rodin and a landscape of Monet's were claiming the exclusive attention of artistic France. I went back to the studio and resumed my work. It was a Renaissance screen, which Boris wanted me to paint for Geneviève's boudoir. But the small boy who was unwillingly dawdling through a series of poses for it to-day refused all bribes to be good. He never rested an instant in the same position, and inside of five minutes I had as many different outlines of the little beggar.

"Are you posing or are you executing a song and dance, my friend?" I inquired.

"Whichever monsieur pleases," he replied, with an angelic smile.

Of course I dismissed him for the day, and of course I paid him for the full time, that being the way we spoil our models.

After the young imp had gone, I made a few perfunctory daubs at my work, but was so thoroughly out of humor that it took me the rest of the afternoon to undo the damage I had done, so at last I scraped my palette, stuck my brushes in a bowl of black soap, and strolled into the smoking-room. I really believe that, excepting Geneviève's apartments, no room in the house was so free from the perfume of tobacco as this one. It was a queer chaos of odds and ends hung with threadbare tapestry. A sweet-toned old spinet in good repair stood by the window. There were stands of weapons, some old and dull, others bright and modern, festoons of Indian and Turkish armor over the mantel, two or three good pictures, and a pipe-rack. It was here that we used to come for new sensations in smoking. I doubt if any type of pipe ever existed which was not represented in that rack. When we had selected one, we immediately carried it somewhere else and smoked it; for the place was, on the whole, more gloomy and less inviting than any in the house. But this afternoon the twilight was very soothing; the rugs and skins on the floor looked brown and soft and drowsy; the big couch was piled with cushions. I found my pipe and curled up there for an unaccustomed smoke in the smoking-room. I had chosen one with a long, flexible stem, and, lighting it, fell to dreaming. After a while it went out; but I did not stir. I dreamed on and presently fell asleep.

I awoke to the saddest music I had ever heard. The room was quite dark; I had no idea what time it was. A ray of moonlight silvered one edge of the old spinet, and the polished wood seemed to exhale the sounds as perfume floats above a box of sandal-wood. Someone rose in the darkness and came away weeping quietly, and I was fool enough to cry out, "Geneviève!"

She dropped at my voice, and I had time to curse myself while I made a light and tried to raise her from the floor. She shrank away with a murmur of pain. She was very quiet, and asked for Boris. I carried her to the divan, and went to look for him; but he was not in the house, and the servants were gone to bed. Perplexed and anxious, I hurried back to Geneviève. She lay where I had left her, looking very white.

"I can't find Boris nor any of the servants," I said.

"I know," she answered, faintly, "Boris has gone to Ept with Mr. Scott. I did not remember when I sent you for him just now."

"But he can't get back in that case before to-morrow afternoon, and—are you hurt? Did I frighten you into falling? What an awful fool I am, but I was only half awake."

"Boris thought you had gone home before dinner. Do please excuse us for letting you stay here all this time."

"I have had a long nap," I laughed, "so sound that I did not know whether I was still asleep or not when I found myself staring at a figure that was moving towards me, and called out your name. Have you been trying the old spinet? You must have played very softly."

I would tell a thousand more lies worse than that one to see the look of relief that came into her face. She smiled adorably and said, in her natural voice: "Alec, I tripped on that wolf's head, and I think my ankle is sprained. Please call Marie and then go home."

I did as she bade me, and left her there when the maid came in.

III

At noon next day when I called, I found Boris walking restlessly about his studio.

"Geneviève is asleep just now," he told me; "the sprain is nothing, but why should she have such a high fever? The doctor can't account for it; or else he will not," he muttered.

"Geneviève has a fever?" I asked.

"I should say so, and has actually been a little lightheaded at intervals all night. The idea!—gay little Geneviève, without a care in the world—and she keeps saying her heart's broken and she wants to die!"

My own heart stood still.

Boris leaned against the door of his studio, looking down, his hands in his pockets, his kind, keen eyes clouded, a new line of trouble drawn "over the mouth's good mark, that made the smile." The maid had orders to summon him the instant Geneviève opened her eyes. We waited and waited, and Boris, growing restless, wandered about, fussing with modelling-wax and red clay. Suddenly he started for the next room. "Come and see my rose-colored bath full of death," he cried.

"Is it death?" I asked, to humor his mood.

"You are not prepared to call it life, I suppose," he answered. As he spoke he plucked a solitary goldfish squirming and twisting out of its globe. "We'll send this one after the other—wherever that is," he said. There was feverish excitement in his voice. A dull weight of fever lay on my limbs and on my brain as I followed him to the fair crystal pool with its pink-tinted sides; and he dropped the creature in. Falling, its scales flashed with a hot, orange gleam in its angry twistings and contortions; the moment it struck the liquid it became rigid and sank heavily to the bottom. Then came the milky foam, the splendid hues radiating on the surface, and then the shaft of pure, serene light broke through from seemingly infinite depths. Boris plunged in his hand and drew out an exquisite marble thing, blue veined, rose tinted, and glistening with opalescent drops.

"Child's play," he muttered, and looked wearily, longingly, at me—as if I could answer such questions! But Jack Scott came in and entered into the "game," as he called it, with ardor. Nothing would do but to try the experiment on the white rabbit then and there. I was willing that Boris should find distraction from his cares, but I hated to see the life go out of a warm, living creature, and I declined to be present. Picking up a book at random, I sat down in the studio to read. Alas, I had found "The King in Yellow." After a few moments, which seemed ages, I was putting it away with a nervous shudder, when Boris and Jack came in, bringing their marble rabbit. At the same time the bell rang above and a cry came from the sickroom. Boris was gone like a flash, and the next moment he called: "Jack, run for the doctor; bring him back with you. Alec, come here."

I went and stood at her door. A frightened maid came out in haste and ran away to fetch some remedy. Geneviève, sitting bolt upright, with crimson cheeks and glittering eyes, babbled incessantly and resisted Boris's gentle restraint. He called me to help. At my first touch she sighed and sank back, closing her eyes, and then—then—as we still bent above her, she opened them again, looked straight into Boris's face, poor, fever-crazed girl, and told her secret. At the same instant our three lives turned into new channels; the bond that had held us so long together snapped forever, and a new bond was forged in its place, for she had spoken my name, and, as the fever tortured her, her heart poured out its load of hidden sorrow. Amazed and dumb, I bowed my head, while my face burned like a live coal, and the blood surged in my ears, stupefying me with its clamor. Incapable of movement, incapable of speech, I listened to her feverish words in an agony of shame and sorrow. I could not silence her, I could not look at Boris. Then I felt an arm upon my shoulder, and Boris turned a bloodless face to mine.

"It is not your fault, Alec; don't grieve so if she loves you—" But he could not finish; and as the doctor stepped swiftly into the room, saying, "Ah, the fever!" I seized Jack Scott and hurried him to the street, saying, "Boris would rather be alone." We crossed the street to our own apartments, and that night, seeing I was going to be ill, too, he went for the doctor again. The last thing I recollect with any distinctness was hearing Jack say, "For Heaven's sake, doctor, what ails him, to wear a face like that?" and I thought of "The King in Yellow" and the Pallid Mask.

I was very ill, for the strain of two years which I had endured since that fatal May morning when Geneviève murmured, "I love you, but I think I love Boris best," told on me at last. I had never imagined that it could become more than I could endure. Outwardly tranquil, I had deceived myself. Although the inward battle raged night after night, and I, lying alone in my room, cursed myself for rebellious thoughts unloyal to Boris and unworthy of

Geneviève, the morning always brought relief, and I returned to Geneviève and to my dear Boris with a heart washed clean by the tempests of the night.

Never in word or deed or thought while with them had I betrayed my sorrow even to myself.

The mask of self-deception was no longer a mask for me; it was a part of me. Night lifted it, laying bare the stifled truth below; but there was no one to see except myself, and when day broke the mask fell back again of its own accord. These thoughts passed through my troubled mind as I lay sick, but they were hopelessly entangled with visions of white creatures, heavy as stone, crawling about in Boris's basin—of the wolf's head on the rug, foaming and snapping at Geneviève, who lay smiling beside it. I thought, too, of the King in Yellow wrapped in the fantastic colors of his tattered mantle, and that bitter cry of Cassilda, "Not upon us, O King, not upon us!" Feverishly I struggled to put it from me, but I saw the Lake of Hali, thin and blank, without a ripple or wind to stir it, and I saw the towers of Carcosa behind the moon. Aldebaran, the Hyades, Alar, Hastur, glided through the cloud rifts which fluttered and flapped as they passed like the scalloped tatters of the King in Yellow. Among all these, one sane thought persisted. It never wavered, no matter what else was going on in my disordered mind, that my chief reason for existing was to meet some requirement of Boris and Geneviève. What this obligation was, its nature, was never clear; sometimes it seemed to be protection, sometimes support, through a great crisis. Whatever it seemed to be for the time, its weight rested only on me, and I was never so ill or so weak that I did not respond with my whole soul. There were always crowds of faces about me, mostly strange, but a few I recognized, Boris among them. Afterwards they told me that this could not have been, but I know that once at least he bent over me. It was only a touch, a faint echo of his voice, then the clouds settled back on my senses, and I lost him, but he *did* stand there and bend over me *once* at least.

At last, one morning I awoke to find the sunlight falling across my bed, and Jack Scott reading beside me. I had not strength enough to speak aloud, neither could I think, much less remember, but I could smile feebly as Jack's eye met mine, and, when he jumped up and asked eagerly if I wanted anything, I could whisper, "Yes, Boris." Jack moved to the head of my bed, and leaned down to arrange my pillow; I did not see his face, but he answered, heartily, "You must wait, Alec, you are too weak to see even Boris."

I waited and I grew strong; in a few days I was able to see whom I would, but meanwhile I had thought and remembered. From the moment when all the past grew clear again in my mind, I never doubted what I should do when the time came, and I felt sure that Boris would have resolved upon the same course so far as he was concerned; as for what pertained to me alone, I knew he would see that also as I did. I no longer asked for any one. I never inquired why no message came from them; why, during the week I lay there, waiting and growing stronger, I never heard their names spoken. Preoccupied with my own searchings for the right way, and with my feeble but determined fight against despair, I simply acquiesced in Jack's reticence, taking for granted that he was afraid to speak of them, lest I should turn unruly and insist on seeing them. Meanwhile I said over and over to myself how it would be when life began again for us all. We would take up our relations exactly as they were before Geneviève fell ill. Boris and I would look into each other's eyes, and there would be neither rancor nor cowardice nor mistrust in that glance. I would be with them again for a little while in the dear intimacy of their home, and then, without pretext or explanation, I would disappear from their lives forever. Boris would know; Geneviève—the only comfort was that she would never know. It seemed, as I thought it over, that I had found the meaning of that sense of obligation which had persisted all through my delirium, and the only possible answer to it. So, when I was quite ready, I beckoned Jack to me one day, and said:

"Jack, I want Boris at once, and take my dearest greeting to Geneviève. . . ."

When at last he made me understand that they were both dead, I fell into a wild rage that tore all my little convalescent strength to atoms. I raved and cursed myself into a relapse, from which I crawled forth some weeks afterwards a boy of twenty-one who believed that his youth was gone forever. I seemed to be past the capability of further suffering, and one day, when Jack handed me a letter and the keys to Boris's house, I took them without a tremor and asked him to tell me all. It was cruel of me to ask him, but there was no help for it, and he leaned wearily on his thin hands to reopen the wound which could never entirely heal. He began very quietly.

"Alec, unless you have a clue that I know nothing about, you will not be able to explain any more than I what has happened. I suspect that you would rather not hear these details, but you must learn them, else I would spare you the relation. God knows I wish I could be spared the telling. I shall use few words.

"That day when I left you in the doctor's care and came back to Boris, I found him working on 'The Fates.' Geneviève, he said, was sleeping under the influence of drugs. She had been quite out of her mind, he said. He kept on working, not talking any more, and I watched him. Before long I saw that the third figure of the group—the one looking straight ahead, out over the world—bore his face; not as you ever saw it, but as it looked then and to the end. This is one thing for which I should like to find an explanation, but I never shall.

"Well, he worked and I watched him in silence, and we went on that way until nearly midnight. Then we heard a door open and shut sharply, and a swift rush in the next room. Boris sprang through the door-way, and I followed; but we were too late. She lay at the bottom of the pool, her hands across her breast. Then Boris shot himself through the heart." Jack stopped speaking, drops of sweat stood under his eyes, and his thin cheeks twitched. "I carried Boris to his room. Then I went back and let that hellish fluid out of the pool, and, turning on all the water, washed the marble clean of every drop. When at length I dared descend the steps, I found her lying there as white as snow. At last, when I had decided what was best to do, I went into the laboratory, and first emptied the solution in the basin into the waste-pipe; then I poured the contents of every jar and bottle after it. There was wood in the fireplace, so I built a fire, and, breaking the locks of Boris's cabinet, I burned every paper, note-book, and letter that I found there. With a mallet from the studio I smashed to pieces all the empty bottles, then, loading them into a coal-scuttle, I carried them to the cellar and threw them over the red-hot bed of the furnace. Six times I made the journey, and at last not a vestige remained of anything which might again aid one seeking for the formula which Boris had found. Then at last I dared call the doctor. He is a good man, and together we struggled to keep it from the public. Without him I never could have succeeded. At last we got the servants paid and sent away into the country, where old Rosier keeps them quiet with stories of Boris's and Geneviève's travels in distant lands, whence they will not return for years. We buried Boris in the little cemetery of Sèvres. The doctor is a good creature, and knows when to pity a man who can bear no more. He gave his certificate of heart disease and asked no questions of me."

Then, lifting his head from his hands, he said, "Open the letter, Alec; it is for us both."

I tore it open. It was Boris's will, dated a year before. He left everything to Geneviève, and, in case of her dying childless, I was to take control of the house in the Rue Sainte-Cécile, and Jack Scott the management at Ept. On our deaths the property reverted to his mother's family in Russia, with the exception of the sculptured marbles executed by himself. These he left to me.

The page blurred under our eyes, and Jack got up and walked to the window. Presently he returned and sat down again. I dreaded to hear what he was going to say; but he spoke with the same simplicity and gentleness.

"Geneviève lies before the 'Madonna' in the marble-room. The 'Madonna' bends tenderly above her, and Geneviève smiles back into that calm face that never would have been except for her."

His voice broke, but he grasped my hand, saying, "Courage, Alec." Next morning he left for Ept to fulfil his trust.

IV

The same evening I took the keys and went into the house I had known so well. Everything was in order, but the silence was terrible. Though I went twice to the door of the marble-room, I could not force myself to enter. It was beyond my strength. I went into the smoking-room and sat down before the spinet. A small lace handkerchief lay on the keys, and I turned away, choking. It was plain I could not stay, so I locked every door, every window, and the three front and back gates, and went away. Next morning Alcide packed my valise, and, leaving him in charge of my apartments, I took the Orient Express for Constantinople. During the two years that I wandered through the East, at first, in our letters, we never mentioned Geneviève and Boris, but gradually their names crept in. I recollect particularly a passage in one of Jack's letters replying to one of mine:

"What you tell me of seeing Boris bending over you while you lay ill, and feeling his touch on your face and hearing his voice, of course troubles me. This that you describe must have happened a fortnight after he died. I say to myself that you were dreaming, that it was part of your delirium, but the explanation does not satisfy me, nor would it you."

Towards the end of the second year a letter came from Jack to me in India so unlike anything that I had ever known of him that I decided to return at once to Paris. He wrote: "I am well, and sell all my pictures, as artists do who have no need of money. I have not a care of my own; but I am more restless than if I had. I am unable to shake off a strange anxiety about you. It is not apprehension, it is rather a breathless expectancy—of what, God knows! I can only say it is wearing me out. Nights I dream always of you and Boris. I can never recall anything afterwards; but I wake in the morning with my heart beating, and all day the excitement increases until I fall asleep at night to recall the same experience.

I am quite exhausted by it, and have determined to break up this morbid condition. I must see you. Shall I go to Bombay or will you come to Paris?"

I telegraphed him to expect me by the next steamer.

When we met I thought he had changed very little; I, he insisted, looked in splendid health. It was good to hear his voice again, and as we sat and chatted about what life still held for us we felt that it was pleasant to be alive in the bright spring weather.

We stayed in Paris together a week, and then I went for a week to Ept with him, but first of all we went to the cemetery at Sèvres, where Boris lay.

"Shall we place 'The Fates' in the little grove above him?" Jack asked, and I answered:

"I think only the 'Madonna' should watch over Boris's grave." But Jack was none the better for my home-coming. The dreams, of which he could not retain even the least definite outline, continued, and he said that at times the sense of breathless expectancy was suffocating.

"You see, I do you harm and not good," I said. "Try a change without me." So he started alone for a ramble among the Channel Islands, and I went back to Paris. I had not yet entered Boris's house, now mine, since my return, but I knew it must be done. It had been kept in order by Jack; there were servants there, so I gave up my own apartment and went there to live. Instead of the agitation I had feared, I found myself able to paint there tranquilly. I visited all the rooms—all but one. I could not bring myself to enter the marble-room, where Geneviève lay, and yet I felt the longing growing daily to look upon her face, to kneel beside her.

One April afternoon I lay dreaming in the smoking-room, just as I had lain two years before, and mechanically I looked among the tawny Eastern rugs for the wolf-skin. At last I distinguished the pointed ears and flat, cruel head, and I thought of my dream, where I saw Geneviève lying beside it. The helmets still hung against the threadbare tapestry, among them the old Spanish morion which I remembered Geneviève had once put on when we were amusing ourselves with the ancient bits of mail. I turned my eyes to the spinet; every yellow key seemed eloquent of her caressing hand, and I rose, drawn by the strength of my life's passion to the sealed door of the marble-room. The heavy doors swung inward under my trembling hands. Sunlight poured through the window, tipping with gold the wings of Cupid, and lingered like a nimbus over the brows of the "Madonna." Her tender face bent in compassion over a marble form so exquisitely pure that I knelt and signed myself. Geneviève lay in the shadow under the "Madonna," and yet, through her white arms, I saw the pale azure vein, and beneath her softly clasped hands the folds of her dress were tinged with rose, as if from some faint, warm light within her breast.

Bending, with a breaking heart, I touched the marble drapery with my lips, then crept back into the silent house.

A maid came and brought me a letter, and I sat down in the little conservatory to read it; but as I was about to break the seal, seeing the girl lingering, I asked her what she wanted.

She stammered something about a white rabbit that had been caught in the house, and asked what should be done with it. I told her to let it loose in the walled garden behind the house, and opened my letter. It was from Jack, but so incoherent that I thought he must have lost his reason. It was nothing but a series of prayers to me not to leave the house until he could get back; he could not tell me why; there were the dreams, he said—he could explain nothing, but he was sure that I must not leave the house in the Rue Sainte-Cécile.

As I finished reading I raised my eyes and saw the same maid-servant standing in the door-way holding a glass dish in which two gold-fish were swimming. "Put them back into the tank and tell me what you mean by interrupting me," I said.

With a half-suppressed whimper she emptied water and fish into an aquarium at the end of the conservatory, and, turning to me, asked my permission to leave my service. She said people were playing tricks on her, evidently with a design of getting her into trouble; the marble rabbit had been stolen and a live one had been brought into the house; the two beautiful marble fish were gone, and she had just found those common live things flopping on the dining-room floor. I reassured her and sent her away, saying I would look about myself. I went into the studio; there was nothing there but my canvases and some casts, except the marble of the Easter lily. I saw it on a table across the room. Then I strode angrily over to it. But the flower I lifted from the table was fresh and fragile, and filled the air with perfume.

Then suddenly I comprehended, and sprang through the hall-way to the marble-room. The doors flew open, the sunlight streamed into my face, and through it, in a heavenly glory, the "Madonna" smiled, as Geneviève lifted her flushed face from her marble couch and opened her sleepy eyes.

THE YELLOW SIGN

I

"Let the red dawn surmise
What we shall do,
When this blue starlight dies
And all is through."

THERE ARE SO MANY THINGS WHICH ARE IMPOSSIBLE TO explain! Why should certain chords in music make me think of the brown and golden tints of autumn foliage? Why should the Mass of Sainte-Cécile send my thoughts wandering among caverns whose walls blaze with ragged masses of virgin silver? What was it in the roar and turmoil of Broadway at six o'clock that flashed before my eyes the picture of a still Breton forest where sunlight filtered through spring foliage, and Sylvia bent, half curiously, half tenderly, over a small, green lizard, murmuring, "To think that this also is a little ward of God?"

When I first saw the watchman his back was towards me. I looked at him indifferently, until he went into the church. I paid no more attention to him than I had to any other man who lounged through Washington Square that morning, and when I shut my window and turned back into my studio I had forgotten him. Late in the afternoon, the day being warm, I raised the window again and leaned out to get a sniff of air. A man was standing in the courtyard of the church, and I noticed him again with as little interest as I had that morning. I looked across the square to where the fountain was playing, and then, with my mind filled with vague impressions of trees, asphalt drives, and the moving groups of nursemaids and holiday-makers, I started to walk back to my easel. As I turned, my listless glance included the man below in the church-yard. His face was towards me now, and with a perfectly involuntary movement I bent to see it. At the same moment he raised his head and looked at me. Instantly I thought of a coffin-worm. Whatever it was about the man that repelled me, I did not know, but the impression of a plump, white grave-worm was so intense and nauseating that I must have shown it in my expression, for he turned his puffy face away with a movement which made me think of a disturbed grub in a chestnut.

I went back to my easel and motioned the model to resume her pose. After working awhile, I was satisfied that I was spoiling what I had done as rapidly as possible, and I took up a palette-knife and scraped the color out again. The flesh tones were sallow and unhealthy, and I did not understand how I could have painted such sickly color into a study which before that had glowed with healthy tones.

I looked at Tessie. She had not changed, and the clear flush of health dyed her neck and cheeks as I frowned.

"Is it something I've done?" she asked.

"No; I've made a mess of this arm, and for the life of me I can't see how I came to paint such mud as that into the canvas," I replied.

"Don't I pose well?" she insisted.

"Of course, perfectly."

"Then it's not my fault?"

"No. It's my own."

"I'm very sorry," she said.

I told her she could rest while I applied rag and turpentine to the plague-spot on my canvas, and she went off to smoke a cigarette and look over the illustrations in the *Courier Français*.

I did not know whether it was something in the turpentine or a defect in the canvas, but the more I scrubbed the more that gangrene seemed to spread. I worked like a beaver to get it out, and yet the disease appeared to creep from limb to limb of the study before me. Alarmed, I strove to arrest it, but now the color on the breast changed and the whole figure seemed to absorb the infection as a sponge soaks up water. Vigorously I plied palette-knife, turpentine, and scraper, thinking all the time what a séance I should hold with Duval, who had sold me the canvas; but soon I noticed that it was not the canvas which was defective, nor yet the colors of Edward. "It must be the turpentine," I thought, angrily, "or else my eyes have become so blurred and confused by the afternoon light that I can't see straight." I called Tessie, the model. She came and leaned over my chair, blowing rings of smoke into the air.

"What *have* you been doing to it?" she exclaimed.

"Nothing," I growled; "it must be this turpentine!"

"What a horrible color it is now," she continued. "Do you think my flesh resembles green cheese?"

"No, I don't," I said, angrily, "did you ever know me to paint like that before?"

"No, indeed!"

"Well, then!"

"It must be the turpentine, or something," she admitted.

She slipped on a Japanese robe and walked to the window. I scraped and rubbed until I was tired, and finally picked up my brushes and hurled them through the canvas with a forcible expression, the tone alone of which reached Tessie's ears.

Nevertheless she promptly began: "That's it! Swear and act silly and ruin your brushes! You have been three weeks on that study, and now look! What's the good of ripping the canvas? What creatures artists are!"

I felt about as much ashamed as I usually did after such an outbreak, and I turned the ruined canvas to the wall. Tessie helped me clean my brushes, and then danced away to dress. From the screen she regaled me with bits of advice concerning whole or partial loss of temper, until thinking perhaps I had been tormented sufficiently, she came out to implore me to button her waist where she could not reach it on the shoulder.

"Everything went wrong from the time you came back from the window and talked about that horrid-looking man you saw in the church-yard," she announced.

"Yes, he probably bewitched the picture," I said, yawning. I looked at my watch.

"It's after six, I know," said Tessie, adjusting her hat before the mirror.

"Yes," I replied, "I didn't mean to keep you so long." I leaned out of the window, but recoiled with disgust, for the young man with the pasty face stood below in the church-yard. Tessie saw my gesture of disapproval, and leaned from the window.

"Is that the man you don't like?" she whispered.

I nodded.

"I can't see his face, but he does look fat and soft. Someway or other," she continued, turning to look at me, "he reminds me of a dream—an awful dream—I once had. Or," she mused, looking down at her shapely shoes, "was it a dream after all?"

"How should I know?" I smiled.

Tessie smiled in reply.

"You were in it," she said, "so perhaps you might know something about it."

"Tessie! Tessie!" I protested, "don't you dare flatter by saying that you dream about me!"

"But I did," she insisted. "Shall I tell you about it?"

"Go ahead," I replied, lighting a cigarette.

Tessie leaned back on the open window-sill and began, very seriously:

"One night last winter I was lying in bed thinking about nothing at all in particular. I had been posing for you and I was tired out, yet it seemed impossible for me to sleep. I heard the bells in the city ring ten, eleven, and midnight. I must have fallen asleep about midnight, because I don't remember hearing the bells after that. It seemed to me that I had scarcely closed my eyes when I dreamed that something impelled me to go to the window. I rose, and, raising the sash, leaned out. Twenty-fifth Street was deserted as far as I could see. I began to be afraid; everything outside seemed so—so black and uncomfortable. Then the sound of wheels in the distance came to my ears, and it seemed to me as though that was what I must wait for. Very slowly the wheels approached, and, finally, I could make out a vehicle moving along the street. It came nearer and nearer, and when it passed beneath my window I saw it was a hearse. Then, as I trembled with fear, the driver turned and looked straight at me. When I awoke I was standing by the open window shivering with cold, but the black-plumed hearse and the driver were gone. I dreamed this dream again in March last, and again awoke beside the open window. Last night the dream came again. You remember how it was raining; when I awoke, standing at the open window, my night-dress was soaked."

"But where did I come into the dream?" I asked.

"You—you were in the coffin; but you were not dead."

"In the coffin?"

"Yes."

"How did you know? Could you see me?"

"No; I only knew you were there."

"Had you been eating Welsh rarebits, or lobster salad?" I began, laughing, but the girl interrupted me with a frightened cry.

"Hello! What's up?" I said, as she shrank into the embrasure by the window.

"The—the man below in the church-yard; he drove the hearse."

"Nonsense," I said; but Tessie's eyes were wide with terror. I went to the window and looked out. The man was gone. "Come, Tessie," I urged, "don't be foolish. You have posed too long; you are nervous."

"Do you think I could forget that face?" she murmured. "Three times I saw the hearse pass below my window, and every time the driver turned and looked up at me. Oh, his face was so white and—and soft! It looked dead—it looked as if it had been dead a long time."

I induced the girl to sit down and swallow a glass of Marsala. Then I sat down beside her and tried to give her some advice.

"Look here, Tessie," I said, "you go to the country for a week or two, and you'll have no more dreams about hearses. You pose all day, and when night comes your nerves are upset. You can't keep this up. Then again, instead of going to bed when your day's work is done, you run off to picnics at Sulzer's Park, or go to the

Eldorado or Coney Island, and when you come down here next morning you are fagged out. There was no real hearse. That was a softshell-crab dream."

She smiled faintly.

"What about the man in the church-yard?"

"Oh, he's only an ordinary, unhealthy, every-day creature."

"As true as my name is Tessie Rearden, I swear to you, Mr. Scott, that the face of the man below in the church-yard is the face of the man who drove the hearse!"

"What of it?" I said. "It's an honest trade."

"Then you think I *did* see the hearse?"

"Oh," I said, diplomatically, "if you really did, it might not be unlikely that the man below drove it. There is nothing in that."

Tessie rose, unrolled her scented handkerchief, and, taking a bit of gum from a knot in the hem, placed it in her mouth. Then, drawing on her gloves, she offered me her hand with a frank "Good-night, Mr. Scott," and walked out.

II

The next morning, Thomas, the bell-boy, brought me the *Herald* and a bit of news. The church next door had been sold. I thanked Heaven for it, not that I, being a Catholic, had any repugnance for the congregation next door, but because my nerves were shattered by a blatant exhorter, whose every word echoed through the aisle of the church as if it had been my own rooms, and who insisted on his r's with a nasal persistence which revolted my every instinct. Then, too, there was a fiend in human shape, an organist, who reeled off some of the grand old hymns with an interpretation of his own, and I longed for the blood of a creature who could play the "Doxology" with an amendment of minor chords which one hears only in a quartet of very young undergraduates. I believe the minister was a good man, but when he bellowed, "And the Lorrrd said unto Moses, the Lorrrd is a man of war; the Lorrrd is his name. My wrath shall wax hot, and I will kill you with the sworrrd!" I wondered how many centuries of purgatory it would take to atone for such a sin.

"Who bought the property?" I asked Thomas.

"Nobody that I knows, sir. They do say the gent wot owns this 'ere 'Amilton flats was lookin' at it. 'E might be a bildin' more studios."

I walked to the window. The young man with the unhealthy face stood by the church-yard gate, and at the mere sight of him the same overwhelming repugnance took possession of me.

"By-the-way, Thomas," I said, "who is that fellow down there?"

Thomas sniffed. "That there worm, sir? 'E's night-watchman of the church, sir. 'E maikes me tired a-sittin' out all night on them steps and lookin' at you insultin' like. I'd 'a' punched 'is 'ed, sir—beg pardon, sir—"

"Go on, Thomas."

"One night a comin' 'ome with 'Arry, the other English boy, I sees 'im a sittin' there on them steps. We 'ad Molly and Jen with us, sir, the two girls on the tray service, an' 'e looks so insultin' at us that I up and sez, 'Wat you lookin' hat, you fat slug?'—beg pardon, sir, but that's 'ow I sez, sir. Then 'e don't say nothin', and I sez, 'Come out and I'll punch that puddin' 'ed.' Then I hopens the gate an' goes in, but 'e don't say nothin', only looks insultin' like. Then I 'its 'im one; but, ugh! 'is 'ed was that cold and mushy it ud sicken you to touch 'im."

"What did he do then?" I asked, curiously.

"'Im? Nawthin'."

"And you, Thomas?"

The young fellow flushed with embarrassment, and smiled uneasily.

"Mr. Scott, sir, I ain't no coward, an' I can't make it out at all why I run. I was in the Fifth Lawncers, sir, bugler at Tel-el-Kebir, an' was shot by the wells."

"You don't mean to say you ran away?"

"Yes, sir; I run."

"Why?"

"That's just what I want to know, sir. I grabbed Molly an' run, an' the rest was as frightened as I."

"But what were they frightened at?"

Thomas refused to answer for a while; but now my curiosity was aroused about the repulsive young man below, and I pressed him. Three years' sojourn in America had not only modified Thomas's cockney dialect, but had given him the American's fear of ridicule.

"You won't believe me, Mr. Scott, sir?"

"Yes, I will."

"You will lawf at me, sir?"

"Nonsense!"

He hesitated. "Well, sir, it's Gawd's truth, that when I 'it 'im, 'e grabbed me wrists, sir, and when I twisted 'is soft, mushy fist one of 'is fingers come off in me 'and."

The utter loathing and horror of Thomas's face must have been reflected in my own, for he added:

"It's orful, an' now when I see 'im I just go away. 'E maikes me hill."

When Thomas had gone I went to the window. The man stood beside the church railing, with both hands on the gate; but I hastily retreated to my easel again, sickened and horrified, for I saw that the middle finger of his right hand was missing.

At nine o'clock Tessie appeared and vanished behind the screen, with a merry "Good-morning, Mr. Scott." When she had reappeared and taken her pose upon the model-stand I started a new canvas, much to her delight. She remained silent as long as I was on the drawing, but as soon as the scrape of the charcoal ceased, and I took up my fixative, she began to chatter.

"Oh, I had such a lovely time last night. We went to Tony Pastor's."

"Who are 'we'?" I demanded.

"Oh, Maggie—you know, Mr. Whyte's model—and Pinkie McCormick—we call her Pinkie because she's got that beautiful red hair you artists like so much—and Lizzie Burke."

I sent a shower of spray from the fixative over the canvas, and said, "Well, go on."

"We saw Kelly, and Baby Barnes, the skirt-dancer, and—and all the rest. I made a mash."

"Then you have gone back on me, Tessie?"

She laughed and shook her head.

"He's Lizzie Burke's brother, Ed. He's a perfect gen'l'man."

I felt constrained to give her some parental advice concerning mashing, which she took with a bright smile.

"Oh, I can take care of a strange mash," she said, examining her chewing-gum, "but Ed is different. Lizzie is my best friend."

Then she related how Ed had come back from the stocking-mill in Lowell, Massachusetts, to find her and Lizzie grown up—and what an accomplished young man he was—and how he thought nothing of squandering half a dollar for ice-cream and oysters to celebrate his entry as clerk into the woollen department of Macy's. Before she finished I began to paint, and she resumed the pose, smiling and chattering like a sparrow. By noon I had the study fairly well rubbed in and Tessie came to look at it.

"That's better," she said.

I thought so, too, and ate my lunch with a satisfied feeling that all was going well. Tessie spread her lunch on a drawing-table opposite me, and we drank our claret from the same bottle and lighted our cigarettes from the same match. I was very much attached to Tessie. I had watched her shoot up into a slender but exquisitely formed woman from a frail, awkward child. She had posed for me during the last three years, and among all my models she was my favorite. It would have troubled me very much indeed had she become "tough" or "fly," as the phrase goes; but I never noticed any deterioration of her manner, and felt at heart that she was all right. She and I never discussed morals at all, and I had no intention of doing so, partly because I had none myself, and partly because I knew she would do what she liked in spite of me. Still I did hope she would steer clear of complications, because I wished her well, and then also I had a selfish desire to retain the best model I had. I knew that mashing, as she termed it, had no significance with girls like Tessie, and that such things in America did not resemble in the least the same things in Paris. Yet, having lived with my eyes open, I also knew that somebody would take Tessie away some day, in one manner or another, and though I professed to myself that marriage was nonsense, I sincerely hoped that, in this case, there would be a priest at the end of the vista. I am a Catholic. When I listen to high mass, when I sign myself, I feel that everything, including myself, is more cheerful; and when I confess, it does me good. A man who lives as much alone as I do must confess to somebody. Then, again, Sylvia was Catholic, and it was reason enough for me. But I was speaking of Tessie, which is very different. Tessie also was Catholic, and much more devout than I, so, taking it all in all, I had little fear for my pretty model until she should fall in love. But *then* I knew that fate alone would decide her future for her, and I prayed inwardly that fate would keep her away from men like me and throw into her path nothing but Ed Burkes and Jimmy McCormicks, bless her sweet face!

Tessie sat blowing rings of smoke up to the ceiling and tinkling the ice in her tumbler.

"Do you know that I also had a dream last night?" I observed.

"Not about that man?" she asked, laughing.

"Exactly. A dream similar to yours, only much worse."

It was foolish and thoughtless of me to say this, but you know how little tact the average painter has.

"I must have fallen asleep about ten o'clock," I continued, "and after a while I dreamed that I awoke. So plainly did I hear the midnight bells, the wind in the tree-branches, and the whistle of steamers from the bay, that even now I can scarcely believe I was not awake. I seemed to be lying in a box which had a glass cover. Dimly I saw the street lamps as I passed, for I must tell you, Tessie, the box in which I reclined appeared to lie in a cushioned wagon which jolted me over a stony pavement. After a while I became impatient and tried to move, but the box was too narrow. My hands were crossed on my breast so I could not raise them to help myself. I listened and then tried to call. My voice was gone. I could hear the trample of the horses attached to the wagon, and even the breathing of the driver. Then another sound broke upon my ears like the raising of a window-sash. I managed to turn my head a little, and found I could look, not only through the glass cover of my box, but also through the glass panes in the side of the covered vehicle. I saw houses, empty and silent, with neither light nor life about any of them excepting one. In that house a window was open on the first floor and a figure all in white stood looking down into the street. It was you."

Tessie had turned her face away from me and leaned on the table with her elbow.

"I could see your face," I resumed, "and it seemed to me to be very sorrowful. Then we passed on and turned into a narrow, black lane. Presently the horses stopped. I waited and waited, closing my eyes with fear and impatience, but all was silent as the grave. After what seemed to me hours, I began to feel uncomfortable. A sense that somebody was close to me made me unclose my eyes. Then I saw the white face of the hearse-driver looking at me through the coffinlid—"

A sob from Tessie interrupted me. She was trembling like a leaf. I saw I had made an ass of myself, and attempted to repair the damage.

"Why, Tess," I said, "I only told you this to show you what influence your story might have on another person's dreams. You don't suppose I really lay in a coffin, do you? What are you trembling for? Don't you see that your dream and my unreasonable dislike for that inoffensive watchman of the church simply set my brain working as soon as I fell asleep?"

She laid her head between her arms and sobbed as if her heart would break. What a precious triple donkey I had made of myself! But I was about to break my record. I went over and put my arm about her.

"Tessie, dear, forgive me," I said; "I had no business to frighten you with such nonsense. You are too sensible a girl, too good a Catholic to believe in dreams."

Her hand tightened on mine and her head fell back upon my shoulder, but she still trembled and I petted her and comforted her.

"Come, Tess, open your eyes and smile."

Her eyes opened with a slow, languid movement and met mine, but their expression was so queer that I hastened to reassure her again.

"It's all humbug, Tessie. You surely are not afraid that any harm will come to you because of that?"

"No," she said, but her scarlet lips quivered.

"Then what's the matter? Are you afraid?"

"Yes. Not for myself."

"For me, then?" I demanded, gayly.

"For you," she murmured, in a voice almost inaudible. "I—I care for you."

At first I started to laugh, but when I understood her a shock passed through me, and I sat like one turned to stone. This was the crowning bit of idiocy I had committed. During the moment which elapsed between her reply and my answer I thought of a thousand responses to that innocent confession. I could pass it by with a laugh, I could misunderstand her and reassure her as to my health, I could simply point out that it was impossible she could love me. But my reply was quicker than my thoughts, and I might think and think now when it was too late, for I had kissed her on the mouth.

That evening I took my usual walk in Washington Park, pondering over the occurrences of the day. I was thoroughly committed. There was no back-out now, and I stared the future straight in the face. I was not good, not even scrupulous, but I had no idea of deceiving either myself or Tessie. The one passion of my life lay buried in the sunlit forests of Brittany. Was it buried forever? Hope cried "No!" For three years I had been listening to the voice of Hope, and for three years I had waited for a footstep on my threshold. Had Sylvia forgotten? "No!" cried Hope.

I said that I was not good. That is true, but still I was not exactly a comic-opera villain. I had led an easy-going, reckless life, taking what invited me of pleasure, deploring and sometimes bitterly regretting consequences. In one thing alone, except my painting, was I serious, and that was something which lay hidden if not lost in the Breton forests.

It was too late now for me to regret what had occurred during the day. Whatever it had been, pity, a sudden tenderness for sorrow, or the more brutal instinct of gratified vanity, it was all the same now, and unless I wished to bruise an innocent heart my path lay marked before me. The fire and strength, the depth of passion of a love which I had never even suspected, with all my imagined experience in the world, left me no alternative but to respond or send her away. Whether because I am so cowardly about giving pain to others, or whether it was that I have little of the gloomy Puritan in me, I do not know, but I shrank from disclaiming responsibility for that thoughtless kiss, and, in fact, had no time to do so before the gates of her heart opened and the flood poured forth. Others who habitually do their duty and find a sullen satisfaction in making themselves and everybody else unhappy, might have withstood it. I did not. I dared not. After the storm had abated I did tell her that she might better have loved Ed Burke and worn a plain gold ring, but she would not hear of it, and I thought perhaps that as long as she had decided to love somebody she could not marry, it had better be me. I at least could treat her with an intelligent affection, and whenever she became tired of her infatuation she could go none the worse for it. For I was decided on that point, although I knew how hard it would be. I remembered the usual termination of platonic *liaisons,* and thought how disgusted I had been whenever I heard of one. I knew I was undertaking a great deal for so unscrupulous a man as I was, and I dreaded the future, but never for one moment did I doubt that she was safe with me. Had it been anybody but Tessie, I should not have bothered my head about scruples. For it did not occur to me to sacrifice Tessie as I would have sacrificed a woman of the world. I looked the future squarely in the face, and saw the several probable endings to the affair. She would either tire of the whole thing, or become so unhappy that I should have either to marry her or go away. If I married her we would be unhappy, I with a wife unsuited to me, and she with a husband unsuitable for any woman. For my past life could scarcely entitle me to marry. If I went away she might either fall ill, recover, and marry some Eddie Burke, or she might recklessly or deliberately go and do something foolish. On the other hand, if she tired of me, then her whole life would be before her with beautiful vistas of Eddie Burkes and marriage rings, and twins, and Harlem flats, and Heaven knows what. As I strolled along through the trees by the Washington Arch, I decided that she should find a substantial friend in me anyway, and the future could take care of itself. Then I went into the house and put on my evening dress, for the little, faintly perfumed note on my dresser said, "Have a cab at the stage door at eleven," and the note was signed "Edith Carmichel, Metropolitan Theatre."

I took supper that night, or, rather, we took supper, Miss Carmichel and I, at Solari's, and the dawn was just beginning to gild the cross on the Memorial Church as I entered Washington Square after leaving Edith at the Brunswick. There was not a soul in the park as I passed among the trees and took the walk which leads from the Garibaldi statue to the Hamilton apartment house, but as I passed the church-yard I saw a figure sitting on the stone steps. In spite of myself a chill crept over me at the sight of the white, puffy face, and I hastened to pass. Then he said something which might have been addressed to me or might merely have been a mutter to himself, but a sudden furious anger flamed up within me that such a creature should address me. For an instant I felt like wheeling about and smashing my stick over his head, but I walked on, and, entering the Hamilton, went to my apartment. For some time I tossed about the bed trying to get the sound of his voice out of my ears, but could not. It filled my head, that muttering sound, like thick, oily smoke from a fat-rendering vat or an odor of noisome decay. And as I lay and tossed about, the voice in my ears seemed more distinct, and I began to understand the words he had muttered. They came to me slowly, as if I had forgotten them, and at last I could make some sense out of the sounds. It was this:

"Have you found the Yellow Sign?"

"Have you found the Yellow Sign?"

"Have you found the Yellow Sign?"

I was furious. What did he mean by that? Then with a curse upon him and his I rolled over and went to sleep, but when I awoke later I looked pale and haggard, for I had dreamed the dream of the night before, and it troubled me more than I cared to think.

I dressed and went down into my studio. Tessie sat by the window, but as I came in she rose and put both arms around my neck for an innocent kiss. She looked so sweet and dainty that I kissed her again, and then sat down before the easel.

"Hello! Where's the study I began yesterday?" I asked.

Tessie looked conscious, but did not answer. I began to hunt among the piles of canvases, saying: "Hurry up, Tess, and get ready; we must take advantage of the morning light."

When at last I gave up the search among the other canvases and turned to look around the room for the missing study, I noticed Tessie standing by the screen with her clothes still on.

"What's the matter," I asked, "don't you feel well?"

"Yes."

"Then hurry."

"Do you want me to pose as—as I have always posed?"

Then I understood. Here was a new complication. I had lost, of course, the best nude model I had ever seen. I looked at Tessie. Her face was scarlet. Alas! Alas! We had eaten of the tree of knowledge, and Eden and native innocence were dreams of the past—I mean for her.

I suppose she noticed the disappointment on my face, for she said: "I will pose if you wish. The study is behind the screen here where I put it."

"No," I said, "we will begin something new"; and I went into my wardrobe and picked out a Moorish costume which fairly blazed with tinsel. It was a genuine costume, and Tessie retired to the screen with it, enchanted. When she came forth again I was astonished. Her long, black hair was bound above her forehead with a circlet of turquoises, and the ends curled about her glittering girdle. Her feet were encased in the embroidered pointed slippers, and the skirt of her costume, curiously wrought with arabesques in silver, fell to her ankles. The deep metallic blue vest, embroidered with silver, and the short Mauresque jacket, spangled and sewn with turquoises, became her wonderfully. She came up to me and held up her face, smiling. I slipped my hand into my pocket, and, drawing out a gold chain with a cross attached, dropped it over her head.

"It's yours, Tessie."

"Mine?" she faltered.

"Yours. Now go and pose." Then with a radiant smile she ran behind the screen, and presently reappeared with a little box on which was written my name.

"I had intended to give it to you when I went home to-night," she said, "but I can't wait now."

I opened the box. On the pink cotton inside lay a clasp of black onyx, on which was inlaid a curious symbol or letter in gold. It was neither Arabic nor Chinese, nor, as I found afterwards, did it belong to any human script.

"It's all I had to give you for a keepsake," she said, timidly.

I was annoyed, but I told her how much I should prize it, and promised to wear it always. She fastened it on my coat beneath the lapel.

"How foolish, Tess, to go and buy me such a beautiful thing as this," I said.

"I did not buy it," she laughed.

"Where did you get it?"

Then she told me how she had found it one day while coming from the aquarium in the Battery, how she had advertised it and watched the papers, but at last gave up all hopes of finding the owner.

"That was last winter," she said, "the very day I had the first horrid dream about the hearse."

I remembered my dream of the previous night but said nothing, and presently my charcoal was flying over a new canvas, and Tessie stood motionless on the model-stand.

III

The day following was a disastrous one for me. While moving a framed canvas from one easel to another my foot slipped on the polished floor and I fell heavily on both wrists. They were so badly sprained that it was useless to attempt to hold a brush, and I was obliged to wander about the studio, glaring at unfinished drawings and sketches, until despair seized me and I sat down to smoke and twiddle my thumbs with rage. The rain blew against the windows and rattled on the roof of the church, driving me into a nervous fit with its interminable patter. Tessie sat sewing by the window, and every now and then raised her head and looked at me with such innocent compassion that I began to feel ashamed of my irritation and looked about for something to occupy me. I had read all the papers and all the books in the library, but for the sake of something to do I went to the bookcases and shoved them open with my elbow. I knew every volume by its color and examined them all, passing slowly around the library and whistling to keep up my spirits. I was turning to go into the dining-room when my eye fell upon a book bound in serpent-skin standing in a corner of the top shelf of the last bookcase. I did not remember it, and from the floor could not decipher the pale lettering on the back, so I went to the smoking-room and called Tessie. She came in from the studio and climbed up to reach the book.

"What is it?" I asked.

"'The King in Yellow.'"

I was dumfounded. Who had placed it there? How came it in my rooms? I had long ago decided that I should never open that book, and nothing on earth could have persuaded me to buy it. Fearful lest curiosity might tempt me to open it, I had never even looked at it in book-stores. If I ever had had any curiosity to read it, the awful tragedy of young Castaigne, whom I knew, prevented me from exploring its wicked pages. I had always refused to listen to any description of it, and, indeed, nobody ever ventured to discuss the second part aloud, so I had absolutely no knowledge of what those leaves might reveal. I stared at the poisonous, mottled binding as I would at a snake.

"Don't touch it, Tessie," I said; "come down."

Of course my admonition was enough to arouse her curiosity, and before I could prevent it she took the book, and, laughing, danced off into the studio with it. I called to her, but she slipped away with a tormenting smile at my helpless hands, and I followed her with some impatience.

"Tessie!" I cried, entering the library, "listen; I am serious. Put that book away. I do not wish you to open it!" The library was empty. I went into both drawing-rooms, then into the bedrooms, laundry, kitchen, and finally returned to the library and began a systematic search. She had hidden herself so well that it was half an hour later when I discovered her crouching white and silent by the latticed window in the store-room above. At the first glance I saw she had been punished for her foolishness. "The King in Yellow" lay at her feet; but the book was open at the second part. I looked at Tessie and saw it was too late. She had opened "The King in Yellow." Then I took her by the hand and led her into the studio. She seemed dazed, and when I told her to lie down on the sofa she obeyed me without a word. After a while she closed her eyes and her breathing became regular and deep; but I could not determine whether or not she slept. For a long while I sat silently beside her, but she neither stirred nor spoke, and at last I rose and, entering the unused store-room, took the book in my least injured hand. It seemed heavy as lead; but I carried it into the studio again, and, sitting down on the rug beside the sofa, opened it and read it through from beginning to end.

When, faint with the excess of my emotions, I dropped the volume and leaned wearily back against the sofa, Tessie opened her eyes and looked at me.

We had been speaking for some time in a dull, monotonous strain before I realized that we were discussing "The King in Yellow." Oh the sin of writing such words—words which are clear as crystal, limpid and musical as bubbling springs, words which sparkle and glow like the poisoned diamonds of the Medicis! Oh the wickedness, the hopeless damnation, of a soul who could fascinate and paralyze human creatures with such words—words understood by the ignorant and wise alike, words which are more precious than jewels, more soothing than music, more awful than death!

We talked on, unmindful of the gathering shadows, and she was begging me to throw away the clasp of black onyx quaintly inlaid with what we now knew to be the Yellow Sign. I never shall know why I refused, though even at this hour, here in my bedroom as I write this confession, I should be glad to know *what* it was that prevented me from tearing the Yellow Sign from my breast and casting it into the fire. I am sure I wished to do so, and yet Tessie pleaded with me in vain. Night fell, and the hours dragged on, but still we murmured to each other of the King and the Pallid Mask, and midnight sounded from the misty spires in the fog-wrapped city. We spoke of Hastur and of Cassilda, while outside the fog rolled against the blank window-panes as the cloud waves roll and break on the shores of Hali.

The house was very silent now, and not a sound came up from the misty streets. Tessie lay among the cushions, her face a gray blot in the gloom, but her hands were clasped in mine, and I knew that she knew and read my thoughts as I read hers, for we had understood the mystery of the Hyades, and the Phantom of Truth was laid. Then, as we answered each other, swiftly, silently, thought on thought, the shadows stirred in the gloom about us, and far in the distant streets we heard a sound. Nearer and nearer it came—the dull crunching of wheels, nearer and yet nearer, and now, outside, before the door, it ceased, and I dragged myself to the window and saw a black-plumed hearse. The gate below opened and shut, and I crept, shaking, to my door, and bolted it, but I knew no bolts, no locks, could keep that creature out who was coming for the Yellow Sign. And now I heard him moving very softly along the hall. Now he was at the door, and the bolts rotted at his touch. Now he had entered. With eyes starting from my head I peered into the darkness, but when he came into the room I did not see him. It was only when I felt him envelop me in his cold, soft grasp that I cried out and struggled with deadly fury, but my hands were useless, and he tore the onyx clasp from my coat and struck me full in the face. Then, as I fell, I heard Tessie's soft cry, and her spirit fled; and even while falling I longed to follow her, for I knew that the King in Yellow had opened his tattered mantle and there was only God to cry to now.

I could tell more, but I cannot see what help it will be to the world. As for me, I am past human help or hope. As I lie here, writing, careless even whether or not I die before I finish, I can see the doctor gathering up his powders and phials with a vague gesture to the good priest beside me, which I understand.

They will be very curious to know the tragedy—they of the outside world who write books and print millions of newspapers, but I shall write no more, and the father confessor will seal my last words with the seal of sanctity when his holy office is done. They of the outside world may send their creatures into wrecked homes and death-smitten firesides, and their newspapers will batten on blood and tears, but with me their spies must halt before the confessional. They know that Tessie is dead, and that I am dying. They know how the people in the house, aroused by an infernal scream, rushed into my room, and found one living and two dead, but they do not know what I shall tell them now; they do not know that the doctor said, as he pointed to a horrible, decomposed heap on the floor—the livid corpse of the watchman from the church: "I have no theory, no explanation. That man must have been dead for months!"

I think I am dying. I wish the priest would—

THE DEMOISELLE D'YS

"Mais je croy que je
Suis descendu on puiz
Ténébreux onquel disoit
Heraclytus estre Vérité cachée."

"There be three things which are too wonderful for me—yea, four which I know not:

"The way of an eagle in the air; the way of a serpent upon a rock; the way of a ship in the midst of the sea; and the way of a man with a maid."

I

THE UTTER DESOLATION OF THE SCENE BEGAN TO HAVE ITS effect; I sat down to face the situation and, if possible, recall to mind some landmark which might aid me in extricating myself from my present position. If I could only find the ocean again, all would be clear, for I knew one could see the island of Groix from the cliffs.

I laid down my gun, and, kneeling behind a rock, lighted a pipe. Then I looked at my watch. It was nearly four o'clock. I might have wandered far from Kerselec since daybreak.

Standing the day before on the cliffs below Kerselec with Goulven, looking out over the sombre moors among which I had now lost my way, these downs had appeared to me level as a meadow, stretching to the horizon, and, although I knew how deceptive is distance, I could not realize that what, from Kerselec, seemed to be mere grassy hollows, were great valleys covered with gorse and heather, and what looked like scattered bowlders were, in reality, enormous cliffs of granite.

"It's a bad place for a stranger," old Goulven had said; "you'd better take a guide"; and I had replied, "I shall not lose myself." Now I knew that I had lost myself, as I sat there smoking, with the sea-wind blowing in my face. On every side stretched the moorland, covered with flowering gorse and heath and granite bowlders. There was not a tree in sight, much less a house. After a while I picked up the gun, and, turning my back on the sun, tramped on again.

There was little use in following any of the brawling streams which every now and then crossed my path, for, instead of flowing into the sea, they ran inland to reedy pools in the hollows of the moors. I had followed several, but they all led me to swamps or silent little ponds from which the snipe rose, peeping, and wheeled away in an ecstasy of fright. I began to feel fatigued, and the gun galled my shoulder in spite of the double pads. The sun sank lower and lower, shining level across yellow gorse and the moorland pools.

As I walked, my own gigantic shadow led me on, seeming to lengthen at every step. The gorse scraped against my leggings, crackled beneath my feet, showering the brown earth with blossoms, and the brake bowed and billowed along my path. From tufts of heath rabbits scurried away through the bracken, and among the swamp grass I heard the wild duck's drowsy quack. Once a fox stole across my path, and again, as I stooped to drink at a hurrying rill, a heron flapped heavily from the reeds beside me. I turned to look at the sun. It seemed to touch the edges of the plain. When at last I decided that it was useless to go on, and that I must make up my mind to spend at least one night on the moors, I threw myself down thoroughly fagged out. The evening sunlight slanted warm across my body, but the sea-winds began to rise, and I felt a chill strike through me from my wet shooting-boots. High overhead gulls were wheeling and tossing like bits of white paper; from some distant marsh a solitary curlew called. Little by little the sun sank into the plain, and the zenith flushed with the after-glow. I watched the sky change from palest gold to pink, and then to smouldering fire. Clouds of midges danced above me, and high in the calm air a bat dipped and soared. My eyelids began to droop. Then, as I shook off the drowsiness, a sudden crash among the bracken roused me. I raised my eyes. A great bird hung quivering in the air above my face. For an instant I stared, incapable of motion; then something leaped past me in the ferns, and the bird rose, wheeled, and pitched headlong into the brake.

I was on my feet in an instant peering through the gorse. There came the sound of a struggle from a bunch of heather close by, and then all was quiet. I stepped forward, my gun poised, but when I came to the heather the gun fell under my arm again, and I stood motionless in silent astonishment. A dead hare lay on the ground, and on the hare stood a magnificent falcon, one talon buried in the creature's neck, the other planted firmly on its limp flank. But what astonished me was not the mere sight of a falcon sitting upon its prey. I had seen that more than once. It was that the falcon was fitted with a sort of leash about both talons, and from the leash hung a round bit of metal like a sleigh-bell. The bird turned its fierce yellow eyes on me, and then stooped and struck its curved beak into the quarry. At the same instant hurried steps sounded among the heather, and a girl sprang into the covert in front. Without a glance at me she walked up to the falcon, and, passing her gloved hand under its breast, raised it from the quarry. Then she deftly slipped a small hood over the bird's head, and, holding it out on her gauntlet, stooped and picked up the hare.

She passed a cord about the animal's legs and fastened the end of the thong to her girdle. Then she started to retrace her steps through the covert. As she passed me I raised my cap and she acknowledged my presence with a scarcely perceptible inclination. I had been so astonished, so lost in admiration of the scene before my eyes, that it had not occurred to me that here was my salvation. But as she moved away I recollected that unless I wanted to sleep on a windy moor that night I had better recover my speech without delay. At my first word she hesitated, and as I stepped before her I thought a look of fear came into her beautiful eyes; but as I humbly explained my unpleasant plight her face flushed and she looked at me in wonder.

"Surely you did not come from Kerselec!" she repeated.

Her sweet voice had no trace of the Breton accent, nor of any accent which I knew, and yet there was something in it I seemed to have heard before, something quaint and indefinable, like the theme of an old song.

I explained that I was an American, unacquainted with Finistère, shooting there for my own amusement.

"An American," she repeated, in the same quaint, musical tones. "I have never before seen an American."

For a moment she stood silent, then, looking at me, she said: "If you should walk all night you could not reach Kerselec now, even if you had a guide."

This was pleasant news.

"But," I began, "if I could only find a peasant's hut, where I might get something to eat, and shelter."

The falcon on her wrist fluttered and shook its head. The girl smoothed its glossy back and glanced at me.

"Look around," she said, gently. "Can you see the end of these moors? Look north, south, east, west. Can you see anything but moorland and bracken?"

"No," I said.

"The moor is wild and desolate. It is easy to enter, but sometimes they who enter never leave it. There are no peasants' huts here."

"Well," I said, "if you will tell me in which direction Kerselec lies, to-morrow it will take me no longer to go back than it has to come."

She looked at me again with an expression almost like pity.

"Ah," she said, "to come is easy and takes hours; to go is different—and may take centuries."

I stared at her in amazement, but decided that I had misunderstood her. Then, before I had time to speak, she drew a whistle from her belt and sounded it.

"Sit down and rest," she said to me; "you have come a long distance and are tired."

She gathered up her pleated skirts, and, motioning me to follow, picked her dainty way through the gorse to a flat rock among the ferns.

"They will be here directly," she said, and, taking a seat at one end of the rock, invited me to sit down on the other edge. The after-glow was beginning to fade in the sky and a single star twinkled faintly through the rosy haze. A long, wavering triangle of waterfowl drifted southward over our heads, and from the swamps around plover were calling.

"They are very beautiful—these moors," she said, quietly.

"Beautiful, but cruel to strangers," I answered.

"Beautiful and cruel," she repeated, dreamily—"beautiful and cruel."

"Like a woman," I said, stupidly.

"Oh," she cried, with a little catch in her breath, and looked at me. Her dark eyes met mine, and I thought she seemed angry or frightened.

"Like a woman," she repeated, under her breath; "how cruel to say so!" Then, after a pause, as though speaking aloud to herself, "How cruel for him to say that."

I don't know what sort of an apology I offered for my inane, though harmless, speech, but I know that she seemed so troubled about it that I began to think I had said something very dreadful without knowing it, and remembered with horror the pitfalls and snares which the French language sets for foreigners. While I was trying to imagine what I might have said, a sound of voices came across the moor, and the girl rose to her feet.

"No," she said, with a trace of a smile on her pale face, "I will not accept your apologies, monsieur; but I must prove you wrong, and that shall be my revenge. Look. Here come Hastur and Raoul."

Two men loomed up in the twilight. One had a sack across his shoulders and the other carried a hoop before him as a waiter carries a tray. The hoop was fastened with straps to his shoulders, and around the edge of the circlet sat three hooded falcons fitted with tinkling bells. The girl stepped up to the falconer, and with a quick turn of her wrist transferred her falcon to the hoop, where it quickly sidled off and nestled among its mates, who shook their hooded heads and ruffled their feathers till the belled jesses tinkled again. The other man stepped forward and, bowing respectfully, took up the hare and dropped it into the game-sack.

"These are my *piqueurs,"* said the girl, turning to me with a gentle dignity. "Raoul is a good *fauconnier* and I shall some day make him *grand veneur.* Hastur is incomparable."

The two silent men saluted me respectfully.

"Did I not tell you, monsieur, that I should prove you wrong?" she continued. "This, then, is my revenge, that you do me the courtesy of accepting food and shelter at my own house."

Before I could answer she spoke to the falconers, who started instantly across the heath, and with a gracious gesture to me she followed. I don't know whether I made her understand how profoundly grateful I felt, but she seemed pleased to listen as we walked over the dewy heather.

"Are you not very tired?" she asked.

I had clean forgotten my fatigue in her presence, and I told her so.

"Don't you think your gallantry is a little old-fashioned?" she said; and when I looked confused and humbled, she added, quietly, "Oh, I like it; I like everything old-fashioned, and it is delightful to hear you say such pretty things."

The moorland around us was very still now under its ghostly sheet of mist. The plover had ceased their calling; the crickets and all the little creatures of the fields were silent as we passed, yet it seemed to me as if I could hear them beginning again far behind us. Well in advance the two tall falconers strode across the heather, and the faint jingling of the hawk's bells came to our ears in distant, murmuring chimes.

Suddenly a splendid hound dashed out of the mist in front, followed by another and another, until half a dozen or more were bounding and leaping around the girl beside me. She caressed and quieted them with her gloved hand, speaking to them in quaint terms which I remembered to have seen in old French manuscripts.

Then the falcons on the circlet borne by the falconer ahead began to beat their wings and scream, and from somewhere out of sight the notes of a hunting-horn floated across the moor. The hounds sprang away before us and vanished in the twilight, the falcons flapped and squealed upon their perch, and the girl, taking up the song of the horn, began to hum. Clear and mellow her voice sounded in the night air:

> "Chasseur, chasseur, chassez encore,
> Quittez Rosette et Jeanneton,
> Tonton, tonton, tontaine, tonton,
> Ou, pour, rabattre, dès l'aurore,
> Que les Amours soient de planton,
> Tonton, tontaine, tonton."

As I listened to her lovely voice, a gray mass which rapidly grew more distinct loomed up in front, and the horn rang out joyously through the tumult of the hounds and falcons. A torch glimmered at a gate, a light streamed through an opening door, and we stepped upon a wooden bridge which trembled under our feet, and rose creaking and straining behind us as we passed over the moat and into a small stone court, walled on every side. From an open door-way a man came, and, bending in salutation, presented a cup to the girl beside me. She took the cup and touched it with her lips, then lowering it, turned to me and said, in a low voice, "I bid you welcome."

At that moment one of the falconers came with another cup, but before handing it to me presented it to the girl, who tasted it. The falconer made a gesture to receive it, but she hesitated a moment, and then, stepping forward, offered me the cup with her own hands. I felt this to be an act of extraordinary graciousness, but hardly knew what was expected of me, and did not raise it to my lips at once. The girl flushed crimson. I saw that I must act quickly.

"Mademoiselle," I faltered, "a stranger whom you have saved from dangers he may never realize, empties this cup to the gentlest and loveliest hostess of France."

"In His name," she murmured, crossing herself as I drained the cup. Then, stepping into the door-way, she turned to me with a pretty gesture, and taking my hand in hers led me into the house, saying again and again: "You are very welcome—indeed, you are welcome to the Château d'Ys."

II

I awoke next morning with the music of the horn in my ears, and, leaping out of the ancient bed, went to a curtained window where the sunlight filtered through little, deep-set panes. The horn ceased as I looked into the court below.

A man who might have been brother to the two falconers of the night before stood in the midst of a pack of hounds. A curved horn was strapped over his back and in his hand he held a long-lashed whip. The dogs whined and yelped, dancing around him in anticipation; there was the stamp of horses, too, in the walled yard.

"Mount!" cried a voice in Breton, and with a clatter of hoofs the two falconers, with falcons upon their wrists, rode into the court-yard among the hounds. Then I heard another voice which sent the blood throbbing through my heart: "Piriou Louis, hunt the hounds well, and spare neither spur nor whip. Thou, Raoul, and thou, Gaston, see that the *èpervier* does not prove himself *niais,* and if it be best in your judgment, *faites courtoisie à l'oiseau. Jardiner un oiseau* like the *mué* there on Hastur's wrist is not difficult, but thou, Raoul, mayst not find it so simple to govern that *hagard.* Twice last week he foamed *au vif* and lost the *beccade,* although he is used to the *leurre.* The bird acts like a stupid *branchier. Paître un hagard n'est pas si facile."*

Was I dreaming? The old language of falconry, which I had read in yellow manuscripts—the old forgotten French of the Middle Ages, was sounding in my ears while the hounds bayed and the hawk's bells tinkled accompaniment to the stamping horses. She spoke again in the sweet, forgotten language:

"If you would rather attach the *longe* and leave your *hagard au bloc,* Raoul, I shall say nothing; for it were a pity to spoil so fair a day's sport with an ill-trained *sors. Essimer abaisser*—it is possibly the best way. *Ça lui donnera des reins.* I was perhaps hasty with the bird. It takes time to pass *à la filière* and the exercises *d'escap."*

Then the falconer Raoul bowed in his stirrups and replied: "If it be the pleasure of mademoiselle, I shall keep the hawk."

"It is my wish," she answered. "Falconry I know, but you have yet to give me many a lesson in *autourserie,* my poor Raoul. Sieur Piriou Louis, mount!"

The huntsman sprang into an archway and in an instant returned, mounted upon a strong black horse, followed by a *piqueur,* also mounted.

"Ah!" she cried, joyously, "speed Glemarec René! speed! speed all! Sound thy horn, Sieur Piriou!"

The silvery music of the hunting-horn filled the court-yard, the hounds sprang through the gateway, and galloping hoof-beats plunged out of the paved court; loud on the drawbridge, suddenly muffled, then lost in the heather and bracken of the moors. Distant and more distant sounded the horn, until it became so faint that the sudden carol of a soaring lark drowned it in my ears. I heard the voice below responding to some call from within the house.

"I do not regret the chase; I will go another time. Courtesy to the stranger, Pélagie, remember!"

And a feeble voice came quavering from within the house, *"Courtoisie."*

I stripped and rubbed myself from head to foot in the huge earthen basin of icy water which stood upon the stone floor at the foot of my bed. Then I looked about for my clothes. They were gone, but on a settle near the door lay a heap of garments, which I inspected with astonishment. As my clothes had vanished, I was compelled to attire myself in the costume which had evidently been placed there for me to wear while my own clothes dried. Everything was there—cap, shoes, and hunting doublet of silvery gray homespun; but the close-fitting costume and seamless shoes belonged to another century, and I remembered the strange costumes of the three falconers in the courtyard. I was sure that it was not the modern dress of any portion of France or Brittany; but not until I was dressed and stood before a mirror between the windows did I realize that I was clothed much more like a young huntsman of the Middle Ages than like a Breton of that day. I hesitated and picked up the cap. Should I go down and present myself in that strange guise? There seemed to be no help for it; my own clothes were gone, and there was no bell in the ancient chamber to call a servant, so I contented myself with removing a short hawk's feather from the cap, and, opening the door, went down-stairs.

By the fireplace in the large room at the foot of the stairs an old Breton woman sat spinning with a distaff. She looked up at me when I appeared, and, smiling frankly, wished me health in the Breton language, to which I laughingly replied in French. At the same moment my hostess appeared and returned my salutation with a grace and dignity that sent a thrill to my heart. Her lovely head, with its dark, curly hair, was crowned with a head-dress which set all doubts as to the epoch of my own costume at rest. Her slender figure was exquisitely set off in the home-spun hunting-gown edged with silver, and on her gauntlet-covered wrist she bore one of her petted hawks. With perfect simplicity she took my hand and led me into the garden in the court, and seating herself before a table invited me very sweetly to sit beside her. Then she asked me, in her soft, quaint accent, how I had passed the night, and whether I was very much inconvenienced by wearing the clothes which old Pélagie had put there for me while I slept. I looked at my own clothes and shoes, drying in the sun by the garden-wall, and hated them. What horrors they were, compared with the graceful costume which I now wore! I told her this, laughing, but she agreed with me very seriously.

"We will throw them away," she said, in a quiet voice. In my astonishment I attempted to explain that I not only could not think of accepting clothes from anybody, although, for all I knew, it might be the custom of hospitality in that part of the country, but that I should cut an impossible figure if I returned to France clothed as I was then.

She laughed and tossed her pretty head, saying something in old French which I did not understand, and then Pélagie trotted out with a tray on which stood two bowls of milk, a loaf of white bread, fruit, a platter of honeycomb, and a flagon of deep red wine. "You see, I have not yet broken my fast, because I wished you to eat with me. But I am very hungry," she smiled.

"I would rather die than forget one word of what you have said!" I blurted out, while my cheeks burned. "She will think me mad," I added to myself, but she turned to me with sparkling eyes.

"Ah!" she murmured. "Then monsieur knows all that there is of chivalry—"

She crossed herself and broke bread; I sat and watched her white hands, not daring to raise my eyes to hers.

"Will you not eat?" she asked. "Why do you look so troubled?"

Ah, why? I knew it now. I knew I would give my life to touch with my lips those rosy palms; I understood now that from the moment when I looked into her dark eyes there on the moor last night I had loved her. My great and sudden passion held me speechless.

"Are you ill at ease?" she asked again.

Then, like a man who pronounces his own doom, I answered, in a low voice: "Yes, I am ill at ease for love of you." And, as she did not stir nor answer, the same power moved my lips in spite of me, and I said: "I, who am unworthy of the lightest of your thoughts, I, who abuse hospitality and repay your gentle courtesy with bold presumption—I love you."

She leaned her head upon her hands, and answered, softly: "I love you. Your words are very dear to me. I love you."

"Then I shall win you."

"Win me," she replied.

But all the time I had been sitting silent, my face turned towards her. She, also silent, her sweet face resting on her upturned palm, sat facing me, and as her eyes looked into mine I knew that neither she nor I had spoken human speech; but I knew that her soul had answered mine, and I drew myself up, feeling youth and joyous love coursing through every vein. She, with a bright color in her lovely face, seemed as one awakened from a dream, and her eyes sought mine with a questioning glance which made me tremble with delight. We broke our fast, speaking of ourselves. I told her my name and she told me hers—the Demoiselle Jeanne d'Ys.

She spoke of her father and mother's death, and how the nineteen of her years had been passed in the little fortified farm alone with her nurse Pélagie, Glemarec René the *piqueur,* and the four falconers, Raoul, Gaston, Hastur, and the Sieur Piriou Louis, who had served her father. She had never been outside the moorland—never even had seen a human soul before, except the falconers and Pélagie. She did not know how she had heard of Kerselec; perhaps the falconers had spoken of it. She knew the legends of Loup Garou and Jeanne la Flamme from her nurse Pélagie. She embroidered and spun flax. Her hawks and hounds were her only distraction. When she had met me there on the moor she had been so frightened that she almost dropped at the sound of my voice. She had, it was true, seen ships at sea from the cliffs, but, as far as the eye could reach, the moors over which she galloped were destitute of any sign of human life. There was a legend which old Pélagie told, how anybody once lost in the unexplored moorland might never return, because the moors were enchanted. She did not know whether it was true; she never had thought about it until she met me. She did not know whether the falconers had even been outside, or whether they could go if they would. The books in the house which Pélagie the nurse had taught her to read were hundreds of years old.

All this she told me with a sweet seriousness seldom seen in any one but children. My own name she found easy to pronounce, and insisted, because my first name was Philip, I must have French blood in me. She did not seem curious to learn anything about the outside world, and I thought perhaps she considered it had forfeited her interest and respect from the stories of her nurse.

We were still sitting at the table, and she was throwing grapes to the small field-birds which came fearlessly to our very feet.

I began to speak in a vague way of going, but she would not hear of it, and before I knew it I had promised to stay a week and hunt with hawk and hound in their company. I also obtained permission to come again from Kerselec and visit her after my return.

"Why," she said, innocently, "I do not know what I should do if you never came back"; and I, knowing that I had no right to awaken her with the sudden shock which the avowal of my own love would bring to her, sat silent, hardly daring to breathe.

"You will come very often?" she asked.

"Very often," I said.

"Every day?"

"Every day."

"Oh," she sighed, "I am very happy—come and see my hawks."

She rose and took my hand again with a childlike innocence of possession, and we walked through the garden and fruit trees to a grassy lawn which was bordered by a brook. Over the lawn were scattered fifteen or twenty stumps of trees—partially imbedded in the grass—and upon all of these except two sat falcons. They were attached to the stumps by thongs, which were in turn fastened with steel rivets to their legs just above the talons. A little stream of pure spring water flowed in a winding course within easy distance of each perch.

The birds set up a clamor when the girl appeared, but she went from one to another, caressing some, taking others for an instant upon her wrist, or stooping to adjust their jesses.

"Are they not pretty?" she said. "See, here is a falcon-gentil. We call it 'ignoble,' because it takes the quarry in direct chase. This is a blue falcon. In falconry we call it 'noble,' because it rises over the quarry, and, wheeling, drops upon it from above. This white bird is a gerfalcon from the North. It is also 'noble.' Here is a merlin, and this tiercelet is a falcon-heroner."

I asked her how she had learned the old language of falconry. She did not remember, but thought her father must have taught it to her when she was very young.

Then she led me away and showed me the young falcons still in the nest. "They are termed *niais* in falconry," she explained. "A *branchier* is the young bird which is just able to leave the nest and hop from branch to branch. A young bird which has not yet moulted is called a *sors,* and a *mué* is a hawk which has moulted in captivity. When we catch a wild falcon which has changed its plumage we term it a *hagard.* Raoul first taught me to dress a falcon. Shall I teach you how it is done?"

She seated herself on the bank of the stream among the falcons and I threw myself at her feet to listen.

Then the Demoiselle d'Ys held up one rosy-tipped finger and began very gravely.

"First one must catch the falcon."

"I am caught," I answered.

She laughed very prettily and told me my *dressage* would perhaps be difficult, as I was noble.

"I am already tamed," I replied; "jessed and belled."

She laughed, delighted. "Oh, my brave falcon; then you will return at my call?"

"I am yours," I answered, gravely.

She sat silent for a moment. Then the color heightened in her cheeks and she held up her finger again, saying, "Listen, I wish to speak of falconry—"

"I listen, Countess Jeanne d'Ys."

But again she fell into the reverie, and her eyes seemed fixed on something beyond the summer clouds.

"Philip," she said, at last.

"Jeanne," I whispered.

"That is all—that is what I wished," she sighed—"Philip and Jeanne."

She held her hand towards me and I touched it with my lips.

"Win me," she said; but this time it was the body and soul which spoke in unison.

After a while she began again: "Let us speak of falconry."

"Begin," I replied; "we have caught the falcon."

Then Jeanne d'Ys took my hand in both of hers and told me how with infinite patience the young falcon was taught to perch upon the wrist, how little by little it became used to the belled jesses and the *chaperon à cornette.*

"They must first have a good appetite," she said; "then little by little I reduce their nourishment, which in falconry we call *pât.* When, after many nights passed *au bloc,* as these birds are now, I prevail upon the *hagard* to stay quietly on the wrist, then the bird is ready to be taught to come for its food. I fix the *pât* to the end of a thong, or *leurre,* and teach the bird to come to me as soon as I begin to whirl the cord in circles about my head. At first I drop the *pât* when the falcon comes, and he eats the food on the ground. After a little he will learn to seize the *leurre* in motion as I whirl it around my head, or drag it over the ground. After this it is easy to teach the falcon to strike at game, always remembering to '*faire courtoisie à l'oiseau,*' that is, to allow the bird to taste the quarry."

A squeal from one of the falcons interrupted her, and she arose to adjust the *longe* which had become whipped about the *bloc,* but the bird still flapped its wings and screamed.

"What *is* the matter?" she said; "Philip, can you see?"

I looked around, and at first saw nothing to cause the commotion, which was now heightened by the screams and flapping of all the birds. Then my eye fell upon the flat rock beside the stream from which the girl had risen. A gray serpent was moving slowly across the surface of the bowlder, and the eyes in its flat, triangular head sparkled like jet.

"A *couleuvre,*" she said, quietly.

"It is harmless, is it not?" I asked.

She pointed to the black, V-shaped figure on the neck.

"It is certain death," she said; "it is a viper."

We watched the reptile moving slowly over the smooth rock to where the sunlight fell in a broad, warm patch.

I started forward to examine it, but she clung to my arm, crying, "Don't, Philip, I am afraid!"

"For me?"

"For you, Philip—I love you."

Then I took her in my arms and kissed her on the lips, but all I could say was, "Jeanne, Jeanne, Jeanne." And as she lay trembling on my breast something struck my foot in the grass below, but I did not heed it. Then again something struck my ankle, and a sharp pain shot through me. I looked into the sweet face of Jeanne d'Ys and kissed her, and with all my strength lifted her in my arms and flung her from me. Then, bending, I tore the viper from my ankle and set my heel upon its head. I remember feeling weak and numb—I remember falling to the ground. Through my slowly glazing eyes I saw Jeanne's white face bending close to mine, and when the light in my eyes went out I still felt her arms about my neck, and her soft cheek against my drawn lips.

When I opened my eyes I looked around in terror. Jeanne was gone. I saw the stream and the flat rock; I saw the crushed viper in the grass beside me, but the hawks and *blocs* had disappeared. I sprang to my feet. The garden, the fruit trees, the drawbridge, and the walled court were gone. I stared stupidly at a heap of crumbling ruins, ivy-covered and gray, through which great trees had pushed their way. I crept forward, dragging my numbed foot, and as I moved a falcon sailed from the tree-tops among the ruins, and, soaring, mounting in narrowing circles, faded and vanished in the clouds above.

"Jeanne! Jeanne!" I cried, but my voice died on my lips, and I fell on my knees among the weeds. And as God willed it, I, not knowing, had fallen kneeling before a crumbling shrine carved in stone for our Mother of Sorrows. I saw the sad face of the Virgin wrought in the cold stone. I saw the cross and thorns at her feet, and beneath it I read:

PRAY FOR THE SOUL OF THE
DEMOISELLE JEANNE D'YS,
WHO DIED
IN HER YOUTH FOR LOVE OF
PHILIP, A STRANGER.
A.D. 1573.

But upon the icy slab lay a woman's glove still warm and fragrant.

THE PROPHETS' PARADISE

"If but the vine and love-abjuring band
Are in the Prophets' Paradise to stand,
Alack, I doubt the Prophets' Paradise
Were empty as the hollow of one's hand."

THE STUDIO

He smiled, saying, "Seek her throughout the world."

I said: "Why tell me of the world? My world is here, between these walls and the sheet of glass above; here among gilded flagons and dull jewelled arms, tarnished frames and canvases, black chests and high-backed chairs, quaintly carved and stained in blue and gold."

"For whom do you wait?" he said, and I answered, "When she comes I shall know her."

On my hearth a tongue of flame whispered secrets to the whitening ashes. In the street below I heard footsteps, a voice, and a song.

"For whom, then, do you wait?" he said, and I answered, "I shall know her."

Footsteps, a voice, and a song in the street below, and I knew the song, but neither the steps nor the voice.

"Fool!" he cried, "the song is the same, the voice and steps have but changed with years!"

On the hearth a tongue of flame whispered above the whitening ashes: "Wait no more; they have passed—the steps and the voice in the street below."

Then he smiled, saying, "For whom do you wait? Seek her throughout the world!"

I answered: "My world is here between these walls and the sheet of glass above; here among gilded flagons and dull jewelled arms, tarnished frames and canvases, black chests and high-backed chairs, quaintly carved and stained in blue and gold."

THE PHANTOM

The Phantom of the Past would go no further.

"If it is true," she sighed, "that you find in me a friend, let us turn back together. You will forget, here, under the summer sky."

I held her close, pleading, caressing; I seized her, white with anger, but she resisted.

"If it is true," she sighed, "that you find in me a friend, let us turn back together."

The Phantom of the Past would go no further.

THE SACRIFICE

I went into a field of flowers, whose petals are whiter than snow and whose hearts are pure gold.

Far afield a woman cried, "I have killed him I loved!" and from a jar she poured blood upon the flowers whose petals are whiter than snow and whose hearts are pure gold.

Far afield I followed, and on the jar I read a thousand names, while from within the fresh blood bubbled to the brim.

"I have killed him I loved!" she cried. "The world's athirst; now let it drink!" She passed, and far afield I watched her pouring blood upon the flowers whose petals are whiter than snow and whose hearts are pure gold.

DESTINY

I came to the bridge which few may pass.

"Pass!" cried the keeper, but I laughed, saying, "There is time"; and he smiled and shut the gates.

To the bridge which few may pass came young and old. All were refused. Idly I stood and counted them, until, wearied of their noise and lamentations, I came again to the bridge which few may pass.

Those in the throng about the gates shrieked out: "He comes too late!" But I laughed, saying, "There is time."

"Pass!" cried the keeper as I entered; then smiled and shut the gates.

THE GREEN-ROOM

The Clown turned his powdered face to the mirror.

"If to be fair is to be beautiful," he said, "who can compare with me in my white mask?"

"Who can compare with him in his white mask?" I asked of Death beside me.

"Who can compare with me?" said Death, "for I am paler still."

"You are very beautiful," sighed the Clown, turning his powdered face from the mirror.

THE LOVE TEST

"If it is true that you love," said Love, "then wait no longer. Give her these jewels, which would dishonor her and so dishonor you in loving one dishonored. If it is true that you love," said Love, "then wait no longer."

I took the jewels and went to her, but she trod upon them, sobbing, "Teach me to wait—I love you!"

"Then wait, if it is true," said Love.

THE STREET OF THE FOUR WINDS

"Ferme tes yeux à demi,
Croise tes bras sur ton sein,
Et de ton coeur endormi
Chasse à jamais tout dessein.

* * * *

"Je chante la nature,
Les étoiles du soir, les larmes du matin,
Les couchers de soleil à l'horizon lointain,
Le ciel qui parle au coeur d'existence future!"

I

THE ANIMAL PAUSED ON THE THRESHOLD, INTERROGATIVE, alert, ready for flight if necessary. Severn laid down his palette and held out a hand of welcome. The cat remained motionless, her yellow eyes fastened upon Severn.

"Puss," he said, in his low, pleasant voice, "come in."

The tip of her thin tail twitched uncertainly.

"Come in," he said again.

Apparently she found his voice reassuring, for she slowly settled upon all-fours, her eyes still fastened upon him, her tail tucked under her gaunt flanks.

He rose from his easel smiling. She eyed him quietly, and when he walked towards her she watched him bend above her without a wince; her eyes followed his hand until it touched her head. Then she uttered a ragged mew.

It had long been Severn's custom to converse with animals, probably because he lived so much alone; and now he said, "What's the matter, puss?"

Her timid eyes sought his.

"I understand," he said, gently; "you shall have it at once."

Then, moving quietly about, he busied himself with the duties of a host, rinsed a saucer, filled it with the rest of the milk from the bottle on the window-sill, and, kneeling down, crumbled a roll into the hollow of his hand.

The creature rose and crept towards the saucer.

With the handle of a palette-knife he stirred the crumbs and milk together, and stepped back as she thrust her nose into the mess. He watched her in silence. From time to time the saucer klinked upon the tiled floor as she reached for a morsel on the rim; and at last the bread was all gone, and her purple tongue travelled over every unlicked spot until the saucer shone like polished marble. Then she sat up, and, coolly turning her back to him, began her ablutions.

"Keep it up," said Severn, much interested; "you need it."

She flattened one ear, but neither turned nor interrupted her toilet. As the grime was slowly removed, Severn observed that nature had intended her for a white cat. Her fur had disappeared in patches, from disease or the chances of war, her tail was bony, and her spine sharp. But what charms she had were becoming apparent under vigorous licking, and he waited until she had finished before reopening the conversation. When at last she closed her eyes and folded her forepaws under her breast, he began again, very gently: "Puss, tell me your troubles."

At the sound of his voice she broke into a harsh rumbling which he recognized as an attempt to purr. He bent over to rub her cheek and she mewed again, an amiable, inquiring little mew, to which he replied, "Certainly, you are greatly improved, and when you recover your plumage you will be a gorgeous bird." Much flattered, she stood up and marched around and around his legs, pushing her head between them and making pleased remarks, to which he responded with grave politeness.

"Now what sent you here," he said—"here into the Street of the Four Winds, and up five flights to the very door where you would be welcome? What was it that prevented your meditated flight when I turned from my canvas to encounter your yellow eyes? Are you a Latin Quarter cat as I am a Latin Quarter man? And why do you wear a rose-colored flowered garter buckled about your neck?" The cat had climbed into his lap and now sat purring as he passed his hand over her thin coat.

"Excuse me," he continued, in lazy, soothing tones, harmonizing with her purring, "if I seem indelicate, but I cannot help musing on this rose-colored garter, flowered so quaintly and fastened with a silver clasp. For the clasp is silver; I can see the mint-mark on the edge, as is prescribed by the law of the French Republic. Now, why is this garter, woven of rose silk and delicately embroidered—why is this silken garter with its silver clasp about your famished throat? Am I indiscreet when I inquire if its owner is your owner? Is she some aged dame, living in memory of youthful vanities, fond, doting on you, decorating you with her intimate personal attire? The circumference of the garter would suggest this, for your neck is thin, and the garter fits you. But then, again, I notice—I notice most things—that the garter is capable of being much enlarged. These small silver-rimmed eyelets, of which I count five, are proof of that. And now I observe that the fifth eyelet is worn out, as though the tongue of the clasp were accustomed to lie there. That seems to argue a well-rounded form."

The cat curled her toes in contentment. The street was very still outside.

He murmured on: "Why should your mistress decorate you with an article most necessary to her at all times?—Anyway, at most times? How did she come to slip this bit of silk and silver about your neck? Was it the caprice of a moment—when you, before you had lost your pristine plumpness, marched singing into her bedroom to bid her good-morning? Of course, and she sat up among the pillows, her coiled hair tumbling to her shoulders, as you sprang upon the bed purring: 'Good-day, my lady.' Oh, it is very easy to understand," he yawned, resting his head on the back of the chair. The cat still purred, tightening and relaxing her padded claws over his knee.

"Shall I tell you all about her, cat? She is very beautiful—your mistress," he murmured, drowsily, "and her hair is heavy as burnished gold. I could paint her—not on canvas, for I should need shades and tones and hues and dyes more splendid than the iris of a splendid rainbow. I could only paint her with closed eyes, for in dreams alone can such colors as I need be found. For her eyes, I must have azure from skies untroubled by a cloud—the skies of dreamland. For her lips, roses from the palaces of slumberland; and for her brow, snow-drifts from mountains which tower in fantastic pinnacles to the moons—oh, much higher than our moon here; the crystal moons of dreamland. She is—very—beautiful, your mistress."

The words died on his lips and his eyelids drooped.

The cat, too, was asleep, her cheek turned up upon her wasted flank, her paws relaxed and limp.

II

"It is fortunate," said Severn, sitting up and stretching, "that we have tided over the dinner hour, for I have nothing to offer you for supper but what may be purchased with one silver franc."

The cat on his knee rose, arched her back, yawned, and looked up at him.

"What shall it be? A roast chicken with salad? No? Possibly you prefer beef? Of course—and I shall try an egg and some white bread. Now for the wines. Milk for you? Good. I shall take a little water, fresh from the wood," with a motion towards the bucket in the sink.

He put on his hat and left the room. The cat followed to the door, and after he had closed it behind him she settled down, smelling at the cracks, and cocking one ear at every creak from the crazy old building.

The door below opened and shut. The cat looked serious, for a moment doubtful, and her ears flattened in nervous expectation. Presently she rose with a jerk of her tail and started on a noiseless tour of the studio. She sneezed at a pot of turpentine, hastily retreating to the table, which she presently mounted, and, having satisfied her curiosity concerning a roll of red modelling wax, returned to the door and sat down with her eyes on the crack over the threshold. Then she lifted her voice in a thin plaint.

When Severn returned he looked grave, but the cat, joyous and demonstrative, marched around him, rubbing her gaunt body against his legs, driving her head enthusiastically into his hand, and purring until her voice mounted to a squeal.

He placed a bit of meat, wrapped in brown paper, upon the table, and with a penknife cut it into shreds. The milk he took from a bottle which had served for medicine, and poured it into the saucer on the hearth.

The cat crouched before it, purring and lapping at the same time.

He cooked his egg and ate it with a slice of bread, watching her busy with the shredded meat, and when he had finished, and had filled and emptied a cup of water from the bucket in the sink, he sat down, taking her into his lap, where she at once curled up and began her toilet. He began to speak again, touching her caressingly at times by way of emphasis.

"Cat, I have found out where your mistress lives. It is not very far away; it is here, under this same leaky roof, but in the north wing, which I had supposed was uninhabited. My janitor tells me this. By chance, he is almost sober this evening. The butcher on the Rue de Seine, where I bought your meat, knows you, and old Cabane, the baker, identified you with needless sarcasm. They tell me hard tales of your mistress, which I shall not believe. They say she is idle and vain and pleasure-loving; they say she is hare-brained and reckless. The little sculptor on the ground-floor, who was buying rolls from old Cabane, spoke to me to-night for the first time, although we have always bowed to each other. He said she was very good and very beautiful. He has only seen her once, and does not know her name. I thanked him; I don't know why I thanked him so warmly. Cabane said, 'Into this cursed Street of the Four Winds, the four winds blow all things evil.' The sculptor looked confused, but when he went out with his rolls he said to me, 'I am sure, monsieur, that she is as good as she is beautiful.'"

The cat had finished her toilet, and now, springing softly to the floor, went to the door and sniffed. He knelt beside her, and, unclasping the garter, held it for a moment in his hands. After a while he said: "There is a name engraved upon the silver clasp beneath the buckle. It is a pretty name—Sylvia Elven. Sylvia is a woman's name, Elven is the name of a town. In Paris, in this quarter, above all in this Street of the Four Winds, names are worn and put away as the fashions change with the seasons. I know the little town of Elven, for there I met Fate face to face, and Fate was unkind. But do you know that in Elven Fate had another name, and that name was Sylvia?"

He replaced the garter and stood up, looking down at the cat crouched before the closed door.

"The name of Elven has a charm for me. It tells me of meadows and clear rivers. The name of Sylvia troubles me like perfume from dead flowers."

The cat mewed.

"Yes, yes," he said, soothingly, "I will take you back. Your Sylvia is not my Sylvia; the world is wide, and Elven is not unknown. Yet in the darkness and filth of poorer Paris, in the sad shadows of this ancient house, these names are very pleasant to me."

He lifted her in his arms and strode through the silent corridors to the stairs. Down five flights and into the moonlit court, past the little sculptor's den, and then again in at the gate of the north wing and up the worm-eaten stairs he passed, until he came to a closed door. When he had stood knocking for a long time, something moved behind the door; it opened, and he went in. The room was dark. As he crossed the threshold the cat sprang from his arms into the shadows. He listened, but heard nothing. The silence was oppressive, and he struck a match. At his elbow stood a table, and on the table a candle in a gilded candlestick. This he lighted, then looked around. The chamber was vast, the hangings heavy with embroidery. Over the fireplace towered a carved mantel, gray with the ashes of dead fires. In a recess by the deep-set windows stood a bed, from which the bedclothes, soft and fine as lace, trailed to the polished floor. He lifted the candle above his head. A handkerchief lay at his feet. It was faintly perfumed. He turned towards the windows. In front of them was a *canapé,* and over it were flung, pell-mell, a gown of silk, a heap of lacelike garments, white and delicate as spiders' meshes; long, crumpled gloves, and, on the floor beneath, the stockings, the little pointed shoes, and one garter of rosy silk, quaintly flowered and fitted with a silver clasp. Wondering, he stepped forward and drew the heavy curtains from the bed. For a moment the candle flared in his hand; then his eyes met two other eyes, wide open, smiling, and the candle-flame flashed over hair heavy as gold.

She was pale, but not as white as he; her eyes were untroubled as a child's; but he stared, trembling from head to foot, while the candle flickered in his hand.

At last he whispered, "Sylvia, it is I."

Again he said, "It is I."

Then, knowing that she was dead, he kissed her on the mouth. And through the long watches of the night the cat purred on his knee, tightening and relaxing her padded claws, until the sky paled above the Street of the Four Winds.

THE STREET OF THE FIRST SHELL

"Be of good cheer, the sullen month will die,
And a young moon requite us by-and-by:
Look how the old one, meagre, bent, and wan
With age and fast, is fainting from the sky."

I

THE ROOM WAS ALREADY DARK. THE HIGH ROOFS OPPOSITE CUT off what little remained of the December daylight. The girl drew her chair nearer the window and, choosing a large needle, threaded it, knotting the thread over her fingers. Then she smoothed the baby garment across her knees, and, bending, bit off the thread and drew the smaller needle from where it rested in the hem. When she had brushed away the stray threads and bits of lace, she laid it again over her knees caressingly. Then she slipped the threaded needle from her corsage and passed it through a button, but as the button spun down the thread her hand faltered, the thread snapped, and the button rolled across the floor. She raised her head. Her eyes were fixed on a strip of waning light above the chimneys. From somewhere in the city came sounds like the distant beating of drums, and beyond, far beyond, a vague muttering, now growing, swelling, rumbling in the distance like the pounding of surf upon the rocks, now like the surf again, receding, growling, menacing. The cold had become intense—a bitter, piercing cold, which strained and snapped at joist and beam, and turned the slush of yesterday to flint. From the street below every sound broke sharp and metallic—the clatter of sabots, the rattle of shutters, or the rare sound of a human voice. The air was heavy, weighted with the black cold as with a pall. To breathe was painful, to move an effort.

In the desolate sky there was something that wearied, in the brooding clouds something that saddened. It penetrated the freezing city cut by the freezing river, the splendid city with its towers and domes, its quays and bridges and its thousand spires. It entered the squares, it seized the avenues and the palaces, stole across bridges and crept among the narrow streets of the Latin Quarter, gray under the gray of the December sky. Sadness, utter sadness. A fine, icy sleet was falling, powdering the pavement with a tiny crystalline dust. It sifted against the window-panes and drifted in heaps along the sill. The light at the window had nearly failed, and the girl bent low over her work. Presently she raised her head, brushing the curls from her eyes.

"Jack!"

"Dearest?"

"Don't forget to clean your palette."

He said, "All right," and, picking up the palette, sat down upon the floor in front of the stove. His head and shoulders were in the shadow, but the firelight fell across his knees and glimmered red on the blade of the palette-knife. Full in the firelight beside him stood a color-box. On the lid was carved,

J. TRENT.

École des Beaux Arts.

1870.

This inscription was ornamented with an American and a French flag.

The sleet blew against the window-panes, covering them with stars and diamonds, then, melting from the warmer air within, ran down and froze again in fernlike traceries.

A dog whined and the patter of small paws sounded on the zinc behind the stove.

"Jack, dear, do you think Hercules is hungry?"

The patter of paws was redoubled behind the stove.

"He's whining," she continued, nervously, "and if it isn't because he's hungry it is because—"

Her voice faltered. A loud humming filled the air, the windows vibrated.

"Oh, Jack," she cried, "another—" But her voice was drowned in the scream of a shell tearing through the clouds overhead.

"That is the nearest yet," she murmured.

"Oh no," he answered, cheerfully; "it probably fell way over by Montmartre," and, as she did not answer, he said again, with exaggerated unconcern, "They wouldn't take the trouble to fire at the Latin Quarter; anyway, they haven't a battery that can hurt it."

After a while she spoke up brightly: "Jack, dear, when are you going to take me to see Monsieur West's statues?"

"I will bet," he said, throwing down his palette and walking over to the window beside her, "that Colette has been here to-day."

"Why?" she asked, opening her eyes very wide. Then, "Oh, it's too bad!—really, men are tiresome when they think they know everything! And I warn you that if Monsieur West is vain enough to imagine that Colette—"

From the north another shell came whistling and quavering through the sky, passing above them with long-drawn screech which left the windows singing.

"That," he blurted out, "was too near for comfort."

They were silent for a while, then he spoke again, gayly: "Go on, Sylvia, and wither poor West."

But she only sighed: "Oh, dear, I can never seem to get used to the shells."

He sat down on the arm of the chair beside her.

Her scissors fell jingling to the floor; she tossed the unfinished frock after them, and, putting both arms about his neck, drew him down into her lap.

"Don't go out to-night, Jack."

He kissed her uplifted face. "You know I must; don't make it hard for me."

"But when I hear the shells and—and know you are out in the city—"

"But they all fall in Montmartre—"

"They may all fall in the Beaux Arts. You said yourself that two struck the Quai d'Orsay—"

"Mere accident—"

"Jack, have pity on me! Take me with you!"

"And who will there be to get dinner?"

She rose and flung herself on the bed.

"Oh, I can't get used to it, and I know you must go, but I beg you not to be late to dinner. If you knew what I suffer! I—I—cannot help it, and you must be patient with me, dear."

He said, "It is as safe there as it is in our own house."

She watched him fill for her the alcohol lamp, and when he had lighted it and had taken his hat to go she jumped up and clung to him in silence. After a moment he said, "Now, Sylvia, remember my courage is sustained by yours. Come, I must go!" She did not move, and he repeated, "I must go." Then she stepped back, and he thought she was going to speak and waited, but she only looked at him, and, a little impatiently, he kissed her again saying, "Don't worry, dearest."

When he had reached the last flight of stairs on his way to the street a woman hobbled out of the housekeeper's lodge, waving a letter and calling, "Monsieur Jack! Monsieur Jack! This was left by Monsieur Fallowby!"

He took the letter, and, leaning on the threshold of the lodge, read it:

> "Dear Jack,
>
> I believe Braith is dead-broke and I'm sure Fallowby is. Braith swears he isn't, and Fallowby swears he is, so you can draw your own conclusions. I've got a scheme for a dinner, and if it works I will let you fellows in.
>
> "Yours faithfully,
>
> "West.
>
> "P.S.—Fallowby has shaken Hartman and his gang, thank the Lord! There is something rotten there—or, it may be, he's only a miser.

"P.P.S.—I'm more desperately in love than ever, but I'm sure she does not care a straw for me."

"All right," said Trent, with a smile, to the concierge; "but tell me, how is papa Cottard?"

The old woman shook her head and pointed to the curtained bed in the lodge.

"Père Cottard!" he cried, cheerily, "how goes the wound to-day?"

He walked over to the bed and drew the curtains. An old man was lying among the tumbled sheets.

"Better?" smiled Trent.

"Better," repeated the man, wearily; and, after a pause, "Have you any news, Monsieur Jack?"

"I haven't been out to-day. I will bring you any rumor I may hear, though, goodness knows, I've got enough of rumors," he muttered to himself. Then aloud, "Cheer up; you're looking better."

"And the sortie?"

"Oh, the sortie, that's for this week. General Trochu sent orders last night."

"It will be terrible."

"It will be sickening," thought Trent, as he went out into the street and turned the corner towards the Rue de Seine. "Slaughter—slaughter I Phew! I'm glad I'm not going."

The street was almost deserted. A few women muffled in tattered military capes crept along the frozen pavement, and a wretchedly clad gamin hovered over the sewer-hole on the corner of the boulevard. A rope around his waist held his rags together. From the rope hung a rat, still warm and bleeding.

"There's another in there," he yelled at Trent; "I hit him, but he got away."

Trent crossed the street and asked, "How much?"

"Two francs for a quarter of a fat one; that's what they give at the St. Germain market."

A violent fit of coughing interrupted him, but he wiped his face with the palm of his hand and looked cunningly at Trent.

"Last week you could buy a rat for six francs, but"—and here he swore vilely—"the rats have quit the Rue de Seine, and they kill them now over by the new hospital. I'll let you have this for seven francs; I can sell it for ten in the Isle St. Louis."

"You lie," said Trent; "and let me tell you that if you try to swindle anybody in this quarter the people will make short work of you and your rats."

He stood a moment eying the gamin, who pretended to snivel. Then he tossed him a franc, laughing. The child caught it, and, thrusting it into his mouth, wheeled about to the sewer-hole. For a second he crouched, motionless, alert, his eyes on the bars of the drain, then, leaping forward, he hurled a stone into the gutter, and Trent left him to finish a fierce, gray rat that writhed squealing at the mouth of the sewer.

"Suppose Braith should come to that," he thought; "poor little chap"; and, hurrying, he turned in the dirty Passage des Beaux Arts and entered the third house to the left.

"Monsieur is at home," quavered the old concierge.

Home? A garret absolutely bare, save for the iron bedstead in the corner and the iron basin and pitcher on the floor.

West appeared at the door, winking with much mystery, and motioned Trent to enter. Braith, who was painting in bed to keep warm, looked up, laughed, and shook hands.

"Any news?"

The perfunctory question was answered as usual by, "Nothing but the cannon."

Trent sat down on the bed.

"Where on earth did you get that?" he demanded, pointing to the half-finished chicken nestling in a wash-basin.

West grinned.

"Are you millionaires, you two? Out with it."

Braith, looking a little ashamed, began: "Oh, it's one of West's exploits," but was cut short by West, who said he would tell the story himself.

"You see, before the siege, I had a letter of introduction to a 'type' here, a fat banker, German-American variety. You know the species, I see. Well, of course, I forgot to present the letter; but this morning, judging it to be a favorable opportunity, I called on him.

"The villain lives in comfort—fires, my boy—fires in the anterooms! The Buttons finally condescends to carry my letter and card up, leaving me standing in the hall-way, which I did not like, so I entered the first room I saw and nearly fainted at the sight of a banquet on a table by the fire. Down comes Buttons, very insolent. No, oh no, his master 'is not at home, and in fact is too busy to receive letters of introduction just now; the siege, and many business difficulties—'

"I deliver a kick to Buttons, pick up this chicken from the table, toss my card on to the empty plate, and, addressing Buttons as a species of Prussian pig, march out with the honors of war."

Trent shook his head.

"I forgot to say that Hartman often dines there, and I draw my own conclusions," continued West. "Now about this chicken, half of it is for Braith and myself and half for Colette, but of course you will help me eat my part, because I'm not hungry."

"Neither am I," began Braith, but Trent, with a smile at the pinched faces before him, shook his head, saying, "What nonsense! You know I'm never hungry!"

West hesitated, reddened, and then, slicing off Braith's portion, but not eating any himself, said good-night and hurried away to No. 470 Rue Serpente, where lived a pretty girl named Colette, orphan after Sedan, and Heaven alone knew where she got the roses in her cheeks, for the siege came hard on the poor.

"That chicken will delight her, but I really believe she's in love with West," said Trent. Then, walking over to the bed, "See here, old man, no dodging, you know—how much have you left?"

The other hesitated, and flushed.

"Come, old chap," insisted Trent.

Braith drew a purse from beneath his bolster and handed it to his friend with a simplicity that touched him.

"Seven sous," he counted; "you make me tired! Why on earth don't you come to me? I take it damned ill, Braith! How many times must I go over the same thing, and explain to you that, because I have money, it is my duty to share it, and your duty, and the duty of every American, to share it with me? You can't get a cent, the city's blockaded, and the American Minister has his hands full with all the German riffraff and deuce knows what! Why don't you act sensibly?"

"I—I will, Trent, but it's an obligation that perhaps I can never, even in part, repay; I'm poor and—"

"Of course you'll pay me! If I were a usurer I would take your talent for security. When you are rich and famous—"

"Don't, Trent—"

"All right, only no more monkey business."

He slipped a dozen gold pieces into the purse, and, tucking it again under the mattress, smiled at Braith.

"How old are you?" he demanded.

"Sixteen."

Trent laid his hand lightly on his friend's shoulder. "I'm twenty-two, and I have the rights of a grandfather, as far as you are concerned. You'll do as I say until you're twenty-one."

"The siege will be over then, I hope," said Braith, trying to laugh, but the prayer in their hearts—"How long, O Lord, how long!"—was answered by the swift scream of a shell soaring among the storm-clouds of that December night.

II

West, standing in the door-way of a house in the Rue Serpente, was speaking angrily. He said he didn't care whether Hartman liked it or not; he was telling him, not arguing with him.

"You call yourself an American!" he sneered; "Berlin and hell are full of that kind of American. You come loafing about Colette with your pockets stuffed with white bread and beef, and a bottle of wine at thirty francs, and you can't really afford to give a dollar to the American Ambulance and Public Assistance, which Braith does, and he's half starved!"

Hartman retreated to the curbstone, but West followed him, his face like a thunder-cloud. "Don't you dare to call yourself a countryman of mine," he growled, "no—nor an artist, either! Artists don't worm themselves into the service of the Public Defence where they do nothing but feed like rats on the people's food! And I'll tell you now," he continued, dropping his voice, for Hartman had started as though stung, "you might better keep away from that Alsatian Brasserie and the smug-faced thieves who haunt it. You know what they do with suspects!"

"You lie, you hound!" screamed Hartman, and flung the bottle in his hand straight at West's face. West had him by the throat in a second, and, forcing him against the dead wall, shook him wickedly.

"Now you listen to me," he muttered, through his clenched teeth. "You are already a suspect, and—I swear—I believe you are a paid spy! It isn't my business to detect such vermin, and I don't intend to denounce you, but understand this: Colette don't like you, and I can't stand you, and if I catch you in this street again I'll make it somewhat unpleasant. Get out, you sleek Prussian!"

Hartman had managed to drag a knife from his pocket, but West tore it from him and hurled him into the gutter. A gamin who had seen this burst into a peal of laughter, which rattled harshly in the silent street. Then everywhere windows were raised, and rows of haggard faces appeared demanding to know why people should laugh in the starving city.

"Is it a victory?" murmured one.

"Look at that," cried West, as Hartman picked himself up from the pavement—"look, you miser! look at those faces!" But Hartman gave *him* a look which he never forgot, and walked away without a word. Trent, who suddenly appeared at the corner, glanced curiously at West, who merely nodded towards his door, saying, "Come in; Fallowby's up-stairs."

"What are you doing with that knife?" demanded Fallowby, as he and Trent entered the studio.

West looked at his wounded hand, which still clutched the knife, but saying, "Cut myself by accident," tossed it into a corner and washed the blood from his fingers.

Fallowby, fat and lazy, watched him without comment, but Trent, half divining how things had turned, walked over to Fallowby smiling.

"I've a bone to pick with you," he said.

"Where is it? I'm hungry," replied Fallowby, with affected eagerness, but Trent, frowning, told him to listen.

"How much did I advance you a week ago?"

"Three hundred and eighty francs," replied the other, with a squirm of contrition.

"Where is it?"

Fallowby began a series of intricate explanations, which were soon cut short by Trent.

"I know; you blew it in; you always blow it in. I don't care a rap what you did before the siege; I know you are rich, and have a right to dispose of your money as you wish to, and I also know that, generally speaking, it is none of my business. But *now* it is my business, as I have to supply the funds until you get some more, which you won't until the siege is ended one way or another. I wish to share what I have, but I won't see it thrown out of the window. Oh yes, of course I know you will reimburse me, but that isn't the question; and, anyway, it's the opinion of your friends, old man, that you will not be worse off for a little abstinence from fleshly pleasures. You are positively a freak in this famine-cursed city of skeletons."

"I *am* rather stout," he admitted.

"Is it true you are out of money?" demanded Trent.

"Yes, I am," sighed the other.

"That roast sucking-pig on the Rue St. Honoré—is it there yet?" continued Trent.

"Wh-at?" stammered the feeble one.

"Ah—I thought so! I caught you in ecstasy before that sucking-pig at least a dozen times."

Then, laughing, he presented Fallowby with a roll of twenty-franc pieces, saying, "If these go for luxuries, you must live on your own flesh," and went over to aid West, who sat beside the wash-basin binding up his hand.

West suffered him to tie the knot, and then said: "You remember, yesterday, when I left you and Braith to take the chicken to Colette."

"Chicken! Good heavens!" moaned Fallowby.

"Chicken," repeated West, enjoying Fallowby's grief; "I—that is, I must explain that things are changed. Colette and I—are to be married—"

"What—what about the chicken?" groaned Fallowby.

"Shut up!" laughed Trent, and, slipping his arm through West's, walked to the stair-way.

"The poor little thing," said West—"just think, not a splinter of firewood for a week and wouldn't tell me because she thought I needed it for my clay figure. Whew! When I heard it I smashed that smirking, clay nymph to pieces, and the rest can freeze and be hanged!" After a moment he added, timidly: "Won't you call on your way down and say *bon soir?* It's No. 17."

"Yes," said Trent, and he went out, softly closing the door behind.

He stopped on the third landing, lighted a match, scanned the numbers over the row of dingy doors, and knocked at No. 17.

"C'est toi, Georges?" The door opened.

"Oh, pardon, Monsieur Jack, I thought it was Monsieur West"; then, blushing furiously: "Oh, I see you have heard! Oh, thank you so much for your wishes, and I'm sure we love each other very much—and I'm dying to see Sylvia and tell her, and—"

"And what," laughed Trent.

"I am very happy," she sighed.

"He's pure gold," returned Trent, and then, gayly: "I want you and George to come and dine with us tonight. It's a little treat—you see to-morrow is Sylvia's *fête.* She will be nineteen. I have written to Thorn, and the Guernalecs will come with their cousin Odile. Fallowby has engaged not to bring anybody but himself."

The girl accepted shyly, charging him with loads of loving messages to Sylvia, and he said good-night.

He started up the street, walking swiftly, for it was bitter cold, and, cutting across the Rue de la Lune, he entered the Rue de Seine. The early winter night had fallen, almost without warning; but the sky was clear, and myriads of stars glittered in the heavens. The bombardment had become furious—a steady rolling thunder from the Prussian cannon punctuated by the heavy shocks from Mont Valérien.

The shells streamed across the sky, leaving trails like shooting-stars, and now, as he turned to look back, rockets blue and red flared above the horizon from the Fort of Issy, and the Fortress of the North flamed like a bonfire.

"Good news!" a man shouted over by the Boulevard St. Germain. As if by magic the streets were filled with people—shivering, chattering people with shrunken eyes.

"Jacques!" cried one, "the Army of the Loire!"

"Eh! *Mon vieux,* it has come, then, at last! I told thee! I told thee! To-morrow—to-morrow—who knows?"

"Is it true? Is it a sortie?"

Some one said: "O God—a sortie—and my son?" Another cried: "To the Seine? They say one can see the signals of the Army of the Loire from the Pont Neuf."

There was a child standing near Trent who kept repeating: "Mamma, mamma, then to-morrow we may eat white bread?" And beside him an old man, swaying, stumbling, his shrivelled hands crushed to his breast, muttering as if insane.

"Could it be true? Who has heard the news? The shoemaker on the Rue de Buci had it from a Mobile who had heard a franc-tireur repeat it to a captain of the National Guard."

Trent followed the throng surging through the Rue de Seine to the river.

Rocket after rocket clove the sky, and now, from Montmartre, the cannon clanged, and the batteries on Montparnasse joined in with a crash. The bridge was packed with people.

Trent asked: "Who has seen the signals of the Army of the Loire?"

"We are waiting," was the reply.

He looked towards the north. Suddenly the huge silhouette of the Arc de Triomphe sprang into black relief against the flash of a cannon. The boom of the gun rolled along the quay and the old bridge vibrated.

Again over by the Point du Jour a flash and heavy explosion shook the bridge, and then the whole eastern bastion of the fortifications blazed and crackled, sending a red flame into the sky.

"Has any one seen the signals yet?" he asked, again.

"We are waiting," was the reply.

"Yes, waiting," murmured a man behind him—"waiting—sick, starved, freezing, but waiting. Is it a sortie? They go gladly. Is it to starve? They starve. They have no time to think of surrender. Are they heroes—these Parisians? Answer me, Trent!"

The American ambulance surgeon turned about and scanned the parapets of the bridge.

"Any news, doctor?" asked Trent, mechanically.

"News?" said the doctor; "I don't know any—I haven't time to know any. What are these people after?"

"They say that the Army of the Loire has signalled Mont Valérien."

"Poor devils!" The doctor glanced about him for an instant, and then: "I'm so harried and worried that I don't know what to do. After the last sortie we had the work of fifty ambulances on our poor little corps. To-morrow there's another sortie, and I wish you fellows could come over to headquarters. We may need volunteers. How is madame?" he added, abruptly.

"Well," replied Trent; "but she seems to grow more nervous every day. I ought to be with her now."

"Take care of her," said the doctor; then, with a sharp look at the people: "I can't stop now—goodnight!" and he hurried away, muttering, "Poor devils!"

Trent leaned over the parapet and blinked at the black river surging through the arches. Dark objects, carried swiftly on the breast of the current, struck with a grinding, tearing noise against the stone piers, spun around for an instant, and hurried away into the darkness. The ice from the Marne.

As he stood staring into the water a hand was laid on his shoulder. "Hello, Southwark!" he cried, turning around; "this is a queer place for you!"

"Trent, I have something to tell you. Don't stay here—don't believe in the Army of the Loire"; and the *attaché* of the American

Legation slipped his arm through Trent's and drew him towards the Louvre.

"Then it's another lie!" said Trent, bitterly.

"Worse—we know at the Legation—I can't speak of it. But that's not what I have to say. Something happened this afternoon. The Alsatian Brasserie was visited and an American named Hartman has been arrested. Do you know him?"

"I know a German who calls himself an American; his name is Hartman."

"Well, he was arrested about two hours ago. They mean to shoot him."

"What!"

"Of course we at the Legation can't allow them to shoot him off-hand; but the evidence seems conclusive."

"Is he a spy?"

"Well, the papers seized in his rooms are pretty damning proofs, and, besides, he was caught, they say, swindling the Public Food Committee. He drew rations for fifty—how, I don't know. He claims to be an American artist here, and we have been obliged to take notice of it at the Legation. It's a nasty affair."

"To cheat the people at such a time is worse than robbing the poor-box," cried Trent, angrily. "Let them shoot him!"

"He's an American citizen."

"Yes, oh yes," said the other, with bitterness. "American citizenship is a precious privilege when every goggle-eyed German—" His anger choked him.

Southwark shook hands with him warmly. "It can't be helped, we must own the carrion. I am afraid you may be called upon to identify him as an American artist," he said, with a ghost of a smile on his deep-lined face, and walked away through the Cours de la Reine.

Trent swore silently for a moment, and then drew out his watch. Seven o'clock. "Sylvia will be anxious," he thought, and hurried back to the river. The crowd still huddled shivering on the bridge, a sombre, pitiful congregation, peering out into the night for the signals of the Army of the Loire; and their hearts beat time to the pounding of the guns, their eyes lighted with each flash from the bastions, and hope rose with the drifting rockets.

A black cloud hung over the fortifications. From horizon to horizon the cannon smoke stretched in wavering bands, now capping the spires and domes with cloud, now blowing in streamers and shreds along the streets, now descending from the house-tops, enveloping quays, bridges, and river in a sulphurous mist. And through the smoke pall the lightning of the cannon played, while from time to time a rift above showed a fathomless black vault set with stars.

He turned again into the Rue de Seine, that sad, abandoned street, with its rows of closed shutters and desolate ranks of unlighted lamps. He was a little nervous, and wished once or twice for a revolver, but the slinking forms which passed him in the darkness were too weak with hunger to be dangerous, he thought, and he passed on unmolested to his door-way. But there somebody sprang at his throat. Over and over the icy pavement he rolled with his assailant, tearing at the noose about his neck, and then with a wrench sprang to his feet.

"Get up," he cried to the other.

Slowly and with great deliberation a small gamin picked himself out of the gutter and surveyed Trent with disgust.

"That's a nice, clean trick," said Trent; "a whelp of your age! You'll finish against a dead wall. Give me that cord."

The urchin handed him the noose without a word.

Trent struck a match and looked at his assailant. It was the rat-killer of the day before.

"H'm! I thought so," he muttered.

"Tiens, c'est toi?" said the gamin, tranquilly.

The impudence, the overpowering audacity, of the ragamuffin took Trent's breath away.

"Do you know, you young strangler," he gasped, "that they shoot thieves of your age?"

The child turned a passionless face to Trent.

"Shoot, then."

That was too much, and he turned on his heel and entered his hotel.

Groping up the unlighted stair-way, he at last reached his own landing and felt about in the darkness for the door. From his studio came the sound of voices—West's hearty laugh and Fallowby's chuckle—and at last he found the knob, and, pushing back the door, stood a moment confused by the light.

"Hello, Jack!" cried West, "you're a pleasant creature, inviting people to dine and letting them wait. Here's Fallowby weeping with hunger—"

"Shut up," observed the latter; "perhaps he's been out to buy a turkey."

"He's been out garroting; look at his noose!" laughed Guernalec.

"So now we know where you get your cash!" added West; "vive le coup du Père François!"

Trent shook hands with everybody and laughed at Sylvia's pale face.

"I didn't mean to be late; I stopped on the bridge a moment to watch the bombardment. Were you anxious, Sylvia?"

She smiled and murmured, "Oh no!" but her hand dropped into his and tightened convulsively.

"To the table!" shouted Fallowby, and uttered a joyous whoop.

"Take it easy," observed Thorne, with a remnant of manners; "you are not the host, you know."

Marie Guernalec, who had been chattering with Colette, jumped up and took Thorne's arm, and Monsieur Guernalec drew Odile's arm through his.

Trent, bowing gravely, offered his own arm to Colette, West took in Sylvia, and Fallowby hovered anxiously in the rear.

"You march around the table three times singing the Marseillaise," explained Sylvia, "and Monsieur Fallowby pounds on the table and beats time."

Fallowby suggested that they could sing after dinner, but his protest was drowned in the ringing chorus:

"Aux armes!
Formez vos bataillons!"

Around the room they marched, singing,

"Marchons! Marchons!"

with all their might, while Fallowby, with very bad grace, hammered on the table, consoling himself a little with the hope that the exercise would increase his appetite. Hercules, the black-and-tan, fled under the bed, from which retreat he yapped and whined until dragged out by Guernalec and placed in Odile's lap.

"And now," said Trent, gravely, when everybody was seated, "listen!" and he read the menu:

"'Beef Soup à la Siège de Paris.

———

Fish.
Sardines à la Père Lachaise.
(White Wine.)

———

Rôti.
(Red Wine.)
Fresh Beef à la Sortie.

———

Vegetables.
Canned Beans à la Chassepot,
Canned Peas Gravelotte,
Potatoes Irlandaises,
Miscellaneous.

———

Cold Corned Beef à la Thiers,
Stewed Prunes à la Garibaldi.

———

Dessert.
Dried Prunes—White Bread,

Currant Jelly,
Tea—Café,
Liqueurs,
Pipes and Cigarettes.'"

Fallowby applauded frantically, and Sylvia served the soup.

"Isn't it delicious?" sighed Odile.

Marie Guernalec sipped her soup in rapture.

"Not at all like horse, and, I don't care what they say, horse doesn't taste like beef," whispered Colette to West. Fallowby, who had finished, began to caress his chin and eye the tureen.

"Have some more, old chap?" inquired Trent.

"Monsieur Fallowby cannot have any more," announced Sylvia; "I am saving this for the concierge." Fallowby transferred his eyes to the fish.

The sardines, hot from the grille, were a great success. While the others were eating, Sylvia ran downstairs with the soup for the old concierge and her husband, and when she hurried back, flushed and breathless, and had slipped into her chair with a happy smile at Trent, that young man arose, and silence fell over the table. For an instant he looked at Sylvia, and thought he had never seen her so beautiful.

"You all know," he began, "that to-day is my wife's nineteenth birthday—"

Fallowby, bubbling with enthusiasm, waved his glass in circles about his head, to the terror of Odile and Colette, his neighbors, and Thorne, West, and Guernalec refilled their glasses three times before the storm of applause, which the toast of Sylvia had provoked, subsided.

Three times the glasses were filled and emptied to Sylvia, and again to Trent, who protested.

"This is irregular," he cried; "the next toast is to the twin Republics—France and America."

"To the Republics! To the Republics!" they cried, and the toast was drunk amid shouts of "Vive la France!" "Vive l'Amérique!" "Vive la Nation!"

Then Trent, with a smile at West, offered the toast, "To a Happy Pair!" and everybody understood, and Sylvia leaned over and kissed Colette, while Trent bowed to West.

The beef was eaten in comparative calm, but when it was finished, and a portion of it set aside for the old people below, Trent cried: "Drink to Paris! May she rise from her ruins and crush the invader!" and the cheers rang out, drowning for a moment the monotonous thunder of the Prussian guns.

Pipes and cigarettes were lighted, and Trent listened an instant to the animated chatter around him, broken by ripples of laughter from the girls or the mellow chuckle of Fallowby. Then he turned to West.

"There is going to be a sortie to-night," he said. "I saw the American ambulance surgeon just before I came in and he asked me to speak to you fellows. Any aid we can give him will not come amiss."

Then, dropping his voice and speaking in English: "As for me, I shall go out with the ambulance tomorrow morning. There is, of course, no danger, but it's just as well to keep it from Sylvia."

West nodded. Thorne and Guernalec, who had heard, broke in and offered assistance, and Fallowby volunteered with a groan.

"All right," said Trent, rapidly, "no more now, but meet me at Ambulance Headquarters to-morrow morning at eight."

Sylvia and Colette, who were becoming uneasy at the conversation in English, now demanded to know what they were talking about.

"What does a sculptor usually talk about?" cried West, with a laugh.

Odile glanced reproachfully at Thorne, her *fiancé.*

"You are not French, you know, and it is none of your business, this war," said Odile, with much dignity.

Thorne looked meek, but West assumed an air of outraged virtue.

"It seems," he said to Fallowby, "that a fellow cannot discuss the beauties of Greek sculpture in his mother tongue without being openly suspected."

Colette placed her hand over his mouth, and, turning to Sylvia, murmured, "They are horridly untruthful, these men."

"I believe the word for ambulance is the same in both languages," said Marie Guernalec, saucily; "Sylvia, don't trust Monsieur Trent."

"Jack," whispered Sylvia, "promise me—"

A knock at the studio door interrupted her.

"Come in!" cried Fallowby, but Trent sprang up and, opening the door, looked out. Then, with a hasty excuse to the rest, he stepped into the hall-way and closed the door.

When he returned he was grumbling.

"What is it, Jack?" cried West.

"What is it?" repeated Trent, savagely; "I'll tell you what it is. I have received a despatch from the American Minister to go at once and identify and claim, as a fellow-countryman and a brother artist, a rascally thief and a German spy!"

"Don't go," suggested Fallowby.

"If I don't, they'll shoot him at once."

"Let them," growled Thorne.

"Do you fellows know who it is?"

"Hartman!" shouted West, inspired.

Sylvia sprang up deathly white, but Odile slipped her arm around her and supported her to a chair, saying, calmly, "Sylvia has fainted—it's the hot room—bring some water."

Trent brought it at once.

Sylvia opened her eyes, and after a moment rose, and, supported by Marie Guernalec and Trent, passed into the bedroom.

It was the signal for breaking-up, and everybody came and shook hands with Trent, saying they hoped Sylvia would sleep it off, and that it would be nothing.

When Marie Guernalec took leave of him, she avoided his eyes, but he spoke to her cordially and thanked her for her aid.

"Anything I can do, Jack?" inquired West, lingering, and then hurried down-stairs to catch up with the rest.

Trent leaned over the banisters, listening to their footsteps and chatter, and then the lower door banged and the house was silent. He lingered, staring down into the blackness, biting his lips; then, with an impatient movement, "I am crazy!" he muttered, and, lighting a candle, went into the bedroom. Sylvia was lying on the bed. He bent over her, smoothing the curly hair on her forehead.

"Are you better, dear Sylvia?"

She did not answer, but raised her eyes to his. For an instant he met her gaze, but what he read there sent a chill to his heart, and he sat down, covering his face with his hands.

At last she spoke in a voice changed and strained, a voice which he had never heard, and he dropped his hands and listened, bolt upright in his chair.

"Jack, it has come at last. I have feared it and trembled—ah! how often have I lain awake at night with this on my heart and prayed that I might die before you should ever know of it! For I love you, Jack, and if you go away I cannot live. I have deceived you; it happened before I knew you, but since that first day, when you found me weeping in the Luxembourg and spoke to me, Jack, I have been faithful to you in every thought and deed. I loved you from the first, and did not dare to tell you this, fearing that you would go away; and since then my love has grown—grown—and, oh! I suffered! but I dared not tell you. And now you know, but you do not know the worst. For him—now—what do I care? He was cruel—oh, so cruel!"

She hid her face in her arms.

"Must I go on? Must I tell you—can you not imagine, oh, Jack!—"

He did not stir; his eyes seemed dead.

"I—I was so young, I knew nothing, and he said—said that he loved me—I must finish! When you told me you loved me—you—you asked me nothing; but then, even then, it was too late, and *that other life* which binds me to him must stand forever between you and me! For there *is another* whom he has claimed, and is good to. He must not die—they cannot shoot him, for that *other's* sake!"

Trent sat motionless, but his thoughts ran on in an interminable whirl.

Sylvia, little Sylvia, who shared with him his student life—who bore with him the dreary desolation of the siege without complaint—this slender, blue-eyed girl, whom he was so quietly fond of, whom he teased or caressed as the whim suited, who sometimes made him the least bit impatient with her passionate devotion to him—could this be the same Sylvia who lay weeping there in the darkness?"

Then he clenched his teeth. "Let him die! Let him die!"—but then, for Sylvia's sake, and for that *other's* sake? Yes, he would go—he *must* go—his duty was plain before him. But Sylvia, he could not be what he had been to her, and yet a vague terror seized him, now all was said. Trembling, he struck a light.

She lay there, her curly hair tumbled about her face, her small, white hands pressed to her breast.

He could not leave her, and he could not stay. He never knew before that he loved her. She had been a mere comrade, this girl-wife of his. Ah! he loved her now with all his heart and soul, and he knew it, only when it was too late. Too late? Why? Then he thought of the *other* one, binding her, linking her forever to the creature who stood in danger of his life. With an oath he sprang to the door, but the door would not open—or was it that he pressed it back—locked it, and flung himself on his knees beside the bed, knowing that he dared not for his life's sake leave what was his all in life.

III

It was four in the morning when he came out of the Prison of the Condemned with the Secretary of the American Legation. A knot of people had gathered around the American Minister's carriage, which stood in front of the prison, the horses stamping and pawing in the icy street, the coachman huddled on the box, wrapped in furs. Southwark helped the Secretary into the carriage and shook hands with Trent, thanking him for coming.

"How the scoundrel did stare!" he said. "Your evidence was worse than a kick, but it saved his skin for the moment, at least, and prevented complications."

The Secretary sighed. "We have done our part. Now let them prove him a spy, and we wash our hands of him. Jump in, Captain! Come along, Trent!"

"I have a word to say to Captain Southwark; I won't detain him," said Trent, hastily, and, dropping his voice, "Southwark, help *me* now. You know the story from the blackguard. You know the—the child is at his rooms. Get it, and take it to my own apartment, and if he is shot I will provide a home for it."

"I understand," said the Captain, gravely

"Will you do this at once?"

"At once," he replied.

Their hands met in a warm clasp, and then Captain Southwark climbed into the carriage, motioning Trent to follow; but he shook his head, saying "Good-bye," and the carriage rolled away.

He watched the carriage to the end of the street, then started towards his own quarter, but, after a step or two, hesitated, stopped, and finally turned away in the opposite direction. Something—perhaps it was the sight of the prisoner he had so recently confronted—nauseated him. He felt the need of solitude and quiet to collect his thoughts. The events of the evening had shaken him terribly, but he would walk it off, forget, bury everything, and then go back to Sylvia. He started on swiftly, and for a time the bitter thoughts seemed to fade, but when he paused at last, breathless, under the Arc de Triomphe, the bitterness and the wretchedness of the whole thing—yes, of his whole misspent life—came back with a pang. Then the face of the prisoner, stamped with the horrible grimace of fear, grew in the shadows before his eyes.

Sick at heart, he wandered up and down under the great Arc, striving to occupy his mind, peering up at the sculptured cornices to read the names of the heroes and battles which he knew were engraved there, but always the ashen face of Hartman followed him, grinning with terror—or was it terror?—was it not triumph? At the thought he leaped like a man who feels a knife at his throat, but, after a savage tramp around the square, came back again and sat down to battle with his misery.

The air was cold, but his cheeks were burning with angry shame. Shame? Why? Was it because he had married a girl whom chance had made a mother? *Did* he love her? Was this miserable bohemian existence, then, his end and aim in life? He turned his eyes upon the secrets of his heart, and read an evil story—the story of the past, and he covered his face for shame; while, keeping time to the dull pain throbbing in his head, his heart beat out the story for the future. Shame and disgrace.

Roused at last from a lethargy which had begun to numb the bitterness of his thoughts, he raised his head and looked about. A sudden fog had settled in the streets; the arches of the Arc were choked with it. He would go home. A great horror of being alone seized him. *But he was not alone.* The fog was peopled with phantoms. All around him in the mist they moved, drifting through the arches in lengthening lines, and vanished, while from the fog others rose up, swept past, and were engulfed. He was not alone, for even at his side they crowded, touched him, swarmed before him, beside him, behind him, pressed him back, seized and bore him with them through the mist. Down a dim avenue, through lanes and alleys white with fog, they moved, and if they spoke their voices were dull as the vapor which shrouded them. At last, in front, a bank of masonry and earth cut by a massive, iron-barred gate towered up in the fog. Slowly and more slowly they glided, shoulder to shoulder and thigh to thigh. Then all movement ceased. A sudden breeze stirred the fog. It wavered and eddied. Objects became more distinct. A pallor crept above the horizon, touching the edges of the watery clouds, and drew dull sparks from a thousand bayonets. Bayonets—they were everywhere, cleaving the fog or flowing beneath it in rivers of steel. High on the wall of masonry and earth a great gun loomed, and around it figures moved in silhouettes. Below, a broad torrent of bayonets swept through the iron-barred gateway, out into the shadowy plain. It became lighter. Faces grew more distinct among the marching masses, and he recognized one.

"You, Philippe!"

The figure turned its head.

Trent cried, "Is there room for me?" but the other only waved his arm in a vague adieu, and was gone with the rest. Presently the cavalry began to pass, squadron on squadron, crowding out into darkness; then many cannon, then an ambulance, then again the endless lines of bayonets. Beside him a cuirassier sat on his steaming horse, and in front, among a group of mounted officers he saw a general, with the Astrakhan collar of his dolman turned up about his bloodless face.

Some women were weeping near him, and one was struggling to force a loaf of black bread into a soldier's haversack. The soldier tried to aid her, but the sack was fastened, and his rifle bothered him, so Trent held it while the woman unbuttoned the sack and forced in the bread, now all wet with her tears. The rifle was not heavy. Trent found it wonderfully manageable. Was the bayonet sharp? He tried it. Then a sudden longing, a fierce, imperative desire took possession of him.

"Chouette!" cried the gamin, clinging to the barred gate; "encore toi, mon vieux?"

Trent looked up, and the rat-killer laughed in his face. But when the soldier had taken the rifle again, and, thanking him, ran hard to catch his battalion, he plunged into the throng about the gate-way.

"Are you going?" he cried to a marine who sat in the gutter bandaging his foot.

"Yes."

Then a girl—a mere child—caught him by the hand and led him into the café which faced the gate. The room was crowded with soldiers, some, white and silent, sitting on the floor, others groaning on the leather-covered settees. The air was sour and suffocating.

"Choose!" said the girl, with a little gesture of pity; "they can't go!"

In a heap of clothing on the floor he found a capote and képi.

She helped him buckle his knapsack, cartridge-box, and belt, and showed him how to load the chassepot rifle, holding it on her knees.

When he thanked her she started to her feet.

"You are a foreigner?"

"American," he said, moving towards the door, but the child barred his way.

"I am a Bretonne. My father is up there with the cannon of the marine. He will shoot you if you are a spy."

They faced each other for a moment. Then, sighing, he bent over and kissed the child. "Pray for France, little one," he murmured, and she repeated, with a pale smile, "For France and you, beau monsieur."

He ran across the street and through the gate-way. Once outside, he edged into line and shouldered his way along the road. A corporal passed, looked at him, repassed, and finally called an officer. "You belong to the 60th," growled the corporal, looking at the number on his képi."

"We have no use for francs-tireurs," added the officer, catching sight of his black trousers."

"I wish to volunteer in place of a comrade," said Trent, and the officer shrugged his shoulders and passed on.

Nobody paid much attention to him, one or two merely glancing at his trousers. The road was deep with slush and mud ploughed and torn by wheels and hoofs. A soldier in front of him wrenched his foot in an icy rut and dragged himself to the edge of the embankment groaning. The plain on either side of them was gray with melting snow. Here and there behind dismantled hedgerows stood wagons, bearing white flags with red crosses. Sometimes the driver was a priest in rusty hat and gown, sometimes a crippled Mobile. Once they passed a wagon driven by a Sister of Charity. Silent, empty houses, with great rents in their walls, and every window blank, huddled along the road. Farther on, within the zone of danger, nothing of human habitation remained except here and there a pile of frozen bricks or a blackened cellar choked with snow.

For some time Trent had been annoyed by the man behind him, who kept treading on his heels. Convinced at last that it was intentional, he turned to remonstrate and found himself face to face with a fellow-student from the Beaux Arts. Trent stared.

"I thought you were in the hospital!"

The other shook his head, pointing to his bandaged jaw.

"I see—you can't speak. Can I do anything?"

The wounded man rummaged in his haversack and produced a crust of black bread.

"He can't eat it, his jaw is smashed, and he wants you to chew it for him," said the soldier next to him.

Trent took the crust, and, grinding it in his teeth morsel by morsel, passed it back to the starving man.

From time to time mounted orderlies sped to the front, covering them with slush. It was a chilly, silent march through sodden meadows, wreathed in fog. Along the railroad embankment, across the ditch, another column moved parallel to their own. Trent watched it, a sombre mass, now distinct, now vague, now blotted out in a puff of fog. Once, for half an hour, he lost it, but when again it came into view he noticed a thin line detach itself from the flank, and, bellying in the middle, swing rapidly to the west. At the same moment a prolonged crackling broke out in the fog in front. Other lines began to slough off from the column, swinging east and west, and the crackling became continuous. A battery passed at full gallop, and he drew back with his comrades to give it way. It went into action a little to the right of his battalion, and, as the shot from the first rifled piece boomed through the mist, the cannon from the fortifications opened with a mighty roar. An officer galloped by shouting something which Trent did not catch, but he saw the ranks in front suddenly part company with his own and disappear in the twilight. More officers rode up, and stood beside him peering into the fog. Away in front the crackling had become one prolonged crash. It was dreary waiting. Trent chewed some bread for the man behind, who tried to swallow it, and, after a while, shook his head, motioning Trent to eat the rest himself. A corporal offered him a little brandy, and he drank it, but when he turned around to return the flask the corporal was lying on the ground. Alarmed, he looked at the soldier next to him, who shrugged his shoulders and opened his mouth to speak, but something struck him, and he rolled over and over into the ditch below. At that moment the horse of one of the officers gave a bound, and backed into the battalion, lashing out with his heels. One man was ridden down; another was kicked in the chest and hurled through the ranks. The officer sank his spurs into the horse, and forced him to the front again, where he stood trembling. The cannonade seemed to draw nearer. A staff officer, riding slowly up and down the battalion, suddenly collapsed in his saddle and clung to his horse's mane. One of his boots dangled, crimsoned and dripping, from the stirrup. Then, out of the mist in front, men came running. The roads, the fields, the ditches, were full of them, and many of them fell. For an instant he imagined he saw horsemen riding about like ghosts in the vapors beyond, and a man behind him cursed horribly, declaring he, too, had seen them, and that they were Uhlans; but the battalion stood inactive, and the mist fell again over the meadows.

The Colonel sat heavily upon his horse, his bullet-shaped head buried in the Astrakhan collar of his dolman, his fat legs sticking straight out in the stirrups.

The buglers clustered about him, with bugles poised, and behind him a staff officer, in a pale-blue jacket, smoked a cigarette and chatted with a captain of Hussars. From the road in front came the sound of furious galloping, and an orderly reined up beside the Colonel, who motioned him to the rear without turning his head. Then on the left a confused murmur arose which ended in a shout. A Hussar passed like the wind, followed by another and another, and then squadron after squadron whirled by them into the sheeted mists. At that instant the Colonel reared in his saddle, the bugles clanged, and the whole battalion scrambled down the embankment, over the ditch, and started across the soggy meadow. Almost at once Trent lost his cap. Something snatched it from his head—he thought it was a tree branch. A good many of his comrades rolled over in the slush and ice, and he imagined that they had slipped. One pitched right across his path, and he stopped to help him up, but the man screamed when he touched him, and an officer shouted, "Forward! forward!" So he ran on again. It was a long jog through the mist, and he was often obliged to shift his rifle. When at last they lay panting behind the railroad embankment, he looked about him. He had felt the need of action, of a desperate physical struggle, of killing and crushing. He had been seized with a desire to fling himself among masses and tear right and left. He longed to fire, to use the thin, sharp bayonet on his chassepot. He had not expected this. He wished to become exhausted, to struggle and cut until incapable of lifting his arm. Then he had intended to go home. He heard a man say that half the battalion had gone down in the charge, and he saw another examining a corpse under the embankment. The body, still warm, was clothed in a strange uniform, but, even when he noticed the spiked helmet lying a few inches farther away, he did not realize what had happened.

The Colonel sat on his horse a few feet to the left, his eyes sparkling under the crimson képi. Trent heard him reply to an officer: "I can hold it, but another charge and I won't have enough men left to sound a bugle."

"Were the Prussians here?" Trent asked of a soldier who sat wiping the blood trickling from his hair.

"Yes. The Hussars cleaned them out. We caught their cross-fire."

"We are supporting a battery on the embankment," said another.

Then the battalion crawled over the embankment and moved along the lines of twisted rails. Trent rolled up his trousers and tucked them into his woollen socks, but they halted again, and some of the men sat down on the dismantled railroad track. Trent looked for his wounded comrade from the Beaux Arts. He was standing in his place, very pale. The cannonade had become terrific. For a moment the mist lifted. He caught a glimpse of the first battalion motionless on the railroad track in front, of regiments on either flank, and then, as the fog settled again, the drums beat and the music of the bugles began away on the extreme left. A restless movement passed among the troops, the Colonel threw up his arm, the drums rolled, and the battalion moved off through the fog. They were near the front now, for the first battalion was firing as it advanced. Ambulances galloped along the base of the embankment to the rear, and the Hussars passed and repassed like phantoms. They were in the front at last, for all about them was movement and turmoil, while from the fog, close at hand, came cries and groans and crashing volleys. Shells fell everywhere, bursting along the embankment, splashing them with frozen slush. Trent was frightened. He began to dread the unknown, which lay there crackling and flaming in obscurity. The shock of the cannon sickened him. He could even see the fog light up with a dull orange as the thunder shook the earth. It was near, he felt certain, for the Colonel shouted "Forward!" and the first battalion was hastening into it. He felt its breath, he trembled, but hurried on. A fearful discharge in front terrified him. Somewhere in the fog men were cheering, and the Colonel's horse, streaming with blood, plunged about in the smoke.

Another blast and shock, right in his face, almost stunned him, and he faltered. All the men to the right were down. His head swam; the fog and smoke stupefied him. He put out his hand for a support, and caught something. It was the wheel of a gun carriage, and a man sprang from behind it, aiming a blow at his head with a rammer, but stumbled back shrieking, with a bayonet through his neck, and Trent knew that he had killed. Mechanically he stooped to pick up his rifle, but the bayonet was still in the man who lay beating with red hands against the sod. It sickened him, and he leaned on the cannon. Men were fighting all around him now, and the air was foul with smoke and sweat. Somebody seized him from behind, and another in front, but others in turn seized them or struck them solid blows. The click! click! click! of bayonets infuriated him, and he grasped the rammer and struck out blindly until it was shivered to pieces.

A man threw his arm around his neck and bore him to the ground, but he throttled him and raised himself on his knees. He saw a comrade seize the cannon and fall across it with his skull crushed in; he saw the Colonel tumble clean out of his saddle into the mud; then consciousness fled.

When he came to himself he was lying on the embankment among the twisted rails. On every side huddled men who cried out and cursed and fled away into the fog, and he staggered to his feet and followed them. Once he stopped to help a comrade with a bandaged jaw, who could not speak, but clung to his arm for a time, and then fell dead in the freezing mire; and again he aided another, who groaned, "Trent, c'est moi—Philippe," until a sudden volley in the mist relieved him of his charge.

An icy wind swept down from the heights, cutting the fog into shreds. For an instant, with an evil leer, the sun peered through the naked woods of Vincennes, sank like a blood-clot in the battery smoke, lower, lower, into the blood-soaked plain.

IV

When midnight sounded from the belfry of St. Sulpice, the gates of Paris were still choked with fragments of what had once been an army.

They entered with the night, a sullen horde, spattered with slime, faint with hunger and exhaustion. There was little disorder at first, and the throng at the gates parted silently as the troops tramped along the freezing streets. Confusion came as the hours passed. Swiftly, and more swiftly, crowding squadron after squadron and battery on battery, horses plunging and caissons jolting, the remnants from the front surged through the gates, a chaos of cavalry and artillery struggling for the right of way. Close upon them stumbled the infantry; here a skeleton of a regiment marching with a desperate attempt at order; there a riotous mob of Mobiles crushing their way to the streets; then a turmoil of horsemen, cannon, troops without officers, officers without men, then again a line of ambulances, the wheels groaning under their heavy loads.

Dumb with misery, the crowd looked on.

All through the day the ambulances had been arriving, and all day long the ragged throng whimpered and shivered by the barriers. At noon the crowd was increased tenfold, filling the squares about the gates and swarming over the inner fortifications.

At four o'clock in the afternoon the German batteries suddenly wreathed themselves in smoke, and the shells fell fast on

Montparnasse. At twenty minutes after four two projectiles struck a house in the Rue de Bac, and a moment later the first shell fell in the Latin Quarter.

Braith was painting in bed when West came in, very much scared.

"I wish you would come down; our house has been knocked into a cocked hat, and I'm afraid that some of the pillagers may take it into their heads to pay us a visit to-night."

Braith jumped out of bed and bundled himself into a garment which had once been an overcoat.

"Anybody hurt?" he inquired, struggling with a sleeve full of dilapidated lining.

"No. Colette is barricaded in the cellar, and the concierge ran away to the fortifications. There will be a rough gang there if the bombardment keeps up. You might help us—"

"Of course," said Braith; but it was not until they had reached the Rue Serpente, and had turned in the passage which led to West's cellar, that the latter cried, "Have you seen Jack Trent to-day?"

"No," replied Braith, looking troubled, "he was not at Ambulance Headquarters."

"He stayed to take care of Sylvia, I suppose."

A bomb came crashing through the roof of a house at the end of the alley and burst in the basement, showering the street with slate and plaster. A second struck a chimney and plunged into the garden, followed by an avalanche of bricks; and another exploded with a deafening report in the next street.

They hurried along the passage to the steps which led to the cellar. Here again Braith stopped.

"Don't you think I had better run up to see if Jack and Sylvia are well intrenched? I can get back before dark."

"No. Go in and find Colette, and I'll go."

"No, no, let me go; there's no danger."

"I know it," replied West, calmly; and, dragging Braith into the alley, pointed to the cellar-steps. The iron door was barred.

"Colette! Colette!" he called. The door swung inward, and the girl sprang up the steps to meet them. At that instant Braith, glancing behind him, gave a startled cry, and, pushing the two before him into the cellar, jumped down after them and slammed the iron door. A few seconds later a heavy jar from the outside shook the hinges.

"They are here," muttered West, very pale.

"That door," observed Colette, calmly, "will hold forever."

Braith examined the low iron structure, now trembling with the blows rained on it from without. West glanced anxiously at Colette, who displayed no agitation, and this comforted him.

"I don't believe they will spend much time here," said Braith; "they only rummage in cellars for spirits, I imagine."

"Unless they hear that valuables are buried there."

"But surely nothing is buried here?" exclaimed Braith, uneasily.

"Unfortunately there is," growled West. "That miserly landlord of mine—"

A crash from the outside, followed by a yell, cut him short; then blow after blow shook the doors until there came a sharp snap, a clinking of metal, and a triangular bit of iron fell inward, leaving a hole through which struggled a ray of light.

Instantly West knelt, and, shoving his revolver through the aperture, fired every cartridge. For a moment the alley resounded with the racket of the revolver, then absolute silence followed.

Presently a single questioning blow fell upon the door, and a moment later another, and another, and then a sudden crack zigzagged across the iron plate.

"Here," said West, seizing Colette by the wrist; "you follow me, Braith!" and he ran swiftly towards a circular spot of light at the farther end of the cellar. The spot of light came from a barred manhole above. West motioned Braith to mount on his shoulders.

"Push it over. You *must!*"

With little effort Braith lifted the barred cover, scrambled out on his stomach, and easily raised Colette from West's shoulders.

"Quick, old chap!" cried the latter.

Braith twisted his legs around a fence chain and leaned down again. The cellar was flooded with a yellow light, and the air reeked with the stench of petroleum torches. The iron door still held, but a whole plate of metal was gone; and now, as they looked, a figure came creeping through, holding a torch.

"Quick!" whispered Braith. "Jump!" and West hung dangling, until Colette grasped him by the collar and he was dragged out. Then her nerves gave way, and she wept hysterically, but West threw his arm around her and led her across the gardens into the next street, where Braith, after replacing the manhole cover, and piling some stone slabs from the wall over it, rejoined them. It was almost dark. They hurried through the street, now only lighted by burning buildings or the swift glare of the shells. They gave wide berth to the fires, but at a distance saw the flitting forms of pillagers among the débris. Sometimes they passed a female, fury-crazed with drink, shrieking anathemas upon the world, or some slouching lout whose blackened face and hands betrayed his share in the work of destruction. At last they reached the Seine and passed the bridge, and then Braith said, "I must go back. I am not sure of Jack and Sylvia." As he spoke he made way for a crowd which came trampling across the bridge and along the river-wall by the d'Orsay barracks. In the midst of it West caught the measured tread of a platoon. A lantern passed, a file of bayonets, then another lantern which glimmered on a deathly face behind, and Colette gasped, "Hartman!" and he was gone. They peered fearfully across the embankment, holding their breath. There was a shuffle of feet on the quay and the gate of the barracks slammed. A lantern shone for a moment at the postern, the crowd pressed to the grille, then came the clang of the volley from the stone parade.

One by one the petroleum torches flared up along the embankment, and now the whole square was in motion. Down from the Champs Élysées, and across the Place de la Concorde, straggled the fragments of the battle, a company here and a mob there. They poured in from every street, followed by women and children, and a great murmur, borne on the icy wind, swept through the Arc de Triomphe, and down the dark avenue—"Perdus! perdus!"

A ragged end of a battalion was pressing past, the spectre of annihilation. West groaned. Then a figure sprang from the shadowy ranks and called West's name, and when he saw it was Trent he cried out. Trent seized him, white with terror.

"Sylvia?"

West stared speechless, but Colette moaned, "Oh, Sylvia! Sylvia! and they are shelling the Quarter!"

"Trent!" shouted Braith; but he was gone, and they could not overtake him.

The bombardment ceased as Trent crossed the Boulevard St. Germain, but the entrance to the Rue de Seine was blocked by a heap of smoking bricks. Everywhere the shells had torn great holes in the pavement. The café was a wreck of splinters and glass, the bookstore tottered, ripped from roof to basement, and the little bakery, long since closed, bulged outward above a mass of slate and tin.

He climbed over the steaming bricks and hurried into the Rue de Tournon. On the corner a fire blazed, lighting up his own street, and on the blank wall, beneath a shattered gas-lamp, a child was writing with a bit of cinder,

HERE FELL THE FIRST SHELL.

The letters stared him in the face. The rat-killer finished and stepped back to view his work, but, catching sight of Trent's bayonet, screamed and fled; and as Trent staggered across the shattered street, from holes and crannies in the ruins fierce women fled from their work of pillage, cursing him.

At first he could not find his house, for the tears blinded him, but he felt along the wall and reached the door. A lantern burned in the concierge's lodge, and the old man lay dead beside it. Faint with fright, he leaned a moment on his rifle, then, snatching the lantern, sprang up the stairs. He tried to call, but his tongue hardly moved. On the second floor he saw plaster on the stair-way, and on the third the floor was torn and the concierge lay in a pool of blood across the landing. The next floor was his—*theirs.* The door hung from its hinges, the walls gaped. He crept in and sank down by the bed, and there two arms were flung around his neck and a tear-stained face sought his own.

"Sylvia!"

"Oh, Jack! Jack! Jack!"

From the tumbled pillow beside them a child wailed.

"They brought it; it is mine," she sobbed.

"Ours," he whispered, with his arms around them both.

Then from the stairs below came Braith's anxious voice.

"Trent! Is all well?"

THE STREET OF OUR LADY OF THE FIELDS

"Et tous les jours passés dans la tristesse
Nous sont comptés comme des jours heureux!"

I

The street is not fashionable, neither is it shabby. It is a pariah among streets—a street without a Quarter. It is generally understood to lie outside the pale of the aristocratic Avenue de l'Observatoire. The students of the Montparnasse Quarter consider it swell and will have none of it. The Latin Quarter, from the Luxembourg, its northern frontier, sneers at its respectability, and regards with disfavor the correctly costumed students who haunt it. Few strangers go into it. At times, however, the Latin Quarter students use it as a thoroughfare between the Rue de Rennes and the Bullier, but except for that, and the weekly afternoon visits of parents and guardians to the convent near the Rue Vavin, the street of Our Lady of the Fields is as quiet as a Passy boulevard. Perhaps the most respectable portion lies between the Rue de la Grande Chaumière and the Rue Vavin; at least this was the conclusion arrived at by the Rev. Joel Byram as he rambled through it with Hastings in charge. To Hastings the street looked pleasant in the bright June weather, and he had begun to hope for its selection. The Reverend Byram shied violently at the cross on the convent opposite, sucked in his lips, and looked about him. He was impressed by the evident respectability of the surroundings. Then, frowning at the convent, he took Hastings's arm and shuffled across the street to an iron gate-way which bore the number 201 *bis* painted in white on a blue ground. Below this was a notice printed in English:

1. For Porter please oppress once.
2. For Servant please oppress twice.
3. For Parlor please oppress thrice.

Hastings touched the electric button three times, and they were ushered through the garden and into the parlor by a trim maid. The dining-room door, just beyond, was open, and from the table, in plain view, a stout woman hastily arose and came towards them. Hastings caught a glimpse of a young man with a big head and several snuffy old gentlemen at breakfast before the door closed, and the stout woman waddled into the room, bringing with her an aroma of coffee and a black poodle.

"It ees a plaisir to you receive!" she cried; "monsieur is Anglish? No? Américain? Off course. My pension it ees for Américains surtout. Here all spik Angleesh, c'est-à-dire, ze personelle; ze sairvants do spik, plus ou moins, a little. I am happy to have you comme pensionaires—"

"Madame," began Dr. Byram, but was cut short again.

"Ah, yess, I know, ah! mon Dieu! you do not spik Frainch, but you have come to lairne! My husband does spik Frainch wiss ze pensionaires. We have at ze moment a family Américaine who learn of my husband Frainch—"

Here the poodle growled at Dr. Byram and was promptly cuffed by his mistress.

"Veux-tu!" she cried, with a slap—"veux-tu! Oh! le vilain, oh! le vilain!"

"Mais, madame," said Hastings, smiling, "il n'a pas l'air très féroce."

The poodle fled, and his mistress cried, "Ah, ze accent charming! He does spik already Frainch like a Parisien young gentleman!"

Then Dr. Byram managed to get in a word or two, and gathered more or less information in regard to prices.

"It ees a pension sérieux; my clientèle ees of ze best—indeed, a pension de famille, where one ees at 'ome."

Then they went up-stairs to examine Hastings's future quarters, test the bed-springs, and arrange for the weekly towel allowance. Dr. Byram appeared satisfied.

Madame Marotte accompanied them to the door and rang for the maid, but, as Hastings stepped out into the gravel walk, his guide and mentor paused a moment and fixed madame with his watery eyes.

"You understand," he said, "that he is a youth of most careful bringing-up, and his character and morals are without a stain. He is young and has never been abroad—never even seen a large city—and his parents have requested me, as an old family friend living in Paris, to see that he is placed under good influences. He is to study art, but on no account would his parents wish him to live in the Latin Quarter if they knew of the immorality which is rife there."

A sound like the click of a latch interrupted him, and he raised his eyes, but not in time to see the maid slap the big-headed young man behind the parlor door.

Madame coughed, cast a deadly glance behind her, and then beamed on Dr. Byram.

"It ees well zat he come here. The pension more serious, il n'en existe pas, eet ees not any!" she announced, with conviction.

So, as there was nothing more to add, Dr. Byram joined Hastings at the gate.

"I trust," he said, "that you will make few acquaintances among the students."

Hastings looked at the convent until a pretty girl passed before the gray façade, and then he looked at her. A young fellow with a paint-box and canvas came swinging along, stopped before the pretty girl, said something during a brief but vigorous handshake at which they both laughed, and he went his way, calling back, "A demain, Valentine!" as in the same breath she cried, "A demain!"

"Valentine," thought Hastings—"what a quaint name!" and he started to follow the Rev. Joel Byram, who was shuffling towards the nearest tramway station.

II

"An' you are pleas wiz Paris, Monsieur 'Astang?" demanded Madame Marotte the next morning, as Hastings came into the breakfast-room of the pension rosy from his plunge in the limited bath above.

"I am sure I shall like it," he replied, wondering at his own depression of spirits.

The maid brought him coffee and rolls. He returned the vacant glance of the big-headed young man, and acknowledged diffidently the salutes of the snuffy old gentlemen. He did not try to finish his coffee, and sat crumbling a roll, unconscious of the sympathetic glances of Madame Marotte, who had tact enough not to bother him.

Presently a maid entered with a tray on which was balanced two bowls of chocolate, and the snuffy old gentlemen leered at her ankles. The maid deposited the chocolate at a table near the window and smiled at Hastings. Then a thin young lady, followed by her counterpart in all except years, marched into the room and took the table near the window. They were evidently American, but Hastings, if he expected any sign of recognition, was disappointed. To be ignored by compatriots intensified his depression. He fumbled with his knife and looked at his plate.

The thin young lady was talkative enough. She was quite aware of Hastings's presence, ready to be flattered if he looked at her, but, on the other hand, she felt her superiority, for she had been three weeks in Paris, and he, it was easy to see, had not yet unpacked his steamer-trunk.

Her conversation was complacent. She argued with her mother upon the relative merits of the Louvre and the Bon Marché, but her mother's part of the discussion was mostly confined to the observation, "Why, Susie!"

The snuffy old gentlemen had left the room in a body, outwardly polite and inwardly raging. They could not endure the Americans, who filled the room with their chatter.

The big-headed young man looked after them with a knowing cough, murmuring, "Gay old birds!"

"They look like bad old men, Mr. Bladen," said the girl.

To this Mr. Bladen smiled, and said, "They've had their day," in a tone which implied that he was now having his.

"And that's why they all have baggy eyes," cried the girl. "I think it's a shame for young gentlemen—"

"Why, Susie!" said the mother, and the conversation lagged.

After a while Mr. Bladen threw down the *Petit Journal,* which he daily studied at the expense of the house, and, turning to Hastings, started to make himself agreeable. He began by saying, "I see you are an American."

To this brilliant and original opening, Hastings, deadly homesick, replied gratefully, and the conversation was judiciously nourished by observations from Miss Susie Byng, distinctly addressed to Mr. Bladen. In the course of events, Miss Susie, forgetting to address herself exclusively to Mr. Bladen, and Hastings replying to her general question, the *entente cordiale* was established, and Susie and her mother extended a protectorate over what was clearly neutral territory.

"Mr. Hastings, you must not desert the pension every evening as Mr. Bladen does. Paris is an awful place for young gentlemen, and Mr. Bladen is a horrid cynic."

Mr. Bladen looked gratified.

Hastings answered, "I shall be at the studio all day, and I imagine I shall be glad enough to come back at night."

Mr. Bladen, who, at a salary of fifteen dollars a week, acted as agent for the Pewly Manufacturing Company of Troy, New York, smiled a sceptical smile, and withdrew to keep an appointment with a customer on the Boulevard Magenta.

Hastings walked into the garden with Mrs. Byng and Susie, and, at their invitation, sat down in the shade before the iron gate.

The chestnut-trees still bore their fragrant spikes of pink and white, and the bees hummed among the roses trellised on the white-walled house.

A faint freshness was in the air. The watering-carts moved up and down the street, and a clear stream bubbled over the spotless gutters of the Rue de la Grande Chaumière. The sparrows were merry along the curbstones, taking bath after bath in the water and ruffling their feathers with delight. In a walled garden across the street a pair of blackbirds whistled among the almond-trees.

Hastings swallowed the lump in his throat, for the song of the birds and the ripple of water in a Paris gutter brought back to him the sunny meadows of Millbrook.

"That's a blackbird," observed Miss Byng; "see him there on the bush with pink blossoms. He's all black except his bill, and that looks as if it had been dipped in an omelet, as some Frenchman says—"

"Why, Susie!" said Mrs. Byng.

"That garden belongs to a studio inhabited by two Americans," continued the girl, serenely, "and I often see them pass. They seem to need a great many models, mostly young and feminine—"

"Why, Susie!"

"Perhaps they prefer painting that kind, but I don't see why they should invite five, with three more young gentlemen, and all get into two cabs and drive away singing. This street," she continued, "is dull. There is nothing to see except the garden and a glimpse of the Boulevard Montparnasse through the Rue de la Grande Chaumière. No one ever passes except a policeman. There is a convent on the corner."

"I thought it was a Jesuit college," began Hastings, but was at once overwhelmed with a Baedeker description of the place, ending with, "On one side stand the palatial hôtels of Jean Paul Laurens and Guillaume Bouguereau, and opposite, in the little Passage Stanislas, Carolus Duran paints the masterpieces which charm the world."

The blackbird burst into a ripple of golden, throaty notes, and from some distant green spot in the city an unknown wild bird answered with a frenzy of liquid trills until the sparrows paused in their ablutions to look up with restless chirps.

Then a butterfly came and sat on a cluster of heliotrope and waved his crimson-banded wings in the hot sunshine. Hastings knew him for a friend, and before his eyes there came a vision of tall mullins and scented milkweed, alive with painted wings, a vision of a white house and woodbine-covered piazza—a glimpse of a man reading and a woman leaning over the pansy-bed—and his heart was full. He was startled a moment later by Miss Byng.

"I believe you are homesick!" Hastings blushed. Miss Byng looked at him with a sympathetic sigh, and continued: "Whenever I felt homesick, at first, I used to go with mamma and walk in the Luxembourg Gardens. I don't know why it is, but those old-fashioned gardens seem to bring me nearer home than anything in this artificial city."

"But they are full of marble statues," said Mrs. Byng, mildly. "I don't see the resemblance myself."

"Where is the Luxembourg?" inquired Hastings, after a silence.

"Come with me to the gate," said Miss Byng. He rose and followed her, and she pointed out the Rue Vavin at the foot of the street.

"You pass by the convent to the right," she smiled; and Hastings went.

III

The Luxembourg was a blaze of flowers.

He walked slowly through the long avenues of trees, past mossy marbles and old-time columns, and, threading the grove by the bronze lion, came upon the tree-crowned terrace above the fountain. Below lay the basin shining in the sunlight. Flowering almonds encircled the terrace, and, in a greater spiral, groves of chestnuts wound in and out and down among the moist thickets by the western palace wing. At one end of the avenue of trees the Observatory rose, its white domes piled up like an eastern mosque; at the other end stood the heavy palace, with every window-pane ablaze in the fierce sun of June.

Around the fountain children and white-capped nurses, armed with bamboo poles, were pushing toy boats, whose sails hung limp in the sunshine. A park policeman, wearing red epaulets and a dress sword, watched them for a while, and then went away to remonstrate with a young man who had unchained his dog. The dog was pleasantly occupied in rubbing grass and dirt into his back while his legs waved in the air.

The policeman pointed at the dog. He was speechless with indignation.

"Well, Captain?" smiled the young fellow.

"Well, Monsieur Student?" growled the policeman.

"What do you come and complain to me for?"

"If you don't chain him, I'll take him," shouted the policeman.

"What's that to me, mon Capitaine?"

"Wha-t! Isn't that bull-dog yours?"

"If it was, don't you suppose I'd chain him?"

The officer glared for a moment in silence, then, deciding that as he was a student he was wicked, grabbed at the dog, who promptly dodged. Around and around the flower-beds they raced; and when the officer came too near for comfort, the bull-dog cut across a flower-bed, which, perhaps, was not playing fair.

The young man was amused, and the dog also seemed to enjoy the exercise.

The policeman noticed this, and decided to strike at the fountain-head of the evil. He stormed up to the student and said, "As the owner of this public nuisance, I arrest you!"

"But," objected the other, "I disclaim the dog."

That was a poser. It was useless to attempt to catch the dog until three gardeners lent a hand, but then the dog simply ran away and disappeared in the Rue de Medici.

The policeman shambled off to find consolation among the white-capped nurses, and the student, looking at his watch, stood up yawning. Then, catching sight of Hastings, he smiled and bowed. Hastings walked over to the marble, laughing.

"Why, Clifford," he said, "I didn't recognize you."

"It's my mustache," sighed the other. "I sacrificed it to humor a whim of—of—a friend. What do you think of my dog?"

"Then he is yours?" cried Hastings.

"Of course. It's a pleasant change for him, this playing tag with policemen, but he is known now, and I'll have to stop it. He's gone home. He always does when the gardeners take a hand. It's a pity; he's fond of rolling on lawns." Then they chatted for a moment of Hastings's prospects, and Clifford politely offered to stand his sponsor at the studio.

"You see, old tabby—I mean Dr. Byram—told me about you before I met you," explained Clifford, "and Elliott and I will be glad to do anything we can." Then, looking at his watch again, he muttered, "I have just ten minutes to catch the Versailles train; au revoir," and started to go, but, catching sight of a girl advancing by the fountain, took off his hat with a confused smile.

"Why are you not at Versailles?" she said, with an almost imperceptible acknowledgment of Hastings's presence.

"I—I'm going," murmured Clifford.

For a moment they faced each other, and then Clifford, very red, stammered, "With your permission, I have the honor of presenting to you my friend, Monsieur Hastings."

Hastings bowed low. She smiled very sweetly, but there was something of malice in the quiet inclination of her small Parisienne head.

"I could have wished," she said, "that Monsieur Clifford might spare me more time when he brings with him so charming an American."

"Must—must I go, Valentine?" began Clifford.

"Certainly," she replied.

Clifford took his leave with very bad grace, wincing when she added, "And give my dearest love to Cécile!" As he disappeared in the Rue d'Assas the girl turned, as if to go, but then, suddenly remembering Hastings, looked at him and shook her head.

"Monsieur Clifford is so perfectly hare-brained," she smiled, "it is embarrassing sometimes. You have heard, of course, all about his success at the Salon?"

He looked puzzled, and she noticed it.

"You have been to the Salon, of course?"

"Why, no," he answered, "I only arrived in Paris three days ago."

She seemed to pay little heed to his explanation, but continued: "Nobody imagined he had the energy to do anything good, but on varnishing day the Salon was astonished by the entrance of Monsieur Clifford, who strolled about as bland as you please, with an orchid in his button-hole and a beautiful picture on the line."

She smiled to herself at the reminiscence, and looked at the fountain.

"Monsieur Bouguereau told me that Monsieur Julian was so astonished that he only shook hands with Monsieur Clifford in a dazed manner, and actually forgot to pat him on the back! Fancy," she continued, with much merriment—"fancy Papa Julian forgetting to pat one on the back."

Hastings, wondering at her acquaintance with the great Bouguereau, looked at her with respect. "May I ask," he said, diffidently, "whether you are a pupil of Monsieur Bouguereau?"

"I," she said, in some surprise. Then she looked at him curiously. Was he permitting himself the liberty of joking on such short acquaintance?

His pleasant, serious face questioned hers.

"Tiens," she thought, "what a droll man."

"You surely study art?" he said.

She leaned back on the crooked stick of her parasol and looked at him. "Why do you think so?"

"Because you speak as if you did."

"You are making fun of me," she said, "and it is not good taste."

She stopped, confused, as he colored to the roots of his hair.

"How long have you been in Paris?" she said, at length.

"Three days," he replied, gravely.

"But—but—surely you are not a nouveau! You speak French too well!"

Then, after a pause, "Really, are you a nouveau?"

"I am," he said.

She sat down on the marble bench lately occupied by Clifford, and, tilting her parasol over her small head, looked at him.

"I don't believe it."

He felt the compliment, and for a moment hesitated to declare himself one of the despised. Then mustering up his courage, he told her how new and green he was, and all with a frankness which made her blue eyes open very wide and her lips part in the sweetest of smiles.

"You have never seen a studio?"

"Never."

"Nor a model?"

"No."

"How funny," she said, solemnly. Then they both laughed.

"And you," he said, "have seen studios?"

"Hundreds."

"And models?"

"Millions."

"And you know Bouguereau?"

"Yes, and Henner, and Constant, and Laurens, and Puvis de Chavannes, and Dagnan, and Courtois, and—and all the rest of them!"

"And yet you say you are not an artist."

"Pardon," she said, gravely, "did I say I was not?"

"Won't you tell me?" he hesitated.

At first she looked at him, shaking her head and smiling, then of a sudden her eyes fell and she began tracing figures with her parasol in the gravel at her feet. Hastings had taken a place on the seat, and now, with his elbows on his knees, sat watching the spray drifting above the fountain-jet. A small boy, dressed as a sailor, stood poking his yacht and crying, "I won't go home! I won't go home!" His nurse raised her hands to heaven.

"Just like a little American boy," thought Hastings, and a pang of homesickness shot through him.

Presently the nurse captured the boat and the small boy stood at bay.

"Monsieur René, when you decide to come here you may have your boat."

The boy backed away, scowling.

"Give me my boat, I say," he cried, "and don't call me René, for my name's Randall, and you know it!"

"Hello!" said Hastings—"Randall?—that's English."

"I am American," announced the boy, in perfectly good English, turning to look at Hastings, "and she's such a fool she calls me René because mamma calls me Ranny—"

Here he dodged the exasperated nurse and took up his station behind Hastings, who laughed, and, catching him around the waist, lifted him into his lap.

"One of my countrymen," he said to the girl beside him. He smiled while he spoke, but there was a queer feeling in his throat.

"Don't you see the stars and stripes on my yacht?" demanded Randall. Sure enough, the American colors hung limply under the nurse's arm.

"Oh," cried the girl, "he is charming," and impulsively stooped to kiss him, but the infant Randall wriggled out of Hastings's arms and his nurse pounced upon him with an angry glance at the girl.

She reddened, and then bit her lips, as the nurse, with her eyes still fixed on her, dragged the child away and ostentatiously wiped his lips with her handkerchief.

Then she stole a look at Hastings, and bit her lip again.

"What an ill-tempered woman!" he said. "In America most nurses are flattered when people kiss their children."

For an instant she tipped the parasol to hide her face, then closed it with a snap and looked at him defiantly.

"Do you think it strange that she objected?"

"Why not?" he said, in surprise.

Again she looked at him with quick, searching eyes.

His eyes were clear and bright, and he smiled back, repeating, "Why not?"

"You *are* droll," she murmured, bending her head.

"Why?"

But she made no answer, and sat silent, tracing curves and circles in the dust with her parasol. After a while he said: "I am glad to see that young people have so much liberty here. I understood that the French were not at all like us. You know in America—or at least where I live, in Millbrook—girls have every liberty: go out alone and receive their friends alone, and I was afraid I should miss it here. But I see how it is now, and I am glad I was mistaken."

She raised her eyes to his and kept them there.

He continued, pleasantly: "Since I have sat here I have seen a lot of pretty girls walking alone on the terrace there—and, then, *you* are alone, too. Tell me, for I do not know French customs, do you have the liberty of going to the theatre without a chaperon?"

For a long time she studied his face, and then, with a trembling smile, said, "Why do you ask me?"

"Because you must know, of course," he said, gayly.

"Yes," she replied, indifferently, "I know."

He waited for an answer; but, getting none, decided that perhaps she had misunderstood him.

"I hope you don't think I mean to presume on our short acquaintance," he began; "in fact, it is very odd, but I don't know your name. When Mr. Clifford presented me he only mentioned mine. Is that the custom in France?"

"It is the custom in the Latin Quarter," she said, with a queer light in her eyes. Then suddenly she began talking, almost feverishly. "You must know, Monsieur Hastings, that we are all un peu sans gêne here in the Latin Quarter. We are very Bohemian, and etiquette and ceremony are out of place. It was for that Monsieur Clifford presented you to me with small ceremony, and left us together with less—only for that, and I am his friend, and I have many friends in the Latin Quarter, and we all know each other very well—and I am not studying art, but—but—"

"But what?" he said, bewildered.

"I shall not tell you—it is a secret," she said, with an uncertain smile. On both cheeks a pink spot was burning, and her eyes were very bright.

Then in a moment her face fell. "Do you know Monsieur Clifford very intimately?"

"Not very."

After a while she turned to him, grave and a little pale.

"My name is Valentine—Valentine Tissot. Might—might I ask a service of you on such very short acquaintance?"

"Oh," he cried, "I should be honored."

"It is only this," she said, gently, "it is not much. Promise me not to speak to Monsieur Clifford about me. Promise me that you will speak to no one about me."

"I promise," he said, greatly puzzled.

She laughed nervously. "I wish to remain a mystery. It is a caprice."

"But," he began, "I had wished—I had hoped that you might give Monsieur Clifford permission to bring me, to present me at your house."

"My—my house!" she repeated.

"I mean, where you live; in fact, to present me to your family."

The change in the girl's face shocked him.

"I beg your pardon," he cried, "I have hurt you."

And as quick as a flash she understood him because she was a woman.

"My parents are dead," she said.

Presently he began again, very gently.

"Would it displease you if I beg you to receive me? Is it the custom?"

"I cannot," she answered. Then, glancing up at him, "I am sorry; I should like to; but, believe me, I cannot."

He bowed seriously and looked vaguely uneasy.

"It isn't because I don't wish to. I—I like you; you are very kind to me."

"Kind?" he cried, surprised and puzzled.

"I like you," she said, slowly, "and we will see each other sometimes if you will."

"At friends' houses?"

"No, not at friends' houses."

"Where?"

"Here," she said, with defiant eyes.

"Why," he cried, "in Paris you are much more liberal in your views than we are."

She looked at him curiously.

"Yes, we are very Bohemian."

"I think it is charming," he declared.

"You see, we shall be in the best of society," she ventured, timidly, with a pretty gesture towards the statues of the dead queens, ranged in stately ranks above the terrace.

He looked at her, delighted, and she brightened at the success of her innocent little pleasantry.

"Indeed," she smiled, "I shall be well chaperoned, because you see we are under the protection of the gods themselves; look, there are Apollo and Juno and Venus, on their pedestals," counting them on her small, gloved fingers, "and Ceres, Hercules, and—but I can't make out—"

Hastings turned to look up at the winged god under whose shadow they were seated.

"Why, it's Love," he said.

IV

"There is a nouveau here," drawled Laffat, leaning around his easel and addressing his friend Bowles—"there is a nouveau here who is so tender and green and appetizing that Heaven help him if he should fall into a salad-bowl."

"Hayseed?" inquired Bowles, plastering in a background with a broken palette-knife and squinting at the effect with approval.

"Yes, Squeedunk or Oshkosh, and how he ever grew up among the daisies and escaped the cows, Heaven alone knows!"

Bowles rubbed his thumb across the outlines of his study to "throw in a little atmosphere," as he said, glared at the model, pulled at his pipe, and, finding it out, struck a match on his neighbor's back to relight it.

"His name," continued Laffat, hurling a bit of bread at the hat-rack—"his name is Hastings. He *is* a berry. He knows no more about the world"—and here Mr. Laffat's face spoke volumes for his own knowledge of that planet—"than a maiden cat on its first moonlight stroll."

Bowles now having succeeded in lighting his pipe, repeated the thumb touch on the other edge of the study and said, "Ah!"

"Yes," continued his friend, "and would you imagine it, he seems to think that everything here goes on as it does in his damned little backwoods ranch at home; talks about the pretty girls who walk alone in the street; says how sensible it is; and how French parents are misrepresented in America; says that for his part he finds French girls—and he confessed to only knowing one—as jolly as American girls. I tried to set him right, tried to give him a pointer as to what sort of ladies walk about alone or with students, and he was either too stupid or too innocent to catch on. Then I gave it to him straight, and he said I was a vile-minded fool, and marched off."

"Did you assist him with your shoe?" inquired Bowles, languidly interested.

"Well, no."

"He called you a vile-minded fool."

"He was correct," said Clifford, from his easel in front.

"What—what do you mean?" demanded Laffat, turning red.

"That," replied Clifford.

"Who spoke to you? Is this your business?" sneered Bowles, but nearly lost his balance as Clifford swung about and eyed him.

"Yes," he said, slowly, "it's my business."

No one spoke for some time.

Then Clifford sang out, "I say, Hastings!"

And when Hastings left his easel and came around, he nodded towards the astonished Laffat.

"This man has been disagreeable to you, and I want to tell you that any time you feel inclined to kick him, why, I will hold the other creature."

Hastings, embarrassed, said, "Why, no. I don't agree with his ideas, nothing more."

Clifford said, "Naturally," and, slipping his arm through Hastings's, strolled about with him, and introduced him to several of his own friends, at which all the *nouveaux* opened their eyes with envy, and the studio were given to understand that

Hastings, although prepared to do menial work as the latest *nouveau,* was already within the charmed circle of the old, respected, and feared, the truly great.

The rest finished, the model resumed his place, and work went on in a chorus of songs and yells, and every ear-splitting noise which the art student utters when studying the beautiful.

Five o'clock struck. The model yawned, stretched, and climbed into his trousers, and the noisy contents of six studios crowded through the hall and down into the street. Ten minutes later Hastings found himself on top of a Montrouge tram, and shortly afterwards was joined by Clifford.

They climbed down at the Rue Gay Lussac.

"I always stop here," observed Clifford. "I like the walk through the Luxembourg."

"By the-way," said Hastings, "how can I call on you when I don't know where you live?"

"Why, I live opposite you."

"What—the studio in the garden where the almond-trees are, and the blackbirds—"

"Exactly," said Clifford. "I'm with my friend Elliott."

Hastings thought of the description of the two American artists which he had heard from Miss Susie Byng, and looked blank.

Clifford continued: "Perhaps you had better let me know when you think of coming, so—so that I will be sure to—to be there," he ended, rather lamely.

"I shouldn't care to meet any of your model friends there," said Hastings, smiling. "You know—my ideas are rather strait-laced—I suppose you would say, Puritanical. I shouldn't enjoy it, and wouldn't know how to behave."

"Oh, I understand," said Clifford, but added, with great cordiality, "I'm sure we'll be friends, although you may not approve of me and my set; but you will like Severn and Selby, because—because, well, they are like yourself, old chap."

After a moment he continued: "There is something I want to speak about. You see, when I introduced you last week in the Luxembourg to Valentine—"

"Not a word!" cried Hastings, smiling; "you must not tell me a word of her!"

"Why—"

"No—not a word!" he said, gayly; "I insist—promise me upon your honor you will not speak of her until I give you permission; promise!"

"I promise," said Clifford, amazed.

"She is a charming girl. We had such a delightful chat after you left, and I thank you for presenting me, but not another word about her until I give you permission."

"Oh!" murmured Clifford.

"Remember your promise," he smiled, as he turned into his gate-way.

Clifford strolled across the street and, traversing the ivy-covered alley, entered his garden.

He felt for his studio key, muttering, "I wonder—I wonder—but of course he doesn't!"

He entered the hall-way, and, fitting the key into the door, stood staring at the two cards tacked over the panels.

FOXHALL CLIFFORD.

RICHARD OSBORNE ELLIOTT.

"Why the devil doesn't he want me to speak of her?"

He opened the door, and, discouraging the caresses of two brindle bull-dogs, sank down on the sofa.

Elliott sat smoking and sketching with a piece of charcoal by the window.

"Hello," he said, without looking around.

Clifford gazed absently at the back of his head, murmuring, "I'm afraid, I'm afraid that man is too innocent. I say, Elliott," he said, at last, "Hastings—you know the chap that old Tabby

Byram came around here to tell us about—the day you had to hide Colette in the armoire—"

"Yes, what's up?"

"Oh, nothing. He's a brick."

"Yes?" said Elliott, without enthusiasm.

"Don't you think so?" demanded Clifford.

"Why, yes, but he is going to have a tough time when some of his illusions are dispelled."

"More shame to those who dispel 'em!"

"Yes—wait until he comes to pay his call on us, unexpectedly, of course—"

Clifford looked virtuous and lighted a cigar.

"I was just going to say," he observed, "that I have asked him not to come without letting us know, so I can postpone any orgie you may have intended—"

"Ah!" cried Elliott, indignantly, "I suppose you put it to him in that way."

"Not exactly," grinned Clifford. Then, more seriously, "I don't want anything to occur here to bother him. He's a brick, and it's a pity we can't be more like him."

"I am," observed Elliott, complacently, "only living with you—"

"Listen!" cried the other. "I have managed to put my foot in it in great style. Do you know what I've done? Well, the first time I met him in the street, or, rather, it was in the Luxembourg—I introduced him to Valentine!"

"Did he object?"

"Believe me," said Clifford, solemnly, "this rustic Hastings has no more idea that Valentine is—is—in fact, is Valentine, than he has that he himself is a beautiful example of moral decency in a Quarter where morals are as rare as elephants. I heard enough in a conversation between that blackguard Laffat and the little immoral eruption Bowles to open my eyes. I tell you, Hastings is a trump! He's a healthy, clean-minded young fellow, bred in a small country village, brought up with the idea that saloons are way-stations to hell—and as for women—"

"Well?" demanded Elliott.

"Well," said Clifford, "his idea of the dangerous woman is probably a painted Jezebel."

"Probably," replied the other.

"He's a trump!" said Clifford, "and if he swears the world is as good and pure as his own heart, I'll swear he's right."

Elliott rubbed his charcoal on his file to get a point, and turned to his sketch, saying, "He will never hear any pessimism from Richard Osborne E."

"He's a lesson to me," said Clifford. Then he unfolded a small, perfumed note, written on rose-colored paper, which had been lying on the table before him.

He read it, smiled, whistled a bar or two from "Miss Helyett," and sat down to answer it on his best cream-laid note-paper. When it was written and sealed, he picked up his stick and marched up and down the studio two or three times, whistling.

"Going out?" inquired the other, without turning.

"Yes," he said, but lingered a moment over Elliott's shoulder, watching him pick out the lights in his sketch with a bit of bread.

"To-morrow is Sunday," he observed, after a moment's silence.

"Well?" inquired Elliott.

"Have you seen Colette?"

"No, I will to-night. She and Rowden and Jacqueline are coming to Boulant's. I suppose you and Cécile will be there?"

"Well, no," replied Clifford. "Cécile dines at home to-night, and I—I had an idea of going to Mignon's."

Elliott looked at him with disapproval.

"You can make all the arrangements for La Roche without me," he continued, avoiding Elliott's eyes.

"What are you up to now?"

"Nothing," protested Clifford.

"Don't tell me," replied his chum, with scorn; "fellows don't rush off to Mignon's when the set dine at Boulant's. Who is it now?—but no, I won't ask that; what's the use!" Then he lifted up his voice in complaint and beat upon the table with his pipe. "What's the use of ever trying to keep track of you? What will

Cécile say—oh yes, what will she say? It's a pity you can't be constant two months—yes, by Jove! and the Quarter is indulgent; but you abuse its good nature—and mine, too!"

Presently he arose, and, jamming his hat on his head, marched to the door.

"Heaven alone knows why any one puts up with your antics; but they all do, and so do I. If I were Cécile, or any of the other pretty fools after whom you have toddled, and will, in all human probabilities, continue to toddle—I say, if I were Cécile, I'd spank you! Now I'm going to Boulant's, and, as usual, I shall make excuses for you and arrange the affair; and I don't care a continental where you are going, but, by the skull of the studio skeleton! if you don't turn up to-morrow with your sketching-kit under one arm and Cécile under the other—if you don't turn up in good shape, I'm done with you, and the rest can think what they please. Good-night."

Clifford said good-night with as pleasant a smile as he could muster, and then sat down with his eyes on the door. He took out his watch and gave Elliott ten minutes to vanish, then rang the concierge's call, murmuring, "Oh, dear! oh, dear! why the devil do I do it?"

"Alfred," he said, as that gimlet-eyed person answered the call, "make yourself clean and proper, Alfred, and replace your sabots with a pair of shoes. Then put on your best hat and take this letter to the big white house in the Rue de Dragon. There is no answer, mon petit Alfred."

The concierge departed with a snort, in which unwillingness for the errand and affection for M. Clifford were blended. Then, with great care, the young fellow arrayed himself in all the beauties of his and Elliott's wardrobe. He took his time about it, and occasionally interrupted his toilet to play his banjo or make pleasing diversion for the bull-dogs by gambolling about on all fours. "I've got two hours before me," he thought, and borrowed a pair of Elliott's silken foot-gear, with which he and the dogs played ball, until he decided to put them on. Then he lighted a cigarette and inspected his dress-coat. When he had emptied it of four handkerchiefs, a fan, and a pair of crumpled gloves as long as his arm, he decided it was not suited to add *éclat* to his charms, and cast about in his mind for a substitute. Elliott was too thin, and, anyway, his coats were now under lock and key. Rowden probably was as badly off as himself. Hastings! Hastings was the man! But when he threw on a smoking-jacket and sauntered over to Hastings's house, he was informed that he had been gone over an hour.

"Now where in the name of all that's reasonable could he have gone!" muttered Clifford, looking down the street.

The maid didn't know, so he bestowed upon her a fascinating smile and lounged back to the studio.

Hastings was not far away. The Luxembourg is within five minutes' walk of the Rue Notre Dame des Champs, and there he sat under the shadow of a winged god, and there he had sat for an hour, poking holes in the dust and watching the steps which lead from the northern terrace to the fountain. The sun hung, a purple globe, above the misty hills of Meudon. Long streamers of clouds touched with rose swept low on the western sky, and the dome of the distant Invalides burned like an opal through the haze. Behind the palace the smoke from a high chimney mounted straight into the air, purple until it crossed the sun, where it changed to a bar of smouldering fire. High above the darkening foliage of the chestnuts the twin towers of St. Sulpice rose, an ever-deepening silhouette.

A sleepy blackbird was carolling in some near thicket, and pigeons passed and repassed with the whisper of soft winds in their wings. The light on the palace windows had died away, and the dome of the Panthéon swam aglow above the northern terrace, a fiery Valhalla in the sky, while below in grim array, along the terrace ranged, the marble ranks of queens looked out into the west.

From the end of the long walk by the northern façade of the palace came the noise of omnibuses and the cries of the street. Hastings looked at the palace clock. Six, and, as his own watch agreed with it, he fell to poking holes in the gravel again. A constant stream of people passed between the Odéon and the fountain. Priests in black, with silver-buckled shoes; line soldiers, slouchy and rakish;

neat girls without hats, bearing milliners' boxes; students with black portfolios and high hats; students with bérets and big canes; nervous, quick-stepping officers, symphonies in turquoise and silver; ponderous, jangling cavalrymen, all over dust; pastry-cooks' boys, skipping along with utter disregard for the safety of the basket balanced on their impish heads; and then the lean outcast, the shambling Paris tramp, slouching, with shoulders bent, and little eyes furtively scanning the ground for smokers' refuse; all these moved in a steady stream across the fountain circle and out into the city by the Odéon, whose long arcades were now beginning to flicker with gas-jets. The melancholy bells of St. Sulpice struck the hour, and the clock-tower of the palace lighted up. Then hurried steps sounded across the gravel, and Hastings raised his head.

"How late you are!" he said, but his voice was hoarse, and only his flushed face told how long had seemed the waiting.

She said, "I was kept—indeed, I was so much annoyed—and—and I may only stay a moment."

She sat down beside him, casting a furtive glance over her shoulder at the god upon his pedestal.

"What a nuisance, that intruding Cupid still there!"

"Wings and arrows, too," said Hastings, unheeding her motion to be seated.

"Wings," she murmured—"oh yes, to fly away with when he's tired of his play. Of course it was a man who conceived the idea of wings, otherwise Cupid would have been insupportable."

"Do you think so?"

"Ma foi, it's what men think."

"And women?"

"Oh," she said, with a toss of her small head, "I really forgot what we were speaking of."

"We were speaking of love," said Hastings.

"*I* was not," said the girl. Then, looking up at the marble god, "I don't care for this one at all. I don't believe he knows how to shoot his arrows—no, indeed, he is a coward; he creeps up like an assassin in the twilight. I don't approve of cowardice," she announced, and turned her back on the statue.

"I think," said Hastings, quietly, "that he does shoot fairly—yes, and even gives one warning."

"Is it your experience, Monsieur Hastings?"

He looked straight into her eyes, and said, "He is warning me."

"Heed the warning, then," she cried, with a nervous laugh. As she spoke she stripped off her gloves, and then carefully proceeded to draw them on again. When this was accomplished she glanced at the palace clock, saying, "Oh, dear, how late it is!" furled her umbrella, then unfurled it, and finally looked at him.

"No," he said, "I shall not heed his warning."

"Oh, dear," she sighed again, "still talking about that tiresome statue!" Then, stealing a glance at his face, "I suppose—I suppose you are in love."

"I don't know," he muttered, "I suppose I am."

She raised her head with a quick gesture. "You seem delighted at the idea," she said, but bit her lip and trembled as his eyes met hers. Then sudden fear came over her, and she sprang up, staring into the gathering shadows.

"Are you cold?" he said, but she only answered, "Oh, dear! oh, dear! it is late—so late! I must go—good-night."

She gave him her gloved hand a moment, and then withdrew it with a start.

"What is it?" he insisted. "Are you frightened?"

She looked at him strangely.

"No—no—not frightened—you are very good to me—"

"By Jove!" he burst out, "what do you mean by saying I'm good to you? That's at least the third time, and I don't understand."

The sound of a drum from the guard-house at the palace cut him short. "Listen," she whispered, "they are going to close. It's late—oh, so late!"

The rolling of the drum came nearer and nearer, and then the silhouette of the drummer cut the sky above the eastern terrace. The fading light lingered a moment on his belt and bayonet, then he passed into the shadows, drumming the echoes awake. The roll became fainter along the eastern terrace, then grew and grew and rattled with increasing sharpness when he passed the avenue by the bronze lion and turned down the western terrace-walk. Louder and louder the drum sounded, and the echoes struck back the notes from the gray palace wall; and now the drummer loomed up before them, his red trousers a dull spot in the gathering gloom, the brass of his drum and bayonet touched with a pale spark, his epaulets tossing on his shoulders. He passed, leaving the crash of the drum in their ears, and far into the alley of trees they saw his little tin cup shining on his haversack. Then the sentinels began the monotonous cry, "On ferme! on fe-rme!" and the bugle blew from the barracks in the Rue de Tournon.

"On ferme! on ferme!"

"Good-night," she whispered, "I must return alone to-night."

He watched her until she reached the northern terrace, and then sat down on the marble seat until a hand on his shoulder and a glimmer of bayonets warned him away.

She passed on through the grove, and, turning into the Rue de Médici, traversed it to the boulevard. At the corner she bought a bunch of violets, and walked on along the boulevard to the Rue des Écoles. A cab was drawn up before Boulant's, and a pretty girl, aided by Elliott, jumped out.

"Valentine!" cried the girl, "come with us!"

"I can't," she said, stopping a moment, "I have a rendezvous at Mignon's."

"Not Victor?" cried the girl, laughing; but she passed with a little shiver, nodding good-night, then, turning into the Boulevard St. Germain, she walked a little faster to escape a gay party sitting before the Café Cluny, who called to her to join them. At the door of the Restaurant Mignon stood a coal-black negro in buttons. He took off his peaked cap as she mounted the carpeted stairs.

"Send Eugène to me," she said at the office, and, passing through the hall-way to the right of the dining-room, stopped before a row of panelled doors. A waiter passed and she repeated her demand for Eugène, who presently appeared, noiselessly skipping, and bowed, murmuring, "Madame."

"Who is here?"

"No one in the cabinets, madame; in the hall, Madame Madelon and Monsieur Gay, Monsieur de Clamart, Monsieur Clisson, Madame Marie, and their set." Then he looked around and, bowing again, murmured, "Monsieur awaits madame since half an hour," and he knocked at one of the panelled doors bearing the number six.

Clifford opened the door and the girl entered.

The garçon bowed her in and, whispering, "Will monsieur have the goodness to ring," vanished.

He helped her off with her jacket, and took her hat and umbrella. When she was seated at the little table, with Clifford opposite, she smiled and leaned forward on both elbows, looking him in the face.

"What are you doing here?" she demanded.

"Waiting," he replied, in accents of adoration.

For an instant she turned and examined herself in the glass. The wide, blue eyes, the curling hair, the straight nose and short, curled lip flashed in the mirror an instant only, and then its depths reflected her pretty neck and back. "Thus do I turn my back on vanity," she said, and then, leaning forward again, "What are you doing here?"

"Waiting for you," repeated Clifford, slightly troubled.

"And Cécile?"

"Now don't, Valentine—"

"Do you know," she said, calmly, "I dislike your conduct?"

He was a little disconcerted, and rang for Eugène to cover his confusion.

The soup was bisque and the wine Pommery, and the courses followed each other with the usual regularity until Eugène brought coffee, and there was nothing left on the table but a small silver lamp.

"Valentine," said Clifford, after having obtained permission to smoke, "is it the Vaudeville or the Eldorado—or both, or the Nouveau Cirque, or—"

"It is here," said Valentine.

"Well," he said, greatly flattered, "I'm afraid I couldn't amuse you—"

"Oh yes, you are funnier than the Eldorado."

"Now see here, don't guy me, Valentine. You always do, and, and—you know what they say—a good laugh kills—"

"What?"

"Er—er—love and all that."

She laughed until her eyes were moist with tears. "Tiens," she cried, "he is dead, then!"

Clifford eyed her with growing alarm.

"Do you know why I came?" she said.

"No," he replied, uneasily, "I don't."

"How long have you made love to me?"

"Well," he admitted, somewhat startled, "I should say for about a year."

"It is a year, I think. Are you not tired?"

He did not answer.

"Don't you know that I like you too well to—to ever fall in love with you?" she said. "Don't you know that we are too good comrades—too old friends for that? And were we not—do you think that I do not know your history, Monsieur Clifford?"

"Don't be—don't be so sarcastic," he urged; "don't be unkind, Valentine."

"I'm not. I'm kind. I'm very kind—to you and to Cécile."

"Cécile is tired of me."

"I hope she is," said the girl, "for she deserves a better fate. Tiens, do you know your reputation in the Quarter? Of the inconstant, the most inconstant, utterly incorrigible, and no more serious than a gnat on a summer night. Poor Cécile!"

Clifford looked so uncomfortable that she spoke more kindly.

"I like you. You know that. Everybody does. You are a spoiled child here. Everything is permitted you and every one makes allowance, but every one cannot be a victim to caprice."

"Caprice!" he cried. "By Jove, if the girls of the Latin Quarter are not capricious—"

"Never mind—never mind about that! You must not sit in judgment—you of all men. Why are you here to-night? Oh," she cried, "I will tell you why! Monsieur receives a little note; he sends a little answer; he dresses in his conquering raiment—"

"I don't," said Clifford, very red.

"You do, and it becomes you," she retorted, with a faint smile. Then again, very quietly, "I am in your power, but I know I am in the power of a friend. I have come to acknowledge it to you here; and it is because of that that I am here to beg of you—a—a favor."

Clifford opened his eyes but said nothing.

"I am in—great distress of mind. It is Monsieur Hastings."

"Well?" said Clifford, in some astonishment.

"I want to ask you," she continued, in a low voice—"I want to ask you to—to—in case you should speak of me before him—not to say—not to say—"

"I shall not speak of you to him," he said, quietly.

"Can—can you prevent others?"

"I might if I was present. May I ask why?"

"That is not fair," she murmured. "You know how—how he considers me—as he considers every woman. You know how different he is from you and the rest. I have never seen a man—such a man as Monsieur Hastings."

He let his cigarette go out unnoticed.

"I am almost afraid of him—afraid he should know—what we all are in the Quarter. Oh, I do not wish him to know! I do not wish him to—to turn from me—to cease from speaking to me as he does! You—you and the rest cannot know what he has been to me. I could not believe him; I could not believe he was so good and—and noble. I do not wish him to know—so soon. He will find out—sooner or later, he will find out for himself, and then he will turn away from me. Why," she cried, passionately—"why should he turn from me and not from *you?*"

Clifford, much embarrassed, eyed his cigarette.

The girl rose, very white. "He is your friend—you have a right to warn him."

"He is my friend," he said, at length.

They looked at each other in silence.

Then she cried, "By all that I hold to me most sacred, you need not warn him."

"I shall trust your word," he said, pleasantly.

V

The month passed quickly for Hastings, and left few definite impressions after it. It did leave some, however. One was a painful impression of meeting Mr. Bladen on the Boulevard des Capucines in company with a very pronounced young person whose laugh dismayed him, and when at last he escaped from the café where Mr. Bladen had hauled him to join them in a bock, he felt as if the whole boulevard was looking at him, and judging him by his company. Later, an instinctive conviction regarding the young person with Mr. Bladen sent the hot blood into his cheek, and he returned to the pension in such a miserable state of mind that Miss Byng was alarmed, and advised him to conquer his homesickness at once.

Another impression was equally vivid. One Saturday morning, feeling lonely, his wanderings about the city brought him to the Gare St. Lazare. It was early for breakfast, but he entered the Hôtel Terminus and took a table near the window. As he wheeled about to give his order, a man passing rapidly along the aisle collided with his head, and, looking up to receive the expected apology, he was met instead by a slap on the shoulder and a hearty, "What the deuce are you doing here, old chap?" It was Rowden, who seized him and told him to come along. So, mildly protesting, he was ushered into a private dining-room, where Clifford, rather red, jumped up from the table and welcomed him with a startled air, which was softened by the unaffected glee of Rowden and the extreme courtesy of Elliott. The latter presented him to three bewitching girls, who welcomed him so charmingly, and seconded Rowden in his demand that Hastings should make one of the party, that he consented at once. While Elliott briefly outlined the projected excursion to La Roche, Hastings delightedly ate his omelet, and returned the smiles of encouragement from Cécile and Colette and Jacqueline. Meantime Clifford, in a bland whisper, was telling Rowden what an ass he was. Poor Rowden looked miserable until Elliott, divining how affairs were turning, frowned on Clifford, and found a moment to let Rowden know that they were all going to make the best of it.

"You shut up," he observed to Clifford; "it's fate, and that settles it."

"It's Rowden, and that settles it," murmured Clifford, concealing a grin. For, after all, he was not Hastings's wet nurse. So it came about that the train which left the Gare St. Lazare at 9.15 A.M. stopped a moment in its career towards Havre and deposited at the red-roofed station of La Roche a merry party, armed with sunshades, trout-rods, and one cane, carried by the non-combatant, Hastings. Then, when they had established their camp in a grove of sycamores which bordered the little River Ept, Clifford, the acknowledged master of all that pertained to sportsmanship, took command.

"You, Rowden," he said, "divide your flies with Elliott, and keep an eye on him, or else he'll be trying to put on a float and sinker. Prevent him by force from grubbing about for worms."

Elliott protested, but was forced to smile in the general laugh.

"You make me ill," he asserted. "Do you think this is my first trout?"

"I shall be delighted to see your first trout," said Clifford, and, dodging a fly-hook, hurled with intent to hit, proceeded to sort and equip three slender rods destined to bring joy and fish to Cécile, Colette, and Jacqueline. With perfect gravity he ornamented each line with four split shot, a small hook, and a brilliant quill float.

"*I* shall never touch the worms," announced Cécile, with a shudder.

Jacqueline and Colette hastened to sustain her, and Hastings pleasantly offered to act in the capacity of general baiter and taker-off of fish. But Cécile, doubtless fascinated by the gaudy flies in Clifford's book, decided to accept lessons from him in the true art, and presently disappeared up the Ept with Clifford in tow.

Elliott looked doubtfully at Colette.

"I prefer gudgeons," said that damsel, with decision, "and you and Monsieur Rowden may go away when you please; may they not, Jacqueline?"

"Certainly," responded Jacqueline.

Elliott, undecided, examined his rod and reel.

"You've got your reel on wrong side up," observed Rowden.

Elliott wavered, and stole a glance at Colette.

"I—I—have almost decided to—er—not to flip the flies about just now," he began. "There's the pole that Cécile left—"

"Don't call it a pole," corrected Rowden.

"*Rod,* then," continued Elliott, and started off in the wake of the two girls, but was promptly collared by Rowden.

"No you don't! Fancy a man fishing with a float and sinker, when he has a fly-rod in his hand! You come along!"

Where the placid little Ept flows down between its thickets to the Seine, a grassy bank shadows the haunt of the gudgeon, and on this bank sat Colette and Jacqueline, and chattered and laughed and watched the swerving of the scarlet quills, while Hastings, his hat over his eyes, his head on a bank of moss, listened to their soft voices and gallantly unhooked the small and indignant gudgeon when a flash of a rod and a half-suppressed scream announced a catch. The sunlight filtered through the leafy thickets, awaking to song the forest birds. Magpies in spotless black and white flitted past, alighting near by with a hop and bound and twitch of the tail. Blue and white jays with rosy breasts shrieked through the trees, and a low-sailing hawk wheeled among the fields of ripening wheat, putting to flight flocks of twittering hedge-birds.

Across the Seine a gull dropped on the water like a plume. The air was pure and still. Scarcely a leaf moved. Sounds from a distant farm came faintly—the shrill cock-crow and dull baying. Now and then a steam-tug with big, raking smoke-pipe, bearing the name *Guêpe* 27, ploughed up the river, dragging its interminable train of barges, or a sailboat dropped down with the current towards sleepy Rouen.

A faint, fresh odor of earth and water hung in the air, and through the sunlight orange-tipped butterflies danced above the marsh-grass, soft, velvety butterflies flapped through the mossy woods.

Hastings was thinking of Valentine. It was two o'clock when Elliott strolled back, and, frankly admitting that he had eluded Rowden, sat down beside Colette and prepared to doze with satisfaction.

"Where are your trout?" said Colette, severely.

"They still live," murmured Elliott, and went fast asleep.

Rowden returned shortly after, and, casting a scornful glance at the slumbering one, displayed three crimson-flecked trout.

"And that," smiled Hastings, lazily—"that is the holy end to which the faithful plod—the slaughter of these small fish with a bit of silk and feather."

Rowden disdained to answer him. Colette caught another gudgeon and awoke Elliott, who protested and gazed about for the lunch-baskets as Clifford and Cécile came up, demanding instant refreshment. Cécile's skirts were soaked, and her gloves torn, but she was happy, and Clifford, dragging out a two-pound trout, stood still to receive the applause of the company.

"Where the deuce did you get that?" demanded Elliott.

Cécile, wet and enthusiastic, recounted the battle, and then Clifford eulogized her powers with the fly, and, in proof, produced from his creel a defunct chub, which, he observed, just missed being a trout.

They were all very merry at luncheon, and Hastings was voted "charming." He enjoyed it immensely—only it seemed to him at moments that flirtation went further in France than in Millbrook, Connecticut, and he thought that Cécile might be a little less enthusiastic about Clifford; that perhaps it would be quite as well if Jacqueline sat farther away from Rowden, and that possibly Colette could have, for a moment, at least, taken her eyes from Elliott's face. Still he enjoyed it—except when his thoughts drifted to Valentine, and then he felt that he was very far away from her. La Roche is at least an hour and a half from Paris. It is true also that he felt a happiness, a quick heart-beat when, at eight o'clock that night, the train which bore them from La Roche rolled into the Gare St. Lazare, and he was once more in the city of Valentine.

"Good-night," they said, pressing around him. "You must come with us next time!"

He promised, and watched them, two by two, drift into the darkening city, and stood so long that, when again he raised his eyes, the vast boulevard was twinkling with gas-jets through which the electric lights stared like moons.

VI

It was with another quick heart-beat that he awoke next morning, for his first thought was of Valentine.

The sun already gilded the towers of Notre Dame, the clatter of workmen's sabots awoke sharp echoes in the street below, and across the way a blackbird in a pink almond-tree was going into an ecstasy of trills.

He determined to awake Clifford for a brisk walk in the country, hoping later to beguile that gentleman into the American church for his soul's sake. He found Alfred the gimlet-eyed washing the asphalt walk which led to the studio.

"Monsieur Elliott?" he replied, to the perfunctory inquiry, "Je ne sais pas."

"And Monsieur Clifford?" began Hastings, somewhat astonished.

"Monsieur Clifford," said the concierge, with fine irony, "will be pleased to see you, as he retired early; in fact, he has just come in."

Hastings hesitated while the concierge pronounced a fiery eulogy on people who never stayed out all night, and then came battering at the lodge-gate during hours which even a gendarme held sacred to sleep. He also discoursed eloquently upon the beauties of temperance, and took an ostentatious draught from the fountain in the court.

"I do not think I will come in," said Hastings.

"Pardon, monsieur," growled the concierge, "perhaps it would be well to see Monsieur Clifford. He possibly needs aid. Me he drives forth with hairbrushes and boots. It is a mercy if he has not set fire to something with his candle."

Hastings hesitated for an instant, but, swallowing his dislike of such a mission, walked slowly through the ivy-covered alley and across the inner garden to the studio. He knocked. Perfect silence. Then he knocked again, and this time something struck the door from within with a crash.

"That," said the concierge, "was a boot." He fitted his duplicate key into the lock and ushered Hastings in. Clifford, in disordered evening dress, sat on the rug in the middle of the room. He held in his hand a shoe, and did not appear astonished to see Hastings.

"Good-morning—do you use Pears' soap?" he inquired, with a vague wave of his hand and a vaguer smile.

Hastings's heart sank. "For Heaven's sake," he said, "Clifford, go to bed."

"Not while that—that Alfred pokes his shaggy head in here an' I have a shoe left."

Hastings blew out the candle, picked up Clifford's hat and cane, and said, with an emotion he could not conceal, "This is terrible, Clifford. I—never knew you did this sort of thing."

"Well, I do," said Clifford.

"Where is Elliott?"

"Ole chap," returned Clifford, becoming maudlin, "Providence which feeds—feeds—er—sparrows an' that sort of thing watcheth over the intemperate wanderer—"

"Where is Elliott?"

But Clifford only wagged his head and waved his arm about. "He's out there—somewhere about." Then suddenly feeling a desire to see his missing chum, lifted up his voice and howled for him.

Hastings, thoroughly shocked, sat down on the lounge without a word. Presently, after shedding several scalding tears, Clifford brightened up and rose with great precaution.

"Ole chap," he observed, "do you want to see er—er miracle? Well, here goes. I'm goin' to begin."

He paused, beaming at vacancy.

"Er miracle," he repeated.

Hastings supposed he was alluding to the miracle of his keeping his balance and said nothing.

"I'm goin' to bed," he announced; "poor ole Clifford's goin' to bed, an' that's er miracle."

And he did, with a nice calculation of distance and equilibrium which would have wrung enthusiastic yells of applause from Elliott had he been there to assist *en connaisseur.* But he was not. He had not yet reached the studio. He was on his way, however, and smiled with magnificent condescension on Hastings, who, half an hour later, found him reclining upon a bench in the Luxembourg. He permitted himself to be aroused, dusted, and escorted to the gate. Here, however, he refused all further assistance, and, bestowing a patronizing bow upon Hastings, steered a tolerably true course for the Rue Vavin.

Hastings watched him out of sight, and then slowly retraced his steps towards the fountain. At first he felt gloomy and depressed, but gradually the clear air of the morning lifted the pressure from his heart, and he sat down on the marble seat under the shadow of the winged god.

The air was fresh and sweet with perfume from the orange flowers. Everywhere pigeons were bathing, dashing the water over their iris-hued breasts, flashing in and out of the spray or nestling almost to the neck along the polished basin. The sparrows, too, were abroad in force, soaking their dust-colored feathers in the limpid pool and chirping with might and main. Under the sycamores which surround the duck-pond opposite the fountain of Marie de Médici the waterfowl cropped the herbage or waddled in rows down the bank to embark on some solemn, aimless cruise.

Butterflies, somewhat lame from a chilly night's repose under the lilac leaves, crawled over and over the white phlox or took a rheumatic flight towards some sun-warmed shrub. The bees were already busy among the heliotrope, and one or two great, gray flies with brick-colored eyes sat in a spot of sunlight beside the marble seat, or chased each other about, only to return again to the spot of sunshine and rub their forelegs exulting.

The sentries paced briskly before the painted boxes, pausing at times to look towards the guard-house for their relief.

They came at last, with a shuffle of feet and click of bayonets, the word was passed, the relief fell out, and away they went, crunch, crunch, across the gravel.

A mellow chime floated from the clock-tower of the palace; the deep bell of St. Sulpice echoed the stroke. Hastings sat dreaming in the shadow of the god, and while he mused somebody came and sat down beside him. At first he did not raise his head. It was only when she spoke that he sprang up.

"You! At this hour?"

"I was restless, I could not sleep." Then in a low, happy voice: "And *you!*—at this hour?"

"I—I slept, but the sun awoke me."

"*I* could not sleep," she said; and her eyes seemed, for a moment, touched with an indefinable shadow. Then, smiling: "I am so glad; I seemed to know you were coming. Don't laugh, I believe in dreams."

"Did you really dream of—of my being here?"

"I think I was awake when I dreamed it," she admitted. Then for a time they were mute, acknowledging by silence the happiness of being together. And, after all, their silence was eloquent; for faint smiles and glances, born of their thoughts, crossed and recrossed, until lips moved and words were formed which seemed almost superfluous. What they said was not very profound. Perhaps the most valuable jewel that fell from Hastings's lips bore direct reference to breakfast.

"I have not yet had my chocolate," she confessed; "but what a material man you are!"

"Valentine," he said, impulsively, "I wish—I do wish that you would—just for this once—give me the whole day—just for this once."

"Oh, dear," she smiled, "not only material, but selfish."

"Not selfish—hungry," he said, looking at her.

"A cannibal, too. Oh, dear!"

"Will you, Valentine?"

"But my chocolate—"

"Take it with me."

"But *déjeuner*—"

"Together, at St. Cloud."

"But I can't—"

"Together—all day—all day long. Will you, Valentine?"

She was silent.

"Only for this once."

Again that indefinable shadow fell across her eyes, and when it was gone she sighed. "Yes—together, only for this once."

"All day?" he said, doubting his happiness.

"All day," she smiled; "and, oh, I am so hungry!" He laughed, enchanted.

"What a material young lady it is!"

On the Boulevard St. Michel there is a *crémerie* painted white and blue outside, and neat and clean as a whistle inside. The auburn-haired young woman, who speaks French like a native, and rejoices in the name of Murphy, smiled at them as they entered, and, tossing a fresh napkin over the zinc tête-à-tête table, whisked before them two cups of chocolate and a basket full of crisp, fresh croissons.

The primrose-colored pats of butter, each stamped with a shamrock in relief, seemed saturated with the fragrance of Normandy pastures.

"How delicious!" they said, in the same breath, and then laughed at the coincidence.

"With but a single thought," he began.

"How absurd!" she cried, with cheeks all rosy; "I'm thinking I'd like a croisson."

"So am I," he replied, triumphant; "that proves it."

Then they had a quarrel, she accusing him of behavior unworthy of a child in arms, and he denying it, and bringing counter-charges, until Mademoiselle Murphy laughed in sympathy, and the last croisson was eaten under a flag of truce. Then they rose, and she took his arm with a bright nod to Mademoiselle Murphy, who cried them a merry, “Bonjour, madame! Bonjour, monsieur!” and watched them hail a passing cab and drive away. “Dieu! qu’il est beau,” she sighed, adding, after a moment, “Do they be married, I dunno—ma foi, ils ont bien l’air.”

The cab swung around the Rue de Médici, turned into the Rue de Vaugirard, followed it to where it crosses the Rue de Rennes, and, taking that noisy thoroughfare, drew up before the Gare Montparnasse. They were just in time for a train, and scampered up the stair-way and out to the cars as the last note from the starting-gong rang through the arched station. The guard slammed the door of their compartment, a whistle sounded, answered by a screech from the locomotive, and the long train glided from the station, faster, faster, and sped out into the morning sunshine. The summer wind blew in their faces from the open window, and sent the soft hair dancing on the girl’s forehead.

“We have the compartment to ourselves,” said Hastings.

She leaned against the cushioned window-seat, her eyes bright and wide open, her lips parted. The wind lifted her hat and fluttered the ribbons under her chin. With a quick movement she untied them, and, drawing a long hat-pin from her hat, laid it down on the seat beside her. The train was flying.

The color surged in her cheeks, and with each quick-drawn breath her breast rose and fell under the cluster of lilies at her throat. Trees, houses, ponds danced past, cut by a mist of telegraph poles.

“Faster! faster!” she cried.

His eyes never left her; but hers, wide open and blue as the summer sky, seemed fixed on something far ahead—something which came no nearer, but fled before them as they fled.

Was it the horizon, cut now by the grim fortress on the hill, now by the cross of a country chapel? Was it the summer moon, ghostlike, slipping through the vaguer blue above?

“Faster! faster!” she cried.

Her parted lips burned scarlet.

The car shook and shivered, and the fields streamed by like an emerald torrent. He caught the excitement and his face glowed.

"Oh!" she cried, and with an unconscious movement caught his hand, drawing him to the window beside her. "Look! Lean out with me!"

He only saw her lips move; her voice was drowned in the roar of a trestle, but his hand closed in hers and he clung to the sill. The wind whistled in their ears. "Not so far out, Valentine. Take care!" he gasped.

Below, through the ties of the trestle, a broad river flashed into view and out again, as the train thundered along a tunnel, and away once more through the freshet of green fields. The wind roared about them. The girl was leaning far out from the window, and he caught her by the waist, crying, "Not too far!" But she only murmured, "Faster! faster! Away out of the city, out of the land, faster, faster! Away out of the world!"

"What are you saying all to yourself?" he said, but his voice was broken, and the wind whirled it back into his throat.

She heard him, and, turning from the window, looked down at his arm about her. Then she raised her eyes to his. The car shook and the windows rattled. They were dashing through a forest now, and the sun swept the dewy branches with running flashes of fire. He looked into her troubled eyes; he drew her to him and kissed the half-parted lips, and she cried out, a bitter, hopeless cry, "Not that—not that!"

But he held her close and strong, whispering words of honest love and passion, and when she sobbed, "Not that—not that—I have promised! You must—you must know—I am—not—worthy—" in the purity of his own heart her words were, to him, meaningless then, meaningless forever after. Presently her voice ceased, and her head rested on his breast. He leaned against the window, his ears swept by the furious wind, his heart in a joyous tumult. The forest was passed, and the sun slipped from behind the trees, flooding the earth again with brightness. She raised her eyes and looked out into the world from the window. Then she began to speak, but her voice was faint, and he bent his head close to hers and listened. "I cannot turn from you; I am too weak. You were long ago my master—master of my heart and soul. I have broken my word to one who trusted me, but I have told you all—what matters the rest?" He smiled at her innocence and she worshipped his. She spoke again: "Take me or cast me away—what matters it? Now with a word you can kill me, and it might be easier to die than to look upon happiness as great as mine."

He took her in his arms. "Hush! What are you saying? Look—look out at the sunlight, the meadows, and the streams. We shall be very happy in so bright a world."

She turned to the sunlight. From the window the world below seemed very fair to her.

Trembling with happiness, she sighed: "Is this the world? Then I have never known it."

"Nor have I, God forgive me," he murmured.

Perhaps it was our gentle Lady of the Fields who forgave them both.

RUE BARRÉE

"For let philosopher and doctor preach
Of what they will and what they will not—each
Is but one link in an eternal chain
That none can slip nor break nor overreach."

"Crimson nor yellow roses nor
The savor of the mounting sea
Are worth the perfume I adore
That clings to thee.

"The languid-headed lilies tire,
The changeless waters weary me;
I ache with passionate desire
Of thine and thee.

"There are but these things in the world—
Thy mouth of fire,
Thy breasts, thy hands, thy hair upcurled,
And my desire."

I

One morning at Julian's a student said to Selby, "That is Foxhall Clifford," pointing with his brushes at a young man who sat before an easel, doing nothing.

Selby, shy and nervous, walked over and began: "My name is Selby—I have just arrived in Paris, and bring a letter of introduction—" His voice was lost in the crash of a falling easel, the owner of which promptly assaulted his neighbor, and for a time the noise of battle rolled through the studios of MM. Boulanger and Lefebvre, presently subsiding into a scuffle on the stairs outside. Selby, apprehensive as to his own reception in the studio, looked at Clifford, who sat serenely watching the fight.

"It's a little noisy here," said Clifford, "but you will like the fellows when you know them." His unaffected manner delighted Selby. Then, with a simplicity that won his heart, he presented him to half a dozen students of as many nationalities. Some were cordial, all were polite. Even the majestic creature who held the position of *massier* unbent enough to say: "My friend, when a man speaks French as well as you do, and is also a friend of Monsieur Clifford, he will have no trouble in this studio. You expect, of course, to fill the stove until the next new man comes?"

"Of course."

"And you don't mind chaff?"

"No," replied Selby, who hated it.

Clifford, much amused, put on his hat, saying, "You must expect lots of it at first."

Selby placed his own hat on his head and followed him to the door.

As he passed the model-stand there was a furious cry of "Chapeau! Chapeau!" and a student sprang from his easel, menacing Selby, who reddened but looked at Clifford.

"Take off your hat for them," said the latter, laughing.

A little embarrassed, he turned and saluted the studio.

"Et moi?" cried the model.

"You are charming," replied Selby, astonished at his own audacity, but the studio rose as one man, shouting, "He has done well! he's all right!" while the model, laughing, kissed her hand to him and cried: "À demain, beau jeune homme!"

All that week Selby worked at the studio unmolested. The French students christened him *"L'Enfant Prodigue,"* which was freely translated, "The Prodigious Infant," "The Kid," "Kid Selby," and "Kidby." But the disease soon ran its course from "Kidby" to "Kidney," and then naturally to "Tidbits," where it was arrested by Clifford's authority and ultimately relapsed to "Kid."

Wednesday came, and with it Monsieur Boulanger. For three hours the students writhed under his biting sarcasms—among the others Clifford, who was informed that he knew even less about a work of art than he did about the art of work. Selby was more fortunate. The professor examined his drawing in silence, looked at him sharply, and passed on with a noncommittal gesture. He presently departed arm in arm with Bouguereau, to the relief of Clifford, who was then at liberty to jam his hat on his head and depart.

The next day he did not appear, and Selby, who had counted on seeing him at the studio, a thing which he learned later it was vanity to count on, wandered back to the Latin Quarter alone.

Paris was still strange and new to him. He was vaguely troubled by its splendor. No tender memories stirred his American bosom at the Place du Châtelet, nor even by Notre Dame. The Palais de Justice, with its clock and turrets and stalking sentinels in blue and vermilion; the Place St. Michel, with its jumble of omnibuses and ugly water-spitting griffins; the hill of the Boulevard St. Michel, the tooting trams, the policemen dawdling two by two, and the table-lined terraces of the Café Vachette, were nothing to him as yet, nor did he even know, when he stepped from the stones of the Place St. Michel to the asphalt of the boulevard, that he had crossed the frontier and entered the student zone—the famous Latin Quarter.

A cabman hailed him as *bourgeois,* and urged the superiority of driving over walking. A gamin, with an appearance of great concern, requested the latest telegraphic news from London, and then, standing on his head, invited Selby to feats of strength. A pretty girl gave him a glance from a pair of violet eyes. He did not see her, but she, catching her own reflection in a window, wondered at the color burning in her cheeks. Turning to resume her course, she met Foxhall Clifford, and hurried on. Clifford, open-mouthed, followed her with his eyes; then he looked after Selby, who had turned into the Boulevard St. Germain, towards the Rue de Seine. Then he examined himself in the shop-window. The result seemed to be satisfactory.

"I'm not a beauty," he mused, "but neither am I a hobgoblin. What does she mean by blushing at Selby? I never before saw her look at a fellow in my life—neither has any one in the Quarter. Anyway, I can swear she never looks at me, and goodness knows I have done all that respectful adoration can do."

He sighed, and, murmuring a prophecy concerning the salvation of his immortal soul, swung into that graceful lounge which at all times characterized Clifford. With no apparent exertion, he overtook Selby at the corner, and together they crossed the sunlit boulevard and sat down under the awning of the Café du Cercle. Clifford bowed to everybody on the terrace, saying, "You shall meet them all later, but now let me present you to two of the sights of Paris, Mr. Richard Elliott and Mr. Stanley Rowden."

The "sights" looked amiable, and took vermouth.

"You cut the studio to-day," said Elliott, suddenly turning on Clifford, who avoided his eyes.

"To commune with nature?" observed Rowden.

"What's her name this time?" asked Elliott, and Rowden answered, promptly: "Name, Yvette; nationality, Breton—"

"Wrong," replied Clifford, blandly. "It's Rue Barrée."

The subject changed instantly, and Selby listened in surprise to names which were new to him, and eulogies on the latest Prix de Rome winner. He was delighted to hear opinions boldly expressed and points honestly debated, although the vehicle was mostly slang, both English and French. He longed for the time when he, too, should be plunged into the strife for fame.

The bells of St. Sulpice struck the hour, and the palace of the Luxembourg answered chime on chime. With a glance at the sun, dipping low in the golden dust behind the Palais Bourbon, they rose, and, turning to the east, crossed the Boulevard St. Germain and sauntered towards the École de Médecine. At the corner a girl passed them, walking hurriedly. Clifford smirked, Elliott and Rowden were agitated, but they all bowed, and, without raising her eyes, she returned their salute. But Selby, who had lagged behind, fascinated by some gay shop-window, looked up to meet two of the bluest eyes he had ever seen. The eyes were dropped in an instant, and the young fellow hastened to overtake the others.

"By Jove!" he said, "do you fellows know I have just seen the prettiest girl—"

An exclamation broke from the trio, gloomy, foreboding, like the chorus in a Greek play:

"Rue Barrée."

"What!" cried Selby, bewildered.

The only answer was a vague gesture from Clifford.

Two hours later, during dinner, Clifford turned to Selby and said: "You want to ask me something; I can tell by the way you fidget about."

"Yes, I do," he said, innocently enough; "it's about that girl. Who is she?"

In Rowden's smile there was pity; in Elliott's, bitterness.

"Her name," said Clifford, solemnly, "is unknown to any one—at least," he added, with much conscientiousness, "as far as I can learn. Every fellow in the Quarter bows to her and she returns the salute gravely, but no man has ever been known to obtain more than that. Her profession, judging from her music-roll, is that of a pianist. Her residence is in a small and humble street which is kept in a perpetual process of repair by the city authorities, and from the black letters painted on the barrier which defends the street from traffic she has taken the name by which we know her—Rue Barrée. Mr. Rowden, in his imperfect knowledge of the French tongue, called our attention to it as Roo Barry—"

"I didn't," said Rowden, hotly.

"And Roo Barry, or Rue Barrée, is to-day an object of adoration to every rapin in the Quarter—"

"We are not rapins," corrected Elliott.

"*I* am not," returned Clifford, "and I beg to call to your attention, Selby, that these two gentlemen have, at various and apparently unfortunate moments, offered to lay down life and limb at the feet of Rue Barrée. The lady possesses a chilling smile which she uses on such occasions, and"—here he became gloomily impressive—"I have been forced to believe that neither the scholarly grace of my friend Elliott nor the buxom beauty of my friend Rowden have touched that heart of ice."

Elliott and Rowden, boiling with indignation, cried out, "And you!"

"I," said Clifford, blandly, "do fear to tread where you rush in."

II

Twenty-four hours later Selby had completely forgotten Rue Barrée. During the week he worked with might and main at the studio, and Saturday night found him so tired that he went to bed before dinner and had a nightmare about a river of yellow ochre in which he was drowning. Sunday morning, apropos of nothing at all, he thought of Rue Barrée, and ten seconds afterwards he saw her. It was at the flower-market on the marble bridge. She was examining a pot of pansies. The gardener had evidently thrown heart and soul into the transaction, but Rue Barrée shook her head.

It is a question whether Selby would have stopped then and there to inspect a cabbage-rose had not Clifford unwound for him the yarn of the previous Tuesday. It is possible that his curiosity was piqued, for with the exception of a hen-turkey, a boy of nineteen is the most openly curious biped alive. From twenty until death he tries to conceal it. But, to be fair to Selby, it is also true that the market was attractive. Under a cloudless sky the flowers were packed and heaped along the marble bridge to the parapet. The air was soft, the sun spun a shadowy lacework among the palms and glowed in the hearts of a thousand roses. Spring had come—was full in tide. The watering-carts and sprinklers spread freshness over the boulevard, the sparrows had become vulgarly obtrusive, and the credulous Seine angler anxiously followed his gaudy quill, floating among the soapsuds of the *lavoirs.* The white-spiked chestnuts, clad in tender green, vibrated with the hum of bees. Shoddy butterflies flaunted their winter rags among the heliotrope. There was a smell of fresh earth in the air, an echo of the woodland brook in the ripple of the Seine, and swallows soared and skimmed among the anchored river craft. Somewhere in a window a caged bird was singing its heart out to the sky.

Selby looked at the cabbage-rose and then at the sky. Something in the song of the caged bird may have moved him, or perhaps it was that dangerous sweetness in the air of May.

At first he was hardly conscious that he had stopped, then he was scarcely conscious why he had stopped, then he thought he would move on, then he thought he wouldn't, then he looked at Rue Barrée.

The gardener said: "Mademoiselle, this is undoubtedly a fine pot of pansies."

Rue Barrée shook her head.

The gardener smiled. She evidently did not want the pansies. She had bought many pots of pansies there, two or three every spring, and never argued. What did she want, then? The pansies were evidently a feeler towards a more important transaction. The gardener rubbed his hands and gazed about him.

"These tulips are magnificent," he observed, "and these hyacinths—" He fell into a trance at the mere sight of the scented thickets.

"That," murmured Rue, pointing to a splendid rose-bush with her furled parasol, but, in spite of her, her voice trembled a little. Selby noticed it, more shame to him that he was listening, and the gardener noticed it, and, burying his nose in the roses, scented a bargain. Still, to do him justice, he did not add a centime to the honest value of the plant, for, after all, Rue was probably poor, and any one could see she was charming.

"Fifty francs, mademoiselle."

The gardener's tone was grave. Rue felt that argument would be wasted. They both stood silent for a moment. The gardener did not eulogize his prize—the rose-tree was gorgeous, and any one could see it.

"I will take the pansies," said the girl, and drew two francs from a worn purse. Then she looked up. A tear-drop stood in the way, refracting the light like a diamond, but as it rolled into a little corner by her nose a vision of Selby replaced it, and when a brush of the handkerchief had cleared the startled blue eyes Selby himself appeared, very much embarrassed. He instantly looked up into the sky, apparently devoured with a thirst for astronomical research, and, as he continued his investigations for fully five minutes, the gardener looked up, too, and so did a policeman. Then Selby looked at the tips of his boots, the gardener looked at him, and the policeman slouched on. Rue Barrée had been gone some time.

"What," said the gardener, "may I offer, monsieur?"

Selby never knew why, but he suddenly began to buy flowers. The gardener was electrified. Never before had he sold so many flowers; never at such satisfying prices, and never, never, with such absolute unanimity of opinion with a customer. But he missed the bargaining, the arguing, the calling of Heaven to witness. The transaction lacked spice.

"These tulips are magnificent!"

"They are!" cried Selby, warmly.

"But, alas! they are dear."

"I will take them."

"Dieu!" murmured the gardener, in a perspiration. "He's madder than most Englishmen."

"This cactus—"

"Is gorgeous!"

"Alas—"

"Send it with the rest."

The gardener braced himself against the river wall.

"That splendid rose-bush," he began, faintly.

"That is a beauty. I believe it is fifty francs—" He stopped, very red. The gardener relished his confusion. Then a sudden, cool self-possession took the place of his momentary confusion, and he held the gardener with his eye and bullied him.

"I'll take that bush. Why did not the young lady buy it?"

"Mademoiselle is not wealthy."

"How do you know?"

"Dame, I sell her many pansies; pansies are not expensive."

"Those are the pansies she bought?"

"These, monsieur, the blue and gold."

"Then you intend to send them to her?"

"At mid-day, after the market."

"Take this rose-bush with them, and"—here he glared at the gardener—"don't you dare say from whom they came." The gardener's eyes were like saucers, but Selby, calm and victorious, said: "Send the others to the Hôtel du Sénat, 7 Rue de Tournon. I will leave directions with the concierge."

Then he buttoned his glove with much dignity and stalked off, but when well around the corner and hidden from the gardener's view the conviction that he was an idiot came home to him in a furious blush. Ten minutes later he sat in his room in the Hôtel du Sénat, repeating with an imbecile smile: "What an ass I am—what an ass!"

An hour later found him in the same chair, in the same position, his hat and gloves still on, his stick in his hand; but he was silent, apparently lost in contemplation of his boot toes, and his smile was less imbecile and even a bit retrospective.

III

About five o'clock that afternoon the little, sad-eyed woman who fills the position of concierge at the Hôtel du Sénat held up her hands in amazement to see a wagon-load of flower-bearing shrubs draw up before the door-way. She called Joseph, the intemperate garçon, who, while calculating the value of the flowers in *petits verres,* gloomily disclaimed any knowledge as to their destination.

"Voyons," said the little concierge, "cherchons la femme!"

"You?" he suggested.

The little woman stood a moment pensive and then sighed. Joseph caressed his nose, a nose which for gaudiness could vie with any floral display.

Then the gardener came in, hat in hand, and a few minutes later Selby stood in the middle of his room, his coat off, his shirt-sleeves rolled up. The chamber originally contained, besides the furniture, about two square feet of walking-room, and now this was occupied by a cactus. The bed groaned under crates of pansies, lilies, and heliotrope, the lounge was covered with hyacinths and tulips, and the washstand supported a species of young tree warranted to bear flowers at some time or other.

Clifford came in a little later, fell over a box of sweet-peas, swore a little, apologized, and then, as the full splendor of the floral fête burst upon him, sat down in astonishment upon a geranium. The geranium was a wreck, but Selby said, "Don't mind," and glared at the cactus.

"Are you going to give a ball?" demanded Clifford.

"N—no—I'm very fond of flowers," said Selby, but the statement lacked enthusiasm.

"I should imagine so." Then, after a silence, "That's a fine cactus."

Selby contemplated the cactus, touched it with the air of a *connaisseur,* and pricked his thumb.

Clifford poked a pansy with his stick. Then Joseph came in with the bill, announcing the sum total in a loud voice, partly to impress Clifford, partly to intimidate Selby into disgorging a *pourboire* which he would share, if he chose, with the gardener. Clifford tried to pretend that he had not heard, while Selby paid bill and tribute without a murmur. Then he lounged back into the room with an attempt at indifference, which failed entirely when he tore his trousers on the cactus.

Clifford made some commonplace remark, lighted a cigarette, and looked out of the window to give Selby a chance. Selby tried to take it, but, getting as far as, "Yes, spring is here at last," froze solid. He looked at the back of Clifford's head. It expressed volumes. Those little, perked-up ears seemed tingling with suppressed glee. He made a desperate effort to master the situation, and jumped up to reach for some Russian cigarettes as an incentive to conversation, but was foiled by the cactus, to whom again he fell a prey. The last straw was added.

"Damn the cactus!" This observation was wrung from Selby against his will—against his own instinct of self-preservation, but the thorns on the cactus were long and sharp, and at their repeated prick his pent-up wrath escaped. It was too late now; it was done, and Clifford had wheeled around.

"See here, Selby, why the deuce did you buy these flowers?"

"I'm fond of them," said Selby.

"What are you going to do with them? You can't sleep here."

"I could, if you'd help me take the pansies off the bed."

"Where can you put them?"

"Couldn't I give them to the concierge?"

As soon as he said it he regretted it. What in Heaven's name would Clifford think of him! He had heard the amount of the bill. Would he believe that he had invested in these luxuries as a timid declaration to his concierge? And would the Latin Quarter comment upon it in their own brutal fashion? He dreaded ridicule, and he knew Clifford's reputation.

Then somebody knocked.

Selby looked at Clifford with a hunted expression which touched that young man's heart. It was a confession, and at the same time a supplication. Clifford jumped up, threaded his way through the floral labyrinth, and, putting an eye to the crack of the door, said, "Who the devil is it?"

This graceful style of reception is indigenous to the Quarter.

"It's Elliott," he said, looking back, "and Rowden, too, and their bull-dogs." Then he addressed them through the crack.

"Sit down on the stairs; Selby and I are coming out directly."

Discretion is a virtue. The Latin Quarter possesses few, and discretion seldom figures on the list. They sat down and began to whistle.

Presently Rowden called out, "I smell flowers. They feast within!"

"You ought to know Selby better than that," growled Clifford, behind the door, while the other hurriedly exchanged his torn trousers for others.

"*We* know Selby," said Elliott, with emphasis.

"Yes," said Rowden, "he gives receptions with floral decorations and invites Clifford, while we sit on the stairs."

"Yes, while the youth and beauty of the Quarter revel," suggested Rowden; then, with sudden misgiving, "Is Odette there?"

"See here," demanded Elliott, "is Colette there?"

Then he raised his voice in a plaintive howl, "Are you there, Colette, while I'm kicking my heels on these tiles?"

"Clifford is capable of anything," said Rowden; "his nature is soured since Rue Barrée sat on him."

Elliott raised his voice: "I say, you fellows, we saw some flowers carried into Rue Barrée's house at noon."

"Posies and roses," specified Rowden.

"Probably for her," added Elliott, caressing his bulldog.

Clifford turned with sudden suspicion upon Selby. The latter hummed a tune, selected a pair of gloves, and, choosing a dozen cigarettes, placed them in a case. Then walking over to the cactus, he deliberately detached a blossom, drew it through his buttonhole, and, picking up hat and stick, smiled upon Clifford, at which the latter was mightily troubled.

IV

Monday morning, at Julian's, students fought for places; students with prior claims drove away others who had been anxiously squatting on coveted taborets since the door was opened, in hopes of appropriating them at roll-call; students squabbled over palettes, brushes, portfolios, or rent the air with demands for Ciceri and bread. The former, a dirty ex-model, who had in palmier days posed as Judas, now dispensed stale bread at one sou, and made enough to keep himself in cigarettes. Monsieur Julian walked in, smiled a fatherly smile, and walked out. His disappearance was followed by the apparition of the clerk, a foxy creature who flitted through the battling hordes in search of prey.

Three men who had not paid dues were caught and summoned. A fourth was scented, followed, outflanked, his retreat towards the door cut off, and finally captured behind the stove. About that time, the revolution assuming an acute form, howls rose for "Jules!"

Jules came, umpired two fights with a sad resignation in his big, brown eyes, shook hands with everybody, and melted away in the throng, leaving an atmosphere of peace and good-will. The lions sat down with the lambs, the *massiers* marked the best places for themselves and friends, and, mounting the model-stands, opened the roll-calls.

The word was passed, "They begin with C this week."

They did.

"Clisson!"

Clisson jumped like a flash and marked his name on the floor in chalk before a front seat.

"Caron!"

Caron galloped away to secure his place. Bang! went an easel. "Nom de Dieu!" in French—"Where in hell are you goin'!" in English. Crash! a paintbox fell with brushes and all on board. "Dieu de Dieu de—" Spat! A blow, a short rush, a clinch and scuffle, and the voice of the *massier,* stern and reproachful:

"Cochon!"

Then the roll-call was resumed.

"Clifford!"

The *massier* paused and looked up, one finger between the leaves of the ledger.

"Clifford!"

Clifford was not there. He was about three miles away in a direct line, and every instant increased the distance. Not that he was walking fast—on the contrary, he was strolling with that leisurely gait peculiar to himself. Elliott was beside him and two bulldogs covered the rear. Elliott was reading the *Gil Blas,* from which he seemed to extract amusement, but, deeming boisterous mirth unsuitable to Clifford's state of mind, subdued his amusement to a series of discreet smiles. The latter, moodily aware of this, said nothing, but, leading the way into the Luxembourg Gardens, installed himself upon a bench by the northern terrace and surveyed the landscape with disfavor. Elliott, according to the Luxembourg regulations, tied the two dogs, and then, with an interrogative glance towards his friend, resumed the *Gil Blas* and the discreet smiles.

The day was perfect. The sun hung over Notre Dame, setting the city in a glitter. The tender foliage of the chestnuts cast a shadow over the terrace and flecked the paths and walks with tracery so blue that Clifford might here have found encouragement for his violent "impressions" had he but looked; but, as usual in this period of his career, his thoughts were anywhere except in his profession. Around about, the sparrows quarrelled and chattered their courtship songs, the big, rosy pigeons sailed from tree to tree, the flies whirled in the sunbeams, and the flowers exhaled a thousand perfumes which stirred Clifford with languorous wistfulness. Under this influence he spoke.

"Elliott, you are a true friend—"

"You make me ill," replied the latter, folding his paper. "It's just as I thought—you are tagging after some new petticoat again. And," he continued, wrathfully, "if this is what you've kept me away from Julian's for—if it's to fill me up with the perfections of some little idiot—"

"Not idiot," remonstrated Clifford, gently.

"See here," cried Elliott, "have you the nerve to try to tell me that you are in love again?"

"Again?"

"Yes, again and again and again and—by George, have you?"

"This," observed Clifford, sadly, "is serious."

For a moment Elliott would have laid hands on him, then he laughed from sheer helplessness. "Oh, go on, go on; let's see—there's Clémence, and Marie Tellec, and Cosette, and Fifine, Colette, Marie Verdier—"

"All of whom are charming, most charming, but I never was serious—"

"So help me, Moses!" said Elliott, solemnly. "Each and every one of those named have separately and in turn torn your heart with anguish, and have also made me lose my place at Julian's in this same manner; each and every one, separately and in turn. Do you deny it?"

"What you say may be founded on facts—in a way—but give me the credit of being faithful to one at a time—"

"Until the next came along."

"But this—this is really very different. Elliott, believe me, I am all broken up."

Then, there being nothing else to do, Elliott gnashed his teeth and listened.

"It's—it's Rue Barrée."

"Well," observed Elliott, with scorn, "if you are moping and moaning over *that* girl—the girl who has given you and myself every reason to wish that the ground would open and engulf us—well, go on!"

"I'm going on—I don't care; timidity has fled—"

"Yes, your native timidity."

"I'm desperate, Elliott. Am I in love? Never, never did I feel so damned miserable. I can't sleep; honestly, I'm incapable of eating properly."

"Same symptoms noticed in the case of Colette."

"Listen, will you?"

"Hold on a moment, I know the rest by heart. Now let me ask you something. Is it your belief that Rue Barrée is a pure girl?"

"Yes," said Clifford, turning red.

"Do you love her—not as you dangle and tiptoe after every pretty inanity—I mean, do you honestly love her?"

"Yes," said the other, doggedly. "I would—"

"Hold on a moment; would you marry her?"

Clifford turned scarlet. "Yes," he muttered.

"Pleasant news for your family!" growled Elliott, in suppressed fury. "'Dear father, I have just married a charming grisette, whom I'm sure you'll welcome with open arms, in company with her mother, a most estimable and cleanly washlady.' Good heavens! This seems to have gone a little further than the rest. Thank your stars, young man, that my head is level enough for us both. Still, in this case I have no fear. Rue Barrée sat on your aspirations in a manner unmistakably final."

"Rue Barrée," began Clifford, drawing himself up, but he suddenly ceased, for there where the dappled sunlight glowed in spots of gold, along the sun-flecked path, tripped Rue Barrée. Her gown was spotless, and her big straw hat, tipped a little from the white forehead, threw a shadow across her eyes.

Elliott stood up and bowed. Clifford removed his head-covering with an air so plaintive, so appealing, so utterly humble that Rue Barrée smiled.

The smile was delicious, and when Clifford, incapable of sustaining himself on his legs from sheer astonishment, toppled slightly, she smiled again in spite of herself. A few moments later she took a chair on the terrace, and, drawing a book from her music-roll, turned the pages, found the place, and then, placing it open downward in her lap, sighed a little, smiled a little, and looked out over the city. She had entirely forgotten Foxhall Clifford.

After a while she took up her book again, but, instead of reading, began to adjust a rose in her corsage. The rose was big and red. It glowed like fire there over her heart, and like fire it warmed her heart, now fluttering under the silken petals. Rue Barrée sighed again. She was very happy. The sky was so blue, the air so soft and perfumed, the sunshine so caressing, and her heart sang within her, sang to the rose in her breast. This is what it sang: "Out of the throng of passers-by, out of the world of yesterday, out of the millions passing, one has turned aside to me."

So her heart sang under his rose on her breast. Then two big, mouse-colored pigeons came whistling by and alighted on the terrace, where they bowed and strutted and bobbed and turned until Rue Barrée laughed in delight, and, looking up, beheld Clifford before her. His hat was in his hand, and his face was wreathed in a series of appealing smiles which would have touched the heart of a Bengal tiger.

For an instant Rue Barrée frowned, then she looked curiously at Clifford; then, when she saw the resemblance between his bows and the bobbing pigeons, in spite of herself her lips parted in the most bewitching laugh. Was this Rue Barrée? So changed—so changed that she did not know herself; but, oh! that song in her heart which drowned all else, which trembled on her lips, struggling for utterance, which rippled forth in a laugh at nothing—at a strutting pigeon—and Mr. Clifford.

"And you think because I return the salute of the students in the Quarter that you may be received in particular as a friend? I do not know you, monsieur, but vanity is man's other name; be content, Monsieur Vanity, I shall be punctilious—oh, most punctilious—in returning your salute."

"But I beg—I implore you to let me render you that homage which has so long—"

"Oh, dear, I don't care for homage."

"Let me only be permitted to speak to you now and then—occasionally—very occasionally."

"And if *you,* why not another?"

"Not at all—I will be discretion itself."

"Discretion—why?"

Her eyes were very clear, and Clifford winced for a moment, but only for a moment. Then, the devil of recklessness seizing him, he sat down and offered himself, soul and body, goods and chattels. And all the time he knew he was a fool, and that infatuation is not love, and that each word he uttered bound him in honor from which there was no escape. And all the time Elliott was scowling down on the fountain plaza, and savagely checking both bull-dogs from their desire to rush to Clifford's rescue—for even they felt there was something wrong, as Elliott stormed within himself and growled maledictions.

When Clifford finished, he finished in a glow of excitement; but Rue Barrée's response was long in coming, and his ardor cooled while the situation slowly assumed its just proportions. Then regret began to creep in, but he put that aside and broke out again in protestations. At the first word Rue Barrée checked him.

"I thank you," she said, speaking very gravely. "No man has ever before offered me marriage." She turned and looked out over the city. After a while she spoke again. "You offer me a great deal. I am alone, I have nothing, I am nothing." She turned again and looked at Paris, brilliant, fair, in the sunshine of a perfect day. He followed her eyes.

"Oh," she murmured, "it is hard—hard to work always—always alone, with never a friend you can have in honor, and the love that is offered means the streets, the boulevard—when passion is dead. I know it—*we* know it—we others who have nothing—have no one, and who give ourselves, unquestioning—when we love—yes, unquestioning—heart and soul, knowing the end."

She touched the rose at her breast. For a moment she seemed to forget him, then, quietly, "I thank you, I am very grateful." She opened the book and, plucking a petal from the rose, dropped it between the leaves. Then, looking up, she said, gently, "I cannot accept."

V

It took Clifford a month to entirely recover, although at the end of the first week he was pronounced convalescent by Elliott, who was an authority, and his convalescence was aided by the cordiality with which Rue Barrée acknowledged his solemn salutes. Forty times a day he blessed Rue Barrée for her refusal and thanked his lucky stars, and at the same time—oh, wondrous heart of ours!—he suffered the tortures of the blighted.

Elliott was annoyed, partly by Clifford's reticence, partly by the unexplainable thaw in the frigidity of Rue Barrée. At their frequent encounters, when she, tripping along the Rue de Seine, with music-roll and big straw hat, would pass Clifford and his familiars steering an easterly course to the Café Vachette, and at the respectful uncovering of the band would color and smile at Clifford, Elliott's slumbering suspicions awoke. But he never found out anything, and finally gave it up as beyond his comprehension, merely qualifying Clifford as an idiot and reserving his opinion of Rue Barrée. And all this time Selby was jealous. At first he refused to acknowledge it to himself, and cut the studio for a day in the country, but the woods and fields, of course, aggravated his case, and the brooks babbled of Rue Barrée, and the mowers calling to each other across the meadow ended in a quavering "Rue Bar-rée-e!" That day spent in the country made him angry for a week, and he worked sulkily at Julian's, all the time tormented by a desire to know where Clifford was and what he might be doing. This culminated in an erratic stroll on Sunday which ended at the flower-market on the Pont du Change, began again, was gloomily extended to the morgue, and again ended at the marble bridge. It would never do, and Selby felt it; so he went to see Clifford, who was convalescing on mint-juleps in his garden.

They sat down together and discussed morals and human happiness, and each found the other most entertaining, only Selby failed to pump Clifford, to the other's unfeigned amusement. But the juleps spread balm on the sting of jealousy and trickled hope to the blighted; and when Selby said he must go, Clifford went, too; and when Selby, not to be outdone, insisted on accompanying Clifford back to his door, Clifford determined to see Selby back half-way; and then, finding it hard to part, they decided to dine together and "flit." To flit, a verb applied to Clifford's nocturnal prowls, expressed, perhaps, as well as anything, the gayety proposed. Dinner was ordered at Mignon's, and while Selby interviewed the chef, Clifford kept a fatherly eye on the butler. The dinner was a success, or was of the sort generally termed a success. Towards the dessert Selby heard some one say, as at a great distance, "Kid Selby, drunk as a lord."

A group of men passed near them; it seemed to him that he shook hands and laughed a great deal, and that everybody was very witty. There was Clifford opposite, swearing undying confidence in his chum Selby, and there seemed to be others there, either seated beside them or continually passing with the swish of skirts on the polished floor. The perfume of roses, the rustle of fans, the touch of rounded arms, and the laughter grew vaguer and vaguer. The room seemed enveloped in mist. Then, all in a moment, each object stood out painfully distinct, only forms and visages were distorted and voices piercing. He drew himself up, calm, grave, for the moment master of himself, but very drunk. He knew he was drunk, and was as guarded and alert, as keenly suspicious of himself as he would have been of a thief at his elbow. His self-command enabled Clifford to hold his head safely under some running water, and repair to the street considerably the worse for wear, but never suspecting that his companion was drunk. For a time he kept his self-command. His face was only a bit paler, a bit tighter than usual; he was only a trifle slower and more fastidious in his speech. It was midnight when he left Clifford peacefully slumbering in somebody's armchair, with a long Suède glove dangling in his hand and a plumy boa twisted about his neck to protect his throat from draughts. He walked through the hall and down the stairs, and found himself on the sidewalk in a quarter he did not know. Mechanically he looked up at the name of the street. The name was not familiar. He turned and steered his course towards some lights clustered at the end of the street. They proved farther away than he had anticipated, and after a long quest he came to the conclusion that his eyes had been mysteriously removed from their proper places and had been reset on either side of his head like those of a bird. It grieved him to think of the inconvenience this transformation might occasion him, and he attempted to cock up his head, hen-like, to test the mobility of his neck. Then an immense despair stole over him—tears gathered in the tear-ducts, his heart melted, and he collided with a tree. This shocked him into comprehension; he stifled the violent tenderness in his breast, picked up his hat, and moved on more briskly. His mouth was white and drawn, his teeth tightly clinched. He held his course pretty well and strayed but little, and after an apparently interminable length of time found himself passing a line of cabs. The brilliant lamps, red, yellow, and green, annoyed him, and he felt it might be pleasant to demolish them with his cane, but, mastering this impulse, he passed on. Later an idea struck him that it would save fatigue to take a cab, and he started back with that intention, but the cabs seemed already so far away and the lanterns were so bright and confusing that he gave it up, and, pulling himself together, looked around.

A shadow, a mass, huge, undefined, rose to his right. He recognized the Arc de Triomphe, and gravely shook his cane at it. Its size annoyed him. He felt it was too big. Then he heard something fall clattering to the pavement, and thought probably it was his cane, but it didn't much matter. When he had mastered himself and regained control of his right leg, which betrayed symptoms of insubordination, he found himself traversing the Place de la Concorde at a pace which threatened to land him at the Madeleine. This would never do. He turned sharply to the right, and, crossing the bridge, passed the Palais Bourbon at a trot and wheeled into the Boulevard St. Germain. He got on well enough, although the size of the War Office struck him as a personal insult, and he missed his cane, which it would have been pleasant to drag along the iron railings as he passed. It occurred to him, however, to substitute his hat, but when he found it he forgot what he wanted it for, and replaced it upon his head with gravity. Then he was obliged to battle with a violent inclination to sit down and weep. This lasted until he came to the Rue de Rennes, but there he became absorbed in contemplating the dragon on the balcony overhanging the Cour de Dragon, and time slipped away until he remembered vaguely that he had no business there and marched off again. It was slow work. The inclination to sit down and weep had given place to a desire for solitary and deep reflection. Here his right leg forgot its obedience, and, attacking the left, outflanked it, and brought him up against a wooden board which seemed to bar his path. He tried to walk around it, but found the street closed. He tried to push it over and found he couldn't. Then he noticed a red lantern standing on a pile of paving-stones inside the barrier. This was pleasant. How was he to get home if the boulevard was blocked? But he was not on the boulevard. His treacherous right leg had beguiled him into a détour, for there behind him lay the boulevard with its endless line of lamps—and here, what was this narrow, dilapidated street piled up with earth and mortar and heaps of stone? He looked up. Written in staring black letters on the barrier was

RUE BARRÉE.

He sat down. Two policemen whom he knew came by and advised him to get up, but he argued the question from a standpoint of personal taste, and they passed on, laughing. For he was at that moment absorbed in a problem. It was, how to see Rue Barrée. She was somewhere or other in that big house with the iron balconies, and the door was locked, but what of that? The simple idea struck him to shout until she came. This idea was replaced by another equally lucid—to hammer on the door until she came; but finally, rejecting both of these as too uncertain, he decided to climb into the balcony, and, opening a window, politely inquire for Rue Barrée. There was but one lighted window in the house that he could see. It was on the second floor, and towards this he cast his eyes. Then mounting the wooden barrier and clambering over the piles of stones, he reached the sidewalk and looked up at the façade for a foothold. It seemed impossible. But a sudden fury seized him, a blind, drunken obstinacy, and the blood rushed to his head, leaping, beating in his ears like the dull thunder of an ocean. He set his teeth, and, springing at a window-sill, dragged himself up and hung to the iron bars. Then reason fled;

there surged in his brain the sound of many voices; his heart leaped up, beating a mad tattoo, and, gripping at cornice and ledge, he worked his way along the façade, clung to pipes and shutters, and dragged himself up, over and into the balcony by the lighted window. His hat fell off and rolled against the pane. For a moment he leaned breathless against the railing—then the window was slowly opened from within.

They stared at each other for some time. Presently the girl took two unsteady steps back into the room. He saw her face—all crimsoned now—he saw her sink into a chair by the lamp-lit table, and without a word he followed her into the room, closing the big, doorlike panes behind him. Then they looked at each other in silence.

The room was small and white; everything was white about it—the curtained bed, the little washstand in the corner, the bare walls, the china lamp, and his own face, had he known it; but the face and neck of Rue Barrée were surging in the color that dyed the blossoming rose-tree there on the hearth beside her. It did not occur to him to speak. She seemed not to expect it. His mind was struggling with the impressions of the room. The whiteness, the extreme purity of everything, occupied him—began to trouble him. As his eye became accustomed to the light, other objects grew from the surroundings and took their places in the circle of lamp-light. There was a piano and a coal-scuttle, and a little iron trunk and a bath-tub. Then there was a row of wooden pegs against the door, with a white chintz curtain covering the clothes underneath. On the bed lay an umbrella and a big straw hat, and on the table a music-roll unfurled, an inkstand, and sheets of ruled paper. Behind him stood a wardrobe faced with a mirror, but somehow he did not care to see his own face just then. He was sobering.

The girl sat looking at him without a word. Her face was expressionless; yet the lips, at times, trembled almost imperceptibly. Her eyes, so wonderfully blue in the daylight, seemed dark and soft as velvet, and the color on her neck deepened and whitened with every breath. She seemed smaller and more slender than when he had seen her in the street, and there was now something in the curve of her cheek almost infantine. When at last he turned and caught his own reflection in the mirror behind him a shock passed through him as though he had seen a shameful thing, and his clouded mind and his clouded thoughts grew clearer. For a moment their eyes met, then his sought the floor, his lips tightened, and the struggle within him bowed his head and strained every nerve to the breaking. And now it was over, for the voice within had spoken. He listened, dully interested, but already knowing the end—indeed, it little mattered—the end would always be the same for him—he understood now—always the same for him, and he listened, dully interested, to a voice which grew within him. After a while he stood up, and she rose at once, one small hand resting on the table. Presently he opened the window, picked up his hat, and then closed the window. Then he went over to the rosebush and touched the blossoms with his face. One was standing in a glass of water on the table, and mechanically the girl drew it out, pressed it with her lips, and laid it on the table beside him. He took it without a word, and, crossing the room, opened the door. The landing was dark and silent, but the girl lifted the lamp, and, gliding past him, slipped down the polished stairs to the hall-way. Then, unchaining the bolts, she drew open the iron wicket.

Through this he passed with his rose.

THE END

OTHER TALES OF THE SUPERNATURAL

CONTENTS

THE PURPLE EMPEROR

Un souvenir heureux est peut-être, sur terre,
Plus vrai que le bonheur.

—A. de Musset.

I

The Purple Emperor watched me in silence. I cast again, spinning out six feet more of waterproof silk, and, as the line hissed through the air far across the pool, I saw my three flies fall on the water like drifting thistledown. The Purple Emperor sneered.

"You see," he said, "I am right. There is not a trout in Brittany that will rise to a tailed fly."

"They do in America," I replied.

"Zut! for America!" observed the Purple Emperor.

"And trout take a tailed fly in England," I insisted sharply.

"Now do I care what things or people do in England?" demanded the Purple Emperor.

"You don't care for anything except yourself and your wriggling caterpillars," I said, more annoyed than I had yet been.

The Purple Emperor sniffed. His broad, hairless, sunburnt features bore that obstinate expression which always irritated me. Perhaps the manner in which he wore his hat intensified the irritation, for the flapping brim rested on both ears, and the two little velvet ribbons which hung from the silver buckle in front wiggled and fluttered with every trivial breeze. His cunning eyes and sharp-pointed nose were out of all keeping with his fat red face. When he met my eye, he chuckled.

"I know more about insects than any man in Morbihan—or Finistère either, for that matter," he said.

"The Red Admiral knows as much as you do," I retorted.

"He doesn't," replied the Purple Emperor angrily.

"And his collection of butterflies is twice as large as yours," I added, moving down the stream to a spot directly opposite him.

"It is, is it?" sneered the Purple Emperor. "Well, let me tell you, Monsieur Darrel, in all his collection he hasn't a specimen, a single specimen, of that magnificent butterfly, Apatura Iris, commonly known as the 'Purple Emperor.'"

"Everybody in Brittany knows that," I said, casting across the sparkling water; "but just because you happen to be the only man who ever captured a 'Purple Emperor' in Morbihan, it doesn't follow that you are an authority on sea-trout flies. Why do you say that a Breton sea-trout won't touch a tailed fly?"

"It's so," he replied.

"Why? There are plenty of May-flies about the stream."

"Let 'em fly!" snarled the Purple Emperor, "you won't see a trout touch 'em."

My arm was aching, but I grasped my split bamboo more firmly, and, half turning, waded out into the stream and began to whip the ripples at the head of the pool. A great green dragon-fly came drifting by on the summer breeze and hung a moment above the pool, glittering like an emerald.

"There's a chance! Where is your butterfly net?" I called across the stream.

"What for? That dragon-fly? I've got dozens—Anax Junius, Drury, characteristic, anal angle of posterior wings, in male, round; thorax marked with——"

"That will do," I said fiercely. "Can't I point out an insect in the air without this burst of erudition? Can you tell me, in simple everyday French, what this little fly is—this one, flitting over the eel grass here beside me? See, it has fallen on the water."

"Huh!" sneered the Purple Emperor, "that's a Linnobia annulus."

"What's that?" I demanded.

Before he could answer there came a heavy splash in the pool, and the fly disappeared.

"He! he! he!" tittered the Purple Emperor. "Didn't I tell you the fish knew their business? That was a sea-trout. I hope you don't get him."

He gathered up his butterfly net, collecting box, chloroform bottle, and cyanide jar. Then he rose, swung the box over his shoulder, stuffed the poison bottles into the pockets of his silver-buttoned velvet coat, and lighted his pipe. This latter operation was a demoralizing spectacle, for the Purple Emperor, like all Breton peasants, smoked one of those microscopical Breton pipes which requires ten minutes to find, ten minutes to fill, ten minutes to light, and ten seconds to finish. With true Breton stolidity he went through this solemn rite, blew three puffs of smoke into the air, scratched his pointed nose reflectively, and waddled away, calling back an ironical "Au revoir, and bad luck to all Yankees!"

I watched him out of sight, thinking sadly of the young girl whose life he made a hell upon earth—Lys Trevec, his niece. She never admitted it, but we all knew what the black-and-blue marks meant on her soft, round arm, and it made me sick to see the look of fear come into her eyes when the Purple Emperor waddled into the café of the Groix Inn.

It was commonly said that he half-starved her. This she denied. Marie Joseph and 'Fine Lelocard had seen him strike her the day after the Pardon of the Birds because she had liberated three bullfinches which he had limed the day before. I asked Lys if this were true, and she refused to speak to me for the rest of the week. There was nothing to do about it. If the Purple Emperor had not been avaricious, I should never have seen Lys at all, but he could not resist the thirty francs a week which I offered him; and Lys posed for me all day long, happy as a linnet in a pink thorn hedge. Nevertheless, the Purple Emperor hated me, and constantly threatened to send Lys back to her dreary flax-spinning. He was suspicious, too, and when he had gulped down the single glass of cider which proves fatal to the sobriety of most Bretons, he would pound the long, discoloured oaken table and roar curses on me, on Yves Terrec, and on the Red Admiral. We were the three objects in the world which he most hated: me, because I was a foreigner, and didn't care a rap for him and his butterflies; and the Red Admiral, because he was a rival entomologist.

He had other reasons for hating Terrec.

The Red Admiral, a little wizened wretch, with a badly adjusted glass eye and a passion for brandy, took his name from a butterfly which predominated in his collection. This butterfly, commonly known to amateurs as the "Red Admiral," and to entomologists as Vanessa Atalanta, had been the occasion of scandal among the entomologists of France and Brittany. For the Red Admiral had taken one of these common insects, dyed it a brilliant yellow by the aid of chemicals, and palmed it off on a credulous collector as a South African species, absolutely unique. The fifty francs which he gained by this rascality were, however, absorbed in a suit for damages brought by the outraged amateur a month later; and when he had sat in the Quimperlé jail for a month, he reappeared in the little village of St. Gildas soured, thirsty, and burning for revenge. Of course we named him the Red Admiral, and he accepted the name with suppressed fury.

The Purple Emperor, on the other hand, had gained his imperial title legitimately, for it was an undisputed fact that the only specimen of that beautiful butterfly, Apatura Iris, or the Purple Emperor, as it is called by amateurs—the only specimen that had ever been taken in Finistère or in Morbihan—was captured and brought home alive by Joseph Marie Gloanec, ever afterward to be known as the Purple Emperor.

When the capture of this rare butterfly became known the Red Admiral nearly went crazy. Every day for a week he trotted over to the Groix Inn, where the Purple Emperor lived with his niece, and brought his microscope to bear on the rare newly captured butterfly, in hopes of detecting a fraud. But this specimen was genuine, and he leered through his microscope in vain.

"No chemicals there, Admiral," grinned the Purple Emperor; and the Red Admiral chattered with rage.

To the scientific world of Brittany and France the capture of an Apatura Iris in Morbihan was of great importance. The Museum of Quimper offered to purchase the butterfly, but the Purple Emperor, though a hoarder of gold, was a monomaniac on butterflies, and he jeered at the Curator of the Museum. From all parts of Brittany and France letters of inquiry and congratulation poured in upon him. The French Academy of Sciences awarded him a prize, and the Paris Entomological Society made him an honorary member. Being a Breton peasant, and a more than commonly pigheaded one at that, these honours did not disturb his equanimity; but when the little hamlet of St. Gildas elected him mayor, and, as is the custom in Brittany under such circumstances, he left his thatched house to take up an official life in the little Groix Inn, his head became completely turned. To be mayor in a village of nearly one hundred and fifty people! It was an empire! So he became unbearable, drinking himself viciously drunk every night of his life, maltreating his niece, Lys Trevec, like the barbarous old wretch that he was, and driving the Red Admiral nearly frantic with his eternal harping on the capture of Apatura Iris. Of course he refused to tell where he had caught the butterfly. The Red Admiral stalked his footsteps, but in vain.

"He! he! he!" nagged the Purple Emperor, cuddling his chin over a glass of cider; "I saw you sneaking about the St. Gildas spinny yesterday morning. So you think you can find another Apatura Iris by running after me? It won't do, Admiral, it won't do, d'ye see?"

The Red Admiral turned yellow with mortification and envy, but the next day he actually took to his bed, for the Purple Emperor had brought home not a butterfly but a live chrysalis, which, if successfully hatched, would become a perfect specimen of the invaluable Apatura Iris. This was the last straw. The Red Admiral shut himself up in his little stone cottage, and for weeks now he had been invisible to everybody except 'Fine Lelocard who carried him a loaf of bread and a mullet or langouste every morning.

The withdrawal of the Red Admiral from the society of St. Gildas excited first the derision and finally the suspicion of the Purple Emperor. What deviltry could he be hatching? Was he experimenting with chemicals again, or was he engaged in some deeper plot, the object of which was to discredit the Purple Emperor? Roux, the postman, who carried the mail on foot once a day from Bannalec, a distance of fifteen miles each way, had brought several suspicious letters, bearing English stamps, to the

Red Admiral, and the next day the Admiral had been observed at his window grinning up into the sky and rubbing his hands together. A night or two after this apparition the postman left two packages at the Groix Inn for a moment while he ran across the way to drink a glass of cider with me. The Purple Emperor, who was roaming about the café, snooping into everything that did not concern him, came upon the packages and examined the postmarks and addresses. One of the packages was square and heavy, and felt like a book. The other was also square, but very light, and felt like a pasteboard box. They were both addressed to the Red Admiral, and they bore English stamps.

When Roux, the postman, came back, the Purple Emperor tried to pump him, but the poor little postman knew nothing about the contents of the packages, and after he had taken them around the corner to the cottage of the Red Admiral the Purple Emperor ordered a glass of cider, and deliberately fuddled himself until Lys came in and tearfully supported him to his room. Here he became so abusive and brutal that Lys called to me, and I went and settled the trouble without wasting any words. This also the Purple Emperor remembered, and waited his chance to get even with me.

That had happened a week ago, and until to-day he had not deigned to speak to me.

Lys had posed for me all the week, and today being Saturday, and I lazy, we had decided to take a little relaxation, she to visit and gossip with her little black-eyed friend Yvette in the neighbouring hamlet of St. Julien, and I to try the appetites of the Breton trout with the contents of my American fly book.

I had thrashed the stream very conscientiously for three hours, but not a trout had risen to my cast, and I was piqued. I had begun to believe that there were no trout in the St. Gildas stream, and would probably have given up had I not seen the sea trout snap the little fly which the Purple Emperor had named so scientifically. That set me thinking. Probably the Purple Emperor was right, for he certainly was an expert in everything that crawled and wriggled in Brittany. So I matched, from my American fly book, the fly that the sea trout had snapped up, and withdrawing the cast of three, knotted a new leader to the silk and slipped a fly on the loop. It was a queer fly. It was one of those unnameable experiments which fascinate anglers in sporting stores and which generally prove utterly useless. Moreover, it was a tailed fly, but of course I easily remedied that with a stroke of my penknife. Then I was all ready, and I stepped out into the hurrying rapids and cast straight as an arrow to the spot where the sea trout had risen. Lightly as a plume the fly settled on the bosom of the pool; then came a startling splash, a gleam of silver, and the line tightened from the vibrating rod-tip to the shrieking reel. Almost instantly I checked the fish, and as he floundered for a moment, making the water boil along his glittering sides, I sprang to the bank again, for I saw that the fish was a heavy one and I should probably be in for a long run down the stream. The five-ounce rod swept in a splendid circle, quivering under the strain. "Oh, for a gaff-hook!" I cried aloud, for I was now firmly convinced that I had a salmon to deal with, and no sea trout at all.

Then as I stood, bringing every ounce to bear on the sulking fish, a lithe, slender girl came hurriedly along the opposite bank calling out to me by name.

"Why, Lys!" I said, glancing up for a second, "I thought you were at St. Julien with Yvette."

"Yvette has gone to Bannelec. I went home and found an awful fight going on at the Groix Inn, and I was so frightened that I came to tell you."

The fish dashed off at that moment, carrying all the line my reel held, and I was compelled to follow him at a jump. Lys, active and graceful as a young deer, in spite of her Pont-Aven sabots, followed along the opposite bank until the fish settled in a deep pool, shook the line savagely once or twice, and then relapsed into the sulks.

"Fight at the Groix Inn?" I called across the water. "What fight?"

"Not exactly fight," quavered Lys, "but the Red Admiral has come out of his house at last, and he and my uncle are drinking together and disputing about butterflies. I never saw my uncle so angry, and the Red Admiral is sneering and grinning. Oh, it is almost wicked to see such a face!"

"But Lys," I said, scarcely able to repress a smile, "your uncle and the Red Admiral are always quarrelling and drinking."

"I know—oh, dear me!—but this is different, Monsieur Darrel. The Red Admiral has grown old and fierce since he shut himself up three weeks ago, and—oh, dear! I never saw such a look in my uncle's eyes before. He seemed insane with fury. His eyes—I can't speak of it—and then Terrec came in."

"Oh," I said more gravely, "that was unfortunate. What did the Red Admiral say to his son?"

Lys sat down on a rock among the ferns, and gave me a mutinous glance from her blue eyes.

Yves Terrec, loafer, poacher, and son of Louis Jean Terrec, otherwise the Red Admiral, had been kicked out by his father, and had also been forbidden the village by the Purple Emperor, in his majestic capacity of mayor. Twice the young ruffian had returned: once to rifle the bedroom of the Purple Emperor—an unsuccessful enterprise—and another time to rob his own father. He succeeded in the latter attempt, but was never caught, although he was frequently seen roving about the forests and moors with his gun. He openly menaced the Purple Emperor; vowed that he would marry Lys in spite of all the gendarmes in Quimperlé; and these same gendarmes he led many a long chase through brier-filled swamps and over miles of yellow gorse.

What he did to the Purple Emperor—what he intended to do—disquieted me but little; but I worried over his threat concerning Lys. During the last three months this had bothered me a great deal; for when Lys came to St. Gildas from the convent the first thing she captured was my heart. For a long time I had refused to believe that any tie of blood linked this dainty blue-eyed creature with the Purple Emperor. Although she dressed in the velvet-laced bodice and blue petticoat of Finistère, and wore the bewitching white coiffe of St. Gildas, it seemed like a pretty masquerade. To me she was as sweet and as gently bred as many a maiden of the noble Faubourg who danced with her cousins at a

Louis XV fête champêtre. So when Lys said that Yves Terrec had returned openly to St. Gildas, I felt that I had better be there also.

"What did Terrec say, Lys?" I asked, watching the line vibrating above the placid pool.

The wild rose colour crept into her cheeks. "Oh," she answered, with a little toss of her chin, "you know what he always says."

"That he will carry you away?"

"Yes."

"In spite of the Purple Emperor, the Red Admiral, and the gendarmes?"

"Yes."

"And what do you say, Lys?"

"I? Oh, nothing."

"Then let me say it for you."

Lys looked at her delicate pointed sabots, the sabots from Pont-Aven, made to order. They fitted her little foot. They were her only luxury.

"Will you let me answer for you, Lys?" I asked.

"You, Monsieur Darrel?"

"Yes. Will you let me give him his answer?"

"Mon Dieu, why should you concern yourself, Monsieur Darrel?"

The fish lay very quiet, but the rod in my hand trembled.

"Because I love you, Lys."

The wild rose colour in her cheeks deepened; she gave a gentle gasp, then hid her curly head in her hands.

"I love you, Lys."

"Do you know what you say?" she stammered.

"Yes, I love you."

She raised her sweet face and looked at me across the pool.

"I love you," she said, while the tears stood like stars in her eyes. "Shall I come over the brook to you?"

II

That night Yves Terrec left the village of St. Gildas vowing vengeance against his father, who refused him shelter.

I can see him now, standing in the road, his bare legs rising like pillars of bronze from his straw-stuffed sabots, his short velvet jacket torn and soiled by exposure and dissipation, and his eyes, fierce, roving, bloodshot—while the Red Admiral squeaked curses on him, and hobbled away into his little stone cottage.

"I will not forget you!" cried Yves Terrec, and stretched out his hand toward his father with a terrible gesture. Then he whipped his gun to his cheek and took a short step forward, but I caught him by the throat before he could fire, and a second later we were rolling in the dust of the Bannalec road. I had to hit him a heavy blow behind the ear before he would let go, and then, rising and shaking myself, I dashed his muzzle-loading fowling piece to bits against a wall, and threw his knife into the river. The Purple Emperor was looking on with a queer light in his eyes. It was plain that he was sorry Terrec had not choked me to death.

"He would have killed his father," I said, as I passed him, going toward the Groix Inn.

"That's his business," snarled the Purple Emperor. There was a deadly light in his eyes. For a moment I thought he was going to attack me; but he was merely viciously drunk, so I shoved him out of my way and went to bed, tired and disgusted.

The worst of it was I couldn't sleep, for I feared that the Purple Emperor might begin to abuse Lys. I lay restlessly tossing among the sheets until I could stay there no longer. I did not dress entirely; I merely slipped on a pair of chaussons and sabots, a pair of knickerbockers, a jersey, and a cap. Then, loosely tying a handkerchief about my throat, I went down the worm-eaten stairs and out into the moonlit road. There was a candle flaring in the Purple Emperor's window, but I could not see him.

"He's probably dead drunk," I thought, and looked up at the window where, three years before, I had first seen Lys.

"Asleep, thank Heaven!" I muttered, and wandered out along the road. Passing the small cottage of the Red Admiral, I saw that it was dark, but the door was open. I stepped inside the hedge to shut it, thinking, in case Yves Terrec should be roving about, his father would lose whatever he had left.

Then, after fastening the door with a stone, I wandered on through the dazzling Breton moonlight. A nightingale was singing in a willow swamp below, and from the edge of the mere, among the tall swamp grasses, myriads of frogs chanted a bass chorus.

When I returned, the eastern sky was beginning to lighten, and across the meadows on the cliffs, outlined against the paling horizon, I saw a seaweed gatherer going to his work among the curling breakers on the coast. His long rake was balanced on his shoulder, and the sea wind carried his song across the meadows to me:

St. Gildas!
St. Gildas!
Pray for us,
Shelter us,
Us who toil in the sea.

Passing the shrine at the entrance of the village, I took off my cap and knelt in prayer to Our Lady of Faöuet; and if I neglected myself in that prayer, surely I believed Our Lady of Faöuet would be kinder to Lys. It is said that the shrine casts white shadows. I looked, but saw only the moonlight. Then very peacefully I went to bed again, and was only awakened by the clank of sabres and the trample of horses in the road below my window.

"Good gracious!" I thought, "it must be eleven o'clock, for there are the gendarmes from Quimperlé."

I looked at my watch; it was only half-past eight, and as the gendarmes made their rounds every Thursday at eleven, I wondered what had brought them out so early to St. Gildas.

"Of course," I grumbled, rubbing my eyes, "they are after Terrec," and I jumped into my limited bath.

Before I was completely dressed I heard a timid knock, and opening my door, razor in hand, stood astonished and silent. Lys, her blue eyes wide with terror, leaned on the threshold.

"My darling!" I cried, "what on earth is the matter?" But she only clung to me, panting like a wounded sea gull. At last, when I drew her into the room and raised her face to mine, she spoke in a heart-breaking voice:

"Oh, Dick! they are going to arrest you, but I will die before I believe one word of what they say. No, don't ask me," and she began to sob desperately.

When I found that something really serious was the matter, I flung on my coat and cap, and, slipping one arm about her waist, went down the stairs and out into the road. Four gendarmes sat on their horses in front of the café door; beyond them, the entire population of St. Gildas gaped, ten deep.

"Hello, Durand!" I said to the brigadier, "what the devil is this I hear about arresting me?"

"It's true, mon ami," replied Durand with sepulchral sympathy. I looked him over from the tip of his spurred boots to his sulphur-yellow sabre belt, then upward, button by button, to his disconcerted face.

"What for?" I said scornfully. "Don't try any cheap sleuth work on me! Speak up, man, what's the trouble?"

The Purple Emperor, who sat in the door-way staring at me, started to speak, but thought better of it and got up and went into the house. The gendarmes rolled their eyes mysteriously and looked wise.

"Come, Durand," I said impatiently, "what's the charge?"

"Murder," he said in a faint voice.

"What!" I cried incredulously. "Nonsense! Do I look like a murderer? Get off your horse, you stupid, and tell me who's murdered."

Durand got down, looking very silly, and came up to me, offering his hand with a propitiatory grin.

"It was the Purple Emperor who denounced you! See, they found your handkerchief at his door——"

"Whose door, for Heaven's sake?" I cried.

"Why, the Red Admiral's!"

"The Red Admiral's? What has he done?"

"Nothing—he's only been murdered."

I could scarcely believe my senses, although they took me over to the little stone cottage and pointed out the blood-spattered room. But the horror of the thing was that the corpse of the murdered man had disappeared, and there only remained a nauseating lake of blood on the stone floor, in the centre of which lay a human hand. There was no doubt as to whom the hand belonged, for everybody who had ever seen the Red Admiral knew that the shrivelled bit of flesh which lay in the thickening blood was the hand of the Red Admiral. To me it looked like the severed claw of some gigantic bird.

"Well," I said, "there's been murder committed. Why don't you do something?"

"What?" asked Durand.

"I don't know. Send for the Commissaire."

"He's at Quimperlé. I telegraphed."

"Then send for a doctor, and find out how long this blood has been coagulating."

"The chemist from Quimperlé is here; he's a doctor."

"What does he say?"

"He says that he doesn't know."

"And who are you going to arrest?" I inquired, turning away from the spectacle on the floor.

"I don't know," said the brigadier solemnly; "you are denounced by the Purple Emperor, because he found your handkerchief at the door when he went out this morning."

"Just like a pig-headed Breton!" I exclaimed, thoroughly angry. "Did he not mention Yves Terrec?"

"No."

"Of course not," I said. "He overlooked the fact that Terrec tried to shoot his father last night, and that I took away his gun. All that counts for nothing when he finds my handkerchief at the murdered man's door."

"Come into the café," said Durand, much disturbed, "we can talk it over, there. Of course, Monsieur Darrel, I have never had the faintest idea that you were the murderer!"

The four gendarmes and I walked across the road to the Groix Inn and entered the café. It was crowded with Britons, smoking, drinking, and jabbering in half a dozen dialects, all equally unsatisfactory to a civilized ear; and I pushed through the crowd to where little Max Fortin, the chemist of Quimperlé, stood smoking a vile cigar.

"This is a bad business," he said, shaking hands and offering me the mate to his cigar, which I politely declined.

"Now, Monsieur Fortin," I said, "it appears that the Purple Emperor found my handkerchief near the murdered man's door this morning, and so he concludes"—here I glared at the Purple Emperor—"that I am the assassin. I will now ask him a question," and turning on him suddenly, I shouted, "What were you doing at the Red Admiral's door?"

The Purple Emperor started and turned pale, and I pointed at him triumphantly.

"See what a sudden question will do. Look how embarrassed he is, and yet I do not charge him with murder; and I tell you, gentlemen, that man there knows as well as I do who was the murderer of the Red Admiral!"

"I don't!" bawled the Purple Emperor.

"You do," I said. "It was Yves Terrec."

"I don't believe it," he said obstinately, dropping his voice.

"Of course not, being pig-headed."

"I am not pig-headed," he roared again, "but I am mayor of St. Gildas, and I do not believe that Yves Terrec killed his father."

"You saw him try to kill him last night?"

The mayor grunted.

"And you saw what I did."

He grunted again.

"And," I went on, "you heard Yves Terrec threaten to kill his father. You heard him curse the Red Admiral and swear to kill him. Now the father is murdered and his body is gone."

"And your handkerchief?" sneered the Purple Emperor.

"I dropped it, of course."

"And the seaweed gatherer who saw you last night lurking about the Red Admiral's cottage," grinned the Purple Emperor.

I was startled at the man's malice.

"That will do," I said. "It is perfectly true that I was walking on the Bannalec road last night, and that I stopped to close the Red Admiral's door, which was ajar, although his light was not burning. After that I went up the road to the Dinez Woods, and then walked over by St. Julien, whence I saw the seaweed gatherer on the cliffs. He was near enough for me to hear what he sang. What of that?"

"What did you do then?"

"Then I stopped at the shrine and said a prayer, and then I went to bed and slept until Brigadier Durand's gendarmes awoke me with their clatter."

"Now, Monsieur Darrel," said the Purple Emperor, lifting a fat finger and shooting a wicked glance at me, "Now, Monsieur Darrel, which did you wear last night on your midnight stroll—sabots or shoes?"

I thought a moment. "Shoes—no, sabots. I just slipped on my chaussons and went out in my sabots."

"Which was it, shoes or sabots?" snarled the Purple Emperor.

"Sabots, you fool."

"Are these your sabots?" he asked, lifting up a wooden shoe with my initials cut on the instep.

"Yes," I replied.

"Then how did this blood come on the other one?" he shouted, and held up a sabot, the mate to the first, on which a drop of blood had spattered.

"I haven't the least idea," I said calmly; but my heart was beating very fast and I was furiously angry.

"You blockhead!" I said, controlling my rage, "I'll make you pay for this when they catch Yves Terrec and convict him. Brigadier Durand, do your duty if you think I am under suspicion. Arrest me, but grant me one favour. Put me in the Red Admiral's cottage, and I'll see whether I can't find some clue that you have overlooked. Of course, I won't disturb anything until the Commissaire arrives. Bah! You all make me very ill."

"He's hardened," observed the Purple Emperor, wagging his head.

"What motive had I to kill the Red Admiral?" I asked them all scornfully. And they all cried:

"None! Yves Terrec is the man!"

Passing out of the door I swung around and shook my finger at the Purple Emperor.

"Oh, I'll make you dance for this, my friend," I said; and I followed Brigadier Durand across the street to the cottage of the murdered man.

III

They took me at my word and placed a gendarme with a bared sabre at the gateway by the hedge.

"Give me your parole," said poor Durand, "and I will let you go where you wish." But I refused, and began prowling about the cottage looking for clues. I found lots of things that some people would have considered most important, such as ashes from the Red Admiral's pipe, footprints in a dusty vegetable bin, bottles smelling of Pouldu cider, and dust—oh, lots of dust!—but I was not an expert, only a stupid, everyday amateur; so I defaced the footprints with my thick shooting boots, and I declined to examine the pipe ashes through a microscope, although the Red Admiral's microscope stood on the table close at hand.

At last I found what I had been looking for, some long wisps of straw, curiously depressed and flattened in the middle, and I was certain I had found the evidence that would settle Yves Terrec for the rest of his life. It was plain as the nose on your face. The straws were sabot straws, flattened where the foot had pressed them, and sticking straight out where they projected beyond the sabot. Now nobody in St. Gildas used straw in sabots except a fisherman who lived near St. Julien, and the straw in his sabots was ordinary yellow wheat straw! This straw, or rather these straws, were from the stalks of the red wheat which only grows inland, and which, everybody in St. Gildas knew, Yves Terrec wore in his sabots. I was perfectly satisfied; and when, three hours later, a hoarse shouting from the Bannalec Road brought me to the window, I was not surprised to see Yves Terrec, bloody, dishevelled, hatless, with his strong arms bound behind him, walking with bent head between two mounted gendarmes. The crowd around him swelled every minute, crying: Parricide! parricide! Death to the murderer!" As he passed my window I saw great clots of mud on his dusty sabots, from the heels of which projected wisps of red wheat straw. Then I walked back into the Red Admiral's study, determined to find what the microscope would show on the wheat straws. I examined each one very carefully, and then, my eyes aching, I rested my chin on my hand and leaned back in the chair. I had not been as fortunate as some detectives, for there was no evidence that the straws had ever been used in a sabot at all. Furthermore, directly across the hallway stood a carved Breton chest, and now I noticed for the first time that, from beneath the closed lid, doxens of similar red wheat straws projected, bent exactly as mine were bent by the weight of the lid.

I yawned in disgust. It was apparent that I was not cut out for a detective, and I bitterly pondered over the difference between clues in real life and clues in a detective story. After a while I rose, walked over to the chest and opened the lid. The interior was wadded with the red wheat straws, and on this wadding lay two curious glass jars, two or three small vials, several empty bottles labelled chloroform, a collecting jar of cyanide of potassium, and a book. In a farther corner of the chest were some letters bearing English stamps, and also the torn coverings of two parcels, all from England, and all directed to the Red Admiral under his proper name of "Sieur Louis Jean Terrec, St. Gildas, par Moëlan, Finistère."

All these traps I carried over to the desk, shut the lid of the chest, and sat down to read the letters. They were written in commercial French, evidently by an Englishman.

Freely translated, the contents of the first letter were as follows:

"LONDON, *June 12, 1894.*

"DEAR MONSIEUR (*sic*):

"Your kind favour of the 19th inst. received and contents noted. The latest work on the Lepidoptera of England is Blowzer's How to catch British Butterflies, with notes and tables, and an introduction by Sir Thomas Sniffer. The price of this work (in one volume, calf) is £5 or 125 francs of French money. A post-office order will receive our prompt attention. We beg to remain,

"Yours, etc.,

"FRADLEY & TOOMER,

"470 Regent Square,

London, S. W."

The next letter was even less interesting. It merely stated that the money had been received and the book would be forwarded. The third engaged my attention, and I shall quote it, the translation being a free one:

"DEAR SIR:

"Your letter of the 1st of July was duly received, and we at once referred it to Mr. Fradley himself. Mr. Fradley being much interested in your question, sent your letter to Professor Schweineri, of the Berlin Entomological Society, whose note Blowzer refers to on page 630, in his How to catch British Butterflies. We have just received an answer from Professor Schweineri, which we translate into French—(see inclosed slip). Professor Schweineri begs to present to you two jars of cythyl, prepared under his own supervision. We forward the same to you. Trusting that you will find everything satisfactory, we remain,

"Yours sincerely,

"FRADLEY & TOOMER."

The enclosed slip read as follows:

> "Messrs. FRADLEY & TOOMER,
>
> "GENTLEMEN: Cythaline, a complex hydrocarbon, was first used by Professor Schnoot, of Antwerp, a year ago. I discovered an analogous formula about the same time and named it cythyl. I have used it with great success everywhere. It is as certain as a magnet. I beg to present you three small jars, and would be pleased to have you forward two of them to your correspondent in St. Gildas with my compliments. Blowzer's quotation of me, on page 630 of his glorious work, How to catch British Butterflies, is correct.
>
> "Yours, etc.,
>
> "HEINRICH SCHWEINERI,
>
> PhD, DD, DS, MS."

When I had finished this letter I folded it up and put it into my pocket with the others. Then I opened Blowzer's valuable work, How to catch British Butterflies, and turned to page 630.

Now, although the Red Admiral could only have acquired the book very recently, and although all the other pages were perfectly clean, this particular page was thumbed black, and heavy pencil marks enclosed a paragraph at the bottom of the page. This is the paragraph:

> "Professor Schweineri says: 'Of the two old methods used by collectors for the capture of the swift-winged, high-flying Apatura Iris, or Purple Emperor, the first, which was using a long-handled net, proved successful once in a thousand times; and the second, the placing of bait upon the ground, such as decayed meat, dead cats, rats, etc., was not only disagreeable, even for an enthusiastic collector, but also very uncertain. Once in five hundred times would the splendid butterfly leave the tops of his

> favourite oak trees to circle about the fetid bait offered. I have found cythyl a perfectly sure bait to draw this beautiful butterfly to the ground, where it can be easily captured. An ounce of cythyl placed in a yellow saucer under an oak tree, will draw to it every Apatura Iris within a radius of twenty miles. So, if any collector who possesses a little cythyl, even though it be in a sealed bottle in his pocket—if such a collector does not find a single Apatura Iris fluttering close about him within an hour, let him be satisfied that the Apatura Iris does not inhabit his country.'"

When I had finished reading this note I sat for a long while thinking hard. Then I examined the two jars. They were labelled *"Cythyl."* One was full, the other *nearly full.* "The rest must be on the corpse of the Red Admiral," I thought, "no matter if it is in a corked bottle——"

I took all the things back to the chest, laid them carefully on the straw, and closed the lid. The gendarme sentinel at the gate saluted me respectfully as I crossed over to the Groix Inn. The Inn was surrounded by an excited crowd, and the hallway was choked with gendarmes and peasants. On every side they greeted me cordially, announcing that the real murderer was caught; but I pushed by them without a word and ran upstairs to find Lys. She opened her door when I knocked and threw both arms about my neck. I took her to my breast and kissed her. After a moment I asked her if she would obey me no matter what I commanded, and she said she would, with a proud humility that touched me.

"Then go at once to Yvette in St. Julien," I said. "Ask her to harness the dog-cart and drive you to the convent in Quimperlé. Wait for me there. Will you do this without questioning me, my darling?"

She raised her face to mine. "Kiss me," she said innocently; the next moment she had vanished.

I walked deliberately into the Purple Emperor's room and peered into the gauze-covered box which had held the chrysalis of Apatura Iris. It was as I expected. The chrysalis was empty and transparent, and a great crack ran down the middle of its back, but, on the netting inside the box, a magnificent butterfly slowly waved its burnished purple wings; for the chrysalis had given up its silent tenant, the butterfly symbol of immortality: Then a great fear fell upon me. I know now that it was the fear of the Black Priest, but neither then nor for years after did I know that the Black Priest had ever lived on earth. As I bent over the box I heard a confused murmur outside the house which ended in a furious shout of "Parricide!" and I heard the gendarmes ride away behind a wagon which rattled sharply on the flinty highway. I went to the window. In the wagon sat Yves Terrec, bound and wild-eyed, two gendarmes at either side of him, and all around the wagon rode mounted gendarmes whose bared sabres scarcely kept the crowd away.

"Parricide!" they howled. "Let him die!"

I stepped back and opened the gauze-covered box. Very gently but firmly I took the splendid butterfly by its closed fore wings and lifted it unharmed between my thumb and forefinger. Then, holding it concealed behind my back, I went down into the café.

Of all the crowd that had filled it, shouting for the death of Yves Terrec, only three persons remained seated in front of the huge empty fireplace. They were the Brigadier Durand, Max Fortin, the chemist of Quimperlé, and the Purple Emperor. The latter looked abashed when I entered, but I paid no attention to him and walked straight to the chemist.

"Monsieur Fortin," I said, "do you know much about hydrocarbons?"

"They are my specialty," he said astonished.

"Have you ever heard of such a thing as cythyl?"

"Schweineri's cythyl? Oh, yes! We use it in perfumery."

"Good!" I said. "Has it an odour?"

"No—and, yes. One is always aware of its presence, but really nobody can affirm it has an odour. It is curious," he continued, looking at me, "it is very curious you should have asked me that, for all day I have been imagining I detected the presence of cythyl."

"Do you imagine so now?" I asked.

"Yes, more than ever."

I sprang to the front door and tossed out the butterfly. The splendid creature beat the air for a moment, flitted uncertainly hither and thither, and then, to my astonishment, sailed majestically back into the café and alighted on the hearthstone. For a moment I was nonplussed, but when my eyes rested on the Purple Emperor I comprehended in a flash.

"Lift that hearthstone!" I cried to the Brigadier Durand; "pry it up with your scabbard!"

The Purple Emperor suddenly fell forward in his chair, his face ghastly white, his jaw loose with terror.

"What is cythyl?" I shouted, seizing him by the arm; but he plunged heavily from his chair, face downward on the floor, and at the same moment a cry from the chemist made me turn. There stood the Brigadier Durand, one hand supporting the hearthstone, one hand raised in horror. There stood Max Fortin, the chemist, rigid with excitement, and below, in the hollow bed where the hearthstone had rested, lay a crushed mass of bleeding human flesh, from the midst of which stared a cheap glass eye. I seized the Purple Emperor and dragged him to his feet.

"Look!" I cried; "look at your old friend, the Red Admiral!" but he only smiled in a vacant way, and rolled his head muttering; "Bait for butterflies! Cythyl! Oh, no, no, no! You can't do it, Admiral, d'ye see. I alone own the Purple Emperor! I alone am the Purple Emperor!"

And the same carriage that bore me to Quimperlé to claim my bride, carried him to Quimper, gagged and bound, a foaming, howling lunatic.

* * * * * * *

This, then, is the story of the Purple Emperor. I might tell you a pleasanter story if I chose; but concerning the fish that I had hold of, whether it was a salmon, a grilse, or a sea trout, I may not say, because I have promised Lys, and she has promised me, that no power on earth shall wring from our lips the mortifying confession that the fish escaped.

THE MESSENGER

Little gray messenger,
Robed like painted Death,
Your robe is dust.
Whom do you seek
Among lilies and closed buds
At dusk?

Among lilies and closed buds
At dusk,
Whom do you seek,
Little gray messenger,
Robed in the awful panoply
Of painted Death?

R. W. C.

All-wise,
Hast thou seen all there is to see with thy two eyes?
Dost thou know all there is to know, and so,
Omniscient,
Darest thou still to say thy brother lies?

R. W. C.

"THE BULLET ENTERED HERE," SAID MAX FORTIN, AND HE placed his middle finger over a smooth hole exactly in the centre of the forehead.

I sat down upon a mound of dry seaweed and unslung my fowling piece.

The little chemist cautiously felt the edges of the shot-hole, first with his middle finger, then with his thumb.

"Let me see the skull again," said I.

Max Fortin picked it up from the sod.

"It's like all the others," he observed. I nodded, without offering to take it from him. After a moment he thoughtfully replaced it upon the grass at my feet.

"It's like all the others," he repeated, wiping his glasses on his handkerchief. "I thought you might care to see one of the skulls, so I brought this over from the gravel pit. The men from Bannalec are digging yet. They ought to stop."

"How many skulls are there altogether?" I inquired.

"They found thirty-eight skulls; there are thirty-nine noted in the list. They lie piled up in the gravel pit on the edge of Le Bihan's wheat field. The men are at work yet. Le Bihan is going to stop them."

"Let's go over," said I; and I picked up my gun and started across the cliffs, Fortin on one side, Môme on the other.

"Who has the list?" I asked, lighting my pipe. "You say there is a list?"

"The list was found rolled up in a brass cylinder," said the little chemist. He added: "You should not smoke here. You know that if a single spark drifted into the wheat——"

"Ah, but I have a cover to my pipe," said I, smiling.

Fortin watched me as I closed the pepperbox arrangement over the glowing bowl of the pipe. Then he continued:

"The list was made out on thick yellow paper; the brass tube has preserved it. It is as fresh to-day as it was in 1760. You shall see it."

"Is that the date?"

"The list is dated 'April, 1760.' The Brigadier Durand has it. It is not written in French."

"Not written in French!" I exclaimed.

"No," replied Fortin solemnly, "it is written in Breton."

"But," I protested, "the Breton language was never written or printed in 1760."

"Except by priests," said the chemist.

"I have heard of but one priest who ever wrote the Breton language," I began.

Fortin stole a glance at my face.

"You mean—the Black Priest?" he asked.

I nodded.

Fortin opened his mouth to speak again, hesitated, and finally shut his teeth obstinately over the wheat stem that he was chewing.

"And the Black Priest?" I suggested encouragingly. But I knew it was useless; for it is easier to move the stars from their courses than to make an obstinate Breton talk. We walked on for a minute or two in silence.

"Where is the Brigadier Durand?" I asked, motioning Môme to come out of the wheat, which he was trampling as though it were heather. As I spoke we came in sight of the farther edge of the wheat field and the dark, wet mass of cliffs beyond.

"Durand is down there—you can see him; he stands just behind the Mayor of St. Gildas."

"I see," said I; and we struck straight down, following a sun-baked cattle path across the heather.

When we reached the edge of the wheat field, Le Bihan, the Mayor of St. Gildas, called to me, and I tucked my gun under my arm and skirted the wheat to where he stood.

"Thirty-eight skulls," he said in his thin, high-pitched voice; "there is but one more, and I am opposed to further search. I suppose Fortin told you?"

I shook hands with him, and returned the salute of the Brigadier Durand.

"I am opposed to further search," repeated Le Bihan, nervously picking at the mass of silver buttons which covered the front of his velvet and broadcloth jacket like a breastplate of scale armour.

Durand pursed up his lips, twisted his tremendous mustache, and hooked his thumbs in his sabre belt.

"As for me," he said, "I am in favour of further search."

"Further search for what—for the thirty-ninth skull?" I asked.

Le Bihan nodded. Durand frowned at the sunlit sea, rocking like a bowl of molten gold from the cliffs to the horizon. I followed his eyes. On the dark glistening cliffs, silhouetted against the glare of the sea, sat a cormorant, black, motionless, its horrible head raised toward heaven.

"Where is that list, Durand?" I asked.

The gendarme rummaged in his despatch pouch and produced a brass cylinder about a foot long. Very gravely he unscrewed the head and dumped out a scroll of thick yellow paper closely covered with writing on both sides. At a nod from Le Bihan he handed me the scroll. But I could make nothing of the coarse writing, now faded to a dull brown.

"Come, come, Le Bihan," I said impatiently, "translate it, won't you? You and Max Fortin make a lot of mystery out of nothing, it seems."

Le Bihan went to the edge of the pit where the three Bannalec men were digging, gave an order or two in Breton, and turned to me.

As I came to the edge of the pit the Bannalec men were removing a square piece of sailcloth from what appeared to be a pile of cobblestones.

"Look!" said Le Bihan shrilly. I looked. The pile below was a heap of skulls. After a moment I clambered down the gravel sides of the pit and walked over to the men of Bannalec. They saluted me gravely, leaning on their picks and shovels, and wiping their sweating faces with sunburned hands.

"How many?" said I in Breton.

"Thirty-eight," they replied.

I glanced around. Beyond the heap of skulls lay two piles of human bones. Beside these was a mound of broken, rusted bits of iron and steel. Looking closer, I saw that this mound was composed of rusty bayonets, sabre blades, scythe blades, with here and there a tarnished buckle attached to a bit of leather hard as iron.

I picked up a couple of buttons and a belt plate. The buttons bore the royal arms of England; the belt plate was emblazoned with the English arms, and also with the number "27."

"I have heard my grandfather speak of the terrible English regiment, the 27th Foot, which landed and stormed the fort up there," said one of the Bannalec men.

"Oh!" said I; "then these are the bones of English soldiers?"

"Yes," said the men of Bannalec.

Le Bihan was calling to me from the edge of the pit above, and I handed the belt plate and buttons to the men and climbed the side of the excavation.

"Well," said I, trying to prevent Môme from leaping up and licking my face as I emerged from the pit, "I suppose you know what these bones are. What are you going to do with them?"

"There was a man," said Le Bihan angrily, "an Englishman, who passed here in a dogcart on his way to Quimper about an hour ago, and what do you suppose he wished to do?"

"Buy the relics?" I asked, smiling.

"Exactly—the pig!" piped the mayor of St. Gildas. "Jean Marie Tregunc, who found the bones, was standing there where Max Fortin stands, and do you know what he answered? He spat upon the ground, and said: 'Pig of an Englishman, do you take me for a desecrator of graves?'"

I knew Tregunc, a sober, blue-eyed Breton, who lived from one year's end to the other without being able to afford a single bit of meat for a meal.

"How much did the Englishman offer Tregunc?" I asked.

"Two hundred francs for the skulls alone."

I thought of the relic hunters and the relic buyers on the battlefields of our civil war.

"Seventeen hundred and sixty is long ago," I said.

"Respect for the dead can never die," said Fortin.

"And the English soldiers came here to kill your fathers and burn your homes," I continued.

"They were murderers and thieves, but—they are dead," said Tregunc, coming up from the beach below, his long sea rake balanced on his dripping jersey.

"How much do you earn every year, Jean Marie?" I asked, turning to shake hands with him.

"Two hundred and twenty francs, monsieur."

"Forty-five dollars a year," I said. "Bah! you are worth more, Jean. Will you take care of my garden for me? My wife wished me to ask you. I think it would be worth one hundred francs a month to you and to me. Come on, Le Bihan—come along, Fortin—and you, Durand. I want somebody to translate that list into French for me."

Tregunc stood gazing at me, his blue eyes dilated.

"You may begin at once," I said, smiling, "if the salary suits you?"

"It suits," said Tregunc, fumbling for his pipe in a silly way that annoyed Le Bihan.

"Then go and begin your work," cried the mayor impatiently; and Tregunc started across the moors toward St. Gildas, taking off his velvet-ribboned cap to me and gripping his sea rake very hard.

"You offer him more than my salary," said the mayor, after a moment's contemplation of his silver buttons.

"Pooh!" said I, "what do you do for your salary except play dominoes with Max Fortin at the Groix Inn?"

Le Bihan turned red, but Durand rattled his sabre and winked at Max Fortin, and I slipped my arm through the arm of the sulky magistrate, laughing.

"There's a shady spot under the cliff," I said; "come on, Le Bihan, and read me what is in the scroll."

In a few moments we reached the shadow of the cliff, and I threw myself upon the turf, chin on hand, to listen.

The gendarme, Durand, also sat down, twisting his mustache into needlelike points. Fortin leaned against the cliff, polishing his glasses and examining us with vague, near-sighted eyes; and Le Bihan, the mayor, planted himself in our midst, rolling up the scroll and tucking it under his arm.

"First of all," he began in a shrill voice, "I am going to light my pipe, and while lighting it I shall tell you what I have heard about the attack on the fort yonder. My father told me; his father told him."

He jerked his head in the direction of the ruined fort, a small, square stone structure on the sea cliff, now nothing but crumbling walls. Then he slowly produced a tobacco pouch, a bit of flint and tinder, and a long-stemmed pipe fitted with a microscopical bowl of baked clay. To fill such a pipe requires ten minutes' close attention. To smoke it to a finish takes but four puffs. It is very Breton, this Breton pipe. It is the crystallization of everything Breton.

"Go on," said I, lighting a cigarette.

"The fort," said the mayor, "was built by Louis XIV, and was dismantled twice by the English. Louis XV restored it in 1739. In 1760 it was carried by assault by the English. They came across from the island of Groix—three shiploads—and they stormed the fort and sacked St. Julien yonder, and they started to burn St. Gildas—you can see the marks of their bullets on my house yet; but the men of Bannalec and the men of Lorient fell upon them with pike and scythe and blunderbuss, and those who did not run away lie there below in the gravel pit now—thirty-eight of them."

"And the thirty-ninth skull?" I asked, finishing my cigarette.

The mayor had succeeded in filling his pipe, and now he began to put his tobacco pouch away.

"The thirty-ninth skull," he mumbled, holding the pipestem between his defective teeth—"the thirty-ninth skull is no business of mine. I have told the Bannalec men to cease digging."

"But what is—whose is the missing skull?" I persisted curiously.

The mayor was busy trying to strike a spark to his tinder. Presently he set it aglow, applied it to his pipe, took the prescribed four puffs, knocked the ashes out of the bowl, and gravely replaced the pipe in his pocket.

"The missing skull?" he asked.

"Yes," said I impatiently.

The mayor slowly unrolled the scroll and began to read, translating from the Breton into French. And this is what he read:

"On the Cliffs of St. Gildas,
"April 13, 1760.

"On this day, by order of the Count of Soisic, general in chief of the Breton forces now lying in Kerselec Forest, the bodies of thirty-eight English soldiers of the 27th, 50th, and 72d regiments of Foot were buried in this spot, together with their arms and equipments."

The mayor paused and glanced at me reflectively.

"Go on, Le Bihan," I said.

"With them," continued the mayor, turning the scroll and reading on the other side, "was buried the body of that vile traitor who betrayed the fort to the English. The manner of his death was as follows: By order of the most noble Count of Soisic, the traitor was first branded upon the forehead with the brand of an arrowhead. The iron burned through the flesh, and was pressed heavily so that the brand should even burn into the bone of the skull. The traitor was then led out and bidden to kneel. He admitted having guided the English from the island of Groix. Although a priest and a Frenchman, he had violated his priestly office to aid him in discovering the password to the fort. This password he extorted during confession from a young Breton girl who was in the habit of rowing across from the island of Groix to visit her husband in the fort. When the fort fell, this young girl, crazed by the death of her husband, sought the Count of Soisic and told how the priest had forced her to confess to him all she knew about the fort. The priest was arrested at St. Gildas as he was about to cross the river to Lorient. When arrested he cursed the girl, Marie Trevec——"

"What!" I exclaimed, "Marie Trevec!"

"Marie Trevec," repeated Le Bihan; "the priest cursed Marie Trevec, and all her family and descendants. He was shot as he knelt, having a mask of leather over his face, because the Bretons who composed the squad of execution refused to fire at a priest unless his face was concealed. The priest was l'Abbé Sorgue, commonly known as the Black Priest on account of his dark face and swarthy eyebrows. He was buried with a stake through his heart."

Le Bihan paused, hesitated, looked at me, and handed the manuscript back to Durand. The gendarme took it and slipped it into the brass cylinder.

"So," said I, "the thirty-ninth skull is the skull of the Black Priest."

"Yes," said Fortin. "I hope they won't find it."

"I have forbidden them to proceed," said the mayor querulously. "You heard me, Max Fortin."

I rose and picked up my gun. Môme came and pushed his head into my hand.

"That's a fine dog," observed Durand, also rising.

"Why don't you wish to find his skull?" I asked Le Bihan. "It would be curious to see whether the arrow brand really burned into the bone."

"There is something in that scroll that I didn't read to you," said the mayor grimly. "Do you wish to know what it is?"

"Of course," I replied in surprise.

"Give me the scroll again, Durand," he said; then he read from the bottom: "I, l'Abbé Sorgue, forced to write the above by my executioners, have written it in my own blood; and with it I leave my curse. My curse on St. Gildas, on Marie Trevec, and on her descendants. I will come back to St. Gildas when my remains are disturbed. Woe to that Englishman whom my branded skull shall touch!"

"What rot!" I said. "Do you believe it was really written in his own blood?"

"I am going to test it," said Fortin, "at the request of Monsieur le Maire. I am not anxious for the job, however."

"See," said Le Bihan, holding out the scroll to me, "it is signed, 'l'Abbé Sorgue.'"

I glanced curiously over the paper.

"It must be the Black Priest," I said. "He was the only man who wrote in the Breton language. This is a wonderfully interesting discovery, for now, at last, the mystery of the Black Priest's disappearance is cleared up. You will, of course, send this scroll to Paris, Le Bihan?"

"No," said the mayor obstinately, "it shall be buried in the pit below where the rest of the Black Priest lies."

I looked at him and recognised that argument would be useless. But still I said, "It will be a loss to history, Monsieur Le Bihan."

"All the worse for history, then," said the enlightened Mayor of St. Gildas.

We had sauntered back to the gravel pit while speaking. The men of Bannalec were carrying the bones of the English soldiers toward the St. Gildas cemetery, on the cliffs to the east, where already a knot of white-coiffed women stood in attitudes of prayer; and I saw the sombre robe of a priest among the crosses of the little graveyard.

"They were thieves and assassins; they are dead now," muttered Max Fortin.

"Respect the dead," repeated the Mayor of St. Gildas, looking after the Bannalec men.

"It was written in that scroll that Marie Trevec, of Groix Island, was cursed by the priest—she and her descendants," I said, touching Le Bihan on the arm. "There was a Marie Trevec who married an Yves Trevec of St. Gildas——"

"It is the same," said Le Bihan, looking at me obliquely.

"Oh!" said I; "then they were ancestors of my wife."

"Do you fear the curse?" asked Le Bihan.

"What?" I laughed.

"There was the case of the Purple Emperor," said Max Fortin timidly.

Startled for a moment, I faced him, then shrugged my shoulders and kicked at a smooth bit of rock which lay near the edge of the pit, almost embedded in gravel.

"Do you suppose the Purple Emperor drank himself crazy because he was descended from Marie Trevec?" I asked contemptuously.

"Of course not," said Max Fortin hastily.

"Of course not," piped the mayor. "I only——Hello! what's that you're kicking?"

"What?" said I, glancing down, at the same time involuntarily giving another kick. The smooth bit of rock dislodged itself and rolled out of the loosened gravel at my feet.

"The thirty-ninth skull!" I exclaimed. "By jingo, its the noddle of the Black Priest! See! there is the arrowhead branded on the front!"

The mayor stepped back. Max Fortin also retreated. There was a pause, during which I looked at them, and they looked anywhere but at me.

"I don't like it," said the mayor at last, in a husky, high voice. "I don't like it! The scroll says he will come back to St. Gildas when his remains are disturbed. I—I don't like it, Monsieur Darrel——"

"Bosh!" said I; "the poor wicked devil is where he can't get out. For Heaven's sake, Le Bihan, what is this stuff you are talking in the year of grace 1896?"

The mayor gave me a look.

"And he says 'Englishman.' You are an Englishman, Monsieur Darrel," he announced.

"You know better. You know I'm an American."

"It's all the same," said the Mayor of St. Gildas, obstinately.

"No, it isn't!" I answered, much exasperated, and deliberately pushed the skull till it rolled into the bottom of the gravel pit below.

"Cover it up," said I; "bury the scroll with it too, if you insist, but I think you ought to send it to Paris. Don't look so gloomy, Fortin, unless you believe in were-wolves and ghosts. Hey! what the—what the devil's the matter with you, anyway? What are you staring at, Le Bihan?"

"Come, come," muttered the mayor in a low, tremulous voice, "it's time we got out of this. Did you see? Did you see, Fortin?"

"I saw," whispered Max Fortin, pallid with fright.

The two men were almost running across the sunny pasture now, and I hastened after them, demanding to know what was the matter.

"Matter!" chattered the mayor, gasping with exasperation and terror. "The skull is rolling uphill again!" and he burst into a terrified gallop. Max Fortin followed close behind.

I watched them stampeding across the pasture, then turned toward the gravel pit, mystified, incredulous. The skull was lying on the edge of the pit, exactly where it had been before I pushed it over the edge. For a second I stared at it; a singular chilly feeling crept up my spinal column, and I turned and walked away, sweat starting from the root of every hair on my head. Before I had gone twenty paces the absurdity of the whole thing struck me. I halted, hot with shame and annoyance, and retraced my steps.

There lay the skull.

"I rolled a stone down instead of the skull," I muttered to myself. Then with the butt of my gun I pushed the skull over the edge of the pit and watched it roll to the bottom; and as it struck the bottom of the pit, Môme, my dog, suddenly whipped his tail between his legs, whimpered, and made off across the moor.

"Môme!" I shouted, angry and astonished; but the dog only fled the faster, and I ceased calling from sheer surprise.

"What the mischief is the matter with that dog!" I thought. He had never before played me such a trick.

Mechanically I glanced into the pit, but I could not see the skull. I looked down. The skull lay at my feet again, touching them.

"Good heavens!" I stammered, and struck at it blindly with my gunstock. The ghastly thing flew into the air, whirling over and over, and rolled again down the sides of the pit to the bottom. Breathlessly I stared at it, then, confused and scarcely comprehending, I stepped back from the pit, still facing it, one, ten, twenty paces, my eyes almost starting from my head, as though I expected to see the thing roll up from the bottom of the pit under my very gaze. At last I turned my back to the pit and strode out across the gorse-covered moorland toward my home. As I reached the road that winds from St. Gildas to St. Julien I gave one hasty glance at the pit over my shoulder. The sun shone hot on the sod about the excavation. There was something white and bare and round on the turf at the edge of the pit. It might have been a stone; there were plenty of them lying about.

II

When I entered my garden I saw Môme sprawling on the stone doorstep. He eyed me sideways and flopped his tail.

"Are you not mortified, you idiot dog?" I said, looking about the upper windows for Lys.

Môme rolled over on his back and raised one deprecating forepaw, as though to ward off calamity.

"Don't act as though I was in the habit of beating you to death," I said, disgusted. I had never in my life raised whip to the brute. "But you are a fool dog," I continued. "No, you needn't come to be babied and wept over; Lys can do that, if she insists, but I am ashamed of you, and you can go to the devil."

Môme slunk off into the house, and I followed, mounting directly to my wife's boudoir. It was empty.

"Where has she gone?" I said, looking hard at Môme, who had followed me. "Oh! I see you don't know. Don't pretend you do. Come off that lounge! Do you think Lys wants tan-coloured hairs all over her lounge?"

I rang the bell for Catherine and 'Fine, but they didn't know where "madame" had gone; so I went into my room, bathed, exchanged my somewhat grimy shooting clothes for a suit of warm, soft knickerbockers, and, after lingering some extra moments over my toilet—for I was particular, now that I had married Lys—I went down to the garden and took a chair out under the fig-trees.

"Where can she be?" I wondered. Môme came sneaking out to be comforted, and I forgave him for Lys's sake, whereupon he frisked.

"You bounding cur," said I, "now what on earth started you off across the moor? If you do it again I'll push you along with a charge of dust shot."

As yet I had scarcely dared think about the ghastly hallucination of which I had been a victim, but now I faced it squarely, flushing a little with mortification at the thought of my hasty retreat from the gravel pit.

"To think," I said aloud, "that those old woman's tales of Max Fortin and Le Bihan should have actually made me see what didn't exist at all! I lost my nerve like a schoolboy in a dark bedroom." For I knew now that I had mistaken a round stone for a skull each time, and had pushed a couple of big pebbles into the pit instead of the skull itself.

"By jingo!" said I, "I'm nervous; my liver must be in a devil of a condition if I see such things when I'm awake! Lys will know what to give me."

I felt mortified and irritated and sulky, and thought disgustedly of Le Bihan and Max Fortin.

But after a while I ceased speculating, dismissed the mayor, the chemist, and the skull from my mind, and smoked pensively, watching the sun low dipping in the western ocean. As the twilight fell for a moment over ocean and moorland, a wistful, restless happiness filled my heart, the happiness that all men know—all men who have loved.

Slowly the purple mist crept out over the sea; the cliffs darkened; the forest was shrouded.

Suddenly the sky above burned with the afterglow, and the world was alight again.

Cloud after cloud caught the rose dye; the cliffs were tinted with it; moor and pasture, heather and forest burned and pulsated with the gentle flush. I saw the gulls turning and tossing above the sand bar, their snowy wings tipped with pink; I saw the sea swallows sheering the surface of the still river, stained to its placid depths with warm reflections of the clouds. The twitter of drowsy hedge birds broke out in the stillness; a salmon rolled its shining side above tide-water.

The interminable monotone of the ocean intensified the silence. I sat motionless, holding my breath as one who listens to the first low rumour of an organ. All at once the pure whistle of a nightingale cut the silence, and the first moonbeam silvered the wastes of mist-hung waters.

I raised my head.

Lys stood before me in the garden.

When we had kissed each other, we linked arms and moved up and down the gravel walks, watching the moonbeams sparkle on the sand bar as the tide ebbed and ebbed. The broad beds of white pinks about us were atremble with hovering white moths; the October roses hung all abloom, perfuming the salt wind.

"Sweetheart," I said, "where is Yvonne? Has she promised to spend Christmas with us?"

"Yes, Dick; she drove me down from Plougat this afternoon. She sent her love to you. I am not jealous. What did you shoot?"

"A hare and four partridges. They are in the gun room. I told Catherine not to touch them until you had seen them."

Now I suppose I knew that Lys could not be particularly enthusiastic over game or guns; but she pretended she was, and always scornfully denied that it was for my sake and not for the pure love of sport. So she dragged me off to inspect the rather meagre game bag, and she paid me pretty compliments and gave a little cry of delight and pity as I lifted the enormous hare out of the sack by his ears.

"He'll eat no more of our lettuce," I said, attempting to justify the assassination.

"Unhappy little bunny—and what a beauty! O Dick, you are a splendid shot, are you not?"

I evaded the question and hauled out a partridge.

"Poor little dead things!" said Lys in a whisper; "it seems a pity—doesn't it, Dick? But then you are so clever——"

"We'll have them broiled," I said guardedly; "tell Catherine."

Catherine came in to take away the game, and presently 'Fine Lelocard, Lys's maid, announced dinner, and Lys tripped away to her boudoir.

I stood an instant contemplating her blissfully, thinking, "My boy, you're the happiest fellow in the world—you're in love with your wife!"

I walked into the dining room, beamed at the plates, walked out again; met Tregunc in the hallway, beamed on him; glanced into the kitchen, beamed at Catherine, and went up stairs, still beaming.

Before I could knock at Lys's door it opened, and Lys came hastily out. When she saw me she gave a little cry of relief, and nestled close to my breast.

"There is something peering in at my window," she said.

"What!" I cried angrily.

"A man, I think, disguised as a priest, and he has a mask on. He must have climbed up by the bay tree."

I was down the stairs and out of doors in no time. The moonlit garden was absolutely deserted. Tregunc came up, and together we searched the hedge and shrubbery around the house and out to the road.

"Jean Marie," said I at length, "loose my bulldog—he knows you—and take your supper on the porch where you can watch. My wife says the fellow is disguised as a priest, and wears a mask."

Tregunc showed his white teeth in a smile. "He will not care to venture in here again, I think, Monsieur Darrel."

I went back and found Lys seated quietly at the table.

"The soup is ready, dear," she said. "Don't worry; it was only some foolish lout from Bannalec. No one in St. Gildas or St. Julien would do such a thing."

I was too much exasperated to reply at first, but Lys treated it as a stupid joke, and after a while I began to look at it in that light.

Lys told me about Yvonne, and reminded me of my promise to have Herbert Stuart down to meet her.

"You wicked diplomat!" I protested. "Herbert is in Paris, and hard at work for the Salon."

"Don't you think he might spare a week to flirt with the prettiest girl in Finistère?" inquired Lys innocently.

"Prettiest girl! Not much!" I said.

"Who is, then?" urged Lys.

I laughed a trifle sheepishly.

"I suppose you mean me, Dick," said Lys, colouring up.

"Now I bore you, don't I?"

"Bore me? Ah, no, Dick."

After coffee and cigarettes were served I spoke about Tregunc, and Lys approved.

"Poor Jean! he will be glad, won't he? What a dear fellow you are!"

"Nonsense," said I; "we need a gardener; you said so yourself, Lys."

But Lys leaned over and kissed me, and then bent down and hugged Môme, who whistled through his nose in sentimental appreciation.

"I am a very happy woman," said Lys.

"Môme was a very bad dog to-day," I observed.

"Poor Môme!" said Lys, smiling.

When dinner was over and Môme lay snoring before the blaze—for the October nights are often chilly in Finistère—Lys curled up in the chimney corner with her embroidery, and gave me a swift glance from under her drooping lashes.

"You look like a schoolgirl, Lys," I said teasingly. "I don't believe you are sixteen yet."

She pushed back her heavy burnished hair thoughtfully. Her wrist was as white as surf foam.

"Have we been married four years? I don't believe it," I said.

She gave me another swift glance and touched the embroidery on her knee, smiling faintly.

"I see," said I, also smiling at the embroidered garment. "Do you think it will fit?"

"Fit?" repeated Lys. Then she laughed.

"And," I persisted, "are you perfectly sure that you—er—we shall need it?"

"Perfectly," said Lys. A delicate colour touched her cheeks and neck. She held up the little garment, all fluffy with misty lace and wrought with quaint embroidery.

"It is very gorgeous," said I; "don't use your eyes too much, dearest. May I smoke a pipe?"

"Of course," she said, selecting a skein of pale blue silk.

For a while I sat and smoked in silence, watching her slender fingers among the tinted silks and thread of gold.

Presently she spoke: "What did you say your crest is, Dick?"

"My crest? Oh, something or other rampant on a something or other——"

"Dick!"

"Dearest?"

"Don't be flippant."

"But I really forget. It's an ordinary crest; everybody in New York has them. No family should be without 'em."

"You are disagreeable, Dick. Send Josephine upstairs for my album."

"Are you going to put that crest on the—the—whatever it is?"

"I am; and my own crest, too."

I thought of the Purple Emperor and wondered a little.

"You didn't know I had one, did you?" she smiled.

"What is it?" I replied evasively.

"You shall see. Ring for Josephine."

I rang, and, when 'Fine appeared, Lys gave her some orders in a low voice, and Josephine trotted away, bobbing her white-coiffed head with a "Bien, madame!"

After a few minutes she returned, bearing a tattered, musty volume, from which the gold and blue had mostly disappeared.

I took the book in my hands and examined the ancient emblazoned covers.

"Lilies!" I exclaimed.

"Fleur-de-lis," said my wife demurely.

"Oh!" said I, astonished, and opened the book.

"You have never before seen this book?" asked Lys, with a touch of malice in her eyes.

"You know I haven't. Hello! what's this? Oho! So there should be a *de* before Trevec? Lys de Trevec? Then why in the world did the Purple Emperor——"

"Dick!" cried Lys.

"All right," said I. "Shall I read about the Sieur de Trevec who rode to Saladin's tent alone to seek for medicine for St. Louis? or shall I read about—what is it? Oh, here it is, all down in black and white—about the Marquis de Trevec who drowned himself before Alva's eyes rather than surrender the banner of the fleur-de-lis to Spain? It's all written here. But, dear, how about that soldier named Trevec who was killed in the old fort on the cliff yonder?"

"He dropped the *de*, and the Trevecs since then have been Republicans," said Lys—"all except me."

"That's quite right," said I; "it is time that we Republicans should agree upon some feudal system. My dear, I drink to the king!" and I raised my wine-glass and looked at Lys.

"To the king," said Lys, flushing. She smoothed out the tiny garment on her knees; she touched the glass with her lips; her eyes were very sweet. I drained the glass to the king.

After a silence I said: "I will tell the king stories. His Majesty shall be amused."

"His Majesty," repeated Lys softly.

"Or hers," I laughed. "Who knows?"

"Who knows?" murmured Lys, with a gentle sigh.

"I know some stories about Jack the Giant-Killer," I announced. "Do you, Lys?"

"I? No, not about a giant-killer, but I know all about the were-wolf, and Jeanne-la-Flamme, and the Man in Purple Tatters, and—O dear me! I know lots more."

"You are very wise," said I. "I shall teach his Majesty English."

"And I Breton," cried Lys jealously.

"I shall bring playthings to the king," said I—"big green lizards from the gorse, little gray mullets to swim in glass globes, baby rabbits from the forest of Kerselec——"

"And I," said Lys, "will bring the first primrose, the first branch of aubepine, the first jonquil, to the king—my king."

"Our king," said I; and there was peace in Finistère.

I lay back, idly turning the leaves of the curious old volume.

"I am looking," said I, "for the crest."

"The crest, dear? It is a priest's head with an arrow-shaped mark on the forehead, on a field——"

I sat up and stared at my wife.

"Dick, whatever is the matter?" she smiled. "The story is there in that book. Do you care to read it? No? Shall I tell it to you? Well, then: It happened in the third crusade. There was a monk whom men called the Black Priest. He turned apostate, and sold himself to the enemies of Christ. A Sieur de Trevec burst into the Saracen camp, at the head of only one hundred lances, and carried the Black Priest away out of the very midst of their army."

"So that is how you come by the crest," I said quietly; but I thought of the branded skull in the gravel pit, and wondered.

"Yes," said Lys. "The Sieur de Trevec cut the Black Priest's head off, but first he branded him with an arrow mark on the forehead. The book says it was a pious action, and the Sieur de Trevec got great merit by it. But I think it was cruel, the branding," she sighed.

"Did you ever hear of any other Black Priest?"

"Yes. There was one in the last century, here in St. Gildas. He cast a white shadow in the sun. He wrote in the Breton language. Chronicles, too, I believe. I never saw them. His name was the same as that of the old chronicler, and of the other priest, Jacques

Sorgue. Some said he was a lineal descendant of the traitor. Of course the first Black Priest was bad enough for anything. But if he did have a child, it need not have been the ancestor of the last Jacques Sorgue. They say this one was a holy man. They say he was so good he was not allowed to die, but was caught up to heaven one day," added Lys, with believing eyes.

I smiled.

"But he disappeared," persisted Lys.

"I'm afraid his journey was in another direction," I said jestingly, and thoughtlessly told her the story of the morning. I had utterly forgotten the masked man at her window, but before I finished I remembered him fast enough, and realized what I had done as I saw her face whiten.

"Lys," I urged tenderly, "that was only some clumsy clown's trick. You said so yourself. You are not superstitious, my dear?"

Her eyes were on mine. She slowly drew the little gold cross from her bosom and kissed it. But her lips trembled as they pressed the symbol of faith.

III

About nine o'clock the next morning I walked into the Groix Inn and sat down at the long, discoloured oaken table, nodding good-day to Marianne Bruyère, who in turn bobbed her white coiffe at me.

"My clever Bannalec maid," said I, "what is good for a stirrup-cup at the Groix Inn?"

"Schist?" she inquired in Breton.

"With a dash of red wine, then," I replied.

She brought the delicious Quimperlé cider, and I poured a little Bordeaux into it. Marianne watched me with laughing black eyes.

"What makes your cheeks so red, Marianne?" I asked. "Has Jean Marie been here?"

"We are to be married, Monsieur Darrel," she laughed.

"Ah! Since when has Jean Marie Tregunc lost his head?"

"His head? Oh, Monsieur Darrel—his heart, you mean!"

"So I do," said I. "Jean Marie is a practical fellow."

"It is all due to your kindness——" began the girl, but I raised my hand and held up the glass.

"It's due to himself. To your happiness, Marianne;" and I took a hearty draught of the schist. "Now," said I, "tell me where I can find Le Bihan and Max Fortin."

"Monsieur Le Bihan and Monsieur Fortin are above in the broad room. I believe they are examining the Red Admiral's effects."

"To send them to Paris? Oh, I know. May I go up, Marianne?"

"And God go with you," smiled the girl.

When I knocked at the door of the broad room above little Max Fortin opened it. Dust covered his spectacles and nose; his hat, with the tiny velvet ribbons fluttering, was all awry.

"Come in, Monsieur Darrel," he said; "the mayor and I are packing up the effects of the Purple Emperor and of the poor Red Admiral."

"The collections?" I asked, entering the room. "You must be very careful in packing those butterfly cases; the slightest jar might break wings and antennae, you know."

Le Bihan shook hands with me and pointed to the great pile of boxes.

"They're all cork lined," he said, "but Fortin and I are putting felt around each box. The Entomological Society of Paris pays the freight."

The combined collections of the Red Admiral and the Purple Emperor made a magnificent display.

I lifted and inspected case after case set with gorgeous butterflies and moths, each specimen carefully labelled with the name in Latin. There were cases filled with crimson tiger moths all aflame with colour; cases devoted to the common yellow butterflies; symphonies in orange and pale yellow; cases of soft gray and dun-coloured sphinx moths; and cases of garish nettle-bred butterflies of the numerous family of *Vanessa.*

All alone in a great case by itself was pinned the purple emperor, the Apatura Iris, that fatal specimen that had given the Purple Emperor his name and quietus.

I remembered the butterfly, and stood looking at it with bent eyebrows.

Le Bihan glanced up from the floor where he was nailing down the lid of a box full of cases.

"It is settled, then," said he, "that madame, your wife, gives the Purple Emperor's entire collection to the city of Paris?"

I nodded.

"Without accepting anything for it?"

"It is a gift," I said.

"Including the purple emperor there in the case? That butterfly is worth a great deal of money," persisted Le Bihan.

"You don't suppose that we would wish to sell that specimen, do you?" I answered a trifle sharply.

"If I were you I should destroy it," said the mayor in his high-pitched voice.

"That would be nonsense," said I—"like your burying the brass cylinder and scroll yesterday."

"It was not nonsense," said Le Bihan doggedly, "and I should prefer not to discuss the subject of the scroll."

I looked at Max Fortin, who immediately avoided my eyes.

"You are a pair of superstitious old women," said I, digging my hands into my pockets; "you swallow every nursery tale that is invented."

"What of it?" said Le Bihan sulkily; "there's more truth than lies in most of 'em."

"Oh!" I sneered, "does the Mayor of St. Gildas and St. Julien believe in the Loup-garou?"

"No, not in the Loup-garou."

"In what, then—Jeanne-la-Flamme?"

"That," said Le Bihan with conviction, "is history."

"The devil it is!" said I; "and perhaps, monsieur the mayor, your faith in giants is unimpaired?"

"There were giants—everybody knows it," growled Max Fortin.

"And you a chemist!" I observed scornfully.

"Listen, Monsieur Darrel," squeaked Le Bihan; "you know yourself that the Purple Emperor was a scientific man. Now suppose I should tell you that he always refused to include in his collection a Death's Messenger?"

"A what?" I exclaimed.

"You know what I mean—that moth that flies by night; some call it the Death's Head, but in St. Gildas we call it 'Death's Messenger.'"

"Oh!" said I, "you mean that big sphinx moth that is commonly known as the 'death's-head moth.' Why the mischief should the people here call it death's messenger?"

"For hundreds of years it has been known as death's messenger in St. Gildas," said Max Fortin. "Even Froissart speaks of it in his commentaries on Jacques Sorgue's Chronicles. The book is in your library."

"Sorgue? And who was Jacques Sorgue? I never read his book."

"Jacques Sorgue was the son of some unfrocked priest—I forget. It was during the crusades."

"Good Heavens!" I burst out, "I've been hearing of nothing but crusades and priests and death and sorcery ever since I kicked that skull into the gravel pit, and I am tired of it, I tell you frankly. One would think we lived in the dark ages. Do you know what year of our Lord it is, Le Bihan?"

"Eighteen hundred and ninety-six," replied the mayor.

"And yet you two hulking men are afraid of a death's-head moth."

"I don't care to have one fly into the window," said Max Fortin; "it means evil to the house and the people in it."

"God alone knows why he marked one of his creatures with a yellow death's head on the back," observed Le Bihan piously, "but I take it that he meant it as a warning; and I propose to profit by it," he added triumphantly.

"See here, Le Bihan," I said; "by a stretch of imagination one can make out a skull on the thorax of a certain big sphinx moth. What of it?"

"It is a bad thing to touch," said the mayor, wagging his head.

"It squeaks when handled," added Max Fortin.

"Some creatures squeak all the time," I observed, looking hard at Le Bihan.

"Pigs," added the mayor.

"Yes, and asses," I replied. "Listen, Le Bihan: do you mean to tell me that you saw that skull roll uphill yesterday?"

The mayor shut his mouth tightly and picked up his hammer.

"Don't be obstinate," I said; "I asked you a question."

"And I refuse to answer," snapped Le Bihan. "Fortin saw what I saw; let him talk about it."

I looked searchingly at the little chemist.

"I don't say that I saw it actually roll up out of the pit, all by itself," said Fortin with a shiver, "but—but then, how did it come up out of the pit, if it didn't roll up all by itself?"

"It didn't come up at all; that was a yellow cobblestone that you mistook for the skull again," I replied. "You were nervous, Max."

"A—a very curious cobblestone, Monsieur Darrel," said Fortin.

"I also was a victim to the same hallucination," I continued, "and I regret to say that I took the trouble to roll two innocent cobblestones into the gravel pit, imagining each time that it was the skull I was rolling."

"It was," observed Le Bihan with a morose shrug.

"It just shows," said I, ignoring the mayor's remark, "how easy it is to fix up a train of coincidences so that the result seems to savour of the supernatural. Now, last night my wife imagined that she saw a priest in a mask peer in at her window——"

Fortin and Le Bihan scrambled hastily from their knees, dropping hammer and nails.

"W-h-a-t—what's that?" demanded the mayor.

I repeated what I had said. Max Fortin turned livid.

"My God!" muttered Le Bihan, "the Black Priest is in St. Gildas!"

"D-don't you—you know the old prophecy?" stammered Fortin; "Froissart quotes it from Jacques Sorgue:

> 'When the Black Priest rises from the dead,
> St. Gildas folk shall shriek in bed;
> When the Black Priest rises from his grave,
> May the good God St. Gildas save!'"

"Aristide Le Bihan," I said angrily, "and you, Max Fortin, I've got enough of this nonsense! Some foolish lout from Bannalec has been in St. Gildas playing tricks to frighten old fools like you. If you have nothing better to talk about than nursery legends I'll wait until you come to your senses. Good-morning." And I walked out, more disturbed than I cared to acknowledge to myself.

The day had become misty and overcast. Heavy, wet clouds hung in the east. I heard the surf thundering against the cliffs, and the gray gulls squealed as they tossed and turned high in the sky. The tide was creeping across the river sands, higher, higher, and I saw the seaweed floating on the beach, and the *lançons* springing from the foam, silvery threadlike flashes in the gloom. Curlew were flying up the river in twos and threes; the timid sea swallows skimmed across the moors toward some quiet, lonely pool, safe from the coming tempest. In every hedge field birds were gathering, huddling together, twittering restlessly.

When I reached the cliffs I sat down, resting my chin on my clenched hands. Already a vast curtain of rain, sweeping across the ocean miles away, hid the island of Groix. To the east, behind the white semaphore on the hills, black clouds crowded up over the horizon. After a little the thunder boomed, dull, distant, and slender skeins of lightning unravelled across the crest of the coming storm. Under the cliff at my feet the surf rushed foaming over the shore, and the *lançons* jumped and skipped and quivered until they seemed to be but the reflections of the meshed lightning.

I turned to the east. It was raining over Groix, it was raining at Sainte Barbe, it was raining now at the semaphore. High in the storm whirl a few gulls pitched; a nearer cloud trailed veils of rain in its wake; the sky was spattered with lightning; the thunder boomed.

As I rose to go, a cold raindrop fell upon the back of my hand, and another, and yet another on my face. I gave a last glance at the sea, where the waves were bursting into strange white shapes that seemed to fling out menacing arms toward me. Then something moved on the cliff, something black as the black rock it clutched—a filthy cormorant, craning its hideous head at the sky.

Slowly I plodded homeward across the sombre moorland, where the gorse stems glimmered with a dull metallic green, and the heather, no longer violet and purple, hung drenched and dun-coloured among the dreary rocks. The wet turf creaked under my heavy boots, the black-thorn scraped and grated against knee and elbow. Over all lay a strange light, pallid, ghastly, where the sea spray whirled across the landscape and drove into my face until it grew numb with the cold. In broad bands, rank after rank, billow on billow, the rain burst out across the endless moors, and yet there was no wind to drive it at such a pace.

Lys stood at the door as I turned into the garden, motioning me to hasten; and then for the first time I became conscious that I was soaked to the skin.

"How ever in the world did you come to stay out when such a storm threatened?" she said. "Oh, you are dripping! Go quickly and change; I have laid your warm underwear on the bed, Dick."

I kissed my wife, and went upstairs to change my dripping clothes for something more comfortable.

When I returned to the morning room there was a driftwood fire on the hearth, and Lys sat in the chimney corner embroidering.

"Catherine tells me that the fishing fleet from Lorient is out. Do you think they are in danger, dear?" asked Lys, raising her blue eyes to mine as I entered.

"There is no wind, and there will be no sea," said I, looking out of the window. Far across the moor I could see the black cliffs looming in the mist.

"How it rains!" murmured Lys; "come to the fire, Dick."

I threw myself on the fur rug, my hands in my pockets, my head on Lys's knees.

"Tell me a story," I said. "I feel like a boy of ten."

Lys raised a finger to her scarlet lips. I always waited for her to do that.

"Will you be very still, then?" she said.

"Still as death."

"Death," echoed a voice, very softly.

"Did you speak, Lys?" I asked, turning so that I could see her face.

"No; did you, Dick?"

"Who said 'death'?" I asked, startled.

"Death," echoed a voice, softly.

I sprang up and looked about. Lys rose too, her needles and embroidery falling to the floor. She seemed about to faint, leaning heavily on me, and I led her to the window and opened it a little way to give her air. As I did so the chain lightning split the zenith, the thunder crashed, and a sheet of rain swept into the room, driving with it something that fluttered—something that flapped, and squeaked, and beat upon the rug with soft, moist wings.

We bent over it together, Lys clinging to me, and we saw that it was a death's-head moth drenched with rain.

The dark day passed slowly as we sat beside the fire, hand in hand, her head against my breast, speaking of sorrow and mystery and death. For Lys believed that there were things on earth that none might understand, things that must be nameless forever and ever, until God rolls up the scroll of life and all is ended. We spoke of hope and fear and faith, and the mystery of the saints; we spoke of the beginning and the end, of the shadow of sin, of omens, and of love. The moth still lay on the floor, quivering its sombre wings in the warmth of the fire, the skull and ribs clearly etched upon its neck and body.

"If it is a messenger of death to this house," I said, "why should we fear, Lys?"

"Death should be welcome to those who love God," murmured Lys, and she drew the cross from her breast and kissed it.

"The moth might die if I threw it out into the storm," I said after a silence.

"Let it remain," sighed Lys.

Late that night my wife lay sleeping, and I sat beside her bed and read in the Chronicle of Jacques Sorgue. I shaded the candle, but Lys grew restless, and finally I took the book down into the morning room, where the ashes of the fire rustled and whitened on the hearth.

The death's-head moth lay on the rug before the fire where I had left it. At first I thought it was dead, but, when I looked closer I saw a lambent fire in its amber eyes. The straight white shadow it cast across the floor wavered as the candle flickered.

The pages of the Chronicle of Jacques Sorgue were damp and sticky; the illuminated gold and blue initials left flakes of azure and gilt where my hand brushed them.

"It is not paper at all; it is thin parchment," I said to myself; and I held the discoloured page close to the candle flame and read, translating laboriously:

"I, Jacques Sorgue, saw all these things. And I saw the Black Mass celebrated in the chapel of St. Gildas-on-the-Cliff. And it was said by the Abbé Sorgue, my kinsman: for which deadly sin the apostate priest was seized by the most noble Marquis of Plougastel and by him condemned to be burned with hot irons, until his seared soul quit its body and fly to its master the devil. But when the Black Priest lay in the crypt of Plougastel, his master Satan came at night and set him free, and carried him across land and sea to Mahmoud, which is Soldan or Saladin. And I, Jacques Sorgue, travelling afterward by sea, beheld with my own eyes my kinsman, the Black Priest of St. Gildas, borne along in the air upon a vast black wing, which was the wing of his master Satan. And this was seen also by two men of the crew."

I turned the page. The wings of the moth on the floor began to quiver. I read on and on, my eyes blurring under the shifting candle flame. I read of battles and of saints, and I learned how the great Soldan made his pact with Satan, and then I came to the Sieur de Trevec, and read how he seized the Black Priest in the midst of Saladin's tents and carried him away and cut off his head, first branding him on the forehead. "And before he suffered," said the Chronicle, "he cursed the Sieur de Trevec and his descendants, and he said he would surely return to St. Gildas. 'For the violence you do to me, I will do violence to you. For the evil I suffer at your hands, I will work evil on you and your descendants. Woe to your children, Sieur de Trevec!'" There was a whirr, a beating of strong wings, and my candle flashed up as in a sudden breeze. A humming filled the room; the great moth darted hither and thither, beating, buzzing, on ceiling and wall. I flung down my book and stepped forward. Now it lay fluttering upon the window sill, and for a moment I had it under my hand, but the thing squeaked and I shrank back. Then suddenly it darted across the candle flame; the light flared and went out, and at the same moment a shadow moved in the darkness outside. I raised my eyes to the window. A masked face was peering in at me.

Quick as thought I whipped out my revolver and fired every cartridge, but the face advanced beyond the window, the glass melting away before it like mist, and through the smoke of my revolver I saw something creep swiftly into the room. Then I tried to cry out, but the thing was at my throat, and I fell backward among the ashes of the hearth.

* * * * * * *

When my eyes unclosed I was lying on the hearth, my head among the cold ashes. Slowly I got on my knees, rose painfully, and groped my way to a chair. On the floor lay my revolver, shining in the pale light of early morning. My mind clearing by degrees, I looked, shuddering, at the window. The glass was unbroken. I stooped stiffly, picked up my revolver and opened the cylinder. Every cartridge had been fired. Mechanically I closed the cylinder and placed the revolver in my pocket. The book, the Chronicles of Jacques Sorgue, lay on the table beside me, and as I started to close it I glanced at the page. It was all splashed with rain, and the lettering had run, so that the page was merely a confused blur of gold and red and black. As I stumbled toward the door I cast a fearful glance over my shoulder. The death's-head moth crawled shivering on the rug.

IV

The sun was about three hours high. I must have slept, for I was aroused by the sudden gallop of horses under our window. People were shouting and calling in the road. I sprang up and opened the sash. Le Bihan was there, an image of helplessness, and Max Fortin stood beside him, polishing his glasses. Some gendarmes had just arrived from Quimperlé, and I could hear them around the corner of the house, stamping, and rattling their sabres and carbines, as they led their horses into my stable.

Lys sat up, murmuring half-sleepy, half-anxious questions.

"I don't know," I answered. "I am going out to see what it means."

"It is like the day they came to arrest you," Lys said, giving me a troubled look. But I kissed her, and laughed at her until she smiled too. Then I flung on coat and cap and hurried down the stairs.

The first person I saw standing in the road was the Brigadier Durand.

"Hello!" said I, "have you come to arrest me again? What the devil is all this fuss about, anyway?"

"We were telegraphed for an hour ago," said Durand briskly, "and for a sufficient reason, I think. Look there, Monsieur Darrel!"

He pointed to the ground almost under my feet.

"Good heavens!" I cried, "where did that puddle of blood come from?"

"That's what I want to know, Monsieur Darrel. Max Fortin found it at daybreak. See, it's splashed all over the grass, too. A trail of it leads into your garden, across the flower beds to your very window, the one that opens from the morning room. There is another trail leading from this spot across the road to the cliffs, then to the gravel pit, and thence across the moor to the forest of Kerselec. We are going to mount in a minute and search the bosquets. Will you join us? Bon Dieu! but the fellow bled like an ox. Max Fortin says it's human blood, or I should not have believed it."

The little chemist of Quimperlé came up at that moment, rubbing his glasses with a coloured handkerchief.

"Yes, it is human blood," he said, "but one thing puzzles me: the corpuscles are yellow. I never saw any human blood before with yellow corpuscles. But your English Doctor Thompson asserts that he has——"

"Well, it's human blood, anyway—isn't it?" insisted Durand, impatiently.

"Ye-es," admitted Max Fortin.

"Then it's my business to trail it," said the big gendarme, and he called his men and gave the order to mount.

"Did you hear anything last night?" asked Durand of me.

"I heard the rain. I wonder the rain did not wash away these traces."

"They must have come after the rain ceased. See this thick splash, how it lies over and weighs down the wet grass blades. Pah!"

It was a heavy, evil-looking clot, and I stepped back from it, my throat closing in disgust.

"My theory," said the brigadier, "is this: Some of those Biribi fishermen, probably the Icelanders, got an extra glass of cognac into their hides and quarrelled on the road. Some of them were slashed, and staggered to your house. But there is only one trail, and yet—and yet, how could all that blood come from only one person? Well, the wounded man, let us say, staggered first to your house and then back here, and he wandered off, drunk and dying, God knows where. That's my theory."

"A very good one," said I calmly. "And you are going to trail him?"

"Yes."

"When?"

"At once. Will you come?"

"Not now. I'll gallop over by-and-bye. You are going to the edge of the Kerselec forest?"

"Yes; you will hear us calling. Are you coming, Max Fortin? And you, Le Bihan? Good; take the dog-cart."

The big gendarme tramped around the corner to the stable and presently returned mounted on a strong gray horse; his sabre shone on his saddle; his pale yellow and white facings were spotless. The little crowd of white-coiffed women with their children fell back, as Durand touched spurs and clattered away followed by his two troopers. Soon after Le Bihan and Max Fortin also departed in the mayor's dingy dog-cart.

"Are you coming?" piped Le Bihan shrilly.

"In a quarter of an hour," I replied, and went back to the house.

When I opened the door of the morning room the death's-head moth was beating its strong wings against the window. For a second I hesitated, then walked over and opened the sash. The creature fluttered out, whirred over the flower beds a moment, then darted across the moorland toward the sea. I called the servants together and questioned them. Josephine, Catherine, Jean Marie Tregunc, not one of them had heard the slightest disturbance during the night. Then I told Jean Marie to saddle my horse, and while I was speaking Lys came down.

"Dearest," I began, going to her.

"You must tell me everything you know, Dick," she interrupted, looking me earnestly in the face.

"But there is nothing to tell—only a drunken brawl, and some one wounded."

"And you are going to ride—where, Dick?"

"Well, over to the edge of Kerselec forest. Durand and the mayor, and Max Fortin, have gone on, following a—a trail."

"What trail?"

"Some blood."

"Where did they find it?"

"Out in the road there." Lys crossed herself.

"Does it come near our house?"

"Yes."

"How near?"

"It comes up to the morning-room window," said I, giving in.

Her hand on my arm grew heavy. "I dreamed last night——"

"So did I——" but I thought of the empty cartridges in my revolver, and stopped.

"I dreamed that you were in great danger, and I could not move hand or foot to save you; but you had your revolver, and I called out to you to fire——"

"I did fire!" I cried excitedly.

"You—you fired?"

I took her in my arms. “My darling,” I said, “something strange has happened—something that I can not understand as yet. But, of course, there is an explanation. Last night I thought I fired at the Black Priest.”

“Ah!” gasped Lys.

“Is that what you dreamed?”

“Yes, yes, that was it! I begged you to fire——”

“And I did.”

Her heart was beating against my breast. I held her close in silence.

“Dick,” she said at length, “perhaps you killed the—the thing.”

“If it was human I did not miss,” I answered grimly. “And it was human,” I went on, pulling myself together, ashamed of having so nearly gone to pieces. “Of course it was human! The whole affair is plain enough. Not a drunken brawl, as Durand thinks; it was a drunken lout’s practical joke, for which he has suffered. I suppose I must have filled him pretty full of bullets, and he has crawled away to die in Kerselec forest. It’s a terrible affair; I’m sorry I fired so hastily; but that idiot Le Bihan and Max Fortin have been working on my nerves till I am as hysterical as a schoolgirl,” I ended angrily.

“You fired—but the window glass was not shattered,” said Lys in a low voice.

“Well, the window was open, then. And as for the—the rest—I’ve got nervous indigestion, and a doctor will settle the Black Priest for me, Lys.”

I glanced out of the window at Tregunc waiting with my horse at the gate.

“Dearest, I think I had better go to join Durand and the others.”

“I will go too.”

“Oh, no!”

“Yes, Dick.”

“Don’t, Lys.”

“I shall suffer every moment you are away.”

"The ride is too fatiguing, and we can't tell what unpleasant sight you may come upon. Lys, you don't really think there is anything supernatural in this affair?"

"Dick," she answered gently, "I am a Bretonne." With both arms around my neck, my wife said, "Death is the gift of God. I do not fear it when we are together. But alone—oh, my husband, I should fear a God who could take you away from me!"

We kissed each other soberly, simply, like two children. Then Lys hurried away to change her gown, and I paced up and down the garden waiting for her.

She came, drawing on her slender gauntlets. I swung her into the saddle, gave a hasty order to Jean Marie, and mounted.

Now, to quail under thoughts of terror on a morning like this, with Lys in the saddle beside me, no matter what had happened or might happen, was impossible. Moreover, Môme came sneaking after us. I asked Tregunc to catch him, for I was afraid he might be brained by our horses' hoofs if he followed, but the wily puppy dodged and bolted after Lys, who was trotting along the high-road. "Never mind," I thought; "if he's hit he'll live, for he has no brains to lose."

Lys was waiting for me in the road beside the Shrine of Our Lady of St. Gildas when I joined her. She crossed herself, I doffed my cap, then we shook out our bridles and galloped toward the forest of Kerselec.

We said very little as we rode. I always loved to watch Lys in the saddle. Her exquisite figure and lovely face were the incarnation of youth and grace; her curling hair glistened like threaded gold.

Out of the corner of my eye I saw the spoiled puppy Môme come bounding cheerfully alongside, oblivious of our horses' heels. Our road swung close to the cliffs. A filthy cormorant rose from the black rocks and flapped heavily across our path. Lys's horse reared, but she pulled him down, and pointed at the bird with her riding crop.

"I see," said I; "it seems to be going our way. Curious to see a cormorant in a forest, isn't it?"

"It is a bad sign," said Lys. "You know the Morbihan proverb: 'When the cormorant turns from the sea, Death laughs in the forest, and wise woodsmen build boats.'"

"I wish," said I sincerely, "that there were fewer proverbs in Brittany."

We were in sight of the forest now; across the gorse I could see the sparkle of gendarmes' trappings, and the glitter of Le Bihan's silver-buttoned jacket. The hedge was low and we took it without difficulty, and trotted across the moor to where Le Bihan and Durand stood gesticulating.

They bowed ceremoniously to Lys as we rode up.

"The trail is horrible—it is a river," said the mayor in his squeaky voice. "Monsieur Darrel, I think perhaps madame would scarcely care to come any nearer."

Lys drew bridle and looked at me.

"It is horrible!" said Durand, walking up beside me; "it looks as though a bleeding regiment had passed this way. The trail winds and winds about there in the thickets; we lose it at times, but we always find it again. I can't understand how one man—no, nor twenty—could bleed like that!"

A halloo, answered by another, sounded from the depths of the forest.

"It's my men; they are following the trail," muttered the brigadier. "God alone knows what is at the end!"

"Shall we gallop back, Lys?" I asked.

"No; let us ride along the western edge of the woods and dismount. The sun is so hot now, and I should like to rest for a moment," she said.

"The western forest is clear of anything disagreeable," said Durand.

"Very well," I answered; "call me, Le Bihan, if you find anything."

Lys wheeled her mare, and I followed across the springy heather, Môme trotting cheerfully in the rear.

We entered the sunny woods about a quarter of a kilometre from where we left Durand. I took Lys from her horse, flung both bridles over a limb, and, giving my wife my arm, aided her to a flat mossy rock which overhung a shallow brook gurgling among the beach trees. Lys sat down and drew off her gauntlets. Môme pushed his head into her lap, received an undeserved caress, and came doubtfully toward me. I was weak enough to condone his offence, but I made him lie down at my feet, greatly to his disgust.

I rested my head on Lys's knees, looking up at the sky through the crossed branches of the trees.

"I suppose I have killed him," I said. "It shocks me terribly, Lys."

"You could not have known, dear. He may have been a robber, and—if—not—— Did—have you ever fired your revolver since that day four years ago, when the Red Admiral's son tried to kill you? But I know you have not."

"No," said I, wondering. "It's a fact, I have not. Why?"

"And don't you remember that I asked you to let me load it for you the day when Yves went off, swearing to kill you and his father?"

"Yes, I do remember. Well?"

"Well, I—I took the cartridges first to St. Gildas chapel and dipped them in holy water. You must not laugh, Dick," said Lys gently, laying her cool hands on my lips.

"Laugh, my darling!"

Overhead the October sky was pale amethyst, and the sunlight burned like orange flame through the yellow leaves of beach and oak. Gnats and midges danced and wavered overhead; a spider dropped from a twig halfway to the ground and hung suspended on the end of his gossamer thread.

"Are you sleepy, dear?" asked Lys, bending over me.

"I am—a little; I scarcely slept two hours last night," I answered.

"You may sleep, if you wish," said Lys, and touched my eyes caressingly.

"Is my head heavy on your knees?"

"No, Dick."

I was already in a half doze; still I heard the brook babbling under the beeches and the humming of forest flies overhead. Presently even these were stilled.

The next thing I knew I was sitting bolt upright, my ears ringing with a scream, and I saw Lys cowering beside me, covering her white face with both hands.

As I sprang to my feet she cried again and clung to my knees. I saw my dog rush growling into a thicket, then I heard him whimper, and he came backing out, whining, ears flat, tail down. I stooped and disengaged Lys's hand.

"Don't go, Dick!" she cried. "O God, it's the Black Priest!"

In a moment I had leaped across the brook and pushed my way into the thicket. It was empty. I stared about me; I scanned every tree trunk, every bush. Suddenly I saw him. He was seated on a fallen log, his head resting in his hands, his rusty black robe gathered around him. For a moment my hair stirred under my cap; sweat started on forehead and cheek-bone; then I recovered my reason, and understood that the man was human and was probably wounded to death. Ay, to death; for there, at my feet, lay the wet trail of blood, over leaves and stones, down into the little hollow, across to the figure in black resting silently under the trees.

I saw that he could not escape even if he had the strength, for before him, almost at his very feet, lay a deep, shining swamp.

As I stepped forward my foot broke a twig. At the sound the figure started a little, then its head fell forward again. Its face was masked. Walking up to the man, I bade him tell where he was wounded. Durand and the others broke through the thicket at the same moment and hurried to my side.

"Who are you who hide a masked face in a priest's robe?" said the gendarme loudly.

There was no answer.

"See—see the stiff blood all over his robe!" muttered Le Bihan to Fortin.

"He will not speak," said I.

"He may be too badly wounded," whispered Le Bihan.

"I saw him raise his head," I said; "my wife saw him creep up here,"

Durand stepped forward and touched the figure.

"Speak!" he said.

"Speak!" quavered Fortin.

Durand waited a moment, then with a sudden upward movement he stripped off the mask and threw back the man's head. We were looking into the eye sockets of a skull. Durand stood rigid; the mayor shrieked. The skeleton burst out from its rotting robes and collapsed on the ground before us. From between the staring ribs and the grinning teeth spurted a torrent of black blood, showering the shrinking grasses; then the thing shuddered, and fell over into the black ooze of the bog. Little bubbles of iridescent air appeared from the mud; the bones were slowly engulfed, and, as the last fragments sank out of sight, up from the depths and along the bank crept a creature, shiny, shivering, quivering its wings.

It was a death's-head moth.

* * * * * * *

I wish I had time to tell you how Lys outgrew superstitions—for she never knew the truth about the affair, and she never will know, since she has promised not to read this book. I wish I might tell you about the king and his coronation, and how the coronation robe fitted. I wish that I were able to write how Yvonne and Herbert Stuart rode to a boar hunt in Quimperlé, and how the hounds raced the quarry right through the town, overturning three gendarmes, the notary, and an old woman. But I am becoming garrulous, and Lys is calling me to come and hear the king say that he is sleepy. And his Highness shall not be kept waiting.

THE KING'S CRADLE SONG.

Seal with a seal of gold
The scroll of a life unrolled;
Swathe him deep in his purple stole;
Ashes of diamonds, crystalled coal,
Drops of gold in each scented fold.

Crimson wings of the Little Death,
Stir his hair with your silken breath;
Flaming wings of sins to be,
Splendid pinions of prophecy,
Smother his eyes with hues and dyes,
While the white moon spins and the winds arise,
And the stars drip through the skies.

Wave, O wings of the Little Death!
Seal his sight and stifle his breath,
Cover his breast with the gemmed shroud pressed;
From north to north, from west to west,
Wave, O wings of the Little Death!
Till the white moon reels in the cracking skies,
And the ghosts of God arise.

PASSEUR

O friends, I've served ye food and bed;
O friends, the mist is rising wet;
Then bide a moment, O my dead,
Where, lonely, I must linger yet!

Because man goeth to his long home,
And the mourners go about the streets.

WHEN HE HAD FINISHED HIS PIPE HE TAPPED THE BRIER BOWL against the chimney until the ashes powdered the charred log smouldering across the andirons. Then he sank back in his chair, absently touching the hot pipe-bowl with the tip of each finger until it grew cool enough to be dropped into his coat pocket.

Twice he raised his eyes to the little American clock ticking upon the mantel. He had half an hour to wait.

The three candles that lighted the room might be trimmed to advantage; this would give him something to do. A pair of scissors lay open upon the bureau, and he rose and picked them up. For a while he stood dreamily shutting and opening the scissors, his eyes roaming about the room. There was an easel in the corner, and a pile of dusty canvases behind it; behind the canvases there was a shadow—that gray, menacing shadow that never moved.

When he had trimmed each candle he wiped the smoky scissors on a paint rag and flung them on the bureau again. The clock pointed to ten; he had been occupied exactly three minutes.

The bureau was littered with neckties, pipes, combs and brushes, matches, reels and fly-books, collars, shirt studs, a new pair of Scotch shooting stockings, and a woman's workbasket.

He picked out all the neckties, folded them once, and hung them over a bit of twine that stretched across the looking-glass; the shirt studs he shovelled into the top drawer along with brushes, combs, and stockings; the reels and fly-books he dusted with his handkerchief and placed methodically along the mantel shelf. Twice he stretched out his hand toward the woman's workbasket, but his hand fell to his side again, and he turned away into the room staring at the dying fire.

Outside the snow-sealed window a shutter broke loose and banged monotonously, until he flung open the panes and fastened it. The soft, wet snow, that had choked the window-panes all day, was frozen hard now, and he had to break the polished crust before he could find the rusty shutter hinge.

He leaned out for a moment, his numbed hands resting on the snow, the roar of a rising snow-squall in his ears; and out across the desolate garden and stark hedgerow he saw the flat black river spreading through the gloom.

A candle sputtered and snapped behind him; a sheet of drawing-paper fluttered across the floor, and he closed the panes and turned back into the room, both hands in his worn pockets.

The little American clock on the mantel ticked and ticked, but the hands lagged, for he had not been occupied five minutes in all. He went up to the mantel and watched the hands of the clock. A minute—longer than a year to him—crept by.

Around the room the furniture stood ranged—a chair or two of yellow pine, a table, the easel, and in one corner the broad curtained bed; and behind each lay shadows, menacing shadows that never moved.

A little pale flame started up from the smoking log on the andirons; the room sang with the sudden hiss of escaping wood gases. After a little the back of the log caught fire; jets of blue flared up here and there with mellow sounds like the lighting of gas-burners in a row, and in a moment a thin sheet of yellow flame wrapped the whole charred log.

Then the shadows moved; not the shadows behind the furniture—they never moved—but other shadows, thin, gray, confusing, that came and spread their slim patterns all around him, and trembled and trembled.

He dared not step or tread upon them, they were too real; they meshed the floor around his feet, they ensnared his knees, they fell across his breast like ropes. Some night, in the silence of the moors, when wind and river were still, he feared these strands of shadow might tighten—creep higher around his throat and tighten. But even then he knew that those other shadows would never move, those gray shapes that knelt crouching in every corner.

When he looked up at the clock again ten minutes had straggled past. Time was disturbed in the room; the strands of shadow seemed entangled among the hands of the clock, dragging them back from their rotation. He wondered if the shadows would strangle Time, some still night when the wind and the flat river were silent.

There grew a sudden chill across the floor; the cracks of the boards let it in. He leaned down and drew his sabots toward him from their place near the andirons, and slipped them over his chaussons; and as he straightened up, his eyes mechanically sought the mantel above, where in the dusk another pair of sabots stood, little, slender, delicate sabots, carved from red beach. A year's dust grayed their surface; a year's rust dulled the silver band across the instep. He said this to himself aloud, knowing that it was within a few minutes of the year.

His own sabots came from Mort-Dieu; they were shaved square and banded with steel. But in days past he had thought that no sabot in Mort-Dieu was delicate enough to touch the instep of the Mort-Dieu passeur. So he sent to the shore lighthouse, and they sent to Lorient, where the women are coquettish and show their hair under the coiffe, and wear dainty sabots; and in this town, where vanity corrupts and there is much lace on coiffe and collarette, a pair of delicate sabots was found, banded with silver and chiselled in red beach. The sabots stood on the mantel above the fire now, dusty and tarnished.

There was a sound from the window, the soft murmur of snow blotting glass panes. The wind, too, muttered under the roof eaves. Presently it would begin to whisper to him from the chimney—he knew it—and he held his hands over his ears and stared at the clock.

In the hamlet of Mort-Dieu the pines sing all day of the sea secrets, but in the night the ghosts of little gray birds fill the branches, singing of the sunshine of past years. He heard the song as he sat, and he crushed his hands over his ears; but the gray birds joined with the wind in the chimney, and he heard all that he dared not hear, and he thought all that he dared not hope or think, and the swift tears scalded his eyes.

In Mort-Dieu the nights are longer than anywhere on earth; he knew it—why should he not know? This had been so for a year; it was different before. There were so many things different before; days and nights vanished like minutes then; the pines told no secrets of the sea, and the gray birds had not yet come to Mort-Dieu. Also, there was Jeanne, passeur at the Carmes.

When he first saw her she was poling the square, flat-bottomed ferry skiff from the Carmes to Mort-Dieu, a red handkerchief bound across her silky black hair, a red skirt fluttering just below her knees. The next time he saw her he had to call to her across the placid river, "Ohé! Ohé, passeur!" She came, poling the flat skiff, her deep blue eyes fixed pensively on him, the scarlet skirt and kerchief idly flapping in the April wind. Then day followed day when the far call "Passeur!" grew clearer and more joyous, and the faint answering cry, "I come!" rippled across the water like music tinged with laughter. Then spring came, and with spring came love—love, carried free across the ferry from the Carmes to Mort-Dieu.

The flame above the charred log whistled, flickered, and went out in a jet of wood vapour, only to play like lightning above the gas and relight again. The clock ticked more loudly, and the song from the pines filled the room. But in his straining eyes a summer landscape was reflected, where white clouds sailed and white foam curled under the square bow of a little skiff. And he pressed his numbed hands tighter to his ears to drown the cry, "Passeur! Passeur!"

And now for a moment the clock ceased ticking. It was time to go—who but he should know it, he who went out into the night swinging his lantern? And he went. He had gone each night from the first—from that first strange winter evening when a strange voice had answered him across the river, the voice of the new passeur. He had never heard *her* voice again.

So he passed down the windy wooden stairs, lantern hanging lighted in his hand, and stepped out into the storm. Through sheets of drifting snow, over heaps of frozen seaweed and icy drift he moved, shifting his lantern right and left, until its glimmer on the water warned him. Then he called out into the night, "Passeur!" The frozen spray spattered his face and crusted the lantern; he heard the distant boom of breakers beyond the bar, and the noise of mighty winds among the seaward cliffs.

"Passeur!"

Across the broad flat river, black as a sea of pitch, a tiny light sparkled a moment. Again he cried, "Passeur!"

"I come!"

He turned ghastly white, for it was her voice—or was he crazy?—and he sprang waist deep into the icy current and cried out again, but his voice ended in a sob.

Slowly through the snow the flat skiff took shape, creeping nearer and nearer. But she was not at the pole—he saw that; there was only a tall, thin man, shrouded to the eyes in oilskin; and he leaped into the boat and bade the ferryman hasten.

Halfway across he rose in the skiff, and called, "Jeanne!" But the roar of the storm and the thrashing of icy waves drowned his voice. Yet he heard her again, and she called to him by name.

When at last the boat grated upon the invisible shore, he lifted his lantern, trembling, stumbling among the rocks, and calling to her, as though his voice could silence the voice that had spoken a year ago that night. And it could not. He sank shivering upon his knees, and looked out into the darkness, where an ocean rolled across a world. Then his stiff lips moved, and he repeated her name; but the hand of the ferryman fell gently upon his head.

And when he raised his eyes he saw that the ferryman was Death.

THE KEY TO GRIEF

The moving finger writes, and, having writ,
Moves on; nor all your piety nor wit
Shall lure it back to cancel half a line,
Nor all your tears wash out a word of it.

FITZGERALD.

The wild hawk to the wind-swept sky
The deer to the wholesome wold,
And the heart of a man to the heart of a maid,
As it was in the days of old.

KIPLING.

I

THEY WERE DOING THEIR WORK VERY BADLY. THEY GOT THE rope around his neck, and tied his wrists with moose-bush withes, but again he fell, sprawling, turning, twisting over the leaves, tearing up everything around him like a trapped panther.

He got the rope away from them; he clung to it with bleeding fists; he set his white teeth in it, until the jute strands relaxed, unravelled, and snapped, gnawed through by his white teeth.

Twice Tully struck him with a gum hook. The dull blows fell on flesh rigid as stone.

Panting, foul with forest mould and rotten leaves, hands and face smeared with blood, he sat up on the ground, glaring at the circle of men around him.

"Shoot him!" gasped Tully, dashing the sweat from his bronzed brow; and Bates, breathing heavily, sat down on a log and dragged a revolver from his rear pocket. The man on the ground watched him; there was froth in the corners of his mouth.

"Git back!" whispered Bates, but his voice and hand trembled. "Kent," he stammered, "won't ye hang?"

The man on the ground glared.

"Ye've got to die, Kent," he urged; "they all say so. Ask Lefty Sawyer; ask Dyce; ask Carrots.—He's got to swing fur it—ain't he, Tully?—Kent, fur God's sake, swing fur these here gents!"

The man on the ground panted; his bright eyes never moved.

After a moment Tully sprang on him again. There was a flurry of leaves, a crackle, a gasp and a grunt, then the thumping and thrashing of two bodies writhing in the brush. Dyce and Carrots jumped on the prostrate men. Lefty Sawyer caught the rope again, but the jute strands gave way and he stumbled. Tully began to scream, "He's chokin' me!" Dyce staggered out into the open, moaning over a broken wrist.

"Shoot!" shouted Lefty Sawyer, and dragged Tully aside. "Shoot, Jim Bates! Shoot straight, b' God!"

"Git back!" gasped Bates, rising from the fallen log.

The crowd parted right and left; a quick report rang out—another—another. Then from the whirl of smoke a tall form staggered, dealing blows—blows that sounded sharp as the crack of a whip.

"He's off! Shoot straight!" they cried.

There was a gallop of heavy boots in the woods. Bates, faint and dazed, turned his head.

"Shoot!" shrieked Tully.

But Bates was sick; his smoking revolver fell to the ground; his white face and pale eyes contracted. It lasted only a moment; he started after the others, plunging, wallowing through thickets of osier and hemlock underbrush.

Far ahead he heard Kent crashing on like a young moose in November, and he knew he was making for the shore. The others knew too. Already the gray gleam of the sea cut a straight line along the forest edge; already the soft clash of the surf on the rocks broke faintly through the forest silence.

"He's got a canoe there!" bawled Tully. "He'll be into it!"

And he was into it, kneeling in the bow, driving his paddle to the handle. The rising sun gleamed like red lightning on the flashing blade; the canoe shot to the crest of a wave, hung, bows dripping in the wind, dropped into the depths, glided, tipped, rolled, shot up again, staggered, and plunged on.

Tully ran straight out into the cove surf; the water broke against his chest, bare and wet with sweat. Bates sat down on a worn black rock and watched the canoe listlessly.

The canoe dwindled to a speck of gray and silver; and when Carrots, who had run back to the gum camp for a rifle, returned, the speck on the water might have been easier to hit than a loon's head at twilight. So Carrots, being thrifty by nature, fired once, and was satisfied to save the other cartridges. The canoe was still visible, making for the open sea. Somewhere beyond the horizon lay the keys, a string of rocks bare as skulls, black and slimy where the sea cut their base, white on the crests with the excrement of sea birds.

"He's makin' fur the Key to Grief!" whispered Bates to Dyce.

Dyce, moaning, and nursing his broken wrist, turned a sick face out to sea.

The last rock seaward was the Key to Grief, a splintered pinnacle polished by the sea. From the Key to Grief, seaward a day's paddle, if a man dared, lay the long wooded island in the ocean known as Grief on the charts of the bleak coast.

In the history of the coast, two men had made the voyage to the Key to Grief, and from there to the island. One of these was a rum-crazed pelt hunter, who lived to come back; the other was a college youth; they found his battered canoe at sea, and a day later his battered body was flung up in the cove.

So, when Bates whispered to Dyce, and when Dyce called to the others, they knew that the end was not far off for Kent and his canoe; and they turned away into the forest, sullen, but satisfied that Kent would get his dues when the devil got his.

Lefty spoke vaguely of the wages of sin. Carrots, with an eye to thrift, suggested a plan for an equitable division of Kent's property.

When they reached the gum camp they piled Kent's personal effects on a blanket.

Carrots took the inventory: a revolver, two gum hooks, a fur cap, a nickel-plated watch, a pipe, a pack of new cards, a gum sack, forty pounds of spruce gum, and a frying pan.

Carrots shuffled the cards, picked out the joker, and flipped it pensively into the fire. Then he dealt cold decks all around.

When the goods and chattels of their late companion had been divided by chance—for there was no chance to cheat—somebody remembered Tully.

"He's down there on the coast, starin' after the canoe," said Bates huskily.

He rose and walked toward a heap on the ground covered by a blanket. He started to lift the blanket, hesitated, and finally turned away. Under the blanket lay Tully's brother, shot the night before by Kent.

"Guess we'd better wait till Tully comes," said Carrots uneasily. Bates and Kent had been campmates. An hour later Tully walked into camp.

He spoke to no one that day. In the morning Bates found him down on the coast digging, and said: "Hello, Tully! Guess we ain't much hell on lynchin'!"

"Naw," said Tully. "Git a spade."

"Goin' to plant him there?"

"Yep."

"Where he kin hear them waves?"

"Yep."

"Purty spot."

"Yep."

"Which way will he face?"

"Where he kin watch fur that damned canoe!" cried Tully fiercely.

"He—he can't see," ventured Bates uneasily. "He's dead, ain't he?"

"He'll heave up that there sand when the canoe comes back! An' it's a-comin'! An' Bud Kent'll be in it, dead or alive! Git a spade!"

The pale light of superstition flickered in Bates's eyes. He hesitated.

"The—the dead can't see," he began; "kin they?"

Tully turned a distorted face toward him.

"Yer lie!" he roared. "My brother kin see, dead or livin'! An' he'll see the hangin' of Bud Kent! An' he'll git up outer the grave fur to see it, Bill Bates! I'm tellin' ye! I'm tellin' ye! Deep as I'll plant him, he'll heave that there sand and call to me, when the canoe comes in! I'll hear him; I'll be here! An' we'll live to see the hangin' of Bud Kent!"

About sundown they planted Tully's brother, face to the sea.

II

On the Key to Grief the green waves rub all day. White at the summit, black at the base, the shafted rocks rear splintered pinnacles, slanting like channel buoys. On the polished pillars sea birds brood—white-winged, bright-eyed sea birds, that nestle and preen and flap and clatter their orange-coloured beaks when the sifted spray drives and drifts across the reef.

As the sun rose, painting crimson streaks criss-cross over the waters, the sea birds sidled together, huddling row on row, steeped in downy drowse.

Where the sun of noon burnished the sea, an opal wave washed, listless, noiseless; a sea bird stretched one listless wing.

And into the silence of the waters a canoe glided, bronzed by the sunlight, jewelled by the salt drops stringing from prow to thwart, seaweed a-trail in the diamond-flashing wake, and in the bow a man dripping with sweat.

Up rose the gulls, sweeping in circles, turning, turning over rock and sea, and their clamour filled the sky, starting little rippling echoes among the rocks.

The canoe grated on a shelf of ebony; the seaweed rocked and washed; the little sea crabs sheered sideways, down, down into limpid depths of greenest shadows. Such was the coming of Bud Kent to the Key to Grief.

He drew the canoe halfway up the shelf of rock and sat down, breathing heavily, one brown arm across the bow. For an hour he sat there. The sweat dried under his eyes. The sea birds came back, filling the air with soft querulous notes.

There was a livid mark around his neck, a red, raw circle. The salt wind stung it; the sun burned it into his flesh like a collar of red-hot steel. He touched it at times; once he washed it with cold salt water.

Far in the north a curtain of mist hung on the sea, dense, motionless as the fog on the Grand Banks. He never moved his eyes from it; he knew what it was. Behind it lay the Island of Grief.

All the year round the Island of Grief is hidden by the banks of mist, ramparts of dead white fog encircling it on every side. Ships give it wide berth. Some speak of warm springs on the island whose waters flow far out to sea, rising in steam eternally.

The pelt hunter had come back with tales of forests and deer and flowers everywhere; but he had been drinking much, and much was forgiven him.

The body of the college youth tossed up in the cove on the mainland was battered out of recognition, but some said, when found, one hand clutched a crimson blossom half wilted, but broad as a sap pan.

So Kent lay motionless beside his canoe, burned with thirst, every nerve vibrating, thinking of all these things. It was not fear that whitened the firm flesh under the tan; it was the fear of fear. He must not think—he must throttle dread; his eyes must never falter, his head never turn from that wall of mist across the sea. With set teeth he crushed back terror; with glittering eyes he looked into the hollow eyes of fright. And so he conquered fear.

He rose. The sea birds whirled up into the sky, pitching, tossing, screaming, till the sharp flapping of their pinions set the snapping echoes flying among the rocks.

Under the canoe's sharp prow the kelp bobbed and dipped and parted; the sunlit waves ran out ahead, glittering, dancing. Splash! splash! bow and stern! And now he knelt again, and the polished paddle swung and dipped, and swept and swung and dipped again.

Far behind, the clamour of the sea birds lingered in his ears, till the mellow dip of the paddle drowned all sound and the sea was a sea of silence.

No wind came to cool the hot sweat on cheek and breast. The sun blazed a path of flame before him, and he followed out into the waste of waters. The still ocean divided under the bows and rippled innocently away on either side, tinkling, foaming, sparkling like the current in a woodland brook. He looked around at the world of flattened water, and the fear of fear rose up and gripped his throat again. Then he lowered his head, like a tortured bull, and shook the fear of fear from his throat, and drove the paddle into the sea as a butcher stabs, to the hilt.

So at last he came to the wall of mist. It was thin at first, thin and cool, but it thickened and grew warmer, and the fear of fear dragged at his head, but he would not look behind.

Into the fog the canoe shot; the gray water ran by, high as the gunwales, oily, silent. Shapes flickered across the bows, pillars of mist that rode the waters, robed in films of tattered shadows. Gigantic forms towered to dizzy heights above him, shaking out shredded shrouds of cloud. The vast draperies of the fog swayed and hung and trembled as he brushed them; the white twilight deepened to a sombre gloom. And now it grew thinner; the fog became a mist, and the mist a haze, and the haze floated away and vanished into the blue of the heavens.

All around lay a sea of pearl and sapphire, lapping, lapping on a silver shoal.

So he came to the Island of Grief.

III

On the silver shoal the waves washed and washed, breaking like crushed opals where the sands sang with the humming froth.

Troops of little shore birds, wading on the shoal, tossed their sun-tipped wings and scuttled inland, where, dappled with shadow from the fringing forest, the white beach of the island stretched.

The water all around was shallow, limpid as crystal, and he saw the ribbed sand shining on the bottom, where purple seaweed floated, and delicate sea creatures darted and swarmed and scattered again at the dip of his paddle.

Like velvet rubbed on velvet the canoe brushed across the sand. He staggered to his feet, stumbled out, dragged the canoe high up under the trees, turned it bottom upward, and sank beside it, face downward in the sand. Sleep came to drive away the fear of fear, but hunger, thirst, and fever fought with sleep, and he dreamed—dreamed of a rope that sawed his neck, of the fight in the woods, and the shots. He dreamed, too, of the camp, of his forty pounds of spruce gum, of Tully, and of Bates. He dreamed of the fire and the smoke-scorched kettle, of the foul odour of musty bedding, of the greasy cards, and of his own new pack, hoarded for weeks to please the others. All this he dreamed, lying there face downward in the sand; but he did not dream of the face of the dead.

The shadows of the leaves moved on his blonde head, crisp with clipped curls. A butterfly flitted around him, alighting now on his legs, now on the back of his bronzed hands. All the afternoon the bees hung droning among the wildwood blossoms; the leaves above scarcely rustled; the shore birds brooded along the water's edge; the thin tide, sleeping on the sand, mirrored the sky.

Twilight paled the zenith; a breeze moved in the deeper woods; a star glimmered, went out, glimmered again, faded, and glimmered.

Night came. A moth darted to and fro under the trees; a beetle hummed around a heap of seaweed and fell scrambling in the sand. Somewhere among the trees a sound had become distinct, the song of a little brook, melodious, interminable. He heard it in his dream; it threaded all his dreams like a needle of silver, and like a needle it pricked him—pricked his dry throat and cracked lips. It could not awake him; the cool night swathed him head and foot.

Toward dawn a bird woke up and piped. Other birds stirred, restless, half awakened; a gull spread a cramped wing on the shore, preened its feathers, scratched its tufted neck, and took two drowsy steps toward the sea.

The sea breeze stirred out behind the mist bank; it raised the feathers on the sleeping gulls; it set the leaves whispering. A twig snapped, broke off, and fell. Kent stirred, sighed, trembled, and awoke.

The first thing he heard was the song of the brook, and he stumbled straight into the woods. There it lay, a thin, deep stream in the gray morning light, and he stretched himself beside it and laid his cheek in it. A bird drank in the pool, too—a little fluffy bird, bright-eyed and fearless.

His knees were firmer when at last he rose, heedless of the drops that beaded lips and chin. With his knife he dug and scraped at some white roots that hung half meshed in the bank of the brook, and when he had cleaned them in the pool he ate them.

The sun stained the sky when he went down to the canoe, but the eternal curtain of fog, far out at sea, hid it as yet from sight.

He lifted the canoe, bottom upwards, to his head, and, paddle and pole in either hand, carried it into the forest.

After he had set it down he stood a moment, opening and shutting his knife. Then he looked up into the trees. There were birds there, if he could get at them. He looked at the brook. There were the prints of his fingers in the sand; there, too, was the print of something else—a deer's pointed hoof.

He had nothing but his knife. He opened it again and looked at it.

That day he dug for clams and ate them raw. He waded out into the shallows, too, and jabbed at fish with his setting pole, but hit nothing except a yellow crab.

Fire was what he wanted. He hacked and chipped at flinty-looking pebbles, and scraped tinder from a stick of sun-dried driftwood. His knuckles bled, but no fire came.

That night he heard deer in the woods, and could not sleep for thinking, until the dawn came up behind the wall of mist, and he rose with it to drink his fill at the brook and tear raw clams with his white teeth. Again he fought for fire, craving it as he had never craved water, but his knuckles bled, and the knife scraped on the flint in vain.

His mind, perhaps, had suffered somewhat. The white beach seemed to rise and fall like a white carpet on a gusty hearth. The birds, too, that ran along the sand, seemed big and juicy, like partridges; and he chased them, hurling shells and bits of driftwood at them till he could scarcely keep his feet for the rising, plunging beach—or carpet, whichever it was. That night the deer aroused him at intervals. He heard them splashing and grunting and crackling along the brook. Once he arose and stole after them, knife in hand, till a false step into the brook awoke him to his folly, and he felt his way back to the canoe, trembling.

Morning came, and again he drank at the brook, lying on the sand where countless heart-shaped hoofs had passed leaving clean imprints; and again he ripped the raw clams from their shells and swallowed them, whimpering.

All day long the white beach rose and fell and heaved and flattened under his bright dry eyes. He chased the shore birds at times, till the unsteady beach tripped him up and he fell full length in the sand. Then he would rise moaning, and creep into the shadow of the wood, and watch the little song-birds in the branches, moaning, always moaning.

His hands, sticky with blood, hacked steel and flint together, but so feebly that now even the cold sparks no longer came.

He began to fear the advancing night; he dreaded to hear the big warm deer among the thickets. Fear clutched him suddenly, and he lowered his head and set his teeth and shook fear from his throat again.

Then he started aimlessly into the woods, crowding past bushes, scraping trees, treading on moss and twig and mouldy stump, his bruised hands swinging, always swinging.

The sun set in the mist as he came out of the woods on to another beach—a warm, soft beach, crimsoned by the glow in the evening clouds.

And on the sand at his feet lay a young girl asleep, swathed in the silken garment of her own black hair, round-limbed, brown, smooth as the bloom on the tawny beach.

A gull flapped overhead, screaming. Her eyes, deeper than night, unclosed. Then her lips parted in a cry, soft with sleep, "Ihó!"

She rose, rubbing her velvet eyes. "Ihó!" she cried in wonder; "Inâh!"

The gilded sand settled around her little feet. Her cheeks crimsoned.

"E-hó! E-hó!" she whispered, and hid her face in her hair.

IV

The bridge of the stars spans the sky seas; the sun and the moon are the travellers who pass over it. This was also known in the lodges of the Isantee, hundreds of years ago. Chaské told it to Hârpam, and when Hârpam knew he told it to Hapéda; and so the knowledge spread to Hârka, and from Winona to Wehârka, up and down, across and ever across, woof and web, until it came to the Island of Grief. And how? God knows!

Wehârka, prattling in the tules, may have told Ne-kâ; and Ne-kâ, high in the November clouds, may have told Kay-óshk, who told it to Shinge-bis, who told it to Skeé-skah, who told it to Sé-só-Kah.

Ihó! Inâh! Behold the wonder of it! And this is the fate of all knowledge that comes to the Island of Grief.

* * * * *

As the red glow died in the sky, and the sand swam in shadows, the girl parted the silken curtains of her hair and looked at him.

"Ehó!" she whispered again in soft delight.

For now it was plain to her that he was the sun! He had crossed the bridge of stars in the blue twilight; he had come!

"E-tó!"

She stepped nearer, shivering, faint with the ecstasy of this holy miracle wrought before her.

He was the Sun! His blood streaked the sky at dawn; his blood stained the clouds at even. In his eyes the blue of the sky still lingered, smothering two blue stars; and his body was as white as the breast of the Moon.

She opened both arms, hands timidly stretched, palm upward. Her face was raised to his, her eyes slowly closed; the deep-fringed lids trembled.

Like a young priestess she stood, motionless save for the sudden quiver of a limb, a quick pulse-flutter in the rounded throat. And so she worshipped, naked and unashamed, even after he, reeling, fell heavily forward on his face; even when the evening breeze stealing over the sands stirred the hair on his head, as winds stir the fur of a dead animal in the dust.

* * * * *

When the morning sun peered over the wall of mist, and she saw it was the sun, and she saw him, flung on the sand at her feet, then she knew that he was a man, only a man, pallid as death and smeared with blood.

And yet—miracle of miracles!—the divine wonder in her eyes deepened, and her body seemed to swoon, and fall a-trembling, and swoon again.

For, although it was but a man who lay at her feet, it had been easier for her to look upon a god.

He dreamed that he breathed fire—fire, that he craved as he had never craved water. Mad with delirium, he knelt before the flames, rubbing his torn hands, washing them in the crimson-scented flames. He had water, too, cool scented water, that sprayed his burning flesh, that washed in his eyes, his hair, his throat. After that came hunger, a fierce rending agony, that scorched and clutched and tore at his entrails; but that, too, died away, and he dreamed that he had eaten and all his flesh was warm. Then he dreamed that he slept; and when he slept he dreamed no more.

One day he awoke and found her stretched beside him, soft palms tightly closed, smiling, asleep.

V

Now the days began to run more swiftly than the tide along the tawny beach; and the nights, star-dusted and blue, came and vanished and returned, only to exhale at dawn like perfume from a violet.

They counted hours as they counted the golden bubbles, winking with a million eyes along the foam-flecked shore; and the hours ended, and began, and glimmered, iridescent, and ended as bubbles end in a tiny rainbow haze.

There was still fire in the world; it flashed up at her touch and where she chose. A bow strung with the silk of her own hair, an arrow winged like a sea bird and tipped with shell, a line from the silver tendon of a deer, a hook of polished bone—these were the mysteries he learned, and learned them laughing, her silken head bent close to his.

The first night that the bow was wrought and the glossy string attuned, she stole into the moonlit forest to the brook; and there they stood, whispering, listening, and whispering, though neither understood the voice they loved.

In the deeper woods, Kaug, the porcupine, scraped and snuffed. They heard Wabóse, the rabbit, pit-a-pat, pit-a-pat, loping across dead leaves in the moonlight. Skeé-skah, the wood-duck, sailed past, noiseless, gorgeous as a floating blossom.

Out on the ocean's placid silver, Shinge-bis, the diver, shook the scented silence with his idle laughter, till Kay-óshk, the gray gull, stirred in his slumber. There came a sudden ripple in the stream, a mellow splash, a soft sound on the sand.

"Ihó! Behold!"

"I see nothing."

The beloved voice was only a wordless melody to her.

"Ihó! Ta-hinca, the red deer! E-hó! The buck will follow!"

"Ta-hinca," he repeated, notching the arrow.

"E-tó! Ta-mdóka!"

So he drew the arrow to the head, and the gray gull feathers brushed his ear, and the darkness hummed with the harmony of the singing string.

Thus died Ta-mdóka, the buck deer of seven prongs.

VI

As an apple tossed spinning into the air, so spun the world above the hand that tossed it into space.

And one day in early spring, Sé-só-Kah, the robin, awoke at dawn, and saw a girl at the foot of the blossoming tree holding a babe cradled in the silken sheets of her hair.

At its feeble cry, Kaug, the porcupine, raised his quilled head. Wabóse, the rabbit, sat still with palpitating sides. Kay-óshk, the gray gull, tiptoed along the beach.

Kent knelt with one bronzed arm around them both.

"Ihó! Inâh!" whispered the girl, and held the babe up in the rosy flames of dawn.

But Kent trembled as he looked, and his eyes filled. On the pale green moss their shadows lay—three shadows. But the shadow of the babe was white as froth.

Because it was the firstborn son, they named it Chaské; and the girl sang as she cradled it there in the silken vestments of her hair; all day long in the sunshine she sang:

Wâ-wa, wâ-wa, wâ-wa—yeâ;
Kah-wéen, nee-zhéka Ke-diaus-âi,
Ke-gâh nau-wâi, ne-mé-go S'weén,
Ne-bâun, ne-bâun, ne-dâun-is âis.
E-we wâ-wa, wâ-we—yeá;
E-we wâ-wa, wâ-we—yeá.

Out in the calm ocean, Shinge-bis, the diver, listened, preening his satin breast in silence. In the forest, Ta-hinca, the red deer, turned her delicate head to the wind.

That night Kent thought of the dead, for the first time since he had come to the Key of Grief.

"Aké-u! aké-u!" chirped Sé-só-Kah, the robin. But the dead never come again.

"Beloved, sit close to us," whispered the girl, watching his troubled eyes. "Ma-cânte maséca."

But he looked at the babe and its white shadow on the moss, and he only sighed: "Macânte maséca, beloved! Death sits watching us across the sea."

Now for the first time he knew more than the fear of fear; he knew fear. And with fear came grief.

He never before knew that grief lay hidden there in the forest. Now he knew it. Still, that happiness, eternally reborn when two small hands reached up around his neck, when feeble fingers clutched his hand—that happiness that Sé-só-Kah understood, chirping to his brooding mate—that Ta-mdóka knew, licking his dappled fawns—that happiness gave him heart to meet grief calmly, in dreams or in the forest depths, and it helped him to look into the hollow eyes of fear.

He often thought of the camp now; of Bates, his blanket mate; of Dyce, whose wrist he had broken with a blow; of Tully, whose brother he had shot. He even seemed to hear the shot, the sudden report among the hemlocks; again he saw the haze of smoke, he caught a glimpse of a tall form falling through the bushes.

He remembered every minute incident of the trial: Bates's hand laid on his shoulder; Tully, red-bearded and wild-eyed, demanding his death; while Dyce spat and spat and smoked and kicked at the blackened log-ends projecting from the fire. He remembered, too, the verdict, and Tully's terrible laugh; and the new jute rope that they stripped off the market-sealed gum packs.

He thought of these things, sometimes wading out on the shoals, shell-tipped fish spear poised: at such times he would miss his fish. He thought of it sometimes when he knelt by the forest stream listening for Ta-hinca's splash among the cresses: at such moments the feathered shaft whistled far from the mark, and Tam-dóka stamped and snorted till even the white fisher, stretched on a rotting log, flattened his whiskers and stole away into the forest's blackest depths.

When the child was a year old, hour for hour notched at sunset and sunrise, it prattled with the birds, and called to Ne-Kâ, the wild goose, who called again to the child from the sky: "North-ward! northward, beloved!"

When winter came—there is no frost on the Island of Grief—Ne-Kâ, the wild goose, passing high in the clouds, called: "South-ward! southward, beloved!" And the child answered in a soft whisper of an unknown tongue, till the mother shivered, and covered it with her silken hair.

"O beloved!" said the girl, "Chaské calls to all things living—to Kaug, the porcupine, to Wabóse, to Kay-óshk, the gray gull—he calls, and they understand."

Kent bent and looked into her eyes.

"Hush, beloved; it is not *that* I fear."

"Then what, beloved?"

"His shadow. It is white as surf foam. And at night—I—I have seen——"

"Oh, what?"

"The air about him aglow like a pale rose."

"Ma cânté maséca. The earth alone lasts. I speak as one dying—I know, O beloved!"

Her voice died away like a summer wind.

"Beloved!" he cried.

But there before him she was changing; the air grew misty, and her hair wavered like shreds of fog, and her slender form swayed, and faded, and swerved, like the mist above a pond.

In her arms the babe was a figure of mist, rosy, vague as a breath on a mirror.

"The earth alone lasts. Inâh! It is the end, O beloved!"

The words came from the mist—a mist as formless as the ether—a mist that drove in and crowded him, that came from the sea, from the clouds, from the earth at his feet. Faint with terror, he staggered forward calling, "Beloved! And thou, Chaské, O beloved! Aké u! Aké u!"

Far out at sea a rosy star glimmered an instant in the mist and went out.

A sea bird screamed, soaring over the waste of fog-smothered waters. Again he saw the rosy star; it came nearer; its reflection glimmered in the water.

"Chaské!" he cried.

He heard a voice, dull in the choking mist.

"O beloved, I am here!" he called again.

There was a sound on the shoal, a flicker in the fog, the flare of a torch, a face white, livid, terrible—the face of the dead.

He fell upon his knees; he closed his eyes and opened them. Tully stood beside him with a coil of rope.

* * * * *

Ihó! Behold the end! The earth alone lasts. The sand, the opal wave on the golden beach, the sea of sapphire, the dusted starlight, the wind, and love, shall die. Death also shall die, and lie on the shores of the skies like the bleached skull there on the Key to Grief, polished, empty, with its teeth embedded in the sand.

THE MAKER OF MOONS

I am myself just as much evil as good, and my nation
is—And I say there is in fact no evil;
(Or if there is, I say it is just as important to you, to
the land, or to me, as anything else.

* * * * * *

Each is not for its own sake;
I say the whole earth, and all the stars in the sky, are
for Religion's sake.
I say no man has ever yet been half devout enough;
None has ever yet adored or worshipped half enough;
None has begun to think how divine he himself is, and
how certain the future is."

WALT WHITMAN.

"I have heard what the Talkers were talking,—the talk
Of the beginning and the end;
But I do not talk of the beginning or the end."

I

CONCERNING YUE-LAOU AND THE XIN I KNOW NOTHING MORE than you shall know. I am miserably anxious to clear the matter up. Perhaps what I write may save the United States Government money and lives, perhaps it may arouse the scientific world to action; at any rate it will put an end to the terrible suspense of two people. Certainty is better than suspense.

If the Government dares to disregard this warning and refuses to send a thoroughly equipped expedition at once, the people of the State may take swift vengeance on the whole region and leave a blackened devastated waste where to-day forest and flowering meadow land border the lake in the Cardinal Woods.

You already know part of the story; the New York papers have been full of alleged details. This much is true: Barris caught the "Shiner," red handed, or rather yellow handed, for his pockets and boots and dirty fists were stuffed with lumps of gold. I say gold, advisedly. You may call it what you please. You also know how Barris was—but unless I begin at the beginning of my own experiences you will be none the wiser after all.

On the third of August of this present year I was standing in Tiffany's, chatting with George Godfrey of the designing department. On the glass counter between us lay a coiled serpent, an exquisite specimen of chiselled gold.

"No," replied Godfrey to my question, "it isn't my work; I wish it was. Why, man, it's a masterpiece!"

"Whose?" I asked.

"Now I should be very glad to know also," said Godfrey. "We bought it from an old jay who says he lives in the country somewhere about the Cardinal Woods. That's near Starlit Lake, I believe——"

"Lake of the Stars?" I suggested.

"Some call it Starlit Lake,—it's all the same. Well, my rustic Reuben says that he represents the sculptor of this snake for all practical and business purposes. He got his price too. We hope he'll bring us something more. We have sold this already to the Metropolitan Museum."

I was leaning idly on the glass case, watching the keen eyes of the artist in precious metals as he stooped over the gold serpent.

"A masterpiece!" he muttered to himself, fondling the glittering coil; "look at the texture! whew!" But I was not looking at the serpent. Something was moving,—crawling out of Godfrey's coat pocket,—the pocket nearest to me,—something soft and yellow with crab-like legs all covered with coarse yellow hair.

"What in Heaven's name," said I, "have you got in your pocket? It's crawling out—it's trying to creep up your coat, Godfrey!"

He turned quickly and dragged the creature out with his left hand.

I shrank back as he held the repulsive object dangling before me, and he laughed and placed it on the counter.

"Did you ever see anything like that?" he demanded.

"No," said I truthfully, "and I hope I never shall again. What is it?"

"I don't know. Ask them at the Natural History Museum—they can't tell you. The Smithsonian is all at sea too. It is, I believe, the connecting link between a sea-urchin, a spider, and the devil. It looks venomous but I can't find either fangs or mouth. Is it blind? These things may be eyes but they look as if they were painted. A Japanese sculptor might have produced such an impossible beast, but it is hard to believe that God did. It looks unfinished too. I have a mad idea that this creature is only one of the parts of some larger and more grotesque organism,—it looks so lonely, so hopelessly dependent, so cursedly unfinished. I'm going to use it as a model. If I don't out-Japanese the Japs my name isn't Godfrey."

The creature was moving slowly across the glass case towards me. I drew back.

"Godfrey," I said, "I would execute a man who executed any such work as you propose. What do you want to perpetuate such a reptile for? I can stand the Japanese grotesque but I can't stand that—spider—"

"It's a crab."

"Crab or spider or blind-worm—ugh! What do you want to do it for? It's a nightmare—it's unclean!"

I hated the thing. It was the first living creature that I had ever hated.

For some time I had noticed a damp acrid odour in the air, and Godfrey said it came from the reptile.

"Then kill it and bury it," I said; "and by the way, where did it come from?"

"I don't know that either," laughed Godfrey; "I found it clinging to the box that this gold serpent was brought in. I suppose my old Reuben is responsible."

"If the Cardinal Woods are the lurking places for things like this," said I, "I am sorry that I am going to the Cardinal Woods."

"Are you?" asked Godfrey; "for the shooting?"

"Yes, with Barris and Pierpont. Why don't you kill that creature?"

"Go off on your shooting trip, and let me alone," laughed Godfrey.

I shuddered at the "crab," and bade Godfrey good-bye until December.

That night, Pierpont, Barris, and I sat chatting in the smoking-car of the Quebec Express when the long train pulled out of the Grand Central Depot. Old David had gone forward with the dogs; poor things, they hated to ride in the baggage car, but the Quebec and Northern road provides no sportsman's cars, and David and the three Gordon setters were in for an uncomfortable night.

Except for Pierpont, Barris, and myself, the car was empty. Barris, trim, stout, ruddy, and bronzed, sat drumming on the window ledge, puffing a short fragrant pipe. His gun-case lay beside him on the floor.

"When *I* have white hair and years of discretion," said Pierpont languidly, "I'll not flirt with pretty serving-maids; will you, Roy?"

"No," said I, looking at Barris.

"You mean the maid with the cap in the Pullman car?" asked Barris.

"Yes," said Pierpont.

I smiled, for I had seen it also.

Barris twisted his crisp grey moustache, and yawned.

"You children had better be toddling off to bed," he said. "That lady's-maid is a member of the Secret Service."

"Oh," said Pierpont, "one of your colleagues?"

"You might present us, you know," I said; "the journey is monotonous."

Barris had drawn a telegram from his pocket, and as he sat turning it over and over between his fingers he smiled. After a moment or two he handed it to Pierpont who read it with slightly raised eyebrows.

"It's rot,—I suppose it's cipher," he said; "I see it's signed by General Drummond——"

"Drummond, Chief of the Government Secret Service," said Barris.

"Something interesting?" I enquired, lighting a cigarette.

"Something so interesting," replied Barris, "that I'm going to look into it myself——"

"And break up our shooting trio——"

"No. Do you want to hear about it? Do you Billy Pierpont?"

"Yes," replied that immaculate young man.

Barris rubbed the amber mouth-piece of his pipe on his handkerchief, cleared the stem with a bit of wire, puffed once or twice, and leaned back in his chair.

"Pierpont," he said, "do you remember that evening at the United States Club when General Miles, General Drummond, and

I were examining that gold nugget that Captain Mahan had? You examined it also, I believe."

"I did," said Pierpont.

"Was it gold?" asked Barris, drumming on the window.

"It was," replied Pierpont.

"I saw it too," said I; "of course, it was gold."

"Professor La Grange saw it also," said Barris; "he said it was gold."

"Well?" said Pierpont.

"Well," said Barris, "it was not gold."

After a silence Pierpont asked what tests had been made.

"The usual tests," replied Barris. "The United States Mint is satisfied that it is gold, so is every jeweller who has seen it. But it is not gold,—and yet—it is gold."

Pierpont and I exchanged glances.

"Now," said I, "for Barris's usual coup-de-théâtre: what was the nugget?"

"Practically it was pure gold; but," said Barris, enjoying the situation intensely, "really it was not gold. Pierpont, what is gold?"

"Gold's an element, a metal——"

"Wrong! Billy Pierpont," said Barris coolly.

"Gold was an element when I went to school," said I.

"It has not been an element for two weeks," said Barris; "and, except General Drummond, Professor La Grange, and myself, you two youngsters are the only people, except one, in the world who know it,—or have known it."

"Do you mean to say that gold is a composite metal?" said Pierpont slowly.

"I do. La Grange has made it. He produced a scale of pure gold day before yesterday. That nugget was manufactured gold."

Could Barris be joking? Was this a colossal hoax? I looked at Pierpont. He muttered something about that settling the silver question, and turned his head to Barris, but there was that in Barris's face which forbade jesting, and Pierpont and I sat silently pondering.

"Don't ask me how it's made," said Barris, quietly; "I don't know. But I do know that somewhere in the region of the Cardinal

Woods there is a gang of people who do know how gold is made, and who make it. You understand the danger this is to every civilized nation. It's got to be stopped of course. Drummond and I have decided that I am the man to stop it. Wherever and whoever these people are—these gold makers,—they must be caught, every one of them,—caught or shot."

"Or shot," repeated Pierpont, who was owner of the Cross-Cut Gold Mine and found his income too small; "Professor La Grange will of course be prudent;—science need not know things that would upset the world!"

"Little Willy," said Barris laughing, "your income is safe."

"I suppose," said I, "some flaw in the nugget gave Professor La Grange the tip."

"Exactly. He cut the flaw out before sending the nugget to be tested. He worked on the flaw and separated gold into its three elements."

"He is a great man," said Pierpont, "but he will be the greatest man in the world if he can keep his discovery to himself."

"Who?" said Barris.

"Professor La Grange."

"Professor La Grange was shot through the heart two hours ago," replied Barris slowly.

II

We had been at the shooting box in the Cardinal Woods five days when a telegram was brought to Barris by a mounted messenger from the nearest telegraph station, Cardinal Springs, a hamlet on the lumber railroad which joins the Quebec and Northern at Three Rivers Junction, thirty miles below.

Pierpont and I were sitting out under the trees, loading some special shells as experiments; Barris stood beside us, bronzed, erect, holding his pipe carefully so that no sparks should drift into our powder box. The beat of hoofs over the grass aroused us, and when the lank messenger drew bridle before the door, Barris stepped forward and took the sealed telegram. When he had torn it open he went into the house and presently reappeared, reading something that he had written.

"This should go at once," he said, looking the messenger full in the face.

"At once, Colonel Barris," replied the shabby countryman.

Pierpont glanced up and I smiled at the messenger who was gathering his bridle and settling himself in his stirrups. Barris handed him the written reply and nodded good-bye: there was a thud of hoofs on the greensward, a jingle of bit and spur across the gravel, and the messenger was gone. Barris's pipe went out and he stepped to windward to relight it.

"It is queer," said I, "that your messenger—a battered native,—should speak like a Harvard man."

"He is a Harvard man," said Barris.

"And the plot thickens," said Pierpont; "are the Cardinal Woods full of your Secret Service men, Barris?"

"No," replied Barris, "but the telegraph stations are. How many ounces of shot are you using, Roy?"

I told him, holding up the adjustable steel measuring cup. He nodded. After a moment or two he sat down on a camp-stool beside us and picked up a crimper.

"That telegram was from Drummond," he said; "the messenger was one of my men as you two bright little boys divined. Pooh! If he had spoken the Cardinal County dialect you wouldn't have known."

"His make-up was good," said Pierpont.

Barris twirled the crimper and looked at the pile of loaded shells. Then he picked up one and crimped it.

"Let 'em alone," said Pierpont, "you crimp too tight."

"Does his little gun kick when the shells are crimped too tight?" enquired Barris tenderly; "well, he shall crimp his own shells then,—where's his little man?"

"His little man," was a weird English importation, stiff, very carefully scrubbed, tangled in his aspirates, named Howlett. As valet, gilly, gun-bearer, and crimper, he aided Pierpont to endure the ennui of existence, by doing for him everything except breathing. Lately, however, Barris's taunts had driven Pierpont to do a few things for himself. To his astonishment he found that cleaning his own gun was not a bore, so he timidly loaded a shell or two, was much pleased with himself, loaded some more, crimped them, and went to breakfast with an appetite. So when Barris asked where "his little man" was, Pierpont did not reply but dug a cupful of shot from the bag and poured it solemnly into the half-filled shell.

Old David came out with the dogs and of course there was a pow-wow when "Voyou," my Gordon, wagged his splendid tail across the loading table and sent a dozen unstopped cartridges rolling over the grass, vomiting powder and shot.

"Give the dogs a mile or two," said I; "we will shoot over the Sweet Fern Covert about four o'clock, David."

"Two guns, David," added Barris.

"Are you not going?" asked Pierpont, looking up, as David disappeared with the dogs.

"Bigger game," said Barris shortly. He picked up a mug of ale from the tray which Howlett had just set down beside us and took a long pull. We did the same, silently. Pierpont set his mug on the turf beside him and returned to his loading.

We spoke of the murder of Professor La Grange, of how it had been concealed by the authorities in New York at Drummond's request, of the certainty that it was one of the gang of gold-makers who had done it, and of the possible alertness of the gang.

"Oh, they know that Drummond will be after them sooner or later," said Barris, "but they don't know that the mills of the gods have already begun to grind. Those smart New York papers builded better than they knew when their ferret-eyed reporter poked his red nose into the house on 58th Street and sneaked off with a column on his cuffs about the 'suicide' of Professor La Grange. Billy Pierpont, my revolver is hanging in your room; I'll take yours too——"

"Help yourself," said Pierpont.

"I shall be gone over night," continued Barris; "my poncho and some bread and meat are all I shall take except the 'barkers.'"

"Will they bark to-night?" I asked.

"No, I trust not for several weeks yet. I shall nose about a bit. Roy, did it ever strike you how queer it is that this wonderfully beautiful country should contain no inhabitants?"

"It's like those splendid stretches of pools and rapids which one finds on every trout river and in which one never finds a fish," suggested Pierpont.

"Exactly,—and Heaven alone knows why," said Barris; "I suppose this country is shunned by human beings for the same mysterious reasons."

"The shooting is the better for it," I observed.

"The shooting is good," said Barris, "have you noticed the snipe on the meadow by the lake? Why it's brown with them! That's a wonderful meadow."

"It's a natural one," said Pierpont, "no human being ever cleared that land."

"Then it's supernatural," said Barris; "Pierpont, do you want to come with me?"

Pierpont's handsome face flushed as he answered slowly, "It's awfully good of you,—if I may."

"Bosh," said I, piqued because he had asked Pierpont, "what use is little Willy without his man?"

"True," said Barris gravely, "you can't take Howlett you know."

Pierpont muttered something which ended in "d—n."

"Then," said I, "there will be but one gun on the Sweet Fern Covert this afternoon. Very well, I wish you joy of your cold supper and colder bed. Take your night-gown, Willy, and don't sleep on the damp ground."

"Let Pierpont alone," retorted Barris, "you shall go next time, Roy."

"Oh, all right,—you mean when there's shooting going on?"

"And I?" demanded Pierpont, grieved.

"You too, my son; stop quarelling! Will you ask Howlett to pack our kits—lightly mind you,—no bottles,—they clink."

"My flask doesn't," said Pierpont, and went off to get ready for a night's stalking of dangerous men.

"It is strange," said I, "that nobody ever settles in this region. How many people live in Cardinal Springs, Barris?"

"Twenty counting the telegraph operator and not counting the lumbermen; they are always changing and shifting. I have six men among them."

"Where have you no men? In the Four Hundred?"

"I have men there also,—chums of Billy's only he doesn't know it. David tells me that there was a strong flight of woodcock last night. You ought to pick up some this afternoon."

Then we chatted about alder-cover and swamp until Pierpont came out of the house and it was time to part.

"Au revoir," said Barris, buckling on his kit, "come along, Pierpont, and don't walk in the damp grass."

"If you are not back by to-morrow noon," said I, "I will take Howlett and David and hunt you up. You say your course is due north?"

"Due north," replied Barris, consulting his compass.

"There is a trail for two miles and a spotted lead for two more," said Pierpont.

"Which we won't use for various reasons," added Barris pleasantly; "don't worry, Roy, and keep your confounded expedition out of the way; there*'s* no danger."

He knew, of course, what he was talking about and I held my peace.

When the tip end of Pierpont's shooting coat had disappeared in the Long Covert, I found myself standing alone with Howlett. He bore my gaze for a moment and then politely lowered his eyes.

"Howlett," said I, "take these shells and implements to the gun room, and drop nothing. Did Voyou come to any harm in the briers this morning?"

"No 'arm, Mr. Cardenhe, sir," said Howlett.

"Then be careful not to drop anything else," said I, and walked away leaving him decorously puzzled. For he had dropped no cartridges. Poor Howlett!

III

About four o'clock that afternoon I met David and the dogs at the spinney which leads into the Sweet Fern Covert. The three setters, Voyou, Gamin, and Mioche were in fine feather,—David had killed a woodcock and a brace of grouse over them that morning,—and they were thrashing about the spinney at short range when I came up, gun under arm and pipe lighted.

"What's the prospect, David," I asked, trying to keep my feet in the tangle of wagging, whining dogs; "hello, what's amiss with Mioche?"

"A brier in his foot sir; I drew it and stopped the wound but I guess the gravel's got in. If you have no objection, sir, I might take him back with me."

"It's safer," I said; "take Gamin too, I only want one dog this afternoon. What is the situation?"

"Fair sir; the grouse lie within a quarter of a mile of the oak second-growth. The woodcock are mostly on the alders. I saw any number of snipe on the meadows. There's something else in by the lake,—I can't just tell what, but the wood-duck set up a clatter when I was in the thicket and they come dashing through the wood as if a dozen foxes was snappin' at their tail feathers."

"Probably a fox," I said; "leash those dogs,—they must learn to stand it. I'll be back by dinner time."

"There is one more thing sir," said David, lingering with his gun under his arm.

"Well," said I.

"I saw a man in the woods by the Oak Covert,—at least I think I did."

"A lumberman?"

"I think not sir—at least,—do they have Chinamen among them?"

"Chinese? No. You didn't see a Chinaman in the woods here?"

"I—I think I did sir,—I can't say positively. He was gone when I ran into the covert."

"Did the dogs notice it?"

"I can't say—exactly. They acted queer like. Gamin here lay down an whined—it may have been colic—and Mioche whimpered,—perhaps it was the brier."

"And Voyou?"

"Voyou, he was most remarkable sir, and the hair on his back stood up. I did see a groundhog makin' for a tree near by."

"Then no wonder Voyou bristled. David, your Chinaman was a stump or tussock. Take the dogs now."

"I guess it was sir; good afternoon sir," said David, and walked away with the Gordons leaving me alone with Voyou in the spinney.

I looked at the dog and he looked at me.

"Voyou!"

The dog sat down and danced with his fore feet, his beautiful brown eyes sparkling.

"You're a fraud," I said; "which shall it be, the alders or the upland? Upland? Good!—now for the grouse,—heel, my friend, and show your miraculous self-restraint."

Voyou wheeled into my tracks and followed close, nobly refusing to notice the impudent chipmunks and the thousand and one alluring and important smells which an ordinary dog would have lost no time in investigating.

The brown and yellow autumn woods were crisp with drifting heaps of leaves and twigs that crackled under foot as we turned from the spinney into the forest. Every silent little stream, hurrying toward the lake was gay with painted leaves afloat, scarlet maple or yellow oak. Spots of sunlight fell upon the pools, searching the brown depths, illuminating the gravel bottom where shoals of minnows swam to and fro, and to and fro again, busy with the purpose of their little lives. The crickets were chirping in the long brittle grass on the edge of the woods, but we left them far behind in the silence of the deeper forest.

"Now!" said I to Voyou.

The dog sprang to the front, circled once, zigzagged through the ferns around us and, all in a moment, stiffened stock still, rigid as sculptured bronze. I stepped forward, raising my gun, two paces, three paces, ten perhaps, before a great cock-grouse blundered up from the brake and burst through the thicket fringe toward the deeper growth. There was a flash and puff from my gun, a crash of echoes among the low wooded cliffs, and through the faint veil of smoke something dark dropped from mid-air amid a cloud of feathers, brown as the brown leaves under foot.

"Fetch!"

Up from the ground sprang Voyou, and in a moment he came galloping back, neck arched, tail stiff but waving, holding tenderly in his pink mouth a mass of mottled bronzed feathers. Very gravely he laid the bird at my feet and crouched close beside it, his silky ears across his paws, his muzzle on the ground.

I dropped the grouse into my pocket, held for a moment a silent caressing communion with Voyou, then swung my gun under my arm and motioned the dog on.

It must have been five o'clock when I walked into a little opening in the woods and sat down to breathe. Voyou came and sat down in front of me.

"Well?" I enquired.

Voyou gravely presented one paw which I took.

"We will never get back in time for dinner," said I, "so we might as well take it easy. It's all your fault, you know. Is there a brier in your foot?—let's see,—there! it's out my friend and you are free to nose about and lick it. If you loll your tongue out you'll get it all over twigs and moss. Can't you lie down and try to pant less? No, there is no use in sniffing and looking at that fern patch, for we are going to smoke a little, doze a little, and go home by moonlight. Think what a big dinner we will have! Think of Howlett's despair when we are not in time! Think of all the stories you will have to tell to Gamin and Mioche! Think what a good dog you have been! There—you are tired old chap; take forty winks with me."

Voyou was a little tired. He stretched out on the leaves at my feet but whether or not he really slept I could not be certain, until his hind legs twitched and I knew he was dreaming of mighty deeds.

Now I may have taken forty winks, but the sun seemed to be no lower when I sat up and unclosed my lids. Voyou raised his head, saw in my eyes that I was not going yet, thumped his tail half a dozen times on the dried leaves, and settled back with a sigh.

I looked lazily around, and for the first time noticed what a wonderfully beautiful spot I had chosen for a nap. It was an oval glade in the heart of the forest, level and carpeted with green grass. The trees that surrounded it were gigantic; they formed one towering circular wall of verdure, blotting out all except the turquoise blue of the sky-oval above. And now I noticed that in the centre of the greensward lay a pool of water, crystal clear, glimmering like a mirror in the meadow grass, beside a block of granite. It scarcely seemed possible that the symmetry of tree and lawn and lucent pool could have been one of nature's accidents. I had never before seen this glade nor had I ever heard it spoken of by either Pierpont or Barris. It was a marvel, this diamond clear basin, regular and graceful as a Roman fountain, set in the gem of turf. And these great trees,—they also belonged, not in America but in some legend-haunted forest of France, where moss-grown marbles stand neglected in dim glades, and the twilight of the forest shelters fairies and slender shapes from shadow-land.

I lay and watched the sunlight showering the tangled thicket where masses of crimson Cardinal-flowers glowed, or where one long dusty sunbeam tipped the edge of the floating leaves in the pool, turning them to palest gilt. There were birds too, passing through the dim avenues of trees like jets of flame,—the gorgeous Cardinal-Bird in his deep stained crimson robe,—the bird that gave to the woods, to the village fifteen miles away, to the whole county, the name of Cardinal.

I rolled over on my back and looked up at the sky. How pale,—paler than a robin's egg,—it was. I seemed to be lying at the bottom of a well, walled with verdure, high towering on every side. And, as I lay, all about me the air became sweet scented. Sweeter and sweeter and more penetrating grew the perfume, and

I wondered what stray breeze, blowing over acres of lilies could have brought it. But there was no breeze; the air was still. A gilded fly alighted on my hand,—a honey-fly. It was as troubled as I by the scented silence.

Then, behind me, my dog growled.

I sat quite still at first, hardly breathing, but my eyes were fixed on a shape that moved along the edge of the pool among the meadow grasses. The dog had ceased growling and was now staring, alert and trembling.

At last I rose and walked rapidly down to the pool, my dog following close to heel.

The figure, a woman's, turned slowly toward us.

IV

She was standing still when I approached the pool. The forest around us was so silent that when I spoke the sound of my own voice startled me.

"No," she said,—and her voice was smooth as flowing water, "I have not lost my way. Will he come to me, your beautiful dog?"

Before I could speak, Voyou crept to her and laid his silky head against her knees.

"But surely," said I, "you did not come here alone."

"Alone? I did come alone."

"But the nearest settlement is Cardinal, probably nineteen miles from where we are standing."

"I do not know Cardinal," she said.

"Ste. Croix in Canada is forty miles at least,—how did you come into the Cardinal Woods?" I asked amazed.

"Into the woods?" she repeated a little impatiently.

"Yes."

She did not answer at first, but stood caressing Voyou with gentle phrase and gesture.

"Your beautiful dog I am fond of, but I am not fond of being questioned," she said quietly. "My name is Ysonde and I came to the fountain here to see your dog."

I was properly quenched. After a moment or two I did say that in another hour it would be growing dusky, but she neither replied nor looked at me.

"This," I ventured, "is a beautiful pool,—you call it a fountain,—a delicious fountain: I have never before seen it. It is hard to imagine that nature did all this."

"Is it?" she said.

"Don't you think so?" I asked.

"I haven't thought; I wish when you go you would leave me your dog."

"My—my dog?"

"If you don't mind," she said sweetly, and looked at me for the first time in the face.

For an instant our glances met, then she grew grave, and I saw that her eyes were fixed on my forehead. Suddenly she rose and drew nearer, looking intently at my forehead. There was a faint mark there, a tiny crescent, just over my eyebrow. It was a birthmark.

"Is that a scar?" she demanded drawing nearer.

"That crescent shaped mark? No."

"No? Are you sure?" she insisted.

"Perfectly," I replied, astonished.

"A—a birthmark?"

"Yes,—may I ask why?"

As she drew away from me, I saw that the color had fled from her cheeks. For a second she clasped both hands over her eyes as if to shut out my face, then slowly dropping her hands, she sat down on a long square block of stone which half encircled the basin, and on which to my amazement I saw carving. Voyou went to her again and laid his head in her lap.

"What is your name?" she asked at length.

"Roy Cardenhe."

"Mine is Ysonde. I carved these dragon-flies on the stone, these fishes and shells and butterflies you see."

"You! They are wonderfully delicate,—but those are not American dragon-flies—"

"No—they are more beautiful. See, I have my hammer and chisel with me."

She drew from a queer pouch at her side a small hammer and chisel and held them toward me.

"You are very talented," I said, "where did you study?"

"I? I never studied,—I knew how. I saw things and cut them out of stone. Do you like them? Sometime I will show you other things that I have done. If I had a great lump of bronze I could make your dog, beautiful as he is."

Her hammer fell into the fountain and I leaned over and plunged my arm into the water to find it.

"It is there, shining on the sand," she said, leaning over the pool with me.

"Where," said I, looking at our reflected faces in the water. For it was only in the water that I had dared, as yet, to look her long in the face.

The pool mirrored the exquisite oval of her head, the heavy hair, the eyes. I heard the silken rustle of her girdle, I caught the flash of a white arm, and the hammer was drawn up dripping with spray.

The troubled surface of the pool grew calm and again I saw her eyes reflected.

"Listen," she said in a low voice, "do you think you will come again to my fountain?"

"I will come," I said. My voice was dull; the noise of water filled my ears.

Then a swift shadow sped across the pool; I rubbed my eyes. Where her reflected face had bent beside mine there was nothing mirrored but the rosy evening sky with one pale star glimmering. I drew myself up and turned. She was gone. I saw the faint star twinkling above me in the afterglow, I saw the tall trees motionless in the still evening air, I saw my dog slumbering at my feet.

The sweet scent in the air had faded, leaving in my nostrils the heavy odor of fern and forest mould. A blind fear seized me, and I caught up my gun and and sprang into the darkening woods. The dog followed me, crashing through the undergrowth at my side.

Duller and duller grew the light, but I strode on, the sweat pouring from my face and hair, my mind a chaos. How I reached the spinney I can hardly tell. As I turned up the path I caught a glimpse of a human face peering at me from the darkening thicket,—a horrible human face, yellow and drawn with high-boned cheeks and narrow eyes.

Involuntarily I halted; the dog at my heels snarled. Then I sprang straight at it, floundering blindly through the thicket, but the night had fallen swiftly and I found myself panting and struggling in a maze of twisted shrubbery and twining vines, unable to see the very undergrowth that ensnared me.

It was a pale face, and a scratched one that I carried to a late dinner that night. Howlett served me, dumb reproach in his eyes, for the soup had been standing and the grouse was juiceless.

David brought the dogs in after they had had their supper, and I drew my chair before the blaze and set my ale on a table beside me. The dogs curled up at my feet, blinking gravely at the sparks that snapped and flew in eddying showers from the heavy birch logs.

"David," said I, "did you say you saw a Chinaman today?"

"I did sir."

"What do you think about it now?"

"I may have been mistaken sir——"

"But you think not. What sort of whiskey did you put in my flask today?"

"The usual sir."

"Is there much gone?"

"About three swallows sir, as usual."

"You don't suppose there could have been any mistake about that whiskey,—no medicine could have gotten into it for instance."

David smiled and said, "No sir."

"Well," said I, "I have had an extraordinary dream."

When I said "dream," I felt comforted and reassured. I had scarcely dared to say it before, even to myself.

"An extraordinary dream," I repeated; "I fell asleep in the woods about five o'clock, in that pretty glade where the fountain—I mean the pool is. You know the place?"

"I do not sir."

I described it minutely, twice, but David shook his head.

"Carved stone did you say sir? I never chanced on it. You don't mean the New Spring——"

"No, no! This glade is way beyond that. Is it possible that any people inhabit the forest between here and the Canada line?"

"Nobody short of Ste. Croix; at least I have no knowledge of any."

"Of course," said I, "when I thought I saw a Chinaman, it was imagination. Of course I had been more impressed than I was aware of by your adventure. Of course you saw no Chinaman, David."

"Probably not sir," replied David dubiously.

I sent him off to bed, saying I should keep the dogs with me all night; and when he was gone, I took a good long draught of ale, "just to shame the devil," as Pierpont said, and lighted a cigar. Then I thought of Barris and Pierpont, and their cold bed, for I knew they would not dare build a fire, and, in spite of the hot chimney corner and the crackling blaze, I shivered in sympathy.

"I'll tell Barris and Pierpont the whole story and take them to see the carved stone and the fountain," I thought to myself; what a marvellous dream it was—Ysonde,—if it was a dream."

Then I went to the mirror and examined the faint white mark above my eyebrow.

V

About eight o'clock next morning, as I sat listlessly eyeing my coffee cup which Howlett was filling, Gamin and Mioche set up a howl, and in a moment more I heard Barris's step on the porch.

"Hello, Roy," said Pierpont, stamping into the dining room, "I want my breakfast by jingo! Where's Howlett,—none of your *café au lait* for me,—I want a chop and some eggs. Look at that dog, he'll wag the hinge off his tail in a moment——"

"Pierpont," said I, "this loquacity is astonishing but welcome. Where's Barris? You are soaked from neck to ankle."

Pierpont sat down and tore off his stiff muddy leggings.

"Barris is telephoning to Cardinal Springs,—I believe he wants some of his men,—down! Gamin, you idiot! Howlett, three eggs poached and more toast,—what was I saying? Oh, about Barris; he's struck something or other which he hopes will locate these gold-making fellows. I had a jolly time,—he'll tell you about it."

"Billy! Billy!" I said in pleased amazement, "you are learning to talk! Dear me! You load your own shells and you carry your own gun and you fire it yourself—hello! here's Barris all over mud. You fellows really ought to change your rig—whew! what a frightful odor!"

"It's probably this," said Barris tossing something onto the hearth where it shuddered for a moment and then began to writhe; "I found it in the woods by the lake. Do you know what it can be, Roy?"

To my disgust I saw it was another of those spidery, wormy crab-like creatures that Godfrey had in Tiffany's.

"I thought I recognized that acrid odor," I said; "for the love of the Saints take it away from the breakfast table, Barris!"

"But what is it?" he persisted, unslinging his field-glass and revolver.

"I'll tell you what I know after breakfast," I replied firmly, "Howlett, get a broom and sweep that thing into the road.—what are you laughing at, Pierpont?"

Howlett swept the repulsive creature out and Barris and Pierpont went to change their dew-soaked clothes for drier raiment. David came to take the dogs for an airing and in a few minutes Barris reappeared and sat down in his place at the head of the table.

"Well," said I, "is there a story to tell?"

"Yes, not much. They are near the lake on the other side of the woods,—I mean these gold-makers. I shall collar one of them this evening. I haven't located the main gang with any certainty,—shove the toast rack this way will you, Roy,—no, I am not at all certain, but I've nailed one anyway. Pierpont was a great help, really,—and, what do you think, Roy? He wants to join the Secret Service!"

"Little Willy!"

"Exactly. Oh I'll dissuade him. What sort of a reptile was that I brought in? Did Howlett sweep it away?"

"He can sweep it back again for all I care," I said indifferently, "I've finished my breakfast."

"No," said Barris, hastily swallowing his coffee, "it's of no importance; you can tell me about the beast——"

"Serve you right if I had it brought in on toast," I returned.

Pierpont came in radiant, fresh from the bath.

"Go on with your story, Roy," he said; and I told them about Godfrey and his reptile pet.

"Now what in the name of common sense can Godfrey find interesting in that creature?" I ended, tossing my cigarette into the fireplace.

"It's Japanese, don't you think?" said Pierpont.

"No," said Barris, "it is not artistically grotesque, it's vulgar and horrible,—it looks cheap and unfinished——"

"Unfinished,—exactly," said I, "like an American humorist——"

"Yes," said Pierpont, "cheap. What about that gold serpent?"

"Oh, the Metropolitan Museum bought it; you must see it, it's marvellous."

Barris and Pierpont had lighted their cigarettes and, after a moment, we all rose and strolled out to the lawn, where chairs and hammocks were placed under the maple trees.

David passed, gun under arm, dogs heeling.

"Three guns on the meadows at four this afternoon," said Pierpont.

"Roy," said Barris as David bowed and started on, "what did you do yesterday?"

This was the question that I had been expecting. All night long I had dreamed of Ysonde and the glade in the woods, where, at the bottom of the crystal fountain, I saw the reflection of her eyes. All the morning while bathing and dressing I had been persuading myself that the dream was not worth recounting and that a search for the glade and the imaginary stone carving would be ridiculous. But now, as Barris asked the question, I suddenly decided to tell him the whole story.

"See here, you fellows," I said abruptly, "I am going to tell you something queer. You can laugh as much as you please too, but first I want to ask Barris a question or two. You have been in China, Barris?"

"Yes," said Barris, looking straight into my eyes.

"Would a Chinaman be likely to turn lumberman?"

"Have you seen a Chinaman?" he asked in a quiet voice.

"I don't know; David and I both imagined we did."

Barris and Pierpont exchanged glances.

"Have you seen one also?" I demanded, turning to include Pierpont.

"No," said Barris slowly; "but I know that there is, or has been, a Chinaman in these woods."

"The devil!" said I.

"Yes," said Barris gravely; "the devil, if you like,—a devil,—a member of the Kuen-Yuin."

I drew my chair close to the hammock where Pierpont lay at full length, holding out to me a ball of pure gold.

"Well?" said I, examining the engraving on its surface, which represented a mass of twisted creatures,—dragons, I supposed.

"Well," repeated Barris, extending his hand to take the golden ball, "this globe of gold engraved with reptiles and Chinese hieroglyphics is the symbol of the Kuen-Yuin."

"Where did you get it?" I asked, feeling that something startling was impending.

"Pierpont found it by the lake at sunrise this morning. It is the symbol of the Kuen-Yuin," he repeated, "the terrible Kuen-Yuin, the sorcerers of China, and the most murderously diabolical sect on earth."

We puffed our cigarettes in silence until Barris rose, and began to pace backward and forward among the trees, twisting his grey moustache.

"The Kuen-Yuin are sorcerers," he said, pausing before the hammock where Pierpont lay watching him; "I mean exactly what I say,—sorcerers. I've seen them,—I've seen them at their devilish business, and I repeat to you solemnly, that as there are angels above, there is a race of devils on earth, and they are sorcerers. Bah!" he cried, "talk to me of Indian magic and Yogis and all that clap-trap! Why, Roy, I tell you that the Kuen-Yuin have absolute control of a hundred millions of people, mind and body, body and soul. Do you know what goes on in the interior of China? Does Europe know,—could any human being conceive of the condition of that gigantic hell-pit? You read the papers, you hear diplomatic twaddle about Li Hung Chang and the Emperor, you see accounts of battles on sea and land, and you know that Japan has raised a toy tempest along the jagged edge of the great unknown. But you never before heard of the Kuen-Yuin; no, nor has any European except a stray missionary or two, and yet I tell you that when the fires from this pit of hell have eaten through the continent to the coast, the explosion will inundate half a world,—and God help the other half."

Pierpont's cigarette went out; he lighted another, and looked hard at Barris.

"But," resumed Barris quietly, "'sufficient unto the day,' you know,—I did n't intend to say as much as I did,—it would do no good,—even you and Pierpont will forget it,—it seems so impossible and so far away,—like the burning out of the sun. What I want to discuss is the possibility or probability of a Chinaman,—a member of the Kuen-Yuin, being here, at this moment, in the forest."

"If he is," said Pierpont, "possibly the gold-makers owe their discovery to him."

"I do not doubt it for a second," said Barris earnestly.

I took the little golden globe in my hand, and examined the characters engraved upon it.

"Barris," said Pierpont, "I can't believe in sorcery while I am wearing one of Sanford's shooting suits in the pocket of which rests an uncut volume of the 'Duchess.'"

"Neither can I," I said, "for I read the *Evening Post,* and I know Mr. Godkin would not allow it. Hello! What's the matter with this gold ball?"

"What is the matter?" said Barris grimly.

"Why—why—it's changing color—purple, no, crimson—no, it's green I mean—good Heavens! these dragons are twisting under my fingers——"

"Impossible!" muttered Pierpont, leaning over me; "those are not dragons——"

"No!" I cried excitedly; "they are pictures of that reptile that Barris brought back—see—see how they crawl and turn——"

"Drop it!" commanded Barris; and I threw the ball on the turf. In an instant we had all knelt down on the grass beside it, but the globe was again golden, grotesquely wrought with dragons and strange signs.

Pierpont, a little red in the face, picked it up, and handed it to Barris. He placed it on a chair, and sat down beside me.

"Whew!" said I, wiping the perspiration from my face, "how did you play us that trick, Barris?"

"Trick?" said Barris contemptuously.

I looked at Pierpont, and my heart sank. If this was not a trick, what was it? Pierpont returned my glance and colored, but all he said was, "It's devilish queer," and Barris answered, "Yes, devilish." Then Barris asked me again to tell my story, and I did, beginning from the time I met David in the spinney to the moment when I sprang into the darkening thicket where that yellow mask had grinned like a phantom skull.

"Shall we try to find the fountain?" I asked after a pause.

"Yes,—and—er—the lady," suggested Pierpont vaguely.

"Don't be an ass," I said a little impatiently, "you need not come, you know."

"Oh, I'll come," said Pierpont, "unless you think I am indiscreet——"

"Shut up, Pierpont," said Barris, "this thing is serious; I never heard of such a glade or such a fountain, but it's true that nobody knows this forest thoroughly. It's worth while trying for; Roy, can you find your way back to it?"

"Easily," I answered; "when shall we go?"

"It will knock our snipe shooting on the head," said Pierpont, "but then when one has the opportunity of finding a live dream-lady——"

I rose, deeply offended, but Pierpont was not very penitent and his laughter was irresistible.

"The lady's yours by right of discovery," he said, "I'll promise not to infringe on your dreams,—I'll dream about other ladies——"

"Come, come," said I, "I'll have Howlett put you to bed in a minute. Barris, if you are ready,—we can get back to dinner——"

Barris had risen and was gazing at me earnestly.

"What's the matter?" I asked nervously, for I saw that his eyes were fixed on my forehead, and I thought of Ysonde and the white crescent scar.

"Is that a birthmark?" said Barris.

"Yes—why, Barris?"

"Nothing,—an interesting coincidence——"

"What!—for Heaven's sake!"

"The scar,—or rather the birthmark. It is the print of the dragon's claw,—the crescent symbol of Yue-Laou——"

"And who the devil is Yue-Laou?" I said crossly.

"Yue-Laou,—the Moon Maker, Dzil-Nbu of the Kuen-Yuin;—it's Chinese Mythology, but it is believed that Yue-Laou has returned to rule the Kuen-Yuin——"

"The conversation," interrupted Pierpont, "smacks of peacocks' feathers and yellow-jackets. The chicken-pox has left its card on Roy, and Barris is guying us. Come on, you fellows, and make your call on the dream-lady. Barris, I hear galloping; here come your men."

Two mud-splashed riders clattered up to the porch and dismounted at a motion from Barris. I noticed that both of them carried repeating rifles and heavy Colt's revolvers.

They followed Barris, deferentially, into the dining-room, and presently we heard the tinkle of plates and bottles and the low hum of Barris's musical voice.

Half an hour later they came out again, saluted Pierpont and me, and galloped away in the direction of the Canadian frontier.

Ten minutes passed, and, as Barris did not appear, we rose and went into the house, to find him. He was sitting silently before the table, watching the small golden globe, now glowing with scarlet and orange fire, brilliant as a live coal. Howlett, mouth ajar, and eyes starting from the sockets, stood petrified behind him.

"Are you coming," asked Pierpont, a little startled. Barris did not answer. The globe slowly turned to pale gold again,—but the face that Barris raised to ours was white as a sheet. Then he stood up, and smiled with an effort which was painful to us all.

"Give me a pencil and a bit of paper," he said.

Howlett brought it. Barris went to the window and wrote rapidly. He folded the paper, placed it in the top drawer of his desk, locked the drawer, handed me the key, and motioned us to precede him.

When again we stood under the maples, he turned to me with an impenetrable expression. "You will know when to use the key," he said: "Come, Pierpont, we must try to find Roy's fountain."

VI

At two o'clock that afternoon, at Barris's suggestion, we gave up the search for the fountain in the glade and cut across the forest to the spinney where David and Howlett were waiting with our guns and the three dogs.

Pierpont guyed me unmercifully about the "dream-lady" as he called her, and, but for the significant coincidence of Ysonde's and Barris's questions concerning the white scar on my forehead, I should long ago have been perfectly persuaded that I had dreamed the whole thing. As it was, I had no explanation to offer. We had not been able to find the glade although fifty times I came to landmarks which convinced me that we were just about to enter it. Barris was quiet, scarcely uttering a word to either of us during the entire search. I had never before seen him depressed in spirits. However, when we came in sight of the spinney where a cold bit of grouse and a bottle of Burgundy awaited each, Barris seemed to recover his habitual good humor.

"Here's to the dream-lady!" said Pierpont, raising his glass and standing up.

I did not like it. Even if she was only a dream, it irritated me to hear Pierpont's mocking voice. Perhaps Barris understood,—I don't know, but he bade Pierpont drink his wine without further noise, and that young man obeyed with a childlike confidence which almost made Barris smile.

"What about the snipe, David," I asked; "the meadows should be in good condition."

"There is not a snipe on the meadows, sir," said David solemnly.

"Impossible," exclaimed Barris, "they can't have left."

"They have, sir," said David in a sepulchral voice which I hardly recognized.

We all three looked at the old man curiously, waiting for his explanation of this disappointing but sensational report.

David looked at Howlett and Howlett examined the sky.

"I was going," began the old man, with his eyes fastened on Howlett, "I was going along by the spinney with the dogs when I heard a noise in the covert and I seen Howlett come walkin' very fast toward me. In fact," continued David, "I may say he was runnin'. Was you runnin', Howlett?"

Howlett said "Yes," with a decorous cough.

"I beg pardon," said David, "but I'd rather Howlett told the rest. He saw things which I did not."

"Go on, Howlett," commanded Pierpont, much interested.

Howlett coughed again behind his large red hand.

"What David says is true sir," he began; "I h'observed the dogs at a distance 'ow they was a workin' sir, and David stood a lightin' of 's pipe be'ind the spotted beech when I see a 'ead pop up in the covert 'oldin a stick like 'e was h'aimin' at the dogs sir"—

"A head holding a stick?" said Pierpont severely.

"The 'ead 'ad 'ands, sir," explained Howlett, "'ands that 'eld a painted stick,—like that, sir. 'Owlett, thinks I to meself, this 'ere 's queer, so I jumps in an' runs, but the beggar 'e seen me an' w'en I comes alongside of David, 'e was gone. ''Ello 'Owlett,' sez David, 'what the 'ell'—I beg pardon, sir,—''ow did you come 'ere,' sez 'e very loud. 'Run!' sez I, 'the Chinaman is harryin' the dawgs!' 'For Gawd's sake wot Chinaman?' sez David, h'aimin' 'is gun at every bush. Then I thinks I see 'im an' we run an' run, the dawgs a boundin' close to heel sir, but we don't see no Chinaman."

"I'll tell the rest," said David, as Howlett coughed and stepped in a modest corner behind the dogs.

"Go on," said Barris in a strange voice.

"Well sir, when Howlett and I stopped chasin', we was on the cliff overlooking the south meadow. I noticed that there was hundreds of birds there, mostly yellow-legs and plover, and Howlett seen them too. Then before I could say a word to Howlett, something out in the lake gave a splash—a splash as if the whole cliff had fallen into the water. I was that scared that I jumped straight into the bush and Howlett he sat down quick, and all those snipe wheeled up—there was hundreds,—all a squeelin' with fright, and the wood-duck came bowlin' over the meadows as if the old Nick was behind."

David paused and glanced meditatively at the dogs.

"Go on," said Barris in the same strained voice.

"Nothing more sir. The snipe did not come back."

"But that splash in the lake?"

"I don't know what it was sir."

"A salmon? A salmon couldn't have frightened the duck and the snipe that way?"

"No—oh no, sir. If fifty salmon had jumped they couldn't have made that splash. Could n't they, Howlett?"

"No 'ow," said Howlett.

"Roy," said Barris at length, "what David tells us settles the snipe shooting for to-day. I am going to take Pierpont up to the house. Howlett and David will follow with the dogs,—I have something to say to them. If you care to come, come along; if not, go and shoot a brace of grouse for dinner and be back by eight if you want to see what Pierpont and I discovered last night."

David whistled Gamin and Mioche to heel and followed Howlett and his hamper toward the house. I called Voyou to my side, picked up my gun and turned to Barris.

"I will be back by eight," I said; "you are expecting to catch one of the gold-makers are you not?"

"Yes," said Barris listlessly.

Pierpont began to speak about the Chinaman but Barris motioned him to follow, and, nodding to me, took the path that Howlett and David had followed toward the house. When they disappeared I tucked my gun under my arm and turned sharply into the forest, Voyou trotting close to my heels.

In spite of myself the continued apparition of the Chinaman made me nervous. If he troubled me again I had fully decided to get the drop on him and find out what he was doing in the Cardinal Woods. If he could give no satisfactory account of himself I would march him in to Barris as a gold-making suspect,—I would march him in anyway, I thought, and rid the forest of his ugly face. I wondered what it was that David had heard in the lake. It must have been a big fish, a salmon, I thought; probably David's and Howlett's nerves were overwrought after their Celestial chase.

A whine from the dog broke the thread of my meditation and I raised my head. Then I stopped short in my tracks.

The lost glade lay straight before me.

Already the dog had bounded into it, across the velvet turf to the carved stone where a slim figure sat. I saw my dog lay his silky head lovingly against her silken kirtle; I saw her face bend above him, and I caught my breath and slowly entered the sun-lit glade.

Half timidly she held out one white hand.

"Now that you have come," she said, "I can show you more of my work. I told you that I could do other things besides these dragon-flies and moths carved here in stone. Why do you stare at me so? Are you ill?"

"Ysonde," I stammered.

"Yes," she said, with a faint color under her eyes.

"I—I never expected to see you again," I blurted out, "—you—I—I—thought I had dreamed——"

"Dreamed, of me? Perhaps you did, is that strange?"

"Strange? N—no—but—where did you go when—when we were leaning over the fountain together? I saw your face,—your face reflected beside mine and then—then suddenly I saw the blue sky and only a star twinkling."

"It was because you fell asleep," she said, "was it not?"

"I—asleep?"

"You slept—I thought you were very tired and I went back——"

"Back?—where?"

"Back to my home where I carve my beautiful images; see, here is one I brought to show you to-day."

I took the sculptured creature that she held toward me, a massive golden lizard with frail claw-spread wings of gold so thin that the sunlight burned through and fell on the ground in flaming gilded patches.

"Good Heavens!" I exclaimed, "this is astounding! Where did you learn to do such work? Ysonde, such a thing is beyond price!"

"Oh, I hope so," she said earnestly, "I can't bear to sell my work, but my step-father takes it and sends it away. This is the second thing I have done and yesterday he said I must give it to him. I suppose he is poor."

"I don't see how he can be poor if he gives you gold to model in," I said, astonished.

"Gold!" she exclaimed, "gold! He has a room full of gold! He makes it."

I sat down on the turf at her feet completely unnerved.

"Why do you look at me so?" she asked, a little troubled.

"Where does your step-father live?" I said at last.

"Here."

"Here!"

"In the woods near the lake. You could never find our house."

"A house!"

"Of course. Did you think I lived in a tree? How silly. I live with my step-father in a beautiful house,—a small house, but very beautiful. He makes his gold there but the men who carry it away never come to the house, for they don't know where it is and if they did they could not get in. My step-father carries the gold in lumps to a canvas satchel. When the satchel is full he takes it out into the woods where the men live and I don't know what they do with it. I wish he could sell the gold and become rich for then I could go back to Yian where all the gardens are sweet and the river flows under the thousand bridges."

"Where is this city?" I asked faintly.

"Yian? I don't know. It is sweet with perfume and the sound of silver bells all day long. Yesterday I carried a blossom of dried lotus buds from Yian, in my breast, and all the woods were fragrant. Did you smell it?"

"Yes."

"I wondered, last night, whether you did. How beautiful your dog is; I love him. Yesterday I thought most about your dog but last night——"

"Last night," I repeated below my breath.

"I thought of you. Why do you wear the dragon-claw?"

I raised my hand impulsively to my forehead, covering the scar.

"What do you know of the dragon-claw?" I muttered.

"It is the symbol of Yue-Laou, and Yue-Laou rules the Kuen-Yuin, my step-father says. My step-father tells me everything that I know. We lived in Yian until I was sixteen years old. I am eighteen now; that is two years we have lived in the forest. Look!—see those scarlet birds! What are they? There are birds of the same color in Yian."

"Where is Yian, Ysonde?" I asked with deadly calmness.

"Yian? I don't know."

"But you have lived there?"

"Yes, a very long time."

"Is it across the ocean, Ysonde?"

"It is across seven oceans and the great river which is longer than from the earth to the moon."

"Who told you that?"

"Who? My step-father; he tells me everything."

"Will you tell me his name, Ysonde?"

"I don't know it, he is my step-father, that is all."

"And what is your name?"

"You know it, Ysonde."

"Yes, but what other name."

"That is all, Ysonde. Have you two names? Why do you look at me so impatiently?"

"Does your step-father make gold? Have you seen him make it?"

"Oh yes. He made it also in Yian and I loved to watch the sparks at night whirling like golden bees. Yian is lovely,—if it is all like our garden and the gardens around. I can see the thousand bridges from my garden and the white mountain beyond—"

"And the people—tell me of the people, Ysonde!" I urged gently.

"The people of Yian? I could see them in swarms like ants—oh! many, many millions crossing and recrossing the thousand bridges."

"But how did they look? Did they dress as I do?"

"I don't know. They were very far away, moving specks on the thousand bridges. For sixteen years I saw them every day from my garden but I never went out of my garden into the streets of Yian, for my step-father forbade me."

"You never saw a living creature near by in Yian?" I asked in despair.

"My birds, oh such tall, wise-looking birds, all over grey and rose color."

She leaned over the gleaming water and drew her polished hand across the surface.

"Why do you ask me these questions," she murmured; "are you displeased?"

"Tell me about your step-father," I insisted. "Does he look as I do? Does he dress, does he speak as I do? Is he American?"

"American? I don't know. He does not dress as you do and he does not look as you do. He is old, very, very old. He speaks sometimes as you do, sometimes as they do in Yian. I speak also in both manners."

"Then speak as they do in Yian," I urged impatiently, "speak as—why, Ysonde! why are you crying? Have I hurt you?—I did not intend,—I did not dream of your caring! There Ysonde, forgive me,—see, I beg you on my knees here at your feet."

I stopped, my eyes fastened on a small golden ball which hung from her waist by a golden chain. I saw it trembling against her thigh, I saw it change color, now crimson, now purple, now flaming scarlet. It was the symbol of the Kuen-Yuin.

She bent over me and laid her fingers gently on my arm.

"Why do you ask me such things?" she said, while the tears glistened on her lashes. "It hurts me here,—" she pressed her hand to her breast,—"it pains.—I don't know why. Ah, now your eyes are hard and cold again; you are looking at the golden globe which hangs from my waist. Do you wish to know also what that is?"

"Yes," I muttered, my eyes fixed on the infernal color flames which subsided as I spoke, leaving the ball a pale gilt again.

"It is the symbol of the Kuen-Yuin," she said in a trembling voice; "why do you ask?"

"Is it yours?"

"Y—yes."

"Where did you get it?" I cried harshly.

"My—my step-fa——"

Then she pushed me away from her with all the strength of her slender wrists and covered her face.

If I slipped my arm about her and drew her to me,—if I kissed away the tears that fell slowly between her fingers,—if I told her how I loved her—how it cut me to the heart to see her unhappy,—after all that is my own business. When she smiled through her tears, the pure love and sweetness in her eyes lifted my soul higher than the high moon vaguely glimmering through the sun-lit blue above. My happiness was so sudden, so fierce and overwhelming that I only knelt there, her fingers clasped in mine, my eyes raised to the blue vault and the glimmering moon. Then something in the long grass beside me moved close to my knees and a damp acrid odor filled my nostrils.

"Ysonde!" I cried, but the touch of her hand was already gone and my two clenched fists were cold and damp with dew.

"Ysonde!" I called again, my tongue stiff with fright;—but I called as one awaking from a dream—a horrid dream, for my nostrils quivered with the damp acrid odor and I felt the crab-reptile clinging to my knee. Why had the night fallen so swiftly,—and where was I—where?—stiff, chilled, torn, and bleeding, lying flung like a corpse over my own threshold with Voyou licking my face and Barris stooping above me in the light of a lamp that flared and smoked in the night breeze like a torch. Faugh! the choking stench of the lamp aroused me and I cried out:

"Ysonde!"

"What the devil's the matter with him?" muttered Pierpont, lifting me in his arms like a child, "has he been stabbed, Barris?"

VII

In a few minutes I was able to stand and walk stiffly into my bedroom where Howlett had a hot bath ready and a hotter tumbler of Scotch. Pierpont sponged the blood from my throat where it had coagulated. The cut was slight, almost invisible, a mere puncture from a thorn. A shampoo cleared my mind, and a cold plunge and alcohol friction did the rest.

"Now," said Pierpont, "swallow your hot Scotch and lie down. Do you want a broiled woodcock? Good, I fancy you are coming about."

Barris and Pierpont watched me as I sat on the edge of the bed, solemnly chewing on the woodcock's wishbone and sipping my Bordeaux, very much at my ease.

Pierpont sighed his relief.

"So," he said pleasantly, "it was a mere case of ten dollars or ten days. I thought you had been stabbed——"

"I was not intoxicated," I replied, serenely picking up a bit of celery.

"Only jagged?" enquired Pierpont, full of sympathy.

"Nonsense," said Barris, "let him alone. Want some more celery, Roy?—it will make you sleep."

"I don't want to sleep," I answered; "when are you and Pierpont going to catch your Gold-maker?"

Barris looked at his watch and closed it with a snap.

"In an hour; you don't propose to go with us?"

"But I do,—toss me a cup of coffee, Pierpont, will you,—that's just what I propose to do. Howlett, bring the new box of Panatella's,—the mild imported;—and leave the decanter. Now Barris, I'll be dressing, and you and Pierpont keep still and listen to what I have to say. Is that door shut tight?"

Barris locked it and sat down.

"Thanks," said I, "Barris, where is the city of Yian?"

An expression akin to terror flashed into Barris's eyes and I saw him stop breathing for a moment.

"There is no such city," he said at length, "have I been talking in my sleep?"

"It is a city," I continued, calmly, "where the river winds under the thousand bridges, where the gardens are sweet scented and the air is filled with the music of silver bells——"

"Stop!" gasped Barris, and rose trembling from his chair. He had grown ten years older.

"Roy," interposed Pierpont coolly, "what the deuce are you harrying Barris for?"

I looked at Barris and he looked at me. After a second or two he sat down again.

"Go on, Roy," he said.

"I must," I answered, "for now I am certain that I have not dreamed."

I told them everything; but, even as I told it, the whole thing seemed so vague, so unreal, that at times I stopped with the hot blood tingling in my ears, for it seemed impossible that sensible men, in the year of our Lord 1896 could seriously discuss such matters.

I feared Pierpont, but he did not even smile. As for Barris, he sat with his handsome head sunk on his breast, his unlighted pipe clasped tight in both hands.

When I had finished, Pierpont turned slowly and looked at Barris. Twice he moved his lips as if about to ask something and then remained mute.

"Yian is a city," said Barris, speaking dreamily; "was that what you wished to know, Pierpont?"

We nodded silently.

"Yian is a city," repeated Barris, "where the great river winds under the thousand bridges,—where the gardens are sweet scented, and the air is filled with the music of silver bells."

My lips formed the question, "Where is this city?"

"It lies," said Barris, almost querulously, "across the seven oceans and the river which is longer than from the earth to the moon."

"What do you mean?" said Pierpont.

"Ah," said Barris, rousing himself with an effort and raising his sunken eyes, "I am using the allegories of another land; let it pass. Have I not told you of the Kueu-Yuin? Yian is the centre of the Kuen-Yuin. It lies hidden in that gigantic shadow called China, vague and vast as the midnight Heavens,—a continent unknown, impenetrable."

"Impenetrable," repeated Pierpont below his breath.

"I have seen it," said Barris dreamily. "I have seen the dead plains of Black Cathay and I have crossed the mountains of Death, whose summits are above the atmosphere. I have seen the shadow of Xangi cast across Abaddon. Better to die a million miles from Yezd and Ater Quedah than to have seen the white water-lotus close in the shadow of Xangi! I have slept among the ruins of Xaindu where the winds never cease and the Wulwulleh is wailed by the dead."

"And Yian," I urged gently.

There was an unearthly look on his face as he turned slowly toward me.

"Yian,—I have lived there—and loved there. When the breath of my body shall cease, when the dragon's claw shall fade from my arm,"—he tore up his sleeve, and we saw a white crescent shining above his elbow,—"when the light of my eyes has faded forever, then, even then I shall not forget the city of Yian. Why, it is my home,—mine! The river and the thousand bridges, the white peak beyond, the sweet-scented gardens, the lilies, the pleasant noise of the summer wind laden with bee music and the music of bells,—all these are mine. Do you think because the Kuen-Yuin feared the dragon's claw on my arm that my work with them is ended? Do you think that because Yue-Laou could give, that I acknowledge his right to take away? Is he Xangi in whose shadow the white water-lotus dares not raise its head? No! No!" he cried violently, "it was not from Yue-Laou, the sorcerer, the Maker of Moons, that my happiness came! It was real, it was not a shadow to vanish like a tinted bubble! Can a sorcerer create, and give a man the woman he loves? Is Yue-Laou as great as Xangi then? Xangi is God. In His own time, in His infinite goodness and mercy He will bring me again to the woman I love. And I know she waits for me at God's feet."

In the strained silence that followed I could hear my heart's double beat and I saw Pierpont's face, blanched and pitiful. Barris shook himself and raised his head. The change in his ruddy face frightened me.

"Heed!" he said, with a terrible glance at me; "the print of the dragon's claw is on your forehead and Yue-Laou knows it. If you must love, then love like a man, for you will suffer like a soul in hell, in the end. What is her name again?"

"Ysonde," I answered simply.

VIII

At nine o'clock that night we caught one of the Gold-makers. I do not know how Barris had laid his trap; all I saw of the affair can be told in a minute or two.

We were posted on the Cardinal road about a mile below the house, Pierpont and I with drawn revolvers on one side, under a butternut tree, Barris on the other, a Winchester across his knees.

I had just asked Pierpont the hour, and he was feeling for his watch when far up the road we heard the sound of a galloping horse, nearer, nearer, clattering, thundering past. Then Barris's rifle spat flame and the dark mass, horse and rider, crashed into the dust. Pierpont had the half stunned horseman by the collar in a second,—the horse was stone dead,—and, as we lighted a pine knot to examine the fellow, Barris's two riders galloped up and drew bridle beside us.

"Hm!" said Barris with a scowl, "it's the 'Shiner,' or I'm a moonshiner."

We crowded curiously around to see the "Shiner." He was red-headed, fat and filthy, and his little red eyes burned in his head like the eyes of an angry pig.

Barris went through his pockets methodically while Pierpont held him and I held the torch. The Shiner was a gold mine; pockets, shirt, bootlegs, hat, even his dirty fists, clutched tight and bleeding, were bursting with lumps of soft yellow gold. Barris dropped this "moonshine gold," as we had come to call it, into the pockets of his shooting-coat, and withdrew to question the prisoner. He came back again in a few minutes and motioned his mounted men to take the Shiner in charge. We watched them, rifle on thigh, walking their horses slowly away into the darkness, the Shiner, tightly bound, shuffling sullenly between them.

"Who is the Shiner?" asked Pierpont, slipping the revolver into his pocket again.

"A moonshiner, counterfeiter, forger, and highwayman," said Barris, "and probably a murderer. Drummond will be glad to see him, and I think it likely he will be persuaded to confess to him what he refuses to confess to me."

"Wouldn't he talk?" I asked.

"Not a syllable. Pierpont, there is nothing more for you to do."

"For me to do? Are you not coming back with us, Barris?"

"No," said Barris.

We walked along the dark road in silence for a while, I wondering what Barris intended to do, but he said nothing more until we reached our own verandah. Here he held out his hand, first to Pierpont, then to me, saying good-bye as though he were going on a long journey.

"How soon will you be back?" I called out to him as he turned away toward the gate. He came across the lawn again, and again took our hands with a quiet affection that I had never imagined him capable of.

"I am going," he said, "to put an end to his gold-making to-night. I know that you fellows have never suspected what I was about on my little solitary evening strolls after dinner. I will tell you. Already I have unobtrusively killed four of these gold-makers,—my men put them under ground just below the new wash-out at the four mile stone. There are three left alive,—the Shiner whom we have, another criminal named 'Yellow,' or 'Yaller' in the vernacular, and the third——"

"The third," repeated Pierpont, excitedly.

"The third I have never yet seen. But I know who and what he is,—I know; and if he is of human flesh and blood, his blood will flow to-night."

As he spoke a slight noise across the turf attracted my attention. A mounted man was advancing silently in the starlight over the spongy meadowland. When he came nearer Barris struck a match, and we saw that he bore a corpse across his saddle bow.

"Yaller, Colonel Barris," said the man, touching his slouched hat in salute.

This grim introduction to the corpse made me shudder, and, after a moment's examination of the stiff, wide-eyed dead man, I drew back.

"Identified," said Barris, "take him to the four mile post and carry his effects to Washington,—under seal, mind, Johnstone."

Away cantered the rider with his ghastly burden, and Barris took our hands once more for the last time. Then he went away, gaily, with a jest on his lips, and Pierpont and I turned back into the house.

For an hour we sat moodily smoking in the hall before the fire, saying little until Pierpont burst out with: "I wish Barris had taken one of us with him to-night!"

The same thought had been running in my mind, but I said: "Barris knows what he's about."

This observation neither comforted us nor opened the lane to further conversation, and after a few minutes Pierpont said good night and called for Howlett and hot water. When he had been warmly tucked away by Howlett, I turned out all but one lamp, sent the dogs away with David and dismissed Howlett for the night.

I was not inclined to retire for I knew I could not sleep. There was a book lying open on the table beside the fire and I opened it and read a page or two, but my mind was fixed on other things.

The window shades were raised and I looked out at the star-set firmament. There was no moon that night but the sky was dusted all over with sparkling stars and a pale radiance, brighter even than moonlight, fell over meadow and wood. Far away in the forest I heard the voice of the wind, a soft warm wind that whispered a name, Ysonde.

"Listen," sighed the voice of the wind, and "listen" echoed the swaying trees with every little leaf a-quiver. I listened.

Where the long grasses trembled with the cricket's cadence I heard her name, Ysonde; I heard it in the rustling woodbine where grey moths hovered; I heard it in the drip, drip, drip of the dew from the porch. The silent meadow brook whispered her name, the rippling woodland streams repeated it, Ysonde, Ysonde, until all earth and sky were filled with the soft thrill, Ysonde, Ysonde, Ysonde.

A night-thrush sang in a thicket by the porch and I stole to the verandah to listen. After a while it began again, a little further on. I ventured out into the road. Again I heard it far away in the forest and I followed it, for I knew it was singing of Ysonde.

When I came to the path that leaves the main road and enters the Sweet-Fern Covert below the spinney, I hesitated; but the beauty of the night lured me on and the night-thrushes called me from every thicket. In the starry radiance, shrubs, grasses, field flowers, stood out distinctly, for there was no moon to cast shadows. Meadow and brook, grove and stream, were illuminated by the pale glow. Like great lamps lighted the planets hung from the high domed sky and through their mysterious rays the fixed stars, calm, serene, stared from the heavens like eyes.

I waded on waist deep through fields of dewy golden-rod, through late clover and wild-oat wastes, through crimson fruited sweetbrier, blueberry, and wild plum, until the low whisper of the Wier Brook warned me that the path had ended.

But I would not stop, for the night air was heavy with the perfume of water-lilies and far away, across the low wooded cliffs and the wet meadowland beyond, there was a distant gleam of silver, and I heard the murmur of sleepy waterfowl. I would go to the lake. The way was clear except for the dense young growth and the snares of the moose-bush.

The night-thrushes had ceased but I did not want for the company of living creatures. Slender, quick darting forms crossed my path at intervals, sleek mink, that fled like shadows at my step, wiry weasels and fat musk-rats, hurrying onward to some tryst or killing.

I never had seen so many little woodland creatures on the move at night. I began to wonder where they all were going so fast, why they all hurried on in the same direction. Now I passed a hare hopping through the brushwood, now a rabbit scurrying by, flag hoisted. As I entered the beech second-growth two foxes glided by me; a little further on a doe crashed out of the underbrush, and close behind her stole a lynx, eyes shining like coals.

He neither paid attention to the doe nor to me, but loped away toward the north.

The lynx was in flight.

"From what?" I asked myself, wondering. There was no forest fire, no cyclone, no flood.

If Barris had passed that way could he have stirred up this sudden exodus? Impossible; even a regiment in the forest could scarcely have put to rout these frightened creatures.

"What on earth," thought I, turning to watch the headlong flight of a fisher-cat, "what on earth has started the beasts out at this time of night."

I looked up into the sky. The placid glow of the fixed stars comforted me and I stepped on through the narrow spruce belt that leads down to the borders of the Lake of the Stars.

Wild cranberry and moose-bush entwined my feet, dewy branches spattered me with moisture, and the thick spruce needles scraped my face as I threaded my way over mossy logs and deep spongy tussocks down to the level gravel of the lake shore.

Although there was no wind the little waves were hurrying in from the lake and I heard them splashing among the pebbles. In the pale star glow thousands of water-lilies lifted their half-closed chalices toward the sky.

I threw myself full length upon the shore, and, chin on hand, looked out across the lake.

Splash, splash, came the waves along the shore, higher, nearer, until a film of water, thin and glittering as a knife blade, crept up to my elbows. I could not understand it; the lake was rising, but there had been no rain. All along the shore the water was running up; I heard the waves among the sedge grass; the weeds at my side were awash in the ripples. The lilies rocked on the tiny waves, every wet pad rising on the swells, sinking, rising again until the whole lake was glimmering with undulating blossoms. How sweet and deep was the fragrance from the lilies. And now the water was ebbing, slowly, and the waves receded, shrinking from the shore rim until the white pebbles appeared again, shining like froth on a brimming glass.

No animal swimming out in the darkness along the shore, no heavy salmon surging, could have set the whole shore aflood as though the wash from a great boat were rolling in. Could it have been the overflow, through the Weir Brook, of some cloud-burst far back in the forest? This was the only way I could account for it, and yet when I had crossed the Wier Brook I had not noticed that it was swollen.

And as I lay there thinking, a faint breeze sprang up and I saw the surface of the lake whiten with lifted lily pads.

All around me the alders were sighing; I heard the forest behind me stir; the crossed branches rubbing softly, bark against bark. Something—it may have been an owl—sailed out of the night, dipped, soared, and was again engulfed, and far across the water I heard its faint cry, Ysonde.

Then first, for my heart was full, I cast myself down upon my face, calling on her name. My eyes were wet when I raised my head,—for the spray from the shore was drifting in again,—and my heart beat heavily; "No more, no more." But my heart lied, for even as I raised my face to the calm stars, I saw her standing still, close beside me; and very gently I spoke her name, Ysonde. She held out both hands.

"I was lonely," she said, "and I went to the glade, but the forest is full of frightened creatures and they frightened me. Has anything happened in the woods? The deer are running toward the heights."

Her hand still lay in mine as we moved along the shore, and the lapping of the water on rock and shallow was no lower than our voices.

"Why did you leave me without a word, there at the fountain in the glade?" she said.

"I leave you!——"

"Indeed you did, running swiftly with your dog, plunging through thickets and brush,—oh—you frightened me."

"Did I leave you so?"

"Yes—after——"

"After?"

"You had kissed me——"

Then we leaned down together and looked into the black water set with stars, just as we had bent together over the fountain in the glade.

"Do you remember?" I asked.

"Yes. See, the water is inlaid with silver stars,—everywhere white lilies floating and the stars below, deep, deep down."

"What is the flower you hold in your hand?"

"White water-lotus."

"Tell me about Yue-Laou, Dzil Nbu of the Kuen-Yuin," I whispered, lifting her head so I could see her eyes.

"Would it please you to hear?"

"Yes, Ysonde."

"All that I know is yours, now, as I am yours, all that I am. Bend closer. Is it of Yue-Laou you would know? Yue-Laou is Dzil-Nbu of the Kuen-Yuin. He lived in the Moon. He is old—very, very old, and once, before he came to rule the Kuen-Yuin, he was the old man who unites with a silken cord all predestined couples, after which nothing can prevent their union. But all that is changed since he came to rule the Kuen-Yuin. Now he has perverted the Xin,—the good genii of China,—and has fashioned from their warped bodies a monster which he calls the Xin. This monster is horrible, for it not only lives in its own body, but it has thousands of loathsome satellites,—living creatures without mouths, blind, that move when the Xin moves, like a mandarin and his escort. They are part of the Xin although they are not attached. Yet if one of these satellites is injured the Xin writhes with agony. It is fearful—this huge living bulk and these creatures spread out like severed fingers that wriggle around a hideous hand."

"Who told you this?"

"My step-father."

"Do you believe it?"

"Yes. I have seen one of the Xin's creatures."

"Where, Ysonde?"

"Here in these woods."

"Then you believe there is a Xin here?"

"There must be,—perhaps in the lake——"

"Oh, Xins inhabit lakes?"

"Yes, and the seven seas. I am not afraid here."

"Why?"

"Because I wear the symbol of the Kuen-Yuin."

"Then I am not safe," I smiled.

"Yes you are, for I hold you in my arms. Shall I tell you more about the Xin? When the Xin is about to do to death a man, the Yeth-hounds gallop through the night——"

"What are the Yeth-hounds, Ysonde?"

"The Yeth-hounds are dogs without heads. They are the spirits of murdered children, which pass through the woods at night, making a wailing noise."

"Do you believe this?"

"Yes, for I have worn the yellow lotus——"

"The yellow lotus——"

"Yellow is the symbol of faith——"

"Where?"

"In Yian," she said faintly.

After a while I said, "Ysonde, you know there is a God?"

"God and Xangi are one."

"Have you ever heard of Christ?"

"No," she answered softly.

The wind began again among the tree tops. I felt her hands closing in mine.

"Ysonde," I asked again, "do you believe in sorcerers?"

"Yes, the Kuen-Yuin are sorcerers; Yue-Laou is a sorcerer."

"Have you seen sorcery?"

"Yes, the reptile satellite of the Xin——"

"Anything else?"

"My charm,—the golden ball, the symbol of the Kuen-Yuin. Have you seen it change,—have you seen the reptiles writhe——?"

"Yes," said I shortly, and then remained silent, for a sudden shiver of apprehension had seized me. Barris also had spoken gravely, ominously of the sorcerers, the Kuen-Yuin, and I had seen with my own eyes the graven reptiles turning and twisting on the glowing globe.

"Still," said I aloud, "God lives and sorcery is but a name."

"Ah," murmured Ysonde, drawing closer to me, "they say, in Yian, the Kuen-Yuin live; God is but a name."

"They lie," I whispered fiercely.

"Be careful," she pleaded, "they may hear you. Remember that you have the mark of the dragon's claw on your brow."

"What of it?" I asked, thinking also of the white mark on Barris's arm.

"Ah don't you know that those who are marked with the dragon's claw are followed by Yue-Laou, for good or for evil,—and the evil means death if you offend him?"

"Do you believe that!" I asked impatiently.

"I know it," she sighed.

"Who told you all this? Your step-father? What in Heaven's name is he then,—a Chinaman!"

"I don't know; he is not like you."

"Have—have you told him anything about me?"

"He knows about you—no, I have told him nothing,—ah, what is this—see—it is a cord, a cord of silk about your neck—and about mine!"

"Where did that come from?" I asked astonished.

"It must be—it must be Yue-Laou who binds me to you,—it is as my step-father said—he said Yue-Laou would bind us——"

"Nonsense," I said almost roughly, and seized the silken cord, but to my amazement it melted in my hand like smoke.

"What is all this damnable jugglery!" I whispered angrily, but my anger vanished as the words were spoken, and a convulsive shudder shook me to the feet. Standing on the shore of the lake, a stone's throw away, was a figure, twisted and bent,—a little old man, blowing sparks from a live coal which he held in his naked hand. The coal glowed with increasing radiance, lighting up the skull-like face above it, and threw a red glow over the sands at his feet. But the face!—the ghastly Chinese face on which the light flickered,—and the snaky slitted eyes, sparkling as the coal glowed hotter. Coal! It was not a coal but a golden globe staining the night with crimson flames,—it was the symbol of the Kuen-Yuin.

"See! See!" gasped Ysonde, trembling violently, "see the moon rising from between his fingers! Oh I thought it was my step-father and it is Yue-Laou the Maker of Moons—no! no! it is my step-father—ah God! they are the same!"

Frozen with terror I stumbled to my knees, groping for my revolver which bulged in my coat pocket; but something held me—something which bound me like a web in a thousand strong silky meshes. I struggled and turned but the web grew tighter; it was over us—all around us, drawing, pressing us into each other's arms until we lay side by side, bound hand and body and foot, palpitating, panting like a pair of netted pigeons.

And the creature on the shore below! What was my horror to see a moon, huge, silvery, rise like a bubble from between his fingers, mount higher, higher into the still air and hang aloft in the midnight sky, while another moon rose from his fingers, and another and yet another until the vast span of Heaven was set with moons and the earth sparkled like a diamond in the white glare.

A great wind began to blow from the east and it bore to our ears a long mournful howl,—a cry so unearthly that for a moment our hearts stopped.

"The Yeth-hounds!" sobbed Ysonde, "do you hear!—they are passing through the forest! The Xin is near!"

Then all around us in the dry sedge grasses came a rustle as if some small animals were creeping, and a damp acrid odor filled the air. I knew the smell, I saw the spidery crab-like creatures swarm out around me and drag their soft yellow hairy bodies across the shrinking grasses. They passed, hundreds of them, poisoning the air, tumbling, writhing, crawling with their blind mouthless heads raised. Birds, half asleep and confused by the darkness fluttered away before them in helpless fright, rabbits sprang from their forms, weasels glided away like flying shadows. What remained of the forest creatures rose and fled from the loathsome invasion; I heard the squeak of a terrified hare, the snort of stampeding deer, and the lumbering gallop of a bear; and all the time I was choking, half suffocated by the poisoned air.

Then, as I struggled to free myself from the silken snare about me, I cast a glance of deadly fear at the sorcerer below, and at the same moment I saw him turn in his tracks.

"Halt!" cried a voice from the bushes.

"Barris!" I shouted, half leaping up in my agony.

I saw the sorcerer spring forward, I heard the bang! bang! bang! of a revolver, and, as the sorcerer fell on the water's edge, I saw Barris jump out into the white glare and fire again, once, twice, three times, into the writhing figure at his feet.

Then an awful thing occurred. Up out of the black lake reared a shadow, a nameless shapeless mass, headless, sightless, gigantic, gaping from end to end.

A great wave struck Barris and he fell, another washed him up on the pebbles, another whirled him back into the water and then,—and then the thing fell over him,—and I fainted.

* * * * * *

* * * * * *

* * * * * *

* * * * * *

This, then, is all that I know concerning Yue-Laou and the Xin. I do not fear the ridicule of scientists or of the press for I have told the truth. Barris is gone and the thing that killed him is alive to-day in the Lake of the Stars while the spider-like satellites roam through the Cardinal Woods. The game has fled, the forests around the lake are empty of any living creatures save the reptiles that creep when the Xin moves in the depths of the lake.

General Drummond knows what he has lost in Barris, and we, Pierpont and I, know what we have lost also. His will we found in the drawer, the key of which he had handed me. It was wrapped in a bit of paper on which was written;

"Yue-Laou the sorcerer is here in the Cardinal Woods. I must kill him or he will kill me. He made and gave to me the woman I loved,—he made her,—I saw him,—he made her out of a white water-lotus bud. When our child was born, he came again before me and demanded from me the woman I loved. Then, when I refused, he went away, and that night my wife and child vanished from my side, and I found upon her pillow a white lotus bud. Roy, the woman of your dream, Ysonde, may be my child. God help you if you love her for Yue-Laou will give,—and take away, as though he were Xangi, which is God. I will kill Yue-Laou before I leave this forest,—or he will kill me.

"FRANKLYN BARRIS."

Now the world knows what Barris thought of the Kuen-Yuin and of Yue-Laou. I see that the newspapers are just becoming excited over the glimpses that Li-Hung-Chang has afforded them of Black Cathay and the demons of the Kuen-Yuin. The Kuen-Yuin are on the move.

Pierpont and I have dismantled the shooting-box in the Cardinal Woods. We hold ourselves ready at a moment's notice to join and lead the first Government party to drag the Lake of the Stars and cleanse the forest of the crab reptiles. But it will be necessary that a large force assembles, and a well-armed force, for we never have found the body of Yue-Laou, and, living or dead, I fear him. Is he living?

Pierpont, who found Ysonde and myself lying unconscious on the lake shore, the morning after, saw no trace of corpse or blood on the sands. He may have fallen into the lake, but I fear and Ysonde fears that he is alive. We never were able to find either her dwelling place or the glade and the fountain again. The only thing that remains to her of her former life is the gold serpent in the Metropolitan Museum and her golden globe, the symbol of the Kuen-Yuin; but the latter no longer changes color.

David and the dogs are waiting for me in the court yard as I write. Pierpont is in the gun room loading shells, and Howlett brings him mug after mug of my ale from the wood. Ysonde bends over my desk,—I feel her hand on my arm, and she is saying, "Don't you think you have done enough to-day, dear? How can you write such silly nonsense without a shadow of truth or foundation?"

A PLEASANT EVENING

"Et pis, doucett'ment on s'endort,
On fait sa carne, on fait sa sorgue,
On ronfle, et, comme un tuyau d'orgue,
L'tuyau s'met à ronfler pus fort. . . ."

ARISTIDE BRUANT.

I

As I stepped upon the platform of a Broadway cable-car at Forty-second Street, somebody said; "hello, Hilton, Jamison's looking for you."

"Hello, Curtis," I replied, "what does Jamison want?"

"He wants to know what you've been doing all the week," said Curtis, hanging desperately to the railing as the car lurched forward; "he says you seem to think that the *Manhattan Illustrated Weekly* was created for the sole purpose of providing salary and vacations for you."

"The shifty old tom-cat!" I said, indignantly, "he knows well enough where I've been. Vacation! Does he think the State Camp in June is a snap?"

"Oh," said Curtis, "you've been to Peekskill?"

"I should say so," I replied, my wrath rising as I thought of my assignment.

"Hot?" inquired Curtis, dreamily.

"One hundred and three in the shade," I answered. "Jamison wanted three full pages and three half pages, all for process work, and a lot of line drawings into the bargain. I could have faked them—I wish I had. I was fool enough to hustle and break my neck to get some honest drawings, and that's the thanks I get!"

"Did you have a camera?"

"No. I will next time—I'll waste no more conscientious work on Jamison," I said sulkily.

"It doesn't pay," said Curtis. "When I have military work assigned me, I don't do the dashing sketch-artist act, you bet; I go to my studio, light my pipe, pull out a lot of old *Illustrated London News,* select several suitable battle scenes by Caton Woodville—and use 'em too."

The car shot around the neck-breaking curve at Fourteenth Street.

"Yes," continued Curtis, as the car stopped in front of the Morton House for a moment, then plunged forward again amid a furious clanging of gongs, "it doesn't pay to do decent work for the fat-headed men who run the *Manhattan Illustrated.* They don't appreciate it."

"I think the public does," I said, "but I'm sure Jamison doesn't. It would serve him right if I did what most of you fellows do—take a lot of Caton Woodville's and Thulstrup's drawings, change the uniforms, 'chic' a figure or two, and turn in a drawing labelled 'from life.' I'm sick of this sort of thing anyway. Almost every day this week I've been chasing myself over that tropical camp, or galloping in the wake of those batteries. I've got a full page of the 'camp by moonlight,' full pages of 'artillery drill' and 'light battery in action,' and a dozen smaller drawings that cost me more groans and perspiration than Jamison ever knew in all his lymphatic life!"

"Jamison's got wheels," said Curtis,—"more wheels than there are bicycles in Harlem. He wants you to do a full page by Saturday."

"A what?" I exclaimed, aghast.

"Yes he does—he was going to send Jim Crawford, but Jim expects to go to California for the winter fair, and you've got to do it."

"What is it?" I demanded savagely.

"The animals in Central Park," chuckled Curtis.

I was furious. The animals! Indeed! I'd show Jamison that I was entitled to some consideration! This was Thursday; that gave me a day and a half to finish a full-page drawing for the paper, and, after my work at the State Camp I felt that I was entitled to a little rest. Anyway I objected to the subject. I intended to tell Jamison so—I intended to tell him firmly. However, many of the things that we often intended to tell Jamison were never told. He was a peculiar man, fat-faced, thin-lipped, gentle-voiced, mild-mannered, and soft in his movements as a pussy cat. Just why our firmness should give way when we were actually in his presence, I have never quite been able to determine. He said very little—so did we, although we often entered his presence with other intentions.

The truth was that the *Manhattan Illustrated Weekly* was the best paying, best illustrated paper in America, and we young fellows were not anxious to be cast adrift. Jamison's knowledge of art was probably as extensive as the knowledge of any "Art editor" in the city. Of course that was saying nothing, but the fact merited careful consideration on our part, and we gave it much consideration.

This time, however, I decided to let Jamison know that drawings are not produced by the yard, and that I was neither a floorwalker nor a hand-me-down. I would stand up for my rights; I'd tell old Jamison a few things to set the wheels under his silk hat spinning, and if he attempted any of his pussy-cat ways on me, I'd give him a few plain facts that would curl what hair he had left.

Glowing with a splendid indignation I jumped off the car at the City Hall, followed by Curtis, and a few minutes later entered the office of the *Manhattan Illustrated News.*

"Mr. Jamison would like to see you, sir," said one of the compositors as I passed into the long hallway. I threw my drawings on the table and passed a handkerchief over my forehead.

"Mr. Jamison would like to see you, sir," said a small freckle-faced boy with a smudge of ink on his nose.

"I know it," I said, and started to remove my gloves.

"Mr. Jamison would like to see you, sir," said a lank messenger who was carrying a bundle of proofs to the floor below.

"The deuce take Jamison," I said to myself. I started toward the dark passage that leads to the abode of Jamison, running over in my mind the neat and sarcastic speech which I had been composing during the last ten minutes.

Jamison looked up and nodded softly as I entered the room. I forgot my speech.

"Mr. Hilton," he said, "we want a full page of the Zoo before it is removed to Bronx Park. Saturday afternoon at three o'clock the drawing must be in the engraver's hands. Did you have a pleasant week in camp?"

"It was hot," I muttered, furious to find that I could not remember my little speech.

"The weather," said Jamison, with soft courtesy, "is oppressive everywhere. Are your drawings in, Mr. Hilton?"

"Yes. It was infernally hot and I worked like a nigger——"

"I suppose you were quite overcome. Is that why you took a two days' trip to the Catskills? I trust the mountain air restored you—but—was it prudent to go to Cranston's for the cotillion Tuesday? Dancing in such uncomfortable weather is really unwise. Good-morning, Mr. Hilton, remember the engraver should have your drawings on Saturday by three."

I walked out, half hypnotized, half enraged. Curtis grinned at me as I passed—I could have boxed his ears.

"Why the mischief should I lose my tongue whenever that old tom-cat purrs!" I asked myself as I entered the elevator and was shot down to the first floor. "I'll not put up with this sort of thing much longer—how in the name of all that's foxy did he know that I went to the mountains? I suppose he thinks I'm lazy because I don't wish to be boiled to death. How did he know about the dance at Cranston's? Old cat!"

The roar and turmoil of machinery and busy men filled my ears as I crossed the avenue and turned into the City Hall Park.

From the staff on the tower the flag drooped in the warm sunshine with scarcely a breeze to lift its crimson bars. Overhead stretched a splendid cloudless sky, deep, deep blue, thrilling, scintillating in the gemmed rays of the sun.

Pigeons wheeled and circled about the roof of the grey Post Office or dropped out of the blue above to flutter around the fountain in the square.

On the steps of the City Hall the unlovely politician lounged, exploring his heavy under jaw with wooden toothpick, twisting his drooping black moustache, or distributing tobacco juice over marble steps and close-clipped grass.

My eyes wandered from these human vermin to the calm scornful face of Nathan Hale, on his pedestal, and then to the grey-coated Park policeman whose occupation was to keep little children from the cool grass.

A young man with thin hands and blue circles under his eyes was slumbering on a bench by the fountain, and the policeman walked over to him and struck him on the soles of his shoes with a short club.

The young man rose mechanically, stared about, dazed by the sun, shivered, and limped away. I saw him sit down on the steps of the white marble building, and I went over and spoke to him. He neither looked at me, nor did he notice the coin I offered.

"You're sick," I said, "you had better go to the hospital."

"Where?" he asked vacantly—"I've been, but they wouldn't receive me."

He stooped and tied the bit of string that held what remained of his shoe to his foot.

"You are French," I said.

"Yes."

"Have you no friends? Have you been to the French Consul?"

"The Consul!" he replied; "no, I haven't been to the French Consul."

After a moment I said, "You speak like a gentleman."

He rose to his feet and stood very straight, looking me, for the first time, directly in the eyes.

"Who are you?" I asked abruptly.

"An outcast," he said, without emotion, and limped off thrusting his hands into his ragged pockets.

"Huh!" said the Park policeman who had come up behind me in time to hear my question and the vagabond's answer; "don't you know who that hobo is?—An' you a newspaper man!"

"Who is he, Cusick?" I demanded, watching the thin shabby figure moving across Broadway toward the river.

"On the level you don't know, Mr. Hilton?" repeated Cusick, suspiciously.

"No, I don't; I never before laid eyes on him."

"Why," said the sparrow policeman, "that's 'Soger Charlie';—you remember—that French officer what sold secrets to the Dutch Emperor."

"And was to have been shot? I remember now, four years ago—and he escaped—you mean to say that is the man?"

"Everybody knows it," sniffed Cusick, "I'd a-thought you newspaper gents would have knowed it first."

"What was his name?" I asked after a moment's thought.

"Soger Charlie——"

"I mean his name at home."

"Oh, some French dago name. No Frenchman will speak to him here; sometimes they curse him and kick him. I guess he's dyin' by inches."

I remembered the case now. Two young French cavalry officers were arrested, charged with selling plans of fortifications and other military secrets to the Germans. On the eve of their conviction, one of them, Heaven only knows how, escaped and turned up in New York. The other was duly shot. The affair had made some noise, because both young men were of good families. It was a painful episode, and I had hastened to forget it. Now that it was recalled to my mind, I remembered the newspaper accounts of the case, but I had forgotten the names of the miserable young men.

"Sold his country," observed Cusick, watching a group of children out of the corner of his eyes—"you can't trust no Frenchman nor dagoes nor Dutchmen either. I guess Yankees are about the only white men."

I looked at the noble face of Nathan Hale and nodded.

"Nothin' sneaky about us, eh, Mr. Hilton?"

I thought of Benedict Arnold and looked at my boots.

Then the policeman said, "Well, so long, Mr. Hilton," and went away to frighten a pasty-faced little girl who had climbed upon the railing and was leaning down to sniff the fragrant grass.

"Cheese it, de cop!" cried her shrill-voiced friends, and the whole bevy of small ragamuffins scuttled away across the square.

With a feeling of depression I turned and walked toward Broadway, where the long yellow cable-cars swept up and down, and the din of gongs and the deafening rumble of heavy trucks echoed from the marble walls of the Court House to the granite mass of the Post Office.

Throngs of hurrying busy people passed up town and down town, slim sober-faced clerks, trim cold-eyed brokers, here and there a red-necked politician linking arms with some favourite heeler, here and there a City Hall lawyer, sallow-faced and saturnine. Sometimes a fireman, in his severe blue uniform, passed through the crowd, sometimes a blue-coated policeman, mopping his clipped hair, holding his helmet in his white-gloved hand. There were women too, pale-faced shop girls with pretty eyes, tall blonde girls who might be typewriters and might not, and many, many older women whose business in that part of the city no human being could venture to guess, but who hurried up town and down town, all occupied with *something* that gave to the whole restless throng a common likeness—the expression of one who hastens toward a hopeless goal.

I knew some of those who passed me. There was little Jocelyn of the *Mail and Express;* there was Hood, who had more money than he wanted and was going to have less than he wanted when he left Wall Street; there was Colonel Tidmouse of the 45th Infantry, N.G.S.N.Y., probably coming from the office of the *Army and Navy Journal,* and there was Dick Harding who wrote the best stories of New York life that have been printed. People said his hat no longer fitted,—especially people who also wrote stories of New York life and whose hats threatened to fit as long as they lived.

I looked at the statue of Nathan Hale, then at the human stream that flowed around his pedestal.

"Quand même," I muttered and walked out into Broadway, signalling to the gripman of an uptown cable-car.

II

I passed into the Park by the Fifth Avenue and 59th Street gate; I could never bring myself to enter it through the gate that is guarded by the hideous pigmy statue of Thorwaldsen.

The afternoon sun poured into the windows of the New Netherlands Hotel, setting every orange-curtained pane a-glitter, and tipping the wings of the bronze dragons with flame.

Gorgeous masses of flowers blazed in the sunshine from the grey terraces of the Savoy, from the high grilled court of the Vanderbilt palace, and from the balconies of the Plaza opposite.

The white marble façade of the Metropolitan Club was a grateful relief in the universal glare, and I kept my eyes on it until I had crossed the dusty street and entered the shade of the trees.

Before I came to the Zoo I smelled it. Next week it was to be removed to the fresh cool woods and meadows in Bronx Park, far from the stifling air of the city, far from the infernal noise of the Fifth Avenue omnibuses.

A noble stag stared at me from his enclosure among the trees as I passed down the winding asphalt walk. "Never mind, old fellow." said I, "you will be splashing about in the Bronx River next week and cropping maple shoots to your heart's content."

On I went, past herds of staring deer, past great lumbering elk, and moose, and long-faced African antelopes, until I came to the dens of the great carnivora.

The tigers sprawled in the sunshine, blinking and licking their paws; the lions slept in the shade or squatted on their haunches, yawning gravely. A slim panther travelled to and fro behind her barred cage, pausing at times to peer wistfully out into the free sunny world. My heart ached for caged wild things, and I walked on, glancing up now and then to encounter the blank stare of a tiger or the mean shifty eyes of some ill-smelling hyena.

Across the meadow I could see the elephants swaying and swinging their great heads, the sober bison solemnly slobbering over their cuds, the sarcastic countenances of camels, the wicked little zebras, and a lot more animals of the camel and llama tribe, all resembling each other, all equally ridiculous, stupid, deadly uninteresting.

Somewhere behind the old arsenal an eagle was screaming, probably a Yankee eagle; I heard the "tchug! tchug!" of a blowing hippopotamus, the squeal of a falcon, and the snarling yap! of quarrelling wolves.

"A pleasant place for a hot day!" I pondered bitterly, and I thought some things about Jamison that I shall not insert in this volume. But I lighted a cigarette to deaden the aroma from the hyenas, unclasped my sketching block, sharpened my pencil, and fell to work on a family group of hippopotami.

They may have taken me for a photographer, for they all wore smiles as if "welcoming a friend," and my sketch block presented a series of wide open jaws, behind which shapeless bulky bodies vanished in alarming perspective.

The alligators were easy; they looked to me as though they had not moved since the founding of the Zoo, but I had a bad time with the big bison, who persistently turned his tail to me, looking stolidly around his flank to see how I stood it. So I pretended to be absorbed in the antics of two bear cubs, and the dreary old bison fell into the trap, for I made some good sketches of him and laughed in his face as I closed the book.

There was a bench by the abode of the eagles, and I sat down on it to draw the vultures and condors, motionless as mummies among the piled rocks. Gradually I enlarged the sketch, bringing in the gravel plaza, the steps leading up to Fifth Avenue, the sleepy park policeman in front of the arsenal—and a slim, white-browed girl, dressed in shabby black, who stood silently in the shade of the willow trees.

After a while I found that the sketch, instead of being a study of the eagles, was in reality a composition in which the girl in black occupied the principal point of interest. Unwittingly I had subordinated everything else to her, the brooding vultures, the trees and walks, and the half indicated groups of sun-warmed loungers.

She stood very still, her pallid face bent, her thin white hands loosely clasped before her. "Rather dejected reverie," I thought, "probably she's out of work." Then I caught a glimpse of a sparkling diamond ring on the slender third finger of her left hand.

"She'll not starve with such a stone as that about her," I said to myself, looking curiously at her dark eyes and sensitive mouth. They were both beautiful, eyes and mouth—beautiful, but touched with pain.

After a while I rose and walked back to make a sketch or two of the lions and tigers. I avoided the monkeys—I can't stand them, and they never seem funny to me, poor dwarfish, degraded caricatures of all that is ignoble in ourselves.

"I've enough now," I thought; "I'll go home and manufacture a full page that will probably please Jamison." So I strapped the elastic band around my sketching block, replaced pencil and rubber in my waistcoat pocket, and strolled off toward the Mall to smoke a cigarette in the evening glow before going back to my studio to work until midnight, up to the chin in charcoal grey and Chinese white.

Across the long meadow I could see the roofs of the city faintly looming above the trees. A mist of amethyst, ever deepening, hung low on the horizon, and through it, steeple and dome, roof and tower, and the tall chimneys where thin fillets of smoke curled idly, were transformed into pinnacles of beryl and flaming minarets, swimming in filmy haze. Slowly the enchantment deepened; all that was ugly and shabby and mean had fallen away from the distant city, and now it towered into the evening sky, splendid, gilded, magnificent, purified in the fierce furnace of the setting sun.

The red disk was half hidden now; the tracery of trees, feathery willow and budding birch, darkened against the glow; the fiery rays shot far across the meadow, gilding the dead leaves, staining with soft crimson the dark moist tree trunks around me.

Far across the meadow a shepherd passed in the wake of a huddling flock, his dog at his heels, faint moving blots of grey.

A squirrel sat up on the gravel walk in front of me, ran a few feet, and sat up again, so close that I could see the palpitation of his sleek flanks.

Somewhere in the grass a hidden field insect was rehearsing last summer's solos; I heard the tap! tap! tat-tat-t-t-tat! of a woodpecker among the branches overhead and the querulous note of a sleepy robin.

The twilight deepened; out of the city the music of bells floated over wood and meadow; faint mellow whistles sounded from the river craft along the north shore, and the distant thunder of a gun announced the close of a June day.

The end of my cigarette began to glimmer with a redder light; shepherd and flock were blotted out in the dusk, and I only knew they were still moving when the sheep bells tinkled faintly.

Then suddenly that strange uneasiness that all have known—that half-awakened sense of having seen it all before, of having been through it all, came over me, and I raised my head and slowly turned.

A figure was seated at my side. My mind was struggling with the instinct to remember. Something so vague and yet so familiar—something that eluded thought yet challenged it, something—God knows what! troubled me. And now, as I looked, without interest, at the dark figure beside me, an apprehension, totally involuntary, an impatience to *understand,* came upon me, and I sighed and turned restlessly again to the fading west.

I thought I heard my sigh re-echoed—I scarcely heeded; and in a moment I sighed again, dropping my burned-out cigarette on the gravel beneath my feet.

"Did you speak to me?" said some one in a low voice, so close that I swung around rather sharply.

"No," I said after a moment's silence.

It was a woman. I could not see her face clearly, but I saw on her clasped hands, which lay listlessly in her lap, the sparkle of a great diamond. I knew her at once. It did not need a glance at the shabby dress of black, the white face, a pallid spot in the twilight, to tell me that I had her picture in my sketch-book.

"Do—do you mind if I speak to you?" she asked timidly. The hopeless sadness in her voice touched me, and I said: "Why, no, of course not. Can I do anything for you?"

"Yes," she said, brightening a little, "if you—you only would."

"I will if I can," said I, cheerfully; "what is it? Out of ready cash?"

"No, not that," she said, shrinking back.

I begged her pardon, a little surprised, and withdrew my hand from my change pocket.

"It is only—only that I wish you to take these,"—she drew a thin packet from her breast,—"these two letters."

"I?" I asked astonished.

"Yes, if you will."

"But what am I to do with them?" I demanded.

"I can't tell you; I only know that I must give them to you. Will you take them?"

"Oh, yes, I'll take them," I laughed, "am I to read them?" I added to myself, "It's some clever begging trick."

"No," she answered slowly, "you are not to read them; you are to give them to somebody."

"To whom? Anybody?"

"No, not to anybody. You will know whom to give them to when the time comes."

"Then I am to keep them until further instructions?"

"Your own heart will instruct you," she said, in a scarcely audible voice. She held the thin packet toward me, and to humour her I took it. It was wet.

"The letters fell into the sea," she said; "There was a photograph which should have gone with them but the salt water washed it blank. Will you care if I ask you something else?"

"I? Oh, no."

"Then give me the picture that you made of me to-day."

I laughed again, and demanded how she knew I had drawn her.

"Is it like me?" she said.

"I think it is very like you," I answered truthfully.

"Will you not give it to me?"

Now it was on the tip of my tongue to refuse, but I reflected that I had enough sketches for a full page without that one, so I handed it to her, nodded that she was welcome, and stood up. She rose also, the diamond flashing on her finger.

"You are sure that you are not in want?" I asked, with a tinge of good-natured sarcasm.

"Hark!" she whispered; "listen!—do you hear the bells of the convent!"

I looked out into the misty night.

"There are no bells sounding," I said, "and anyway there are no convent bells here. We are in New York, mademoiselle"—I had noticed her French accent—"we are in Protestant Yankee-land, and the bells that ring are much less mellow than the bells of France."

I turned pleasantly to say good-night. She was gone.

III

"Have you ever drawn a picture of a corpse?" inquired Jamison next morning as I walked into his private room with a sketch of the proposed full page of the Zoo.

"No, and I don't want to," I replied, sullenly.

"Let me see your Central Park page," said Jamison in his gentle voice, and I displayed it. It was about worthless as an artistic production, but it pleased Jamison, as I knew it would.

"Can you finish it by this afternoon?" he asked, looking up at me with persuasive eyes.

"Oh, I suppose so," I said, wearily; "anything else, Mr. Jamison?"

"The corpse," he replied, "I want a sketch by to-morrow—finished."

"What corpse?" I demanded, controlling my indignation as I met Jamison's soft eyes.

There was a mute duel of glances. Jamison passed his hand across his forehead with a slight lifting of the eyebrows.

"I shall want it as soon as possible," he said in his caressing voice.

What I thought was, "Damned purring pussycat!" What I said was, "Where is this corpse?"

"In the Morgue—have you read the morning papers? No? Ah,—as you very rightly observe you are too busy to read the morning papers. Young men must learn industry first, of course, of course. What you are to do is this: the San Francisco police have sent out an alarm regarding the disappearance of a Miss Tufft—the millionaire's daughter, you know. To-day a body was brought to the Morgue here in New York, and it has been identified as the missing young lady,—by a diamond ring. Now I am convinced that it isn't, and I'll show you why, Mr. Hilton."

He picked up a pen and made a sketch of a ring on a margin of that morning's *Tribune.*

"That is the description of her ring as sent on from San Francisco. You notice the diamond is set in the centre of the ring where the two gold serpents' *tails* cross!

Now the ring on the finger of the woman in the Morgue is like this," and he rapidly sketched another ring where the diamond rested in the *fangs* of the two gold serpents.

"That is the difference," he said in his pleasant, even voice.

"Rings like that are not uncommon," said I, remembering that I had seen such a ring on the finger of the white-faced girl in the Park the evening before. Then a sudden thought took shape—perhaps that was the girl whose body lay in the Morgue!

"Well," said Jamison, looking up at me, "what are you thinking about?"

"Nothing," I answered, but the whole scene was before my eyes, the vultures brooding among the rocks, the shabby black dress, and the pallid face,—and the ring, glittering on that slim white hand!

"Nothing," I repeated, "when shall I go, Mr. Jamison? Do you want a portrait—or what?"

"Portrait,—careful drawing of the ring, and,—er—a centre piece of the Morgue at night. Might as well give people the horrors while we're about it."

"But," said I, "the policy of this paper——"

"Never mind, Mr. Hilton," purred Jamison, "I am able to direct the policy of this paper."

"I don't doubt you are," I said angrily.

"I am," he repeated, undisturbed and smiling; "you see this Tufft case interests society. I am—er—also interested."

He held out to me a morning paper and pointed to a heading.

I read: "Miss Tufft Dead! Her Fiancé was Mr. Jamison, the well-known Editor."

"What!" I cried in horrified amazement. But Jamison had left the room, and I heard him chatting and laughing softly with some visitors in the press-room outside.

I flung down the paper and walked out.

"The cold-blooded toad!" I exclaimed again and again;—"making capital out of his fiancée's disappearance! Well, I—I'm d—nd! I knew he was a bloodless, heartless, grip-penny, but I never thought—I never imagined——" Words failed me.

Scarcely conscious of what I did I drew a *Herald* from my pocket and saw the column entitled: "Miss Tufft Found! Identified by a Ring. Wild Grief of Mr. Jamison, her Fiancé."

That was enough. I went out into the street and sat down in City Hall Park. And, as I sat there, a terrible resolution came to me; I would draw that dead girl's face in such a way that it would chill Jamison's sluggish blood, I would crowd the black shadows of the Morgue with forms and ghastly faces, and every face should bear something in it of Jamison. Oh, I'd rouse him from his cold snaky apathy! I'd confront him with Death in such an awful form, that, passionless, base, inhuman as he was, he'd shrink from it as he would from a dagger thrust. Of course I'd lose my place, but that did not bother me, for I had decided to resign anyway, not having a taste for the society of human reptiles. And, as I sat there in the sunny park, furious, trying to plan a picture whose sombre horror should leave in his mind an ineffaceable scar, I suddenly thought of the pale black-robed girl in Central Park. Could it be her poor slender body that lay among the shadows of the grim Morgue! If ever brooding despair was stamped on any face, I had seen its print on hers when she spoke to me in the Park and gave me the letters. The letters! I had not thought of them since, but now I drew them from my pocket and looked at the addresses.

"Curious," I thought, "the letters are still damp; they smell of salt water too."

I looked at the address again, written in the long fine hand of an educated woman who had been bred in a French convent. Both letters bore the same address, in French:

"CAPTAIN D'YNIOL.
(Kindness of a Stranger.)"

"Captain d'Yniol," I repeated aloud—"confound it, I've heard that name! Now, where the deuce—where in the name of all that's queer——" Somebody who had sat down on the bench beside me placed a heavy hand on my shoulder.

It was the Frenchman, "Soger Charlie."

"You spoke my name," he said in apathetic tones.

"Your name!"

"Captain d'Yniol," he repeated; "it is my name."

I recognized him in spite of the black goggles he was wearing, and, at the same moment, it flashed into my mind that d'Yniol was the name of the traitor who had escaped. Ah, I remembered now!

"I am Captain d'Yniol," he said again, and I saw his fingers closing on my coat sleeve.

It may have been my involuntary movement of recoil,—I don't know,—but the fellow dropped my coat and sat straight up on the bench.

"I am Captain d'Yniol," he said for the third time, "charged with treason and under sentence of death."

"And innocent!" I muttered, before I was even conscious of having spoken. What was it that wrung those involuntary words from my lips, I shall never know, perhaps—but it was I, not he, who trembled, seized with a strange agitation, and it was I, not he, whose hand was stretched forth impulsively, touching his.

Without a tremor he took my hand, pressed it almost imperceptibly, and dropped it. Then I held both letters toward him, and, as he neither looked at them nor at me, I placed them in his hand. Then he started.

"Read them," I said, "they are for you."

"Letters!" he gasped in a voice that sounded like nothing human.

"Yes, they are for you,—I know it now——"

"Letters!—letters directed to *me?*"

"Can you not see?" I cried.

Then he raised one frail hand and drew the goggles from his eyes, and, as I looked, I saw two tiny white specks exactly in the centre of both pupils.

"Blind!" I faltered.

"I have been unable to read for two years," he said.

After a moment he placed the tip of one finger on the letters.

"They are wet," I said; "shall—would you like to have me read them?" For a long time he sat silently in the sunshine, fumbling with his cane, and I watched him without speaking. At last he said, "Read, Monsieur," and I took the letters and broke the seals.

The first letter contained a sheet of paper, damp and discoloured, on which a few lines were written:

> "My darling, I knew you were innocent—" Here the writing ended, but, in the blur beneath, I read: "Paris shall know—France shall know, for at last I have the proofs and I am coming to find you, my soldier, and to place them in your own dear brave hands. They know, now, at the War Ministry—they have a copy of the traitor's confession—but they dare not make it public—they dare not withstand the popular astonishment and rage. Therefore I sail on Monday from Cherbourg by the Green Cross Line, to bring you back to your own again, where you will stand before all the world, without fear, without reproach.
>
> "ALINE."

"This—this is terrible!" I stammered; "can God live and see such things done!"

But with his thin hand he gripped my arm again, bidding me read the other letter; and I shuddered at the menace in his voice.

Then, with his sightless eyes on me, I drew the other letter from the wet, stained envelope. And before I was aware—before I understood the purport of what I saw, I had read aloud these half-effaced lines:

"The *Lorient* is sinking—an iceberg—mid-ocean—goodbye—you are innocent—I love——"

"The *Lorient!*" I cried; "it was the French steamer that was never heard from—the *Lorient* of the Green Cross Line! I had forgotten—I——"

The loud crash of a revolver stunned me; my ears rang and ached with it as I shrank back from a ragged dusty figure that collapsed on the bench beside me, shuddered a moment, and tumbled to the asphalt at my feet.

The trampling of the eager hard-eyed crowd, the dust and taint of powder in the hot air, the harsh alarm of the ambulance clattering up Mail Street,—these I remember, as I knelt there, helplessly holding the dead man's hands in mine.

"Soger Charlie," mused the sparrow policeman, "shot his-self, didn't he, Mr. Hilton? You seen him, sir,—blowed the top of his head off, didn't he, Mr. Hilton?"

"Soger Charlie," they repeated, "a French dago what shot his-self;" and the words echoed in my ears long after the ambulance rattled away, and the increasing throng dispersed, sullenly, as a couple of policemen cleared a space around the pool of thick blood on the asphalt.

They wanted me as a witness, and I gave my card to one of the policemen who knew me. The rabble transferred its fascinated stare to me, and I turned away and pushed a path between frightened shop girls and ill-smelling loafers, until I lost myself in the human torrent of Broadway.

The torrent took me with it where it flowed—East? West?—I did not notice nor care, but I passed on through the throng, listless, deadly weary of attempting to solve God's justice—striving to understand His purpose—His laws—His judgments which are "true and righteous altogether."

IV

"More to be desired are they than gold, yea, than much fine gold. Sweeter also than honey and the honey-comb!"

I turned sharply toward the speaker who shambled at my elbow. His sunken eyes were dull and lustreless, his bloodless face gleamed pallid as a death mask above the blood-red jersey—the emblem of the soldiers of Christ.

I don't know why I stopped, lingering, but, as he passed, I said, "Brother, I also was meditating upon God's wisdom and His testimonies."

The pale fanatic shot a glance at me, hesitated, and fell into my own pace, walking by my side. Under the peak of his Salvation Army cap his eyes shone in the shadow with a strange light.

"Tell me more," I said, sinking my voice below the roar of traffic, the clang! clang! of the cable-cars, and the noise of feet on the worn pavements—"tell me of His testimonies."

"Moreover by them is Thy servant warned and in keeping of them there is great reward. Who can understand His errors? Cleanse Thou me from secret faults. Keep back Thy servant also from presumptuous sins. Let them not have dominion over me. Then shall I be upright and I shall be innocent from the great transgression. Let the words of my mouth and the meditation of my heart be acceptable in Thy sight,—O Lord! My strength and my Redeemer!"

"It is Holy Scripture that you quote," I said; "I also can read that when I choose. But it cannot clear for me the reasons—it cannot make me understand——"

"What?" he asked, and muttered to himself.

"That, for instance," I replied, pointing to a cripple, who had been *born* deaf and dumb and horridly misshapen,—a wretched diseased lump on the sidewalk below St. Paul's Churchyard,—a sore-eyed thing that mouthed and mowed and rattled pennies in a tin cup as though the sound of copper could stem the human pack that passed hot on the scent of gold.

Then the man who shambled beside me turned and looked long and earnestly into my eyes. And after a moment a dull recollection stirred within me—a vague something that seemed like the awakening memory of a past, long, long forgotten, dim, dark, too subtle, too frail, too indefinite—ah! the old feeling that all men have known—the old strange uneasiness, that useless struggle to remember when and where it all occurred before.

And the man's head sank on his crimson jersey, and he muttered, muttered to himself of God and love and compassion, until I saw that the fierce heat of the city had touched his brain, and I went away and left him prating of mysteries that none but such as he dare name.

So I passed on through dust and heat; and the hot breath of men touched my cheek and eager eyes looked into mine. Eyes, eyes,—that met my own and looked through them, beyond—far beyond to where gold glittered amid the mirage of eternal hope. Gold! It was in the air where the soft sunlight gilded the floating moats, it was under foot in the dust that the sun made gilt, it glimmered from every window pane where the long red beams struck golden sparks above the gasping gold-hunting hordes of Wall Street.

High, high, in the deepening sky the tall buildings towered, and the breeze from the bay lifted the sun-dyed flags of commerce until they waved above the turmoil of the hives below—waved courage and hope and strength to those who lusted after gold.

The sun dipped low behind Castle William as I turned listlessly into the Battery, and the long straight shadows of the trees stretched away over greensward and asphalt walk.

Already the electric lights were glimmering among the foliage although the bay shimmered like polished brass and the topsails of the ships glowed with a deeper hue, where the red sun rays fall athwart the rigging.

Old men tottered along the sea-wall, tapping the asphalt with worn canes, old women crept to and fro in the coming twilight,—old women who carried baskets that gaped for charity or bulged with mouldy stuffs,—food, clothing?—I could not tell; I did not care to know.

The heavy thunder from the parapets of Castle William died away over the placid bay, the last red arm of the sun shot up out of the sea, and wavered and faded into the sombre tones of the afterglow. Then came the night, timidly at first, touching sky and water with grey fingers, folding the foliage into soft massed shapes, creeping onward, onward, more swiftly now, until colour and form had gone from all the earth and the world was a world of shadows.

And, as I sat there on the dusky sea-wall, gradually the bitter thoughts faded and I looked out into the calm night with something of that peace that comes to all when day is ended.

The death at my very elbow of the poor blind wretch in the Park had left a shock, but now my nerves relaxed their tension and I began to think about it all,—about the letters and the strange woman who had given them to me. I wondered where she had found them,—whether they really were carried by some vagrant current in to the shore from the wreck of the fated *Lorient.*

Nothing but these letters had human eyes encountered from the *Lorient,* although we believed that fire or berg had been her portion; for there had been no storms when the *Lorient* steamed away from Cherbourg.

And what of the pale-faced girl in black who had given these letters to me, saying that my own heart would teach me where to place them?

I felt in my pockets for the letters where I had thrust them all crumpled and wet. They were there, and I decided to turn them over to the police. Then I thought of Cusick and the City Hall Park and these set my mind running on Jamison and my own work,—ah! I had forgotten that,—I had forgotten that I had sworn to stir Jamison's cold, sluggish blood! Trading on his fiancée's reported suicide,—or murder! True, he had told me that he was satisfied that the body at the Morgue was not Miss Tufft's because the ring did not correspond with his fiancée's ring. But what sort of a man was that!—to go crawling and nosing about morgues and graves for a full-page illustration which might sell a few extra thousand papers. I had never known he was such a man. It was strange too—for that was not the sort of illustration that the *Weekly* used; it was against all precedent—against the whole policy of the paper. He would lose a hundred subscribers where he would gain one by such work.

"The callous brute!" I muttered to myself, "I'll wake him up—I'll——"

I sat straight up on the bench and looked steadily at a figure which was moving toward me under the spluttering electric light.

It was the woman I had met in the Park.

She came straight up to me, her pale face gleaming like marble in the dark, her slim hands outstretched.

"I have been looking for you all day—all day," she said, in the same low thrilling tones,—"I want the letters back; have you them here?"

"Yes," I said, "I have them here,—take them in Heaven's name; they have done enough evil for one day!"

She took the letters from my hand; I saw the ring, made of the double serpents, flashing on her slim finger, and I stepped closer, and looked her in the eyes.

"Who are you?" I asked.

"I? My name is of no importance to you," she answered.

"You are right," I said, "I do not care to know your name. That ring of yours——"

"What of my ring?" she murmured.

"Nothing,—a dead woman lying in the Morgue wears such a ring. Do you know what your letters have done? No? Well I read them to a miserable wretch and he blew his brains out!"

"You read them to a man!"

"I did. He killed himself."

"Who was that man?"

"Captain d'Yniol——"

With something between a sob and a laugh she seized my hand and covered it with kisses, and I, astonished and angry, pulled my hand away from her cold lips and sat down on the bench.

"You needn't thank me," I said sharply; "if I had known that,—but no matter. Perhaps after all the poor devil is better off somewhere in other regions with his sweetheart who was drowned,—yes, I imagine he is. He was blind and ill,—and broken-hearted."

"Blind?" she asked gently.

"Yes. Did you know him?"

"I knew him."

"And his sweetheart, Aline?"

"Aline," she repeated softly,—"she is dead.

I come to thank you in her name."

"For what?—for his death?"

"Ah, yes, for that."

"Where did you get those letters?" I asked her, suddenly.

She did not answer, but stood fingering the wet letters.

Before I could speak again she moved away into the shadows of the trees, lightly, silently, and far down the dark walk I saw her diamond flashing.

Grimly brooding, I rose and passed through the Battery to the steps of the Elevated Road. These I climbed, bought my ticket, and stepped out to the damp platform. When a train came I crowded in with the rest, still pondering on my vengeance, feeling and believing that I was to scourge the conscience of the man who speculated on death.

And at last the train stopped at 28th Street, and I hurried out and down the steps and away to the Morgue.

When I entered the Morgue, Skelton, the keeper, was standing before a slab that glistened faintly under the wretched gas jets. He heard my footsteps, and turned around to see who was coming. Then he nodded, saying: "Mr. Hilton, just take a look at this here stiff—I'll be back in a moment—this is the one that all the papers take to be Miss Tufft,—but they're all off, because this stiff has been here now for two weeks."

I drew out my sketching-block and pencils.

"Which is it, Skelton?" I asked, fumbling for my rubber.

"This one, Mr. Hilton, the girl what's smilin'. Picked up off Sandy Hook, too. Looks as if she was asleep, eh?"

"What's she got in her hand—clenched tight? Oh,—a letter. Turn up the gas, Skelton, I want to see her face."

The old man turned the gas jet, and the flame blazed and whistled in the damp, fetid air. Then suddenly my eyes fell on the dead.

Rigid, scarcely breathing, I stared at the ring, made of two twisted serpents set with a great diamond,—I saw the wet letters crushed in her slender hand,—I looked, and—God help me!—I looked upon the dead face of the girl with whom I had been speaking on the Battery!

"Dead for a month at least," said Skelton, calmly.

Then, as I felt my senses leaving me, I screamed out, and at the same instant somebody from behind seized my shoulder and shook me savagely—shook me until I opened my eyes again and gasped and coughed.

"Now then, young feller!" said a Park policeman bending over me, "if you go to sleep on a bench, somebody'll lift your watch!"

I turned, rubbing my eyes desperately.

Then it was all a dream—and no shrinking girl had come to me with damp letters,—I had not gone to the office—there was no such person as Miss Tufft,—Jamison was not an unfeeling villain,—no, indeed!—he treated us all much better than we deserved, and he was kind and generous too. And the ghastly suicide! Thank God that also was a myth,—and the Morgue and the Battery at night where that pale-faced girl had—ugh!

I felt for my sketch-block, found it; turned the pages of all the animals that I had sketched, the hippopotami, the buffalo, the tigers—ah! where was that sketch in which I had made the woman in shabby black the principal figure, with the brooding vultures all around and the crowd in the sunshine—? It was gone.

I hunted everywhere, in every pocket. It was gone.

At last I rose and moved along the narrow asphalt path in the falling twilight.

And as I turned into the broader walk, I was aware of a group, a policeman holding a lantern, some gardeners, and a knot of loungers gathered about something,—a dark mass on the ground.

"Found 'em just so," one of the gardeners was saying, "better not touch 'em until the coroner comes."

The policeman shifted his bull's-eye a little; the rays fell on two faces, on two bodies, half supported against a park bench. On the finger of the girl glittered a splendid diamond, set between the fangs of two gold serpents. The man had shot himself; he clasped two wet letters in his hand. The girl's clothing and hair were wringing wet, and her face was the face of a drowned person.

"Well, sir," said the policeman, looking at me; "you seem to know these two people—by your looks——"

"I never saw them before," I gasped, and walked on, trembling in every nerve.

For among the folds of her shabby black dress I had noticed the end of a paper,—my sketch that I had missed!

THE BRIDAL PAIR

"If I were you," said the elder man, "I should take three months' solid rest."

"A month is enough," said the younger man. "Ozone will do it; the first brace of grouse I bag will do it—" He broke off abruptly, staring at the line of dimly lighted cars, where negro porters stood by the vestibuled sleepers, directing passengers to staterooms and berths.

"Dog all right, doctor?" inquired the elder man pleasantly.

"All right, doctor," replied the younger; "I spoke to the baggage master."

There was a silence; the elder man chewed an unlighted cigar reflectively, watching his companion with keen narrowing eyes.

The younger physician stood full in the white electric light, lean head lowered, apparently preoccupied with a study of his own shadow swimming and quivering on the asphalt at his feet.

"So you fear I may break down?" he observed, without raising his head.

"I think you're tired out," said the other.

"That's a more agreeable way of expressing it," said the young fellow. "I hear"—he hesitated, with a faint trace of irritation—"I understand that Forbes Stanly thinks me mentally unsound."

"He probably suspects what you're up to," said the elder man soberly.

"Well, what will he do when I announce my germ theory? Put me in a strait-jacket?"

"He'll say you're mad, until you prove it; every physician will agree with him—until your radium test shows us the microbe of insanity."

"Doctor," said the young man abruptly, "I'm going to admit something—to *you.*"

"All right; go ahead and admit it."

"Well, I *am* a bit worried about my own condition."

"It's time you were," observed the other.

"Yes—it's about time. Doctor, I am seriously affected."

The elder man looked up sharply.

"Yes, I'm—in love."

"Ah!" muttered the elder physician, amused and a trifle disgusted; "so that's your malady, is it?"

"A malady—yes; not explainable by our germ theory—not affected by radio-activity. Doctor, I'm speaking lightly enough, but there's no happiness in it."

"Never is," commented the other, striking a match and lighting his ragged cigar. After a puff or two the cigar went out. "All I have to say," he added, "is, don't do it just now. Show me a scale of pure radium and I'll give you leave to marry every spinster in New York. In the mean time go and shoot a few dozen harmless, happy grouse; they can't shoot back. But let love alone. . . . By the way, who is she?"

"I don't know."

"You know her name, I suppose?"

The young fellow shook his head. "I don't even know where she lives," he said finally.

After a pause the elder man took him gently by the arm: "Are you subject to this sort of thing? Are you susceptible?"

"No, not at all."

"Ever before in love?"

"Yes—once."

"When?"

"When I was about ten years old. Her name was Rosamund—aged eight. I never had the courage to speak to her. She died recently, I believe."

The reply was so quietly serious, so destitute of any suspicion of humor, that the elder man's smile faded; and again he cast one of his swift, keen glances at his companion.

"Won't you stay away three months?" he asked patiently.

But the other only shook his head, tracing with the point of his walking stick the outline of his own shadow on the asphalt.

A moment later he glanced at his watch, closed it with a snap, silently shook hands with his equally silent friend, and stepped aboard the sleeping car.

Neither had noticed the name of the sleeping car.

It happened to be the *Rosamund.*

Loungers and passengers on Wildwood station drew back from the platform's edge as the towering locomotive shot by them, stunning their ears with the clangor of its melancholy bell.

Slower, slower glided the dusty train, then stopped, jolting; eddying circles of humanity closed around the cars, through which descending passengers pushed.

"Wildwood! Wildwood!" cried the trainmen; trunks tumbling out of the forward car descended with a bang!—a yelping, wagging setter dog landed on the platform, hysterically grateful to be free; and at the same moment a young fellow in tweed shooting clothes, carrying gripsack and gun case, made his way forward toward the baggage master, who was being jerked all over the platform by the frantic dog.

"Much obliged; I'll take the dog," he said, slipping a bit of silver into the official's hand, and receiving the dog's chain in return.

"Hope you'll have good sport," replied the baggage master. "There's a lot o' birds in this country, they tell me. You've got a good dog there."

The young man smiled and nodded, released the chain from his dog's collar, and started off up the dusty village street, followed by an urchin carrying his luggage.

The landlord of the Wildwood Inn stood on the veranda, prepared to receive guests. When a young man, a white setter dog, and a small boy loomed up, his speculative eyes became suffused with benevolence.

"How-de-do, sir?" he said cordially. "Guess you was with us three year since—stayed to supper. Ain't that so?"

"It certainly is," said his guest cheerfully. "I am surprised that you remember me."

"Be ye?" rejoined the landlord, gratified. "Say! I can tell the name of every man, woman, an' child that has ever set down to eat with us. You was here with a pair o' red bird dawgs; shot a mess o' birds before dark, come back pegged out, an' took the ten-thirty to Noo York. Hey? Yaas, an' you was cussin' round because you couldn't stay an' shoot for a month."

"I had to work hard in those days," laughed the young man. "You are right; it was three years ago this month."

"Time's a flyer; it's fitted with triple screws these days," said the landlord. "Come right in an' make yourself to home. Ed! O Ed! Take this bag to 13! We're all full, sir. You ain't scared at No. 13, be ye? Say! if I ain't a liar you had 13 three years ago! Waal, now!—ain't that the dumbdest—But you can have what you want Monday. How long was you calkerlatin' to stay?"

"A month—if the shooting is good."

"It's all right. Orrin Plummer come in last night with a mess o' pa'tridges. He says the woodcock is droppin' in to the birches south o' Sweetbrier Hill."

The young man nodded, and began to remove his gun from the service-worn case of sole leather.

"Ain't startin' right off, be ye?" inquired his host, laughing.

"I can't begin too quickly," said the young man, busy locking barrels to stock, while the dog looked on, thumping the veranda floor with his plumy tail.

The landlord admired the slim, polished weapon. "That's the instrooment!" he observed. "That there's a slick bird dawg, too. Guess I'd better fill my ice box. Your limit's thirty of each—cock an' pa'tridge. After that there's ducks."

"It's a good, sane law," said the young man, dropping his gun under one arm.

The landlord scratched his ear reflectively. "Lemme see," he mused; "wasn't you a doctor? I heard tell that you made up pieces for the papers about the idjits an' loonyticks of Rome an' Roosia an' furrin climes."

"I have written a little on European and Asiatic insanity," replied the doctor good-humoredly.

"Was you over to them parts?"

"For three years." He whistled the dog in from the road, where several yellow curs were walking round and round him, every hair on end.

The landlord said: "You look a little peakèd yourself. Take it easy the fust, is my advice."

His guest nodded abstractedly, lingering on the veranda, preoccupied with the beauty of the village street, which stretched away westward under tall elms. Autumn-tinted hills closed the vista; beyond them spread the blue sky.

"The cemetery lies that way, does it not?" inquired the young man.

"Straight ahead," said the landlord. "Take the road to the Holler."

"Do you"—the doctor hesitated—"do you recall a funeral there three years ago?"

"Whose?" asked his host bluntly.

"I don't know."

"I'll ask my woman; she saves them funeral pieces an' makes a album. . . . Friend o' yours buried there?"

"No."

The landlord sauntered toward the barroom, where two fellow taxpayers stood shuffling their feet impatiently.

"Waal, good luck, Doc," he said, without intentional offense; "supper's at six. We'll try an' make you comfortable."

"Thank you," replied the doctor, stepping out into the road, and motioning the white setter to heel.

"I remember now," he muttered, as he turned northward, where the road forked; "the cemetery lies to the westward; there should be a lane at the next turning——"

He hesitated and stopped, then resumed his course, mumbling to himself: "I can pass the cemetery later; she would not be there; I don't think I shall ever see her again. . . . I—I wonder whether I am—perfectly—well——"

The words were suddenly lost in a sharp indrawn breath; his heart ceased beating, fluttered, then throbbed on violently; and he shook from head to foot.

There was a glimmer of a summer gown under the trees; a figure passed from shadow to sunshine, and again into the cool dusk of a leafy lane.

The pallor of the young fellow's face changed; a heavy flush spread from forehead to neck; he strode forward, dazed, deafened by the tumult of his drumming pulses. The dog, alert, suspicious, led the way, wheeling into the bramble-bordered lane, only to halt, turn back, and fall in behind his master again.

In the lane ahead the light summer gown fluttered under the foliage, bright in the sunlight, almost lost in the shadows. Then he saw her on the hill's breezy crest, poised for a moment against the sky.

When at length he reached the hill, he found her seated in the shade of a pine. She looked up serenely, as though she had expected him, and they faced each other. A moment later his dog left him, sneaking away without a sound.

When he strove to speak, his voice had an unknown tone to him. Her upturned face was his only answer. The breeze in the pinetops, which had been stirring lazily and monotonously, ceased.

Her delicate face was like a blossom lifted in the still air; her upward glance chained him to silence. The first breeze broke the spell: he spoke a word, then speech died on his lips; he stood twisting his shooting cap, confused, not daring to continue.

The girl leaned back, supporting her weight on one arm, fingers almost buried in the deep green moss.

"It is three years to-day," he said, in the dull voice of one who dreams; "three years to-day. May I not speak?"

In her lowered head and eyes he read acquiescence; in her silence, consent.

"Three years ago to-day," he repeated; "the anniversary has given me courage to speak to you. Surely you will not take offense; we have traveled so far together!—from the end of the world to the end of it, and back again, here—to this place of all places in the world! And now to find you here on this day of all days—here within a step of our first meeting place—three years ago to-day! And all the world we have traveled over since, never speaking, yet ever passing on paths parallel—paths which for thousands of miles ran almost within arm's distance——"

She raised her head slowly, looking out from the shadows of the pines into the sunshine. Her dreamy eyes rested on acres of golden-rod and hillside brambles quivering in the September heat; on fern-choked gullies edged with alder; on brown and purple grasses; on pine thickets where slim silver birches glimmered.

"Will you speak to me?" he asked. "I have never even heard the sound of your voice."

She turned and looked at him, touching with idle fingers the soft hair curling on her temples. Then she bent her head once more, the faintest shadow of a smile in her eyes.

"Because," he said humbly, "these long years of silent recognition count for something! And then the strangeness of it!—the fate of it—the quiet destiny that ruled our lives—that rules them now—now as I am speaking, weighting every second with its tiny burden of fate."

She straightened up, lifting her half-buried hand from the moss; and he saw the imprint there where the palm and fingers had rested.

"Three years that end to-day—end with the new moon," he said. "Do you remember?"

"Yes," she said.

He quivered at the sound of her voice. "You were there, just beyond those oaks," he said eagerly; "we can see them from here. The road turns there——"

"Turns by the cemetery," she murmured.

"Yes, yes, by the cemetery! You had been there, I think."

"Do you remember that?" she asked.

"I have never forgotten—never!" he repeated, striving to hold her eyes to his own; "it was not twilight; there was a glimmer of day in the west, but the woods were darkening, and the new moon lay in the sky, and the evening was very clear and still."

Impulsively he dropped on one knee beside her to see her face; and as he spoke, curbing his emotion and impatience with that subtle deference which is inbred in men or never acquired, she stole a glance at him; and his worn visage brightened as though touched with sunlight.

"The second time I saw you was in New York," he said—" only a glimpse of your face in the crowd—but I knew you."

"I saw you," she mused.

"Did you?" he cried, enchanted. "I dared not believe that you recognized me."

"Yes, I knew you. . . . Tell me more."

The thrilling voice set him aflame; faint danger signals tinted her face and neck.

"In December," he went on unsteadily, "I saw you in Paris—I saw only you amid the thousand faces in the candlelight of Notre Dame."

"And I saw you. . . . And then?"

"And then two months of darkness. . . . And at last a light—moonlight—and you on the terrace at Amara."

"There was only a flower bed—a few spikes of white hyacinths between us," she said dreamily.

He strove to speak coolly. "Day and night have built many a wall between us; was that you who passed me in the starlight, so close that our shoulders touched, in that narrow street in Samarcand? And the dark figure with you——"

"Yes, it was I and my attendant."

"And . . . you, there in the fog——"

"At Archangel? Yes, it was I."

"On the Goryn?"

"It was I. . . . And I am here at last—with you. It is our destiny."

So, kneeling there beside her in the shadow of the pines, she absolved him in their dim confessional, holding him guiltless under the destiny that awaits us all.

Again that illumination touched his haggard face as though brightened by a sun ray stealing through the still foliage above. He grew younger under the level beauty of her gaze; care fell from him like a mask; the shadows that had haunted his eyes faded; youth awoke, transfiguring him and all his eyes beheld.

Made prisoner by love, adoring her, fearing her, he knelt beside her, knowing already that she had surrendered, though fearful yet by word or gesture or a glance to claim what destiny was holding for him—holding securely, inexorably, for him alone.

He spoke of her kindness in understanding him, and of his gratitude; of her generosity, of his wonder that she had ever noticed him on his way through the world.

"I cannot believe that we have never before spoken to each other," he said; "that I do not even know your name. Surely there was once a corner in the land of childhood where we sat together when the world was younger."

She said, dreamily: "Have you forgotten?"

"Forgotten?"

"That sunny corner in the land of childhood."

"Had you been there, I should not have forgotten," he replied, troubled.

"Look at me," she said. Her lovely eyes met his; under the penetrating sweetness of her gaze his heart quickened and grew restless and his uneasy soul stirred, awaking memories.

"There was a child," she said, "years ago; a child at school. You sometimes looked at her; you never spoke. Do you remember?"

He rose to his feet, staring down at her.

"Do you remember?" she asked again.

"Rosamund! Do you mean Rosamund? How should you know that?" he faltered.

The struggle for memory focused all his groping senses; his eyes seemed to look her through and through.

"How can you know?" he repeated unsteadily. "You are not Rosamund. . . . Are you? . . . She is dead. I heard that she was dead. . . . *Are you Rosamund?*"

"Do you not know?"

"Yes; you are not Rosamund. . . . What do you know of her?"

"I think she loved you."

"Is she dead?"

The girl looked up at him, smiling, following with delicate perception the sequence of his thoughts; and already his thoughts were far from the child Rosamund, a sweetheart of a day long since immortal; already he had forgotten his question, though the question was of life or death.

Sadness and unrest and the passing of souls concerned not him; she knew that all his thoughts were centered on her; that he was already living over once more the last three years, with all their mystery and charm, savoring their fragrance anew in the exquisite enchantment of her presence.

Through the autumn silence the pines began to sway in a wind unfelt below. She raised her eyes and saw their green crests shimmering and swimming in a cool current; a thrilling sound stole out, and with it floated the pine perfume, exhaling in the sunshine. He heard the dreamy harmony above, looked up; then, troubled, somber, moved by he knew not what, he knelt once more in the shadow beside her—close beside her.

She did not stir. Their destiny was close upon them. It came in the guise of love.

He bent nearer. "I love you," he said. "I loved you from the first. And shall forever. You knew it long ago."

She did not move.

"You knew I loved you?"

"Yes, I knew it."

The emotion in her voice, in every delicate contour of her face, pleaded for mercy. He gave her none, and she bent her head in silence, clasped hands tightening.

And when at last he had had his say, the burning words still rang in her ears through the silence. A curious faintness stole upon her, coming stealthily like a hateful thing. She strove to put it from her, to listen, to remember and understand the words he had spoken, but the dull confusion grew with the sound of the pines.

"Will you love me? Will you try to love me?"

"I love you," she said; "I have loved you so many, many years; I—I am Rosamund——"

She bowed her head and covered her face with both hands.

"Rosamund! Rosamund!" he breathed, enraptured.

She dropped her hands with a little cry; the frightened sweetness of her eyes held back his outstretched arms. "Do not touch me," she whispered; "you will not touch me, will you?—not yet—not now. Wait till I understand!" She pressed her hands to her eyes, then again let them fall, staring straight at him. "I loved you so!" she whispered. "Why did you wait?"

"Rosamund! Rosamund!" he cried sorrowfully, "what are you saying? I do not understand; I can understand nothing save that I worship you. May I not touch you?—touch your hand, Rosamund? I love you so."

"And I love you. I beg you not to touch me—not yet. There is something—some reason why——"

"Tell me, sweetheart."

"Do you not know?"

"By Heaven, I do not!" he said, troubled and amazed.

She cast one desperate, unhappy glance at him, then rose to her full height, gazing out over the hazy valleys to where the mountains began, piled up like dim sun-tipped clouds in the north.

The hill wind stirred her hair and fluttered the white ribbons at waist and shoulder. The goldenrod swayed in the sunshine. Below, amid yellow treetops, the roofs and chimneys of the village glimmered.

"Dear, do you not understand?" she said. "How can I make you understand that I love you—too late?"

"Give yourself to me, Rosamund; let me touch you—let me take you——"

"Will you love me always?"

"In life, in death, which cannot part us. Will you marry me, Rosamund?"

She looked straight into his eyes. "Dear, do you not understand? Have you forgotten? I died three years ago to-day."

The unearthly sweetness of her white face startled him. A terrible light broke in on him; his heart stood still.

In his dull brain words were sounding—his own words, written years ago: "When God takes the mind and leaves the body alive, there grows in it, sometimes, a beauty almost supernatural."

He had seen it in his practice. A thrill of fright penetrated him, piercing every vein with its chill. He strove to speak; his lips seemed frozen; he stood there before her, a ghastly smile stamped on his face, and in his heart, terror.

"What do you mean, Rosamund?" he said at last.

"That I am dead, dear. Did you not understand that? I—I thought you knew it—when you first saw me at the cemetery, after all those years since childhood. . . . Did you not know it?" she asked wistfully. "I must wait for my bridal."

Misery whitened his face as he raised his head and looked out across the sunlit world. Something had smeared and marred the fair earth; the sun grew gray as he stared.

Stupefied by the crash, the ruins of life around him, he stood mute, erect, facing the west.

She whispered, "Do you understand?"

"Yes," he said; "we will wed later. You have been ill, dear; but it is all right now—and will always be—God help us! Love is stronger than all—stronger than death."

"I know it is stronger than death," she said, looking out dreamily over the misty valley.

He followed her gaze, calmly, serenely reviewing all that he must renounce, the happiness of wedlock, children—all that a man desires.

Suddenly instinct stirred, awaking man's only friend—hope. A lifetime for the battle!—for a cure! Hopeless? He laughed in his excitement. Despair?—when the cure lay almost within his grasp!—the work he had given his life to! A month more in the laboratory—two months—three—perhaps a year. What of it? It must surely come—how could he fail when the work of his life meant all in life for her?

The light of exaltation slowly faded from his face; ominous, foreboding thoughts crept in; fear laid a shaky hand on his head which fell heavily forward on his breast.

Science and man's cunning and the wisdom of the world!

"O God," he groaned, "for Him who cured by laying on His hands!"

Now that he had learned her name, and that her father was alive, he stood mutely beside her, staring steadily at the chimneys and stately dormered roof almost hidden behind the crimson maple foliage across the valley—her home.

She had seated herself once more upon the moss, hands clasped upon one knee, looking out into the west with dreamy eyes.

"I shall not be long," he said gently. "Will you wait here for me? I will bring your father with me."

"I will wait for you. But you must come before the new moon. Will you? I must go when the new moon lies in the west."

"Go, dearest? Where?"

"I may not tell you," she sighed, "but you will know very soon—very soon now. And there will be no more sorrow, I think," she added timidly.

"There will be no more sorrow," he repeated quietly.

"For the former things are passing away," she said.

He broke a heavy spray of golden-rod and laid it across her knees; she held out a blossom to him—a blind gentian, blue as her eyes. He kissed it.

"Be with me when the new moon comes," she whispered. "It will be so sweet. I will teach you how divine is death, if you will come."

"You shall teach me the sweetness of life," he said tremulously.

"Yes—life. I did not know you called it by its truest name."

So he went away, trudging sturdily down the lane, gun glistening on his shoulder.

Where the lane joins the shadowy village street his dog skulked up to him, sniffing at his heels.

A mill whistle was sounding; through the red rays of the setting sun people were passing. Along the row of village shops loungers followed him with vacant eyes. He saw nothing, heard nothing, though a kindly voice called after him, and a young girl smiled at him on her short journey through the world.

The landlord of the Wildwood Inn sat sunning himself in the red evening glow.

"Well, doctor," he said, "you look tired to death. Eh? What's that you say?"

The young man repeated his question in a low voice. The landlord shook his head.

"No, sir. The big house on the hill is empty—been empty these three years. No, sir, there ain't no family there now. The old gentleman moved away three years ago."

"You are mistaken," said the doctor; "his daughter tells me he lives there."

"His—his daughter?" repeated the landlord. "Why, doctor, she's dead." He turned to his wife, who sat sewing by the open window: "Ain't it three years, Marthy?"

"Three years to-day," said the woman, biting off her thread. "She's buried in the family vault over the hill. She was a right pretty little thing, too."

"Turned nineteen," mused the landlord, folding his newspaper reflectively.

The great gray house on the hill was closed, windows and doors boarded over, lawn, shrubbery, and hedges tangled with weeds. A few scarlet poppies glimmered above the brown grass. Save for these, and clumps of tall wild phlox, there were no blossoms among the weeds.

His dog, which had sneaked after him, cowered as he turned northward across the fields. Swifter and swifter he strode; and as he stumbled on, the long sunset clouds faded, the golden light in the west died out, leaving a calm, clear sky tinged with faintest green.

Pines hid the west as he crept toward the hill where she awaited him. As he climbed through dusky purple grasses, higher, higher, he saw the new moon's crescent tipping above the hills; and he crushed back the deathly fright that clutched at him and staggered on.

"Rosamund!"

The pines answered him.

"Rosamund!"

The pines replied, answering together. Then the wind died away, and there was no answer when he called.

East and south the darkening thickets, swaying, grew still. He saw the slim silver birches glimmering like the ghosts of young trees dead; he saw on the moss at his feet a broken stalk of golden-rod.

The new moon had drawn a veil across her face; sky and earth were very still.

While the moon lasted he lay, eyes open, listening, his face pillowed on the moss. It was long after sunrise when his dog came to him; later still when men came.

And at first they thought he was asleep.

THE HARBOR-MASTER

I

Because it all seems so improbable—so horribly impossible to me now, sitting here safe and sane in my own library—I hesitate to record an episode which already appears to me less horrible than grotesque. Yet, unless this story is written now, I know I shall never have the courage to tell the truth about the matter—not from fear of ridicule, but because I myself shall soon cease to credit what I now know to be true. Yet scarcely a month has elapsed since I heard the stealthy purring of what I believed to be the shoaling undertow—scarcely a month ago, with my own eyes, I saw that which, even now, I am beginning to believe never existed. As for the harbor-master—and the blow I am now striking at the old order of things—But of that I shall not speak now, or later; I shall try to tell the story simply and truthfully, and let my friends testify as to my probity and the publishers of this book corroborate them.

On the 29th of February I resigned my position under the government and left Washington to accept an offer from Professor Farrago—whose name he kindly permits me to use—and on the first day of April I entered upon my new and congenial duties as general superintendent of the water-fowl department connected with the Zoological Gardens then in course of erection at Bronx Park, New York.

For a week I followed the routine, examining the new foundations, studying the architect's plans, following the surveyors through the Bronx thickets, suggesting arrangements for water-courses and pools destined to be included in the enclosures for swans, geese, pelicans, herons, and such of the waders and swimmers as we might expect to acclimate in Bronx Park.

It was at that time the policy of the trustees and officers of the Zoological Gardens neither to employ collectors nor to send out expeditions in search of specimens. The society decided to depend upon voluntary contributions, and I was always busy, part of the day, in dictating answers to correspondents who wrote offering their services as hunters of big game, collectors of all sorts of fauna, trappers, snarers, and also to those who offered specimens for sale, usually at exorbitant rates.

To the proprietors of five-legged kittens, mangy lynxes, moth-eaten coyotes, and dancing bears I returned courteous but uncompromising refusals—of course, first submitting all such letters, together with my replies, to Professor Farrago.

One day towards the end of May, however, just as I was leaving Bronx Park to return to town, Professor Lesard, of the reptilian department, called out to me that Professor Farrago wanted to see me a moment; so I put my pipe into my pocket again and retraced my steps to the temporary, wooden building occupied by Professor Farrago, general superintendent of the Zoological Gardens. The professor, who was sitting at his desk before a pile of letters and replies submitted for approval by me, pushed his glasses down and looked over them at me with a whimsical smile that suggested amusement, impatience, annoyance, and perhaps a faint trace of apology.

"Now, here's a letter," he said, with a deliberate gesture towards a sheet of paper impaled on a file—"a letter that I suppose you remember." He disengaged the sheet of paper and handed it to me.

"Oh yes," I replied, with a shrug; "of course the man is mistaken—or—"

"Or what?" demanded Professor Farrago, tranquilly, wiping his glasses.

"—Or a liar," I replied.

After a silence he leaned back in his chair and bade me read the letter to him again, and I did so with a contemptuous tolerance for the writer, who must have been either a very innocent victim or a very stupid swindler. I said as much to Professor Farrago, but, to my surprise, he appeared to waver.

"I suppose," he said, with his near-sighted, embarrassed smile, "that nine hundred and ninety-nine men in a thousand would throw that letter aside and condemn the writer as a liar or a fool?"

"In my opinion," said I, "he's one or the other."

"He isn't—in mine," said the professor, placidly.

"What!" I exclaimed. "Here is a man living all alone on a strip of rock and sand between the wilderness and the sea, who wants you to send somebody to take charge of a bird that doesn't exist!"

"How do you know," asked Professor Farrago, "that the bird in question does not exist?"

"It is generally accepted," I replied, sarcastically, "that the great auk has been extinct for years. Therefore I may be pardoned for doubting that our correspondent possesses a pair of them alive."

"Oh, you young fellows," said the professor, smiling wearily, "you embark on a theory for destinations that don't exist."

He leaned back in his chair, his amused eyes searching space for the imagery that made him smile.

"Like swimming squirrels, you navigate with the help of Heaven and a stiff breeze, but you never land where you hope to—do you?"

Rather red in the face, I said: "Don't you believe the great auk to be extinct?"

"Audubon saw the great auk."

"Who has seen a single specimen since?"

"Nobody—except our correspondent here," he replied, laughing.

I laughed, too, considering the interview at an end, but the professor went on, coolly:

"Whatever it is that our correspondent has—and I am daring to believe that it *is* the great auk itself—I want you to secure it for the society."

When my astonishment subsided my first conscious sentiment was one of pity. Clearly, Professor Farrago was on the verge of dotage—ah, what a loss to the world!

I believe now that Professor Farrago perfectly interpreted my thoughts, but he betrayed neither resentment nor impatience. I drew a chair up beside his desk—there was nothing to do but to obey, and this fool's errand was none of my conceiving.

Together we made out a list of articles necessary for me and itemized the expenses I might incur, and I set a date for my return, allowing no margin for a successful termination to the expedition.

"Never mind that," said the professor. "What I want you to do is to get those birds here safely. Now, how many men will you take?"

"None," I replied, bluntly; "it's a useless expense, unless there is something to bring back. If there is I'll wire you, you may be sure."

"Very well," said Professor Farrago, good-humoredly, "you shall have all the assistance you may require. Can you leave to-night?"

The old gentleman was certainly prompt. I nodded, half-sulkily, aware of his amusement.

"So," I said, picking up my hat, "I am to start north to find a place called Black Harbor, where there is a man named Halyard who possesses, among other household utensils, two extinct great auks—"

We were both laughing by this time. I asked him why on earth he credited the assertion of a man he had never before heard of.

"I suppose," he replied, with the same half-apologetic, half-humorous smile, "it is instinct. I feel, somehow, that this man Halyard *has* got an auk—perhaps two. I can't get away from the idea that we are on the eve of acquiring the rarest of living creatures. It's odd for a scientist to talk as I do; doubtless you're shocked—admit it, now!"

But I was not shocked; on the contrary, I was conscious that the same strange hope that Professor Farrago cherished was beginning, in spite of me, to stir my pulses, too.

"If he has—" I began, then stopped.

The professor and I looked hard at each other in silence.

"Go on," he said, encouragingly.

But I had nothing more to say, for the prospect of beholding with my own eyes a living specimen of the great auk produced a series of conflicting emotions within me which rendered speech profanely superfluous.

As I took my leave Professor Farrago came to the door of the temporary, wooden office and handed me the letter written by the man Halyard. I folded it and put it into my pocket, as Halyard might require it for my own identification.

"How much does he want for the pair?" I asked.

"Ten thousand dollars. Don't demur—if the birds are really—"

"I know," I said, hastily, not daring to hope too much.

"One thing more," said Professor Farrago, gravely; "you know, in that last paragraph of his letter, Halyard speaks of something else in the way of specimens—an undiscovered species of amphibious biped—just read that paragraph again, will you?"

I drew the letter from my pocket and read as he directed:

> "When you have seen the two living specimens of the great auk, and have satisfied yourself that I tell the truth, you may be wise enough to listen without prejudice to a statement I shall make concerning the existence of the strangest creature ever fashioned. I will merely say, at this time, that the creature referred to is an amphibious biped and inhabits the ocean near this coast. More I cannot say, for I personally have not seen the animal, but I have a witness who has, and there are many who affirm that they have seen the creature. You will naturally say that my statement amounts to nothing; but when your representative arrives, if he be free from prejudice, I expect his reports to you concerning this sea-biped will confirm the solemn statements of a witness I *know* to be unimpeachable.
>
> "Yours truly,
> "BURTON HALYARD.
> "BLACK HARBOR"

"Well," I said, after a moment's thought, "here goes for the wild-goose chase."

"Wild auk, you mean," said Professor Farrago, shaking hands with me. "You will start to-night, won't you?"

"Yes, but Heaven knows how I'm ever going to land in this man Halyard's door-yard. Good-bye!"

"About that sea-biped—" began Professor Farrago, shyly.

"Oh, don't!" I said; "I can swallow the auks, feathers and claws, but if this fellow Halyard is hinting he's seen an amphibious creature resembling a man—"

"—Or a woman," said the professor, cautiously.

I retired, disgusted, my faith shaken in the mental vigor of Professor Farrago.

II

The three days' voyage by boat and rail was irksome. I bought my kit at Sainte Croix, on the Central Pacific Railroad, and on June 1st I began the last stage of my journey *via* the Sainte Isole broad-gauge, arriving in the wilderness by daylight. A tedious forced march by blazed trail, freshly spotted on the wrong side, of course, brought me to the northern terminus of the rusty, narrow-gauge lumber railway which runs from the heart of the hushed pine wilderness to the sea.

Already a long train of battered flat-cars, piled with sluice-props and roughly hewn sleepers, was moving slowly off into the brooding forest gloom, when I came in sight of the track; but I developed a gratifying and unexpected burst of speed, shouting all the while. The train stopped; I swung myself aboard the last car, where a pleasant young fellow was sitting on the rear brake, chewing spruce and reading a letter.

"Come aboard, sir," he said, looking up with a smile; "I guess you're the man in a hurry."

"I'm looking for a man named Halyard," I said, dropping rifle and knapsack on the fresh-cut, fragrant pile of pine. "Are you Halyard?"

"No, I'm Francis Lee, bossing the mica pit at Port-of-Waves," he replied, "but this letter is from Halyard, asking me to look out for a man in a hurry from Bronx Park, New York."

"I'm that man," said I, filling my pipe and offering him a share of the weed of peace, and we sat side by side smoking very amiably, until a signal from the locomotive sent him forward and I was left alone, lounging at ease, head pillowed on both arms, watching the blue sky flying through the branches overhead.

Long before we came in sight of the ocean I smelled it; the fresh, salt aroma stole into my senses, drowsy with the heated odor of pine and hemlock, and I sat up, peering ahead into the dusky sea of pines.

Fresher and fresher came the wind from the sea, in puffs, in mild, sweet breezes, in steady, freshening currents, blowing the feathery crowns of the pines, setting the balsam's blue tufts rocking.

Lee wandered back over the long line of flats, balancing himself nonchalantly as the cars swung around a sharp curve, where water dripped from a newly propped sluice that suddenly emerged from the depths of the forest to run parallel to the railroad track.

"Built it this spring," he said, surveying his handiwork, which seemed to undulate as the cars swept past. "It runs to the cove—or ought to—" He stopped abruptly with a thoughtful glance at me.

"So you're going over to Halyard's?" he continued, as though answering a question asked by himself.

I nodded.

"You've never been there—of course?"

"No," I said, "and I'm not likely to go again."

I would have told him why I was going if I had not already begun to feel ashamed of my idiotic errand.

"I guess you're going to look at those birds of his," continued Lee, placidly.

"I guess I am," I said, sulkily, glancing askance to see whether he was smiling.

But he only asked me, quite seriously, whether a great auk was really a very rare bird; and I told him that the last one ever seen had been found dead off Labrador in January, 1870. Then I asked him whether these birds of Halyard's were really great auks, and he replied, somewhat indifferently, that he supposed they were—at least, nobody had ever before seen such birds near Port-of-Waves.

"There's something else," he said, running a pine-sliver through his pipe-stem—"something that interests us all here more than auks, big or little. I suppose I might as well speak of it, as you are bound to hear about it sooner or later."

He hesitated, and I could see that he was embarrassed, searching for the exact words to convey his meaning.

"If," said I, "you have anything in this region more important to science than the great auk, I should be very glad to know about it."

Perhaps there was the faintest tinge of sarcasm in my voice, for he shot a sharp glance at me and then turned slightly. After a moment, however, he put his pipe into his pocket, laid hold of the brake with both hands, vaulted to his perch aloft, and glanced down at me.

"Did you ever hear of the harbor-master?" he asked, maliciously.

"Which harbor-master?" I inquired.

"You'll know before long," he observed, with a satisfied glance into perspective.

This rather extraordinary observation puzzled me. I waited for him to resume, and, as he did not, I asked him what he meant.

"If I knew," he said, "I'd tell you. But, come to think of it, I'd be a fool to go into details with a scientific man. You'll hear about the harbor-master—perhaps you will see the harbor-master. In that event I should be glad to converse with you on the subject."

I could not help laughing at his prim and precise manner, and, after a moment, he also laughed, saying:

"It hurts a man's vanity to know he knows a thing that somebody else knows he doesn't know. I'm damned if I say another word about the harbor-master until you've been to Halyard's!"

"A harbor-master," I persisted, "is an official who superintends the mooring of ships—isn't he?"

But he refused to be tempted into conversation, and we lounged silently on the lumber until a long, thin whistle from the locomotive and a rush of stinging salt-wind brought us to our feet. Through the trees I could see the bluish-black ocean, stretching out beyond black headlands to meet the clouds; a great wind was roaring among the trees as the train slowly came to a stand-still on the edge of the primeval forest.

Lee jumped to the ground and aided me with my rifle and pack, and then the train began to back away along a curved side-track which, Lee said, led to the mica-pit and company stores.

"Now what will you do?" he asked, pleasantly. "I can give you a good dinner and a decent bed to-night if you like—and I'm sure Mrs. Lee would be very glad to have you stop with us as long as you choose."

I thanked him, but said that I was anxious to reach Halyard's before dark, and he very kindly led me along the cliffs and pointed out the path.

"This man Halyard," he said, "is an invalid. He lives at a cove called Black Harbor, and all his truck goes through to him over the company's road. We receive it here, and send a pack-mule through once a month. I've met him; he's a bad-tempered hypochondriac, a cynic at heart, and a man whose word is never doubted. If he says he has a great auk, you may be satisfied he has."

My heart was beating with excitement at the prospect; I looked out across the wooded headlands and tangled stretches of dune and hollow, trying to realize what it might mean to me, to Professor Farrago, to the world, if I should lead back to New York a live auk.

"He's a crank," said Lee; "frankly, I don't like him. If you find it unpleasant there, come back to us."

"Does Halyard live alone?" I asked.

"Yes—except for a professional trained nurse—poor thing!"

"A man?"

"No," said Lee, disgustedly.

Presently he gave me a peculiar glance; hesitated, and finally said: "Ask Halyard to tell you about his nurse and—the harbor-master. Good-bye—I'm due at the quarry. Come and stay with us whenever you care to; you will find a welcome at Port-of-Waves."

We shook hands and parted on the cliff, he turning back into the forest along the railway, I starting northward, pack slung, rifle over my shoulder. Once I met a group of quarrymen, faces burned brick-red, scarred hands swinging as they walked. And, as I passed them with a nod, turning, I saw that they also had turned to look after me, and I caught a word or two of their conversation, whirled back to me on the sea-wind.

They were speaking of the harbor-master.

III

Towards sunset I came out on a sheer granite cliff where the sea-birds were whirling and clamoring, and the great breakers dashed, rolling in double-thundered reverberations on the sun-dyed, crimson sands below the rock.

Across the half-moon of beach towered another cliff, and, behind this, I saw a column of smoke rising in the still air. It certainly came from Halyard's chimney, although the opposite cliff prevented me from seeing the house itself.

I rested a moment to refill my pipe, then resumed rifle and pack, and cautiously started to skirt the cliffs. I had descended half-way towards the beach, and was examining the cliff opposite, when something on the very top of the rock arrested my attention—a man darkly outlined against the sky. The next moment, however, I knew it could not be a man, for the object suddenly glided over the face of the cliff and slid down the sheer, smooth lace like a lizard. Before I could get a square look at it, the thing crawled into the surf—or, at least, it seemed to—but the whole episode occurred so suddenly, so unexpectedly, that I was not sure I had seen anything at all.

However, I was curious enough to climb the cliff on the land side and make my way towards the spot where I imagined I saw the man. Of course, there was nothing there—not a trace of a human being, I mean. Something *had* been there—a sea-otter, possibly—for the remains of a freshly killed fish lay on the rock, eaten to the back-bone and tail.

The next moment, below me, I saw the house, a freshly painted, trim, flimsy structure, modern, and very much out of harmony with the splendid savagery surrounding it. It struck a nasty, cheap note in the noble, gray monotony of headland and sea.

The descent was easy enough. I crossed the crescent beach, hard as pink marble, and found a little trodden path among the rocks, that led to the front porch of the house.

There were two people on the porch—I heard their voices before I saw them—and when I set my foot upon the wooden steps, I saw one of them, a woman, rise from her chair and step hastily towards me.

"Come back!" cried the other, a man with a smooth-shaven, deeply lined face, and a pair of angry, blue eyes; and the woman stepped back quietly, acknowledging my lifted hat with a silent inclination.

The man, who was reclining in an invalid's rolling-chair, clapped both large, pale hands to the wheels and pushed himself out along the porch. He had shawls pinned about him, an untidy, drab-colored hat on his head, and, when he looked down at me, he scowled.

"I know who you are," he said, in his acid voice; "you're one of the Zoological men from Bronx Park. You look like it, anyway."

"It is easy to recognize you from your reputation," I replied, irritated at his discourtesy.

"Really," he replied, with something between a sneer and a laugh, "I'm obliged for your frankness. You're after my great auks, are you not?"

"Nothing else would have tempted me into this place," I replied, sincerely.

"Thank Heaven for that," he said. "Sit down a moment; you've interrupted us." Then, turning to the young woman, who wore the neat gown and tiny cap of a professional nurse, he bade her resume what she had been saying. She did so, with a deprecating glance at me, which made the old man sneer again.

"It happened so suddenly," she said, in her low voice, "that I had no chance to get back. The boat was drifting in the cove; I sat in the stern, reading, both oars shipped, and the tiller swinging.

Then I heard a scratching under the boat, but thought it might be seaweed—and, next moment, came those soft thumpings, like the sound of a big fish rubbing its nose against a float."

Halyard clutched the wheels of his chair and stared at the girl in grim displeasure.

"Didn't you know enough to be frightened?" he demanded.

"No—not then," she said, coloring faintly; "but when, after a few moments, I looked up and saw the harbor-master running up and down the beach, I was horribly frightened."

"Really?" said Halyard, sarcastically; "it was about time." Then, turning to me, he rasped out: "And that young lady was obliged to row all the way to Port-of-Waves and call to Lee's quarrymen to take her boat in."

Completely mystified, I looked from Halyard to the girl, not in the least comprehending what all this meant.

"That will do," said Halyard, ungraciously, which curt phrase was apparently the usual dismissal for the nurse.

She rose, and I rose, and she passed me with an inclination, stepping noiselessly into the house.

"I want beef-tea!" bawled Halyard after her; then he gave me an unamiable glance.

"I was a well-bred man," he sneered; "I'm a Harvard graduate, too, but I live as I like, and I do what I like, and I say what I like."

"You certainly are not reticent," I said, disgusted.

"Why should I be?" he rasped; "I pay that young woman for my irritability; it's a bargain between us."

"In your domestic affairs," I said, "there is nothing that interests me. I came to see those auks."

"You probably believe them to be razor-billed auks," he said, contemptuously. "But they're not; they're great auks."

I suggested that he permit me to examine them, and he replied, indifferently, that they were in a pen in his backyard, and that I was free to step around the house when I cared to.

I laid my rifle and pack on the veranda, and hastened off with mixed emotions, among which hope no longer predominated. No man in his senses would keep two such precious prizes in a pen in his backyard, I argued, and I was perfectly prepared to find anything from a puffin to a penguin in that pen.

I shall never forget, as long as I live, my stupor of amazement when I came to the wire-covered enclosure. Not only were there two great auks in the pen, alive, breathing, squatting in bulky majesty on their seaweed bed, but one of them was gravely contemplating two newly hatched chicks, all bill and feet, which nestled sedately at the edge of a puddle of salt-water, where some small fish were swimming.

For a while excitement blinded, nay, deafened me. I tried to realize that I was gazing upon the last individuals of an all but extinct race—the sole survivors of the gigantic auk, which, for thirty years, has been accounted an extinct creature.

I believe that I did not move muscle nor limb until the sun had gone down and the crowding darkness blurred my straining eyes and blotted the great, silent, bright eyed birds from sight.

Even then I could not tear myself away from the enclosure; I listened to the strange, drowsy note of the male bird, the fainter responses of the female, the thin plaints of the chicks, huddling under her breast; I heard their flipper-like, embryotic wings beating sleepily as the birds stretched and yawned their beaks and clacked them, preparing for slumber.

"If you please," came a soft voice from the door, "Mr. Halyard awaits your company to dinner."

IV

I dined well—or, rather, I might have enjoyed my dinner if Mr. Halyard had been eliminated; and the feast consisted exclusively of a joint of beef, the pretty nurse, and myself. She was exceedingly attractive—with a disturbing fashion of lowering her head and raising her dark eyes when spoken to.

As for Halyard, he was unspeakable, bundled up in his snuffy shawls, and making uncouth noises over his gruel. But it is only just to say that his table was worth sitting down to and his wine was sound as a bell.

"Yah!" he snapped, "I'm sick of this cursed soup—and I'll trouble you to fill my glass—"

"It is dangerous for you to touch claret," said the pretty nurse.

"I might as well die at dinner as anywhere," he observed.

"Certainly," said I, cheerfully passing the decanter, but he did not appear overpleased with the attention.

"I can't smoke, either," he snarled, hitching the shawls around until he looked like Richard the Third.

However, he was good enough to shove a box of cigars at me, and I took one and stood up, as the pretty nurse slipped past and vanished into the little parlor beyond.

We sat there for a while without speaking. He picked irritably at the bread-crumbs on the cloth, never glancing in my direction; and I, tired from my long foot-tour, lay back in my chair, silently appreciating one of the best cigars I ever smoked.

"Well," he rasped out at length, "what do you think of my auks—and my veracity?"

I told him that both were unimpeachable.

"Didn't they call me a swindler down there at your museum?" he demanded.

I admitted that I had heard the term applied. Then I made a clean breast of the matter, telling him that it was I who had doubted; that my chief, Professor Farrago, had sent me against my will, and that I was ready and glad to admit that he, Mr. Halyard, was a benefactor of the human race.

"Bosh!" he said. "What good does a confounded wobbly, bandy-toed bird do to the human race?"

But he was pleased, nevertheless; and presently he asked me, not unamiably, to punish his claret again.

"I'm done for," he said; "good things to eat and drink are no good to me. Some day I'll get mad enough to have a fit, and then—"

He paused to yawn.

"Then," he continued, "that little nurse of mine will drink up my claret and go back to civilization, where people are polite."

Somehow or other, in spite of the fact that Halyard was an old pig, what he said touched me. There was certainly not much left in life for him—as he regarded life.

"I'm going to leave her this house," he said, arranging his shawls. "She doesn't know it. I'm going to leave her my money, too. She doesn't know that. Good Lord! What kind of a woman can she be to stand my bad temper for a few dollars a month!"

"I think," said I, "that it's partly because she's poor, partly because she's sorry for you."

He looked up with a ghastly smile.

"You think she really is sorry?"

Before I could answer he went on: "I'm no mawkish sentimentalist, and I won't allow anybody to be sorry for me—do you hear?"

"Oh, I'm not sorry for you!" I said, hastily, and, for the first time since I had seen him, he laughed heartily, without a sneer.

We both seemed to feel better after that; I drank his wine and smoked his cigars, and he appeared to take a certain grim pleasure in watching me.

"There's no fool like a young fool," he observed, presently.

As I had no doubt he referred to me, I paid him no attention.

After fidgeting with his shawls, he gave me an oblique scowl and asked me my age.

"Twenty-four," I replied.

"Sort of a tadpole, aren't you?" he said.

As I took no offence, he repeated the remark.

"Oh, come," said I, "there's no use in trying to irritate me. I see through you; a row acts like a cocktail on you—but you'll have to stick to gruel in my company."

"I call that impudence!" he rasped out, wrathfully.

"I don't care what you call it," I replied, undisturbed, "I am not going to be worried by you. Anyway," I ended, "it is my opinion that you could be very good company if you chose."

The proposition appeared to take his breath away—at least, he said nothing more; and I finished my cigar in peace and tossed the stump into a saucer.

"Now," said I, "what price do you set upon your birds, Mr. Halyard?"

"Ten thousand dollars," he snapped, with an evil smile.

"You will receive a certified check when the birds are delivered," I said, quietly.

"You don't mean to say you agree to that outrageous bargain—and I won't take a cent less, either—Good Lord!—haven't you any spirit left?" he cried, half rising from his pile of shawls.

His piteous eagerness for a dispute sent me into laughter impossible to control, and he eyed me, mouth open, animosity rising visibly.

Then he seized the wheels of his invalid chair and trundled away, too mad to speak; and I strolled out into the parlor, still laughing.

The pretty nurse was there, sewing under a hanging lamp.

"If I am not indiscreet—" I began.

"Indiscretion is the better part of valor," said she, dropping her head but raising her eyes.

So I sat down with a frivolous smile peculiar to the appreciated.

"Doubtless," said I, "you are hemming a 'kerchief."

"Doubtless I am not," she said; "this is a night-cap for Mr. Halyard."

A mental vision of Halyard in a night-cap, very mad, nearly set me laughing again.

"Like the King of Yvetot, he wears his crown in bed," I said, flippantly.

"The King of Yvetot might have made that remark," she observed, re-threading her needle.

It is unpleasant to be reproved. How large and red and hot a man's ears feel.

To cool them, I strolled out to the porch; and, after a while, the pretty nurse came out, too, and sat down in a chair not far away. She probably regretted her lost opportunity to be flirted with.

"I have so little company—it is a great relief to see somebody from the world," she said. "If you can be agreeable, I wish you would."

The idea that she had come out to see me was so agreeable that I remained speechless until she said: "Do tell me what people are doing in New York."

So I seated myself on the steps and talked about the portion of the world inhabited by me, while she sat sewing in the dull light that straggled out from the parlor windows.

She had a certain coquetry of her own, using the usual methods with an individuality that was certainly fetching. For instance, when she lost her needle—and, another time, when we both, on hands and knees, hunted for her thimble.

However, directions for these pastimes may be found in contemporary classics.

I was as entertaining as I could be—perhaps not quite as entertaining as a young man usually thinks he is. However, we got on very well together until I asked her tenderly who the harbor-master might be, whom they all discussed so mysteriously.

"I do not care to speak about it," she said, with a primness of which I had not suspected her capable.

Of course I could scarcely pursue the subject after that—and, indeed, I did not intend to—so I began to tell her how I fancied I had seen a man on the cliff that afternoon, and how the creature slid over the sheer rock like a snake.

To my amazement, she asked me to kindly discontinue the account of my adventures, in an icy tone, which left no room for protest.

"It was only a sea-otter," I tried to explain, thinking perhaps she did not care for snake stories.

But the explanation did not appear to interest her, and I was mortified to observe that my impression upon her was anything but pleasant.

"She doesn't seem to like me and my stories," thought I, "but she is too young, perhaps, to appreciate them."

So I forgave her—for she was even prettier than I had thought her at first—and I took my leave, saying that Mr. Halyard would doubtless direct me to my room.

Halyard was in his library, cleaning a revolver, when I entered.

"Your room is next to mine," he said; "pleasant dreams, and kindly refrain from snoring."

"May I venture an absurd hope that you will do the same!" I replied, politely.

That maddened him, so I hastily withdrew.

I had been asleep for at least two hours when a movement by my bedside and a light in my eyes awakened me. I sat bolt upright in bed, blinking at Halyard, who, clad in a dressing-gown and wearing a night-cap, had wheeled himself into my room with one hand, while with the other he solemnly waved a candle over my head.

"I'm so cursed lonely," he said—"come, there's a good fellow—talk to me in your own original, impudent way."

I objected strenuously, but he looked so worn and thin, so lonely and bad-tempered, so lovelessly grotesque, that I got out of bed and passed a spongeful of cold water over my head.

Then I returned to bed and propped the pillows up for a back-rest, ready to quarrel with him if it might bring some little pleasure into his morbid existence.

"No," he said, amiably, "I'm too worried to quarrel, but I'm much obliged for your kindly offer. I want to tell you something."

"What?" I asked, suspiciously.

"I want to ask you if you ever saw a man with gills like a fish?"

"Gills?" I repeated.

"Yes, gills! Did you?"

"No," I replied, angrily, "and neither did you."

"No, I never did," he said, in a curiously placid voice, "but there's a man with gills like a fish who lives in the ocean out there. Oh, you needn't look that way—nobody ever thinks of doubting my word, and I tell you that there's a man—or a thing that looks like a man—as big as you are, too—all slate-colored—with nasty red gills like a fish!—and I've a witness to prove what I say!"

"Who?" I asked, sarcastically.

"The witness? My nurse."

"Oh! She saw a slate-colored man with gills?"

"Yes, she did. So did Francis Lee, superintendent of the Mica Quarry Company at Port-of-Waves. So have a dozen men who work in the quarry. Oh, you needn't laugh, young man. It's an old story here, and anybody can tell you about the harbor-master."

"The harbor-master!" I exclaimed.

"Yes, that slate-colored thing with gills, that looks like a man—and—by Heaven! *is* a man—that's the harbor-master. Ask any quarryman at Port-of-Waves what it is that comes purring around their boats at the wharf and unties painters and changes the mooring of every cat-boat in the cove at night! Ask Francis Lee what it was he saw running and leaping up and down the shoal at sunset last Friday! Ask anybody along the coast what sort of a thing moves about the cliffs like a man and slides over them into the sea like an otter—"

"I saw it do that!" I burst out.

"Oh, did you? Well, *what was it?*"

Something kept me silent, although a dozen explanations flew to my lips.

After a pause, Halyard said: "You saw the harbor-master, that's what you saw!"

I looked at him without a word.

"Don't mistake me," he said, pettishly; "I don't think that the harbor-master is a spirit or a sprite or a hobgoblin, or any sort of damned rot. Neither do I believe it to be an optical illusion."

"What do you think it is?" I asked.

"I think it's a man—I think it's a branch of the human race—that's what I think. Let me tell you something: the deepest spot in the Atlantic Ocean is a trifle over five miles deep—and I suppose you know that this place lies only about a quarter of a mile off this headland. The British exploring vessel, *Gull,* Captain Marotte, discovered and sounded it, I believe. Anyway, it's there, and it's my belief that the profound depths are inhabited by the remnants of the last race of amphibious human beings!"

This was childish; I did not bother to reply.

"Believe it or not, as you will," he said, angrily; "one thing I know, and that is this: the harbor-master has taken to hanging around my cove, and he is attracted by my nurse! I won't have it! I'll blow his fishy gills out of his head if I ever get a shot at him! I don't care whether it's homicide or not—anyway, it's a new kind of murder and it attracts me!"

I gazed at him incredulously, but he was working himself into a passion, and I did not choose to say what I thought.

"Yes, this slate-colored thing with gills goes purring and grinning and spitting about after my nurse—when she walks, when she rows, when she sits on the beach! Gad! It drives me nearly frantic. I won't tolerate it, I tell you!"

"No," said I, "I wouldn't either." And I rolled over in bed convulsed with laughter.

The next moment I heard my door slam. I smothered my mirth and rose to close the window, for the land-wind blew cold from the forest, and a drizzle was sweeping the carpet as far as my bed.

That luminous glare which sometimes lingers after the stars go out, threw a trembling, nebulous radiance over sand and cove. I heard the seething currents under the breakers' softened thunder—louder than I ever heard it. Then, as I closed my window, lingering for a last look at the crawling tide, I saw a man standing, ankle-deep, in the surf, all alone there in the night. But—was it a man? For the figure suddenly began running over the beach on all fours like a beetle, waving its limbs like feelers. Before I could throw open the window again it darted into the surf, and, when I leaned out into the chilling drizzle, I saw nothing save the flat ebb crawling on the coast—I heard nothing save the purring of bubbles on seething sands.

V

It took me a week to perfect my arrangements for transporting the great auks, by water, to Port-of-Waves, where a lumber schooner was to be sent from Petite Sainte Isole, chartered by me for a voyage to New York.

I had constructed a cage made of osiers, in which my auks were to squat until they arrived at Bronx Park. My telegrams to

Professor Farrago were brief. One merely said "Victory!" Another explained that I wanted no assistance; and a third read: "Schooner chartered. Arrive New York July 1st. Send furniture-van to foot of Bluff Street."

My week as a guest of Mr. Halyard proved interesting. I wrangled with that invalid to his heart's content, I worked all day on my osier cage, I hunted the thimble in the moonlight with the pretty nurse. We sometimes found it.

As for the thing they called the harbor-master, I saw it a dozen times, but always either at night or so far away and so close to the sea that of course no trace of it remained when I reached the spot, rifle in hand.

I had quite made up my mind that the so-called harbor-master was a demented darky—wandered from, Heaven knows where—perhaps shipwrecked and gone mad from his sufferings. Still, it was far from pleasant to know that the creature was strongly attracted by the pretty nurse.

She, however, persisted in regarding the harbor-master as a sea-creature; she earnestly affirmed that it had gills, like a fish's gills, that it had a soft, fleshy hole for a mouth, and its eyes were luminous and lidless and fixed.

"Besides," she said, with a shudder, "it's all slate color, like a porpoise, and it looks as wet as a sheet of india-rubber in a dissecting-room."

The day before I was to set sail with my auks in a catboat bound for Port-of-Waves, Halyard trundled up to me in his chair and announced his intention of going with me.

"Going where?" I asked.

"To Port-of-Waves and then to New York," he replied, tranquilly.

I was doubtful, and my lack of cordiality hurt his feelings.

"Oh, of course, if you need the sea-voyage—" I began.

"I don't; I need you," he said, savagely; "I need the stimulus of our daily quarrel. I never disagreed so pleasantly with anybody in my life; it agrees with me; I am a hundred per cent. better than I was last week."

I was inclined to resent this, but something in the deep-lined face of the invalid softened me. Besides, I had taken a hearty liking to the old pig.

"I don't want any mawkish sentiment about it," he said, observing me closely; "I won't permit anybody to feel sorry for me—do you understand?"

"I'll trouble you to use a different tone in addressing me," I replied, hotly; "I'll feel sorry for you if I choose to!" And our usual quarrel proceeded, to his deep satisfaction.

By six o'clock next evening I had Halyard's luggage stowed away in the cat-boat, and the pretty nurse's effects corded down, with the newly hatched auk-chicks in a hat-box on top. She and I placed the osier cage aboard, securing it firmly, and then, throwing tablecloths over the auks' heads, we led those simple and dignified birds down the path and across the plank at the little wooden pier. Together we locked up the house, while Halyard stormed at us both and wheeled himself furiously up and down the beach below. At the last moment she forgot her thimble. But we found it, I forget where.

"Come on!" shouted Halyard, waving his shawls furiously; "what the devil are you about up there?"

He received our explanation with a sniff, and we trundled him aboard without further ceremony.

"Don't run me across the plank like a steamer trunk!" he shouted, as I shot him dexterously into the cock-pit. But the wind was dying away, and I had no time to dispute with him then.

The sun was setting above the pine-clad ridge as our sail flapped and partly filled, and I cast off, and began a long tack, east by south, to avoid the spouting rocks on our starboard bow.

The sea-birds rose in clouds as we swung across the shoal, the black surf-ducks scuttered out to sea, the gulls tossed their sun-tipped wings in the ocean, riding the rollers like bits of froth.

Already we were sailing slowly out across that great hole in the ocean, five miles deep, the most profound sounding ever taken in the Atlantic. The presence of great heights or great depths, seen or unseen, always impresses the human mind—perhaps oppresses it. We were very silent; the sunlight stain on cliff and beach deepened to crimson, then faded into sombre purple bloom that lingered long after the rose-tint died out in the zenith.

Our progress was slow; at times, although the sail filled with the rising land breeze, we scarcely seemed to move at all.

"Of course," said the pretty nurse, "we couldn't be aground in the deepest hole in the Atlantic."

"Scarcely," said Halyard, sarcastically, "unless we're grounded on a whale."

"What's that soft thumping?" I asked. "Have we run afoul of a barrel or log?"

It was almost too dark to see, but I leaned over the rail and swept the water with my hand.

Instantly something smooth glided under it, like the back of a great fish, and I jerked my hand back to the tiller. At the same moment the whole surface of the water seemed to begin to purr, with a sound like the breaking of froth in a champagne-glass.

"What's the matter with you?" asked Halyard, sharply.

"A fish came up under my hand," I said; "a porpoise or something—"

With a low cry, the pretty nurse clasped my arm in both her hands.

"Listen!" she whispered. "It's purring around the boat."

"What the devil's purring?" shouted Halyard. "I won't have anything purring around me!"

At that moment, to my amazement, I saw that the boat had stopped entirely, although the sail was full and the small pennant fluttered from the mast-head. Something, too, was tugging at the rudder, twisting and jerking it until the tiller strained and creaked in my hand. All at once it snapped; the tiller swung useless and the boat whirled around, heeling in the stiffening wind, and drove shoreward.

It was then that I, ducking to escape the boom, caught a glimpse of something ahead—something that a sudden wave seemed to toss on deck and leave there, wet and flapping—a man with round, fixed, fishy eyes, and soft, slaty skin.

But the horror of the thing were the two gills that swelled and relaxed spasmodically, emitting a rasping, purring sound—two gasping, blood-red gills, all fluted and scolloped and distended.

Frozen with amazement and repugnance, I stared at the creature; I felt the hair stirring on my head and the icy sweat on my forehead.

"It's the harbor-master!" screamed Halyard.

The harbor-master had gathered himself into a wet lump, squatting motionless in the bows under the mast; his lidless eyes were phosphorescent, like the eyes of living codfish. After a while I felt that either fright or disgust was going to strangle me where I sat, but it was only the arms of the pretty nurse clasped around me in a frenzy of terror.

There was not a fire-arm aboard that we could get at. Halyard's hand crept backward where a steel-shod boathook lay, and I also made a clutch at it. The next moment I had it in my hand, and staggered forward, but the boat was already tumbling shoreward among the breakers, and the next I knew the harbor-master ran at me like a colossal rat, just as the boat rolled over and over through the surf, spilling freight and passengers among the seaweed-covered rocks.

When I came to myself I was thrashing about knee-deep in a rocky pool, blinded by the water and half suffocated, while under my feet, like a stranded porpoise, the harbor-master made the water boil in his efforts to upset me. But his limbs seemed soft and boneless; he had no nails, no teeth, and he bounced and thumped and flapped and splashed like a fish, while I rained blows on him with the boat-hook that sounded like blows on a football. And all the while his gills were blowing out and frothing, and purring, and his lidless eyes looked into mine, until, nauseated and trembling, I dragged myself back to the beach, where already the pretty nurse alternately wrung her hands and her petticoats in ornamental despair.

Beyond the cove, Halyard was bobbing up and down, afloat in his invalid's chair, trying to steer shoreward. He was the maddest man I ever saw.

"Have you killed that rubber-headed thing yet?" he roared.

"I can't kill it," I shouted, breathlessly. "I might as well try to kill a football!"

"Can't you punch a hole in it?" he bawled. "If I can only get at him—"

His words were drowned in a thunderous splashing, a roar of great, broad flippers beating the sea, and I saw the gigantic forms of my two great auks, followed by their chicks, blundering past in a shower of spray, driving headlong out into the ocean.

"Oh, Lord!" I said. "I can't stand that," and, for the first time in my life, I fainted peacefully—and appropriately—at the feet of the pretty nurse.

It is within the range of possibility that this story may be doubted. It doesn't matter; nothing can add to the despair of a man who has lost two great auks.

As for Halyard, nothing affects him—except his involuntary sea-bath, and that did him so much good that he writes me from the South that he's going on a walking-tour through Switzerland—if I'll join him. I might have joined him if he had not married the pretty nurse. I wonder whether—But, of course, this is no place for speculation.

In regard to the harbor-master, you may believe it or not, as you choose. But if you hear of any great auks being found, kindly throw a table-cloth over their heads and notify the authorities at the new Zoological Gardens in Bronx Park, New York. The reward is ten thousand dollars.